MATTHEW ZORICH

Maiden of Storms

The Conspiracy of Crows Trilogy Book Two

First published by Raccoon County Press 2025

First edition

ISBN: 979-8-9876861-2-6

Editing by Kavin Space Mage Press
Cover art by David Gardias - Bestselling-covers.com

This book was professionally typeset on Reedsy.
Find out more at reedsy.com

For my Daughter

Preface

~Maiden of Storms~
The Conspiracy of Crows Trilogy
Book Two

The news of the Olde Ridgewatch Massacre ripples across the city-states of Vineland. Newspapers write disturbing details of Holy Imperium soldier's attack on unarmed commoners outside a tavern. Secret meetings occur, subversive pamphlets spread, and thought-provoking books are passed around in back alleys.

Prince Damon moves forward with his Triumphant Masquerade to celebrate his loosely affiliated holdings in the city-states of Vineland while rumors of a storm grow west of the Blightbriar Mountains.

An expeditionary force investigates a burnt-down manor, and the Bastards of Liberty move towards revenge and rebellion, gathering merchants, slavers, and commoners to their cause, hoping a document of paper unifies them against the choking gripe of a sovereign bent on domination.

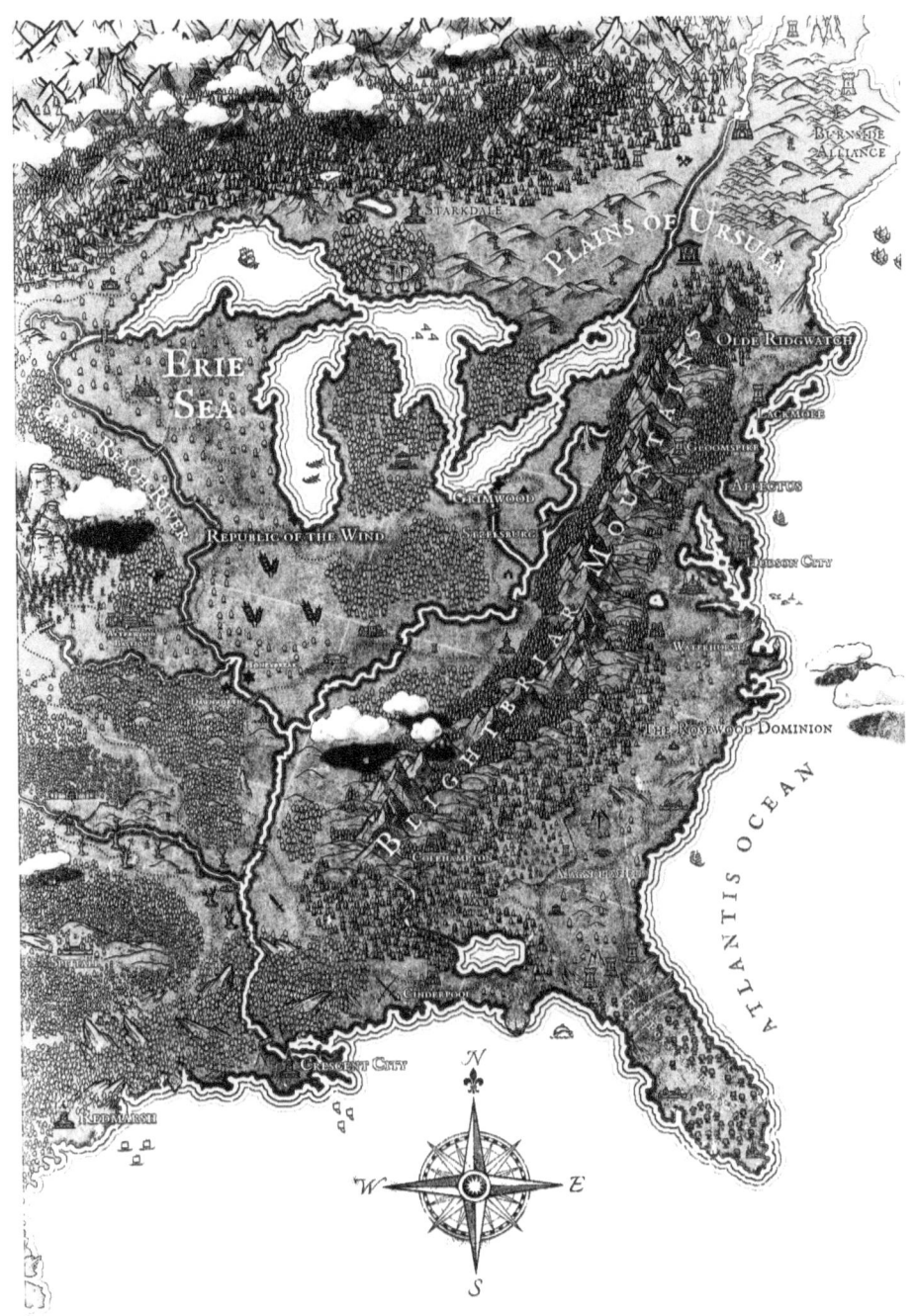

The Holy Imperium - Eastern Vineland

iii

Prologue

The sky shattered last night, spitting lightning and thunder, causing one last snowfall, which was unheard of in Oxfell County.

"Allison, honey, don't veer out too far!" her mother yelled, but she knew her daughter wouldn't listen. Children only listened to their emotions, so Allison walked quicker down the path away from her home.

The Maker herself had shaken the skies to keep the wicked keeper of the night Gothine away from the gates of heaven as the storm shutters trembled and wind pressed against her home's walls. At least that is what her mother said. The snow had melted quickly in the dawn hours and all three now walked towards the tilled fields taking in damage from the storm. Her father was the caretaker of a hunting lodge of Lord Rotherham called Feather Bottom Lodge, used in the summer high season and early autumn for what the nobles and royals called "sport." They would seek out the wicked creatures in the Blightbriar Wilds for trophies to take home. Allison's father, Da, had carved out a large field and built the lodge over the ruins of an old manor on the edge of the Blightbriar Wilds, past Hawkhallow Village and the Razorshine River, and lived on the edge of the property as its caretaker. Those coming to the lodge hoped to hunt briar boars, crucible wolves, and great ruin bears. The types of animals found in storybooks written during the time of King Christopher Goldthorn and Erica the Red were alive well before the Crimson Struggle.

Allison ran ahead of her parents, who walked the path's edge to the main planting field. She ventured down a path in the middle of the field, taking in the tilled earth as it blossomed from the snowfall, smelling of rich minerals and ready for seed. The field was surrounded by oakthorn, black willow, and white spruce trees. She hoped for a fair planting season by the Maker's grace.

The ground was wet but passable, and it felt like the past winter's winds were over, and spring's embrace had begun. Allison remembered knowing the storm was over when she heard blue jays waking her this morning. Now, she listened to the cackle of the three pesky large crows sitting on the scarecrow in the middle of the field. She looked back and saw her parents shaking their heads at a large branch that fell near a path on the other end of the meadow.

Allison walked towards the scarecrow, an old rusty breastplate and helmet with a sharp hole in the head. The crows sat on the cross beam of the scarecrow, laughing with mockery. The armor was her father's, now retired due to a head wound that nearly killed him. After the Battle of the Reaping there were times, he would occasionally have shaking fits and forget to control himself, releasing his bowels at inappropriate times late at night. His battles were over; now, he worked for himself and his family, keeping up an old war friend's hunting lodge.

Her Da called it a grand retirement for a wounded soldier. He said it wasn't too bad a life, and he was lucky to be alive. Saving Lord Rotherham had given them more freedom than living in the slums of Hudson City. They had a home, even if it was on the edge of the Blightbriar Wilds. There was an inn and other farms a day's walk away, maybe a little more as the crow flies, she thought, but smaller crows, not the birds she was looking at now.

"Go away, you stupid birds," Allison said, her eleven-summers hands grasping a rock and tossing it towards the birds, missing easily. The large birds, who were dark in complexion with a slight purple tone, stopped gossiping at each other and looked at the girl, angry at the interruption in their morning talk, and clicked their beaks. *They were large for crows*, Allison thought.

She drew closer, stepping off the walking path into the field, trampling over the finely tilled lines her father and mother had made a few days ago, "Go away, you beasts." She threw another rock, yelling as if the birds would even understand her. The last stone hit the breastplate of the scarecrow dead on. It pinged loudly, drawing her parents' attention a distance away. "That should do it," she said to herself. The three birds shifted their clawed feet.

She looked at them again and realized they were definitely not crows. Their beaks were slightly longer and almost looked sharp, and their clawed feet were gripped entirely around the cross beams. They looked almost muscled in their legs and not afraid of an eleven-summer girl hurling rocks at them.

Allison heard laughter for a moment, and although put off by the birds, she looked back to see what her parents were giggling about. They weren't by the path opening anymore. They must have walked back towards home.

Stepping back, the morning light dimmed as if something crossed the sun, like a fast-moving cloud. She looked back and put her dirty hand up to look at the three odd birds, hoping they had taken flight. They remained and started to screech loudly, putting their beaks to the sky, open and sharp as if they were ready to be fed. Allison spun around, thinking about the size of the mother bird who would feed these three beasts.

She stepped away from the animals, birds, and whatever they were, back over the tilled earth. A slight shiver slowly crept up her side as she turned her head, looking for her parents.

"Ma," she said out loud, "Da, where are you?" The first pings of fear now well ingrained into her thoughts. Goosebumps appeared on her arms as if the air temperature changed. Just then, another shadow crossed the sky, and she felt a slight breeze as the three birds cackled louder behind her.

Something was wrong, and Allison knew it. No other animals danced on the edges of the woods, no bugs buzzed her head, and it was too quiet as if the Blightbriar Wilds knew something dangerous was about, so she no longer walked. She ran back to the path hoping the cover of the trees and the comfort of a trail she cleared herself would lead her back home. Then, there was another shadow from above, on the edge of the field where her Ma and Da had stood, and she slipped and fell on something wet and slimy.

"Ahh," Allison grasped at her knee, and a sharp pain streaked up her leg. She looked down at her sliced kneecap, blood oozing.

Laughter drifted on the wind above her as she gripped her knee, biting down on her lip and putting pressure on it instinctively. The shadow from the sky followed the ground, and suddenly Allison was airborne, leaving the tilled earth and the field below. She felt claws grasp her leg and shoulder, cutting into her skin and slicing muscles, and watched as the ground gave way quickly. Allison was above the tree line now, and there was Feather Bottom Lodge. She screamed out in pain as the claws released, and she dropped for a moment, plummeting toward the ground. A moment later she stopped screaming as the air in her lungs left her and her vision darkened. Her ears rang with laughter again, and she felt the sharp claws of a warhawk grasp at her, slicing into her thigh and shoulder, tearing her apart midair. She choked, feeling weightless pain leave her stomach, and her sight darkened against the sky.

The slender goblin giggled and held tightly onto the warhawks saddle strapped in by thigh and feet. Its giant wings fanned out, and then tightened close to its body as it dove again, and then spread its wings midair, spinning, gliding, and flinging its prey as it tore, ripped, and swallowed bone, and flesh until satisfied. The sky above the Blightbriar Wilds was fresh with delights of the hunt, the warhawk and its riding companion eager to feed on more.

MAIDEN OF STORMS

Sorella - Arrested the Night Before

"I don't think this snow will stop much tonight," hollered Cordial as snow spun and twisted, staggering Sorella and Cordial as they braced against the wind.

"By tomorrow, it will warm and melt, turning everything to muck and shit," shivered Sorella.

Recently, Sorella and Cordial had separated from Stitch, a freed slave and elve, and Duncan, a failed squire, along with their newer friends to meet up in Olde Ridgewatch, a city-state controlled by the Holy Imperium now under martial law. Sorella, an undocumented elve, and Cordial, a wanted pickpocket, had to sneak into the city, risking their lives. They had left a stolen boat behind them on the shores of Bawstone Keep Bay, its dark ink-green waters brushing against its hull.

"We need to find a place to warm up, Cordial," said Sorella. "I don't wanna get caught out here in the streets. It's bad enough I don't have papers. Holy Imperium guards or those damn Black Eagle mercs will call us out for being past curfew, and then we are right and truly," she stopped for a moment, thinking she heard something, "fucked." The wind kissed and cut into their faces.

To the Holy Imperium or the Bitterleak mercenaries known as the Black Eagles patrolling Olde Ridgewatch, they were outlaws, a bunch of sorry bastards who deserved nothing more than the cold floor of a dark cell followed by the noose of a hangman's rope. They jogged to the nearest point of safety, an awning of a closed storefront. Their clothes, a mixture of leather and chain mail, were cold and drenched from rowing from the mainland to Olde

Ridgewatch, the oldest city of Vineland. The last gasp of winter had pushed in from the west and made their passage harrowing.

"I've never felt thunder and lightning like this when it snows," Cordial said. "I thought Judith's time was now bringing the delights of seedtime; this isn't seedtime."

Sorella looked up into the darkness between the buildings at the clouds above and breathed in.

"This is Stribog's last gasp. Tomorrow, there will be sun and warmth. We just need to make it through. Spring and the season of Judith are near." She covered her face with part of her cloak to keep the wind and snow out.

The wind growled, and the snow blinded, punishing Cordial and Sorella as if their sins warranted nature itself to lash at them. They needed a safe place to rest for the night. Their hopes remained low as they rushed about searching for a light in a tavern's window that would accept them in their state. They traveled towards the neighborhood of Mount Whoredom, the prostitution district of Olde Ridgewatch, one of the few places where martial law was lax. Cordial had unfinished contracts from the Society of Shadows in town and creditors that could be looking for him. Still, Sorella was in more danger. Even with her ears cut to look like a human, she was an elve with no papers stating she was free. In cities controlled by the Holy Imperium, any elves, goblins, or orcs needed to carry documents saying they were free citizens of the Holy Imperium, or they would face arrest. She didn't want to end up shipped down to a plantation in the Rosewood Dominion working cotton fields. It was why they separated from the rest of the Bastards of Liberty before attempting to enter the city. Sorella longed for the forests but had to settle for the brothel district of Olde Ridgewatch. The snow blew across the cobbled streets as they slowed at a crossroads.

In most parts of Vineland, elves, goblins, and orcs were considered part of the slave class, whereas dwarves and humans were one step higher. Few city-states allowed freedom for elves, orcs, and goblins, but their numbers dwindled. After the Crimson Struggle ended, Prince Damon's newly crowned Holy Imperium strangled those freedoms into compliance.

"I hear you," Cordial smiled back with the impossibly sharp features of a man born into nobility. Sometimes, Sorella forgot how handsome he was, but she had eyes for another, more extraordinary man she hoped to see soon. Sorella and Wyatt Duncan's connection was intricate and time-worn, with scars from broken hearts and dead lovers. Her heart never fell for Cordial's charm, tricks, or looks; she only truly treasured one man, who was long dead. She thought of him momentarily, and her body warmed at the memory. But unfortunately, he was gone, so she held onto another part, Victor's stepbrother Duncan. Their closeness was that of grief and passion, but she never felt the same way with Duncan as she had with Victor Parish.

"I have an idea; if she is still working, we may be able to warm up in a cellar for a price," Cordial said.

"Anything, even if it's for a few hours," she said. Both their lips were turning darker, and even with her native blood, she feared succumbing to the cold, but even more so, she feared for the lives of her crew, the bastards.

"It's up this block, come on," Cordial said, and they quickly walked as the snow fell, pushing against them and trying to end their night.

Cordial led Sorella to a three-story house, lights still lit, covered by shades casting a red hue. Cordial walked around where the servant's entrance stood to knock three times, paused, and hit twice more.

"Fuck, I hope that was right," he said as the wind gusted. He shoved his hands across his chest and under his armpits.

"Betsy, Betsy, open up; it's your old pal, Cordy," he yelled at the door. The wind blew against him, nearly pushing him back.

The door cracked, "Yes, what? What?" said an eye peeping through the door, light breaking the darkness outside.

"Please let us in. We're friends with Betsy," said Cordial. "It's me, Cord. My mother was friends with Betsy."

She looked at Cordial for a moment but didn't say anything.

"Alright, come in, come in. Don't want a dead vagrant on our doorstep come tomorrow morning," said the person behind the door. Cordial entered, Sorella following. The door slammed shut.

"What are the likes of you two doing outside on a night like this? It's near morning, and it's snowing as if Vulcan's forge has turned cold." The woman who opened the door was a stout older woman, the night cook for the brothel.

"Yeah, sorry, we got in and had nowhere to turn. Is Betsy about?" asked Cordial.

"She is having a lay down, as it were. You two get near the stove and warm up. Don't steal no food. I'll make you a little something here, but you'll need to pay for it," said the woman. She was fifty winters old and dressed in an apron and woolen dress. "You have the coin, don'tcha?"

"Yes, of course," they said, handing over a few coins to tide the woman over. She didn't even look at the amount; she just pocketed it and finished spooning soup and day-old bread into some wooden bowls. "Beggars and bastards this lot." She said to herself.

They warmed themselves by the stove, and their shivering stopped.

"Right, you two eat and finish up. I'll send it to Miss Betsy, and we'll see what to do with the likes of you looking like two wet alley dogs." They ate quickly, and the night cook returned with Miss Betsy, a dwarven woman with red hair dressed in a fur-lined nightgown.

"Well, look what the storm did bring us, the prodigal son Cordy! You look like shit, my boy. Come hug your Aunt Betsy," she said as she stepped toward Cordial. "On second thought, let's not. You're soaked. So, what are you doing in my home?"

"Honestly, we are trying to do a good deed and return a long-lost son to his father."

"In this place? Wonder how much that pays," Betsy snickered to herself aloud.

"Gretchen, clean up my office so we can talk in there. I have two guests to attend, too, and after, don't bother me unless it's important. Let's get you out of those clothes, the two of you, and cover up your weapons. You're going to get us all arrested. No blades in Olde Ridgewatch, per General Ashburn!"

"We know! That's who we're here to see. We're trying to get his son, Runt, to him," said Sorella.

"Maker's sweet saggy tits, you don't say." Miss Betsy put her hands on her hips and thought.

"It's true. We traveled past the Blightbriar Mountains from Steelsburg to deliver the boy to his father. Got caught up in the middle of the wilds and wintered in Mount Nittany University. Hit a spot of mild weather before tonight and just now got in."

Miss Betsy looked Sorella up and down. "And I suppose you, lass, don't have any papers either?"

Cordial nodded and looked at Sorella. "It's all right. Betsy was my governess long before things changed with my family."

"I forgot you come from old money, Cordial. I'm free, Miss Betsy. I've never been a slave and never will be. I don't need papers to tell me or anyone else that."

"Well, here you do. You'll be locked in the stocks without papers and sold down the Atlantis Ocean with a collar on your neck and new chains on your legs. Maker, this land is falling to pieces since Prince Damon showed up to do nothing but send out pamphlets speaking of how he's going to make this land grand," Betsy sighed loudly.

"We need to fix you both up." She put her hand on their faces like a mother would to her children. "Look at me doing something out of the kindness of my own heart. You'd think I'm Cordial himself, the patron saint of lies and fucking. I'll have a basic note of sale for you made up here shortly, showing Cordy owns you. Easier to force that than a true certificate of freedom. Damn, things have a special stamp on them now," Betsy said. "If you want to walk the streets tomorrow, you'll have to stash those weapons too."

Sorella thumbed her tomahawk at her belt.

"Come now. Let's get you to my office. Keep your damn faces covered as best you can. Soldiers are being entertained tonight, so put those wet cloaks around your blades."

They walked near the back of the salon filled with sloped couches, pillows, and an extensive cloud of multi-colored smoke from pipes and hookahs. Nobody took notice of the three as they were engaged in other pursuits. Laughter and piano music rode the smoke in the air. Finally, they made their way into Betsy's office, as she called it. Cordial sat on a wooden chair by a desk and took in the surroundings. It smelled ripe of sex and incense. Betsy had a modest bookshelf, a writing desk, a luxurious bed freshly used, a

5

window, and a chair. In the corner hung a swing set up with a horse harness. Cordial raised his eyebrow.

"Don't judge, sweety, what happens in my house stays in my house. You would be surprised what folks are interested in, even some of those sacred Blue Templar enjoy their sins here. Now, you said you have one of General Ashburn's sons. I don't see him here, so where exactly is the boy?"

Cordial looked at them and let out his breath. "My friend Duncan is with him, bringing Runt in via land route and not a stolen dinghy rowed across the bay. He should be with Stitch."

"You scoundrel, your mother would roll over in her grave if she knew what you were doing now. How far have you fallen to pal around with a native and that rogue Stitch? That little weasel. I miss his face and that evil scarred smile." She grinned. "And his tongue," said Miss Betsy.

Cordial shivered.

"Take your clothes off, both of you, and hang them near the fireplace. I'll warm some wine."

"Stitch should be along eventually," said Cordial. "We split up once we got close to the city. How long has it been under the boot of the Holy Imperium?"

"Oh, the mercenaries are new; they just showed up one day, the Black Eagles of Bitterleak. Mean lot; they rough up my workers too much but can't do anything about it. Safe to say, Cordial, the Society of Shadows has been quiet since the curfew started." She stopped for a moment and said quietly. "There are whispers the leadership is weakening."

Cordial and Sorella looked at each other and nodded at the latest news of the underworld. The politics of their lives were always fluid and adjusting.

They drank wine and watched as Betsy quickly made ownership papers for Cordial to carry. "You might be a bloody heathen, but that doesn't mean people should own you." Sorella's hand curled into a fist, and she squeezed it tight. "Oh Cordial, she's full of fury, and fire this one, fury, and fire best be careful. Both of you get dressed. Your clothes should be dry by now."

They finished two cups of warmed wine. Then, there was a bang at the door.

"Boss better come quick; our guests from the military left in a hurry. We hear there is fighting in the streets, maybe a riot."

"Shit, hurry, both of you, dress and out the back door now!" Miss Betsy stood and hollered back. "Gretchen, I want the windows boarded up immediately. I'll see you two out. You can't stay here. Follow me." She threw a fur-hooded cloak on as she left her office and pushed them to the back door, where they had originally arrived.

"There's a bar, The Empty Gauntlet. They will offer support and care. Find the barkeep and say, 'Comrade, how do you take care of a tree you want to grow?' They should reply, 'With blood and liberty.' That's how you know they are decent people in this area. Some spies are about here and there, even in my own house. Needs to be careful," said Miss Betsy.

"We meant to head that way once we got situated," Cordial nodded. "Thank you again."

Sorella thanked Miss Betsy and walked out of the alley. Snow had fallen to cover their boots.

"Stay in the shadows and alleys a few blocks south of here, and head towards the Atlantis Ocean. You will catch a bright brazier at the foot of the road, and down that alley is the Empty Gauntlet, about eight or so blocks. Now go!" Miss Betsy closed the back door.

Sorella and Cordial walked to the main street, turned, and moved towards a less used area, keeping to themselves and away from a patrol circling it. They were well-armed in a city that had outlawed carrying weapons of any kind under the martial law of the Holy Imperium.

"It's fuckin cold. Wish we could have stayed there." Cordial cupped his hands as they leaned onto a wall and braced against the wind.

"It's three, maybe four more blocks, I think." There was screaming and yelling in the direction they were headed. They were at the edge of an alley, looking down the main street, moved into the light of an owl lamp, a flameless light created by deft dwarven fingers. As they moved towards the noise, they turned left, keeping on the street's walking area, which had less snow. Anxiety and stress strained in their chests as they turned the corner.

"You two rogues stand still! You lads don't move, or we'll feather your backs faster than you can scream for your mother's milk," a voice full of confidence and wine demanded.

Cordial moved his hand towards his belt.

"No, don't do it, son, hands in the air. If you are innocent and obey, you got nothing to worry about from the likes of us."

"Listen to her. She knows what she's speaking about. Comply. Only criminals and thugs don't comply." said another soldier. "Turn around real slow like."

They looked at each other, giving the 'we're truly fucked' look.

The snow came down, skewing them slightly. Sorella moved into the owl lamp light as Cordial turned and stayed out of its shine. As they turned, they came face to face with eight Bitterleak mercenaries.

"Black Eagles, I haven't seen the likes of your outfit in a few years. What are you doing, Vineland side? No more babies' heads to smash in back home?" asked Sorella.

Cordial cringed.

"Well, look at this: we got two armed thugs, and one looks like she's got a mouth on her. She's a heathen hag. Arms up, or we'll pin you full of steel and watch you gag on it until your eyes stop moving."

Four of the Black Eagles carried newly minted dwarven crossbows. The other four had kite shields and short swords. Sorella noted they looked ready to break heads.

They stood hands in the air.

"Sides your mouth full of stupidity, it's illegal to carry weapons in Olde Ridgewatch. I hope you have your papers for this elve. Guess it doesn't matter. An armed heathen will be hanged either way."

"Hands on your heads," said the lead Black Eagles guard. His beard was trimmed to look rounded as if he took care of it, but his eyes were glassy as if he were on drugs. He was fidgety; all their eyes were glassy.

Sorella and Cordial broke into a run, springing in different directions without so much as a nod to each other. Cordial ran to the corresponding direction of the alley and booked it across the street, trying to zig-zag. Sorella heard trash and debris fall over. Cordial knocked objects over to slow their pursuit, and she sprinted the other way.

"Get them! They might be part of the trouble up the way!"

A crossbow bolt flew by Sorella. She banged into a door, but it stuck. *No luck*, and she moved again quickly. No chance to grab at her bow, and she needed to lose whoever was behind her. She heard them running and broke into another street, making a hard right to circle where she started as two Black Eagle guards chased her. The wind pushed the snow into her eyes, causing them to burn. She didn't see the wooden club as she turned her head to look behind her. Pain seared into her face and shocked her neck. She crumbled.

"I got the prick with the loudmouth, boss," said a Black Eagle guard as he wiped his club clean of blood and snot.

"Get those manacles on her. The others will meet us back at Bawstone Keep once they get that other gutter rat."

The Bastards - The Death of Friends

Runt gasped, and blood spewed out of his mouth. "It hurts. Am I going to die?" Then, as he took another breath and choked, his chest shuddered. The late night had given way to the early morning light, but Runt had taken no notice as he tried to breathe in the air around him. He felt a sucking sensation from his chest.

"I know it hurts, Runt," said Maynard. "Just hold on. We're trying to fix you up." He held Runt's hand as he lay on the table in the kitchen. Maynard's spectacles kept fogging. Runt accidentally spit blood onto him when his breath trembled. Maynard looked at Runt and peered down at his shirt, and the metal crossbow bolt pierced through his chest. Runt was going to die, and there was no amount of magic he could perform that would save him.

There had been an incident between soldiers of the Holy Imperium and a group of tavern drinkers, including Maynard's friends Doc, Stitch, and Duncan. The incident left Runt lying on the table in Olde Ridgewatch. They were supposed to deliver a cart of beer and wine to the Empty Gauntlet beer hall and then get Runt to his dad, General Benedict Ashburn. They had traveled from Wolf Hills across the Blightbriar Mountains and were so close to doing the right thing, just this once. A disagreement broke out during a freak spring snowstorm off the Atlantis Ocean. Maynard's friends, the bastards, hadn't known they were smuggling weapons inside beer barrels into the city, but one beer barrel had opened, spilling swords onto the ground, causing an argument between the tavern patrons and Holy Imperium soldiers. Now, poor luck, along with a mixture of stiff drink, led Maynard to hold his friend's bloody hand as he fought to breathe.

The two dwarves who worked with Doc, Runt, Duncan, and Maynard earlier helped drag the wounded Stitch and Runt into a house behind the tavern as the soldiers backed out of the alley. The townspeople yelled and fought, throwing rocks, bottles, and oyster shells at the soldiers as they retreated. Screams, fists, and swords clashed, producing a melee of confusion as snow blinded and wind protested in the alleyway. The soldiers fell back outnumbered, seeking reinforcements, while the townspeople cleaned up and prepared for a potential retribution. Now, the bastards tried to save their friend's lives. Inside the house, Duncan ripped at Runt's shirt to look at Runt's wound as Maynard assessed the situation.

"When will it stop hurting, Maynard?" asked Runt. He moved his right hand towards where the crossbow bolt entered his chest; the movement was uncoordinated and childlike; Maynard grabbed it to keep it away.

"Maynard, hold his fucking arms down by his sides. I am trying to save him," said Duncan. "Doc, how's Stitch!"

Duncan stood next to Runt as he lay on a kitchen table. Maynard stood above Runt, holding him by his shoulders as a bar patron held Runt's feet to ensure he lay still. Duncan looked around and grabbed a knife from a shelf.

"You there, find some clean clothes and bring me some water. Try to cover the windows as well. We don't need the fucking army kicking down the doors while Doc and I have our hands full trying to save these Runt and Stitch," ordered Duncan. His hair was over his face, and although cold, he was sweating and stressed. Blood and snow mixed on the floor under their feet as the dampness mingled with the stress and sweat.

In another room, a few tallow candles lit the living room where Stitch lay on the ground, Doc working on his wound.

"It hurts, Maynard," coughed Runt. "Hurts to," he spat blood, "breathe."

"Soon, Runt, soon. It won't hurt. Duncan will fix you up," said Maynard. He bit his lip. Duncan dug into the wound, blood spewed out, Runt jolted, his chest heaved, and his skin glistened, the house growing colder. Maynard attempted a binding spell, but, as Doc had taught him, working on someone close to you and performing healing magic, which takes concentration, and any emotion ruins the spell. Maynard failed at every attempt. Runt's breaths grew short. He tried to breathe deeply, but blood spewed out of his mouth, and he coughed and wheezed. They huddled in a slight home next to the beer hall, its owner gone or dead, nobody knew. The bottom floor was now a makeshift surgeon's ward. Someone opened the door, letting in snow from outside. "We got more wounded. It's turned into a pitched fight."

"Put them in the fucking hall. We're busy here," yelled Duncan.

"Maynard. Maynard, I don't," wheeze, cough, "I don't," wheeze. "Is there anything after," whispered Runt.

"Yes, there is someplace peaceful, clean, and warm," answered Maynard.

"Don't talk like that, Runt. I'm getting you fixed up. I need to get this fucking bolt out," Duncan gritted and put his hand onto the crossbow bolt sticking out of Runt. "I'm gonna pull it out, Maynard; get a wooden spoon and shove it in his mouth."

"Maynard, don't lie to me," Runt moved his arm stupidly towards Maynard as he lunged for a wooden spoon nearby. Maynard didn't say a word in reply.

"Doc, how's Stitch, man? I'm about to take this bolt out of Runt," yelled Duncan. "May need your help."

"Just because my nickname is Doc doesn't mean I can make miracles. I'm trying here, but I don't know if I can. Crossbows are Gothine's work," yelled Doc from a room over. Maynard looked up, spoon in hand. He saw Doc leaning over Stitch on the floor. Stitch's one leg bent and his other straight. It moved slightly. At least Stitch was moving, not dead. Maynard wasn't thinking clearly. This was far different from practicing healing on already dead corpses at university.

"No, there isn't. There's just darkness, and your body rots in the ground," Maynard said without emotion. He looked at Runt, almost pleading with him with his eyes, saying, "It's not ok."

Runt smiled painfully at Duncan and then looked up at Maynard with bloody lips smeared in a frown.

"Bite on this. Duncan's going to pull the bolt, stuff the wound, and see if we can stop the blood," said Maynard. "I'll try to heal you as best I can and sew you up."

"Maynard, I give you myself, my strength, my power, my soul," Runt spat out blood and froth. Maynard placed the spoon into Runt's mouth. "Take my revenge on all of them," he gnawed through the spoon. Stitch groaned in the other room with Doc, who swore multiple times. Duncan's hand hit the candle, which fell, limiting the light. Duncan looked at Maynard, closed his eyes, knowing what Runt was asking for, and nodded approval hesitantly toward Maynard.

"Maker's tears, not what I meant to do." Duncan got up on the table with a rag in his hand, wet with alcohol, and stood over Runt. "Bite down."

Duncan looked at Runt and Maynard and pulled at the bolt in Runt's chest. There was no sound for a moment; Runt's chest moved up as Duncan pulled at the bolt, his hand slipping, the dwarve holding Runt's feet pushed down, Runt's knees slightly strained, his chest bare, blood, his mouth gripped the spoon, blood, and saliva leaked from his teeth. Then, finally, the bolt heaved through, and Maynard felt Runt's hand lose grip on his. Maynard closed his eyes and drew at Runt in his thoughts, pulled at his wants, dreams, and at Runt's outrage, his sorrow, and loss. He pulled at Runt and his entire being, gripping his hand tighter, even as Runt loosened his grip on him and the material world. Maynard gripped harder, their hands slick with sweat, and as Runt's life slipped away, Maynard tasted sugar and maple sap in his mouth; his eyes closed and flickered open, and he smelled pine trees in the spring, all taken from the thoughts and memories of his friend. Runt and Maynard's eyes flashed again. Runt's chest jolted and slurped, the bolt pulled out, and Duncan fell back, slipping into the wall and down onto the floor. Maynard's eyes shot open after seeing a tree line from a distance and the creek he saw when Runt's house burnt down, and his vision cleared. Runt didn't move, and blood slowly spilled from the hole in his chest. Outside, deep in a forest far away near the burnt village of Wolf Hills, a wolf howled in the night.

Duncan stood up and started to frantically stitch the wound up; the blood continued to pour out, and Runt's chest had stopped pumping air.

* * *

As Doc worked on Stitch, candles flickered in the room, but there wasn't much left to work with as the body's power worked against itself. The half-elve was near the end. Doc could hear his heart beating, and it was slowing.

"Fucking stay with me, boy, you hear me," Doc pulled at Stitch as his eyes rolled back in his head, his face white, and his body limp, closer to the doors of death than to the room of life filled with his closest friends. "I can stop the blood, I can do it, but I need you to be awake, damn it," Doc said as he slapped his face. "I can't replace the blood or your innards, but you have a chance if I stop the wound from bleeding. Come on, young buck, child of the forest, bastard of our civilized world, live or give me all you have left."

Doc worked his hands to the bolt on both sides of Stitch's chest. He quickly took off his coat and glasses, tossed them in a heap in the corner, and looked around. He ripped at a curtain and stood over Stitch.

Doc heard Duncan yell something to him from the other room, but he concentrated on what to do next with the young half-elf. "Ok fucker, I pull this out, and you stay alive for me. I'll stop the blood for a few moments and sew this shut, no painkillers, just plain speed."

Hunter Young, the last battlemage of Vineland, known as Doc, batted the air away as the voices in his mind laughed. The fear of another voice joining the chorus inside gnawed at his self-esteem and courage to save Stitch's life.

Doc stood over Stitch as his legs shifted and closed his eyes to the mage. Doc reached and pulled at the bolt, using the curtain to grip the slippery metal. The motion was quick, and Stitch awoke for a moment. Doc dropped the bolt, took the curtain, wiped the seeping hole in his chest, pushed into it with a finger for a moment, and murmured an old word not heard by others. The blood slowed, seeping from Stitch's chest. Doc went over to his jacket, groped in a pocket, pulled a bone needle and thread, and returned to Stitch to close the wound.

"Stay with me, Stitch. Stay with me," said Doc as his feet wobbled slightly. He was weak now. Performing art took actual time from him, like any other mage or witch. If a magic user did not take their power from a natural source, they took it from inside themselves, taking time in the form of moments, hours, or years from the end of their lives. There was a secondary toll, a curse some would call it, that may not be known to the magic user until after. Some would lose a few pieces of hair or their eyesight temporarily. The toll varied depending on how powerful the spell was and how wise the magic user was.

"These are good people here, don't die on me," ordered Doc. Stitch didn't move. Doc slapped him and continued to sew. Quickly, he finished the front and rolled him onto his side. He looked and saw blood flowing from the back hole. He let go of Stitch and let his body slump onto his back and the dark pool on the floor. He threw the needle back on his coat.

"I'm a doctor of newspaper writing, damn it, I can even stop bleeding for a few moments, but I can't save," Doc stopped, tears trickled down his face, and sat down for a moment next to Stitch. He put his bloody palms into his eyes to relieve the pressure of the moment and to quell the voices resounding inside. Stitch woke momentarily and moved his head towards Doc but couldn't say anything. His fingers moved slightly; Doc watched the elves' hand slowly twitch as the last nerves convulsed, and the rest of the body found the heart emptying and slowing. The finger pointed at Doc accusingly. "I can't do anything more. You've lost too much," he said. Doc took a deep breath and whispered, knowing he would take another year from himself to do what must be done. Doc breathed in profoundly and gripped Stitch's hand. "I take it all, I take your pain, I take your wrath, your sadness," and he breathed in deeply. "Give me what you can, and I will ensure you're not forgotten."

Stitch moved slightly, and the rest of his nerve endings stopped moving. He moaned, and Doc felt a petty rush of anger. Stitch's mouth felt dry, and he coughed, spitting blood. Doc pulled at those feelings, and the spirit slipped away inside Stitch. Doc tasted iron chains and laughter as flashes of a whip and the wrath of hatred coursed through his body. He caught a glimmer of a smile, the love of a mother who was a friend, and the sense of kinship and warmth of fire drifted away.

"I hope this was worth it," Doc said and spat blood out of his mouth and scratched at his chest as if he pierced him as well. "Every time, it's worse but necessary for the needs of Vineland." He whispered to himself. He stood up, put the curtain over Stitch's face, and walked into the kitchen, already finding sunken faces deep in mourning.

* * *

Duncan sat on the floor, legs crossed, and Runt lay on the table. Maynard stood in the kitchen corner, one arm holding the other as if wounded but looking unhurt and unsure of himself, his hands full of the blood from a friend. Tears streamed down his face. Doc walked in, and they looked at him with a slight hope, but it left quickly.

"He's gone too," said Doc. "It wasn't supposed to be like this. One of them was supposed to live. I was sure it was the youngest."

"Fuck are you talking about? Everything and everyone you touch turns to fuckin' mud. The same thing happened to your two best friends, Umar and Jezebel Everfall, up north," said Duncan, standing up and wiping his bloody hands on his pants. "Maker's tits, you killed this kid," he pointed towards Runt as his body released the last of urine and feces. Doc put his hand on his mouth and wiped away the taste of death and its memories. "Like my son, like your daughter, and now Stitch."

Duncan shifted and moved to grab Doc, but Doc grabbed at the air with both hands and pushed towards Duncan with a speed Maynard nor Duncan had ever seen. An invisible force pushed Duncan back, and he knew from the Battle of the Reaping he couldn't do anything.

"Don't take me for some drunken sorcerer that gives two shits about your unintelligent emotions and thoughts," said Doc. An unseen force moved toward Duncan, propelling him on his feet and across the kitchen, slamming him against the wall and shaking the few candles nearby. Maynard looked on at the two but didn't say anything. "Vineland may have been better if Runt stayed alive. Who knows? He would have been dead either way in the war to come. All brave bastards die in war, Duncan, you know that. I looked into the future sober. I looked drunk. I looked blasted out of my head and found the best way, the best way to save his family and him. I was to bring him to his father, and he had a chance to survive that. If not for my interference, he would have burnt alive in a tavern in Wolf Hills. I lost much of myself when I killed Umar and Jezebel on the Plains of Ursula, all for the Maker's damn Holy Imperium. This country was supposed to be better than what

16

we have now." He wiped his bloody hands on his jacket, releasing the spell. "I cursed myself when my daughter died and thousands of others with the Smoldering Plague." He beat down his foot on the board. "The ancient art takes a price, and the price is steep, even when you know the deep truths of the world. What happened to Runt and Stitch? This is the best return I got for using the art to see the future, attempting to make a better country." He sighed. "I didn't want Runt or Stitch to die. If Runt's gone, his siblings survive, which may lead us to a better day. Maybe to a better Vineland."

Maynard looked at them, "Or it may lead to releasing a world of shit and the ruin on us all."

Doc put his arms down, and Duncan fell to the ground and walked towards Maynard, almost challenging him. Maynard stood for a moment and then moved. Doc looked at him and nodded. He moved through the pots and pans, found a small barrel, took a pewter mug, dipped it, and drank. "I'll do my best to not become a monster again, Maynard, Duncan, but when it comes down to it, do you want me at your side or against you?"

Neither replied. It was like having a ruin bear inside a short cave. He could eat honey or rip your face off with his large claws. Doc's mood shifted as if the death of two people he knew no longer rattled inside his broken brain.

"So here we are, time to bring Runt to his father so he can see what he fights for and what his prince of Vineland and the Holy Imperium has done," said Doc. Maynard looked on at Duncan and then Doc and nodded. "I'll clean their bodies myself, as you blame me for their deaths at the hands of Holy Imperium soldiers. Now, walk across the street and bring more beer. This house's beer is shit. We'll rest, drag Runt's corpse to where his father sleeps, and leave the body at his steps. The bastard can bury him."

Duncan stood up, standing over Doc, with no fear in his eyes even after Doc had forced him across the kitchen with the ancient power of magic.

"Fine, and after this, I'm done, done with you and your scheming," said Duncan, walking away. "You took enough from me already."

"You know we ain't done, Duncan, not even close," yelled Doc.

"Doc," said Maynard. "I'm not your equal, but I won't be calling you Master anymore. So, start treating me with more respect, or you will find yourself alone in a country that hates you for all you wish it to be."

The door shut in Doc's face, leaving him with the dead and his ghosts.

Alysha - Goblin Hole

The light in the darkness isn't hope, as some would think. It's a hole in a heart where anger, bitterness, and revenge leak.

Alysha heard this as her breath leaked slightly out of her mouth. She moved her tongue slowly through a hole in the right side of her lower teeth. She tasted copper, opened her mouth slightly, and breathed damp air.

Above, the lightning flies against the dark, the moon is covered by smoke and fire, and their eyes crave life as those around them expire.

Her eyes remained closed in a dull slumber. She felt as if an anvil smashed her head after she drank several bottles of wine.

Make peace with the rain and ease of pain deep inside; it's yours, this wetness of the blood, water, and the company of silence until the thunder rolls and the lightning flashes.

Her last memory was the agony of killing a boy near the altar of Judith, the Maiden of Storms. She remembered cracking Ryan Purenut's skull against a stone altar as he stabbed her with a sword; the force of his blow and gravity killed him and her. His body lay over her. The lightning came as Alysha drifted into extended darkness. Flashes of lightning continued as the rain poured down, washing the blood and hope for a better life away. She felt the storm inside her eyelids, a spark inside giving way to her rage, a shattering of glass in the darkness of life. She opened her mouth again to breathe.

"Oh, there you are, sweetie. Welcome back. It looks as if Judith has more work for you in this world yet," said a familiar voice. "Nice to have you back, although now three are two, and threads are uneven, so you must even it up. Yes, you must make three or make one, never two," said an older woman's voice.

Alysha opened her eyes and tried to understand. She was alive and lying on a bed of moss and leaves. Glass jars stood in corners of the space she lay, each filled with bugs that lit up in yellow and green hues, bringing some brightness around them. It smelled damp and earthy, like a fresh rainstorm. She attempted to make words but didn't move.

"Where," she asked, "how do I live?"

"Drink now, have some water. You have been gone for a few days and must drink and clean up. I did my best, sewed up your chest, and straightened that nose. Your eye looks bad but will heal. Do they work? Can you see child?" asked the old lady.

"Yes, are we underground?" asked Alysha.

"A goblin den we are, safe under the altar of Judith and the storm outside," she said. "You may call me Rowan. That's what my sisters used to call me. One is in the Litchbury Mire south of Grimwood, keeping further Wildcats and Templar from joining their friends. Before, she was called Lady Blacklace, but now, instead of Blacklace, her home is full of dark vines and death. My other sister, Lady Grapeseed, still resides near Hudson City, in the grip of the great and mighty Holy Imperium. She's devoted to the shadows and their machinations and slowly drowns all that defies her."

Alysha sat up and felt her face; her nose felt different, and her right eye hurt and had a scar above and below the eye. She remembered this old woman, Rowan, who lived across the river before her mother's murder and town's destruction at the hands of the Genteel Monks. Why her home and neighbor's cottages were burnt and their lives destroyed by politics, she barely understood, possibly because of her last name, her father a general in Prince Damon's army.

"Alysha Wolfthorn, it is now, no longer Bella Alysha Ashburn; you are new, three, now two, and so now, my three shall be two, and you stronger for it," Rowan Wightland said. "Come now, I have saved your life. I must beg a favor from you. Stand up, stand up, you can walk now, yes, yes," said Rowan.

Alysha stood slightly stooped in the goblin burrow and looked around the den filled with tools found in an apothecary. Bottles were filled with unknown liquids, vials glowed, and herbs hung from the ceiling, mingling with the roots of trees above. Rowan stood somewhat hunched, her hands curved and crooked, her skin sagging and thinned, aged veins, bruises, and brittleness as she shuffled in her movements. Alysha looked at this woman, who, last autumn, was chained up along with her and others from her homestead. They had marched from Wolf Hills towards Counselor City to become slaves to an army of the Holy Imperium, but this woman didn't make it. She attempted to escape and was killed by a bolt of lightning on the altar of Judith, the same one where she had fallen.

"Will you do as I ask, child? Will you? I have the strength but have lost all my time, so I am what's left to you. Do you accept it?" she asked, shuffling over to Alysha and giving her a bowl of dark liquid. Rowan wore a tattered dress, shredded and threaded with blood and silt, yet long ago, it held some form of elegance and noble weight. "You want revenge for your family, and I seek the same. Make the prince of the Holy Imperium fall and crack their hold like a storm that breaks down an army on a battlefield."

Rowan was crazy. Alysha needed to get out of this burrow.

"I appreciate you helping. I can't even understand how I survived," Alysha said.

"Dizzy still, I see. Drink. And promise to topple the prince," said Rowan, urging the bowl into Alysha's hand. She pushed it to her mouth. "For me, for your brother gone and brother that remains."

"What, yes, what do you mean?" she asked, opening her mouth, but Rowan pushed the bowl up, and the liquid fell into Alysha's mouth, burnt, and leaked into her throat as she choked and fell to her knees. The old woman put her hands on Alysha's hair and pulled it down, opening her throat, and she gagged and drank.

"You drank, yes," said Rowan.

"Yes, you nearly choked me with it. What was that?" asked Alysha. Her throat burned as she tasted the bitterness and the sweetness of wildflowers from spring.

"You drank from me, and I give to you. Now I go, and you stay," said the woman.

Alysha stumbled, her eyes rolled back into her head, and she fell back onto the moss and leaf-filled ground of the goblin hole.

* * *

Alysha opened her eyes and tried to understand. She lay against the altar of Judith atop the hill. Ryan's body lay on top of her, smelling of decay and the stench of death. The rain fell, keeping the crows and ravens away as night faded into dawn. She saw his sword lying at her side, his head dented in, his eyes open and staring at the ground. Alysha pushed his body off her and crawled away. She stood on weak legs and checked herself, feeling the stitches where his sword pierced her shoulder and upper chest. Her eyes and head hurt, and the wound to her leg throbbed through her stitches there as well. Everything ached, from her head to her feet, but she lived. She looked at the altar. There were burn marks as if lightning struck it, and she looked to the sky and let the water falling clean the blood from her clothes, and she whispered, "Thank you," to the sky, to Judith, and to herself.

She walked down the hill looking for her bearded maul, Stormkiss, an axe with a hammerhead on one side, crafted from star stone into shimmering black steel with the help of two blacksmiths, Hob and Bob. She was their indentured servant; the blacksmiths had taken care of her after the massacre of Wolf Hills. Then, as their apprentice and friend, at the end of winter, her life abruptly changed again when they were attacked by Holy Imperium scouts looking for wood outside of Counselor City. She had awoken where she had fallen, but her Stormkiss was nowhere to be found.

She placed a knife back into her belt. She remembered having Stormkiss with her at the end when she fell with Ryan against the altar, but it was no longer at the top of the hill. After searching, she went down, stopping by a thicket. Intuition took over as she parted the prickers and brush to find a hole.

"The goblin hole," she mumbled to herself. She crawled in, careful not to reopen her wounds. Her body twisted as she entered. Inside, she found the cave as she remembered. Several jars were lit with bugs, giving natural light to the small cave. At the center was a raised bed of leaves and moss. On top of the bed lay her axe, Stormkiss. Her eyes widened, and she walked towards it, glad for its safety and the strength it gave her; as she walked, she kicked an empty bowl, its dark contents now drained. She instinctively wiped her mouth and whispered, "Revenge."

She looked around but did not see the older woman, Rowan. She grabbed the bearded maul and heard the ground shake as thunder rolled above. She felt no fear, just a calm sense of acknowledgment, and crawled out of the goblin hole and into the morning mists.

Alysha first thought of returning to Hob and Bob's shop. She needed to gather supplies: the Wolfe family heirloom, an ornately carved family pipe, and the newly re-forged Wolfe family sword. Maybe she could return these two items to Junior Wolfe's brother, Felix, and potentially warn the city of Grimwood of the impending siege by the Holy Imperium Army coming from Counselor City. A weak voice deep inside whispered, *find Jared Blackheart and break him open from groin to neck.* She shook her head, trying to forget the thought even as her heart ached for retribution.

She left the goblin hole behind and walked down, leaving the altar of Judith at her back, walking forward to see what remained of Hob and Bob. Halfway down the hill, she saw the remains of bodies torn apart by a pack of wolves, the remains after a fight between herself, Hob, Bob, and a patrol of Holy Imperium soldiers. And she was the only one left. Near the bottom stood the wolves feeding on the bodies. They didn't howl or act aggressively as she came down. She reached out to them through her thoughts.

The lead wolf, a large brown one with slashes of silver in its mane, stopped gnawing on a body and looked at Alysha. At that moment, they knew to leave each other alone. Alysha backed away and walked back toward Counselor City in a daze-filled state. She didn't quite understand how she survived, but thoughts of lightning, rain, and vengeance lingered on her lips.

Austin - Confessions

"There are those defiant against the grace of the Maker, her innocent Child, and the obedient Servant. We see it in the works of Gothine and those who still worship their pagan idols whose names I dare not even say in this blessed church. Even after the great King Christopher and his heathen Queen Erica, the Red conquered Vineland, this rich country held the sins and vice for those who remained weak. Recently, slaves turned on their kind and caring masters while traitorous nobles and merchants griped about taxes and outright refused to kneel to our most holy prince of Vineland. Others suffer and pass sickness around, full of sin, revoking the love and warmth of the Maker's breast. But the unholiest, the bastards of humanity, use power profane in the eyes of the Child of the Maker, breaking the chains of the servants blessed to work our fields and ignoring humanity's loving touch. They draw power from Gothine to make fire from their palms, heal the sick with a vexatious embrace, and drop lightning from the sky," the bishop stopped for effect. "Mages and their deviant ways, slaves revolting from their masters, heathens worshiping Gothine will all whither at the sight of the Maker in all her grace and light. To those who can hear me, I say turn now from your sins, obey your masters, seek the truth like the Child and you will feel the grace of the Maker, bound to her as the servants we justly shall be."

Sir Jasper Pinehard, Sir Austin Casting, and two personal guards known as Wildcats stood next to Prince Damon, the leader of the Holy Imperium, as he knelt, listening to Bishop Devon preach his sermon. Jasper barely paid attention to the words spewing from the bishop's mouth. He tried not to smirk as the bishop's jowls shook and his sparse hair shifted on his head.

Jasper could swear he saw the liver spots moving across the bishop's head as he railed and complained about the sins Jasper indulged in while off duty. The guards were the only ones in the Holy Church's congregation still standing. The rest knelt on rigid wooden panels, including Prince Damon himself. Two Wildcats stood far from the prince in the isle, while Austin and Jasper stood beside the prince on either side. Five weeks ago, a slave attempted regicide on Prince Damon while at church. Austin had bashed the elven slave, a fourteen-year-old boy, in the face with the handle of his sword, and Jasper ran him through, spilling blood in one of the most sacred places in the Holy Imperium. The boy had attempted to throw a fireball the size of a dinky child's toy while the prince knelt during the gospel of Bishop Devon. The Child believed it was the best chance he could take, as it was forbidden to draw blood on Holy Church soil. The slave did not consider that Prince Damon's Wildcat guards didn't give two squirts in a bucket about that rule.

"Our Templar knights broke up an orgy recently," Bishop Devon waited while the last remark hung in the air. He knew the mention of sex in any form would get everyone's attention. And, of course, it did. Jasper watched as various ladies of court straightened their backs and tilted their heads to hear better. Austin, the youngest of Prince Damon's bodyguards, coughed lightly.

"An orgy was uncovered at a private mansion two weeks ago where deviants partook in illicit affairs, betraying the Maker herself. I can say that the monstrosities are too vile to even mention." He paused again and smiled like a cat with a mouse under his paw. "Know that our holy soldiers of the Blue Templar dispatched those in attendance and destroyed the den of vice and disparity. Now, I'm sorry to say none were arrested, but by the Maker's blessing, we will find the culprits."

Jasper didn't believe a word from Bishop Devon, as knights known as the Blue Templar attended the orgy, and he knew because he was enjoying himself with one of them as the door was kicked in. He didn't fear damnation to the pits of Hades ruled over by Gothine. It was all rubbish to him. All Jasper needed was a sharp sword, a wet tongue, and a hard-on, and he'd live one moment at a time because life was short, and Hudson City had thousands of ways to kill him.

Jasper and Austin recently spoke about the strength and number of the Blue Templar in Hudson City with a sense of worry. Their numbers continued to grow, and if left unchecked, they would outnumber the Wildcats and guards around the city. The city guards, known as Copperheads, now walked patrols with a Blue Templar by their sides to help keep the peace and look for hedge mages and witches, checking papers of servants and slaves and verifying all paperwork held the official stamps. They often caused delays in everyday business and more problems than necessary, all for the sake of taxes and safety. The number of official beatings and hangings had gone up, and yet crime in the city persisted.

What worried Jasper further was that Prince Damon asked to speak to him directly after today's sermon. Maybe the prince learned more about the orgy, which could be trouble for the Wildcat Commander.

"Austin, you asked to stay for a moment to pray. You may, but I dislike having Prince Damon guarded by only three knights." Austin nodded as he stood next to Jasper. After the sermon, the congregation shifted and jostled to quickly leave the church, all with solemn faces and bleak expressions. Prince Damon was the first to go, with Jasper and two other guards attending his grace. Austin remained off to the side as he wished to attend confession.

* * *

"Maker, Child, and Servant forgive me for my sins. In choosing to wander off the Path of the Blessed, I failed you. I have sinned against the Holy Church and all your blessings."

Austin knelt for over thirty minutes, lost in prayer, dripping in guilt and the sin of his last outing revelations. He stunk of sex, booze, and rank smoke from the brothels, wine sinks, and gambling halls he attended with his commander, Jasper, the leader of Prince Damon's personal gard, the Wildcats. He was ordered to party with Jasper, but he enjoyed it, Austin thought in silence. He enjoyed himself with women, men, and races not his own, which was illegal in Prince Damon's Holy Imperium. Maker's sweet ass, did he love laying with a dwarven woman and an elvish man, sometimes simultaneously. After a shift of guard duty, he was so tired, yet Jasper would whisper to him to come out into the night and into the East Village to wander in a sea of madness and lust, forgetting about the anxiety of guarding the most important man in Vineland. "Work hard, play hard," is what Jasper said. The locals called the partying in the villages the carnival of the evening, or in the slums, it was called the shitpoke, while the upper classes spoke of it as the night season. The dwarves and human commoners in Hudson City, underpaid servants, said they deserved a stiff drink and a throw at the gambling tables before heading home. The tide of the night called to them.

Hudson City was the most populous city in Vineland and a country on its own. The royals and nobles lived near the Elverstone Citadel and the tallest tower on the peninsula, called Trinity Cloudreach, and the common folk lived in the shadows of the towers, walking the streets of Groanwitch, or the Butcher and Blade neighborhoods. While neighborhoods like Hades Kitchen, where five streets met, or in the East and West Villages of Hudson City all gave life to the wine sinks, brothels, gambling halls, and beer dens settled between factories and other businesses that fed off noble and royal money.

Since Austin's first foray into the East Village with Jasper near the edge of winter, it became a habit for the two Wildcats to finish a week of guard duty, change into commoner clothes, and make their way out of safer noble portions of Hudson City, where the gentry and upper class lived, and travel through tunnels used by slaves and servants into the less refined neighborhoods. They would end up in the East Village, where the morals were looser, at least during the tides of the night. Life was less thought of as a grind if Austin had something to look forward to. Yet raised to worship the Maker, Child, and Servant, the guilt of sin always slipped into his mind as he awoke from his string of iniquities. Seeking absolution through confession to either a priest or priestess of the Holy Church was demanded once a month.

Today, the religious figure in question, hidden behind a screen, made him wait on his knees for a half hour in silence. Austin knew this was a pre-punishment for his confession to come.

The booth was tall, made of ornate wood with a door and room to kneel, connected by a wood frame screen covered in silk to conceal the occupant's face, providing a mask of privacy so those seeking penance could give the truth without fear of public reprisal. The room where priests or priestesses entered was divided by the screen, backed in stone so the other occupants would not know with whom they spoke, although, with only so many clergy members available, a fervent churchgoer could figure it out quickly by voice.

Someone coughed on the other side of the screen. It was a female, which piqued Austin's attention, but he remained eyes cast down, kneeling and attempting to remain pennant in the eyes of the Maker.

"Tell me of your exploits, Sir Austin."

The priestess knew who he was, yet he had no idea what she looked like or anything further about the priestess. The woman's voice was younger, and he'd confessed to her previously.

"I have taken various people to bed and made lavish love to them. I have drunk to indulge, and my fornication tends to lead to the usage of illegal drugs. Sometimes before, sometimes after, and even during the act. I have screamed the Maker's name in anger and lust, and I've done all while under the influence of strong drink and other substances like wizard salt, reefer, and witch pepper. All with other people in attendance watching me or while I watched and," he waited as the guilt lingered and shifted his legs; his knees ached, but he liked the pain. He wanted the pain and her presence.

"Go on," she whispered, a slight urge, and then she caught herself. Austin could feel movement on the screen. "Continue for the Maker, Child, and Servant. I must hear it from you so your sins can be purified by the flame," she finished in a more normal voice.

"I enjoyed it." He smiled and wasn't afraid to hide the smile from her, a priestess of the Maker, right and just.

"You enjoyed it?" she questioned.

"I kill people for a living: I must remain at attention for hours. I have to be prepared for anything. Sometimes, I am sent off to Maker's forsaken nowhere at the request of those I serve, with no questions asked, to kill and destroy a target, and return without so much as a 'Hello, welcome back.' Those I serve, they do not bother to know my name, so yes, I let go and indulge, and I enjoy it."

"Do you wish to absolve your sins, sir knight?"

"Today, I do."

"Pray for another hour in the back pew, on your knees to the Maker, and ask for her forgiveness. And if you can, try to do something decent for those in the villages you treat with your lusts and sins. Make their lives better, and you may do right in this world." the priestess's voice quivered. Austin shifted his knees again. A screen and heavy hardwood separated them.

"May the Path of the Blessed guide your way."

"And also, you." Austin looked closely at the screen and briefly saw bright green eyes before the light of the Holy Church came through. They disappeared as the door opened into the rest of the church.

Austin stepped out and saw the captain of the Wildcats standing at the church's doors, waiting for him. He took a deep breath, walked to the church's back pew, and knelt again. Minutes later, he heard Jasper's footsteps and walked toward his captain.

"Sir, I have another hour of prayer."

"I hate this place. Let's go," Jasper said.

"Hate is a strong word; the Maker, Child, and Servant hate no man. On the contrary, they are the love and light of the world." Austin shifted his weight on his knees, loathing and enjoying the pain of worship. He closed his eyes.

"Look at me. That's an order."

"You can't order me, sir. I'm off duty."

"Then look at me as a," Jasper said, "as a friend. We've drank and broken bread together."

Austin looked at Jasper, that smile, and his young yet lined face.

"Maker loves everyone, you say; don't remind me. The thought makes me sick," his voice echoed in the church. Light from the color-pained windows caught dust as it fell. "Austin, think about it. The Maker loves murderers, rapists, child murderers, and baby rapists," Jasper slightly laughed to himself, his smile forming a smirk on his freshly shaved face. "For me, a god that loves that." He stopped, not wanting to go too far, and looked at Austin and his blind faith peering into his eyes. "Please do me a favor. Just follow orders and leave that shit behind you on duty. Your life is the life of the royal family and

29

the Imperium. You feel guilty for letting loose because you put your life on the line and call it faith. Put your faith in your fellow guards; they'll have your back. Put your belief in the steel at your side." He put his hand on Austin's shoulder. "You'll meet your Maker sooner than you wish. Now, get off your knees. We've got orders." Austin got up, feeling the blood rush to his lower back and legs again.

"I've finished confession."

"You really are a true believer."

"You're not?"

"I believe steel will guide me down the path, whether to light or darkness. It does not matter. Worms don't care."

"I spoke of you in confession," Austin said quietly.

Jasper raised an eyebrow and looked at Austin like a friend. Almost like a father.

"You don't tell them everything, do you? All the sordid details about what you do in the dark during the tides of night," Jasper shook his head. "They want to know all the details because some so-called Holy One profits from our sins."

"What now?"

"Extortion," Jasper said. "They find out who you are and demand favors or money from you."

Austin looked back at the confessional and scratched at his chin nervously.

"Or they store those little details and take care of themselves when they get a free moment. Let's go. You can pray later; Prince Damon has a special assignment for us," said Jasper.

He put his arm around Austin. "Remember why we are here?"

"Yes."

"Why?"

"*Knowledge, obedience, and duty to Vineland. I bleed for you, and you will bleed for me, and we will bleed for the land.*"

"Now, if you must pray, pray you don't take a blade in the stomach, Austin. That is the worst way to go."

They walked on, away from the Holy Church.

"Prince Damon has let me off guard duty, and you as well. We have orders."

"I was wondering how you got off duty today."

"We're to do some recon work out near the Blightbriar Wilds with an attachment of soldiers, some from the Wildcats, some from a mercenary group, a few Blue Templar, and some conscripts," Jasper informed him.

"That doesn't sound like recon; that sounds like a paltry army," said Austin.

"I was also able to get permission to grow the Wildcats. We can take on new members," Austin paused and stepped closer to Jasper. "I don't play court games, but I worry about the influence of the Blue Templar and their strength. You see what they've done lately. We may be the Holy Imperium, but I want this country to be a country of laws, not a country bent by holy rules. Are you with me on that?" pressed Jasper.

Austin had never seen Jasper as serious as he was right now. He looked into his eyes with conviction and sincerity.

"A place where anyone can worship any god as long as they don't hurt someone else," said Jasper.

Austin looked around and nodded.

"We need like-minded people; Prince Damon can be bent. We have his ear."

Austin nodded, again unsure of what to say.

"We're looking for new Wildcats loyal to me. You understand?"

"What's the mission?" Austin asked, changing the subject.

"I have an idea, but we need to get the official orders from above. Some hunting lodge was looted or burnt down; find out who did it, bring them to justice, inform the prince once complete, and come home."

"The Blightbriar Wild is no joke, Jasper. There are warhawks, spiders, bears, tigers, all sorts of evil shit out there, not including wild tribes of orcs, elves, and cave goblins."

"Don't believe all the stories you hear. It's just brigands causing trouble. Maybe leftovers from the war with nothing to do. We take care of this, in and out, and hope the orders don't change."

Austin nodded and felt uneasy at what Jasper had said. He wasn't sure if the anxiety came from going into the Blightbriar Wilds or the politics behind the orders here at the capital.

The Bastards - Poor Mourning

"Forgive me for what I've done and what I may have to do," whispered Doc as he pulled Stitch's body onto the table, resting it next to Runt's. He wasn't sure if he was praying to the Maker or to the pagan gods, and he wasn't sure what really mattered. He just wanted steady hands as the voices whispered in his mind to kill himself and anyone around him.

The crossbow bolts sat in a bucket on the floor, and Doc leaned one body over, pushing the blood out of the seeping wound. He'd pulled the life force from Stitch with difficulty, and the price for gaining another living being's power was unknown to him so far. Doc knew magic was a give-and-take proposition, like a mathematical equation for those born with the talent. Generally, if he were to take something from a living creature, something would need to be returned. Where this energy went, he didn't know, most likely back into nature. He'd already given up his sanity when his daughter lay dying in his hands, and she volunteered to give her innocent life to him, one of the only known children to be born from two mages. After the struggle, the only time he could think straight was to abuse drugs and alcohol, for when he was sober, the dead echoed in his head, causing him to become a wreck of a human. That was the curse of pulling the energy and soul from someone so full of love and sanity that he'd done it again.

His superiors tried to help him by forcing two binding rings onto his fingers, dulling his powers but not the madness, so they jailed him. After escaping the asylum, he returned to Grimwood University, hoping to find answers or solace in its cursed graveyards and library. Still, all he received was Maynard, a promising apprentice now using magic as recklessly as he did after years of

32

teaching and a long, trying journey.

He pushed the stomachs of the corpses, and they released the rest of the food digested in their intestines. Doc lit his pipe, and a thick white smoke poured out, a mixture of Vineland tobacco and reefer. The tobacco was heavily taxed, addictive, and farmed in the south on plantations, and the reefer was illegal, as it was an elvish herb used in their war dances and communes with their gods. At this point, Doc didn't care, and he would burn any Holy Imperium soldier or tax collector who crossed his path if they wanted to complain about his choice of narcotics. He needed it to stay sane and keep his head and the voices quiet.

"Whether it was meant to be this way or not," he mumbled, "Runt's going to get to his father. I promised him that and that Lady Rowan Wightland foresaw it." He took a rag and cleaned Stitch's chest wound, looking at his failure to save the young half-elve life. "My staff, Gaston's Beard, is in General Ashburn's hands; he trades it for Runt's remains, or I'll burn him to cinder where he stands." He shook his head 'no,' defying the voices inside. "There are easier ways," he mumbled.

Doc sewed up their wounds cleanly, and someone brought fresh clothes for each. At least these two would look presentable before internment, and Doc would carry his failure with him until one day, when he would follow them into darkness. Doc stood back and looked at the bodies. "Death is the only forever," he said.

The door slammed open, and the morning sun shined through.

"You fuckin' bastard," said a voice, and Doc squinted as a mass of beard and hair came through the door. He carried a sizable dwarven cast iron pan with sharpened pour spouts on each end. The dwarve swung the pan like an axe, crashing it down toward Doc, who stepped away.

"Did they tell you what happened, Angus?" cried Doc. "Don't make me use force to protect myself."

The large, inebriated dwarve swung again, and Doc stepped back. Blueish-black smoke seeped from Doc's pipe-like ink as it streamed through the air and toward his attacker.

"Angus, settle down. I didn't put a crossbow bolt through either of their chests, you hairy biscuit."

Angus tossed the pan from its handle over his head. Doc ducked, and the pan's spout stuck into the wall from the force of the throw. Angus pulled out an extremely well-maintained butcher knife and cleaver from his belt.

"Runt was nearly my son, you stain. He was your responsibility while I was gone. You failed him, and you failed me. No money or apologies can make up for your failure."

Angus traveled hundreds of miles with Runt, the son of Maria Ashburn, whose corpse was food for the wolves of Runt's town of Wolf Hills last autumn, killed by Holy Imperium soldiers just like him. "His sister was sold into slavery, and you had to get him to his father. Hades, you could have just found his older brother stationed here. We were so close. What have you done?" Angus swung the knife and cleaver at Doc, who held a chair like a shield. The chair was chipped, cut, and broken in several places as Angus screamed at Doc.

Angus dropped his weapons and fell onto his knees, hands on his face, as he sobbed. "He was better than all of us. He wasn't a coward, and he wasn't a murderer, liar, or thief. He could have gone to university and done more with his life than any of us ever have!"

"He was a fine boy, and I thought he was meant for great pursuits," Doc finished dropping the chair. He walked over and kneeled as well and hugged the aged dwarve. They had traveled through Vineland with Runt, and Doc knew Runt meant the world to Angus. The dwarve had watched the young man grow from a baby into a man even after his mother was killed steps away from his home, and now Runt lay dead, killed by the army his father led in the city of Olde Ridgewatch.

Doc listened to Angus cry and held him as he cried tears of blood, yet another curse for using powers he should never touch. Doc waited until Angus cried himself out and wiped his own bloody face.

"I can feel your anger, Angus. All we have left now is to make this right."

"No, there is no right, Doc, not after this. He was the only family I had left. The only thing left now is vengeance."

He stood and put his meat cleaver and butcher knife back into his belt, brushing past Doc and grabbing his large cast iron skillet. "I am taking my

Skull Scrambler here and going to get good and drunk. Hades, help any Holy Imperium soldier who tries to stop me. The bar tab is on you. All of them are now. Any bar I go to, you have a tab open now. Pay it up. It's the least you can do. They will have your full name, what you look like, everything. No place will welcome you unless you pay them. I will be sure of it, you fucking lousy bastard. Find me when you take his body to his father."

Angus walked out the door. The winter storm that blasted through last night was moving across the Atlantis Ocean, heading towards the Empire of Great Brightland on the other side of the ocean, leaving a warming spring sun in its wake.

Doc looked around at the apartment they had commandeered. The ceiling was the only thing not destroyed or sprayed with blood.

"Well, shit. I better find a cart or wheel barrel for these two. I think it's time for Stitch to be buried and for Runt to meet his father."

Doc looked around and crossed the street to the beer hall, where two townsfolk stood outside like guards.

"You need something?"

"I need a cart to carry a body. I'm planning a funeral march; stand in my way, and I'll burn you to the ground."

Having taken Stitch's essence through force, Doc had an excellent source to use his power as a mage, but he was in a poor mood. The two guards didn't know it, but he was extremely dangerous.

"Whatever, you crazy old coot. Get back to your apartment. We are in the middle of something."

"You are in the middle of a riot that has not occurred, and I'm prepared to not let it get out of control. So, I'll take this boy to his father and stop you drunks from getting killed in the next few hours. Now stand aside."

Doc's eyes glowed inking purple fire around their edges and drifted up. This trick is pushed out through emotion. It was unnatural and not seen often. Mages, witches, and sorcerers were not seen in public; if they were, they were in control, bound by a ring procured by the Church of the Holy Imperium.

The two guards fell over themselves, making the Maker's sign across

35

themselves.

"Witch! You're a witch!" one screamed.

"I'm no witch, fool. I'm the last battlemage of Vineland," and he walked through the door. "Now, where is Richard Holmes, the one-legged piker."

The crowd of drunks and merchants parted. Doc saw Maynard, Duncan, and Angus standing at the side of the bar, drinks in their hands. They acknowledged Doc but made no move to stand near his side.

"Excuse me, but everyone shut up!" yelled Doc, raising his voice and breaking up loud conversations of revolution and battle plans.

"You've taken several streets in this old town and plan to take more. You are outnumbered and don't have enough arms to take the town. General Benedict Ashburn is now gathering his soldiers and mercenaries, the elite Brotherhood of Bitterleak, to take what you have here."

"We can take them," one drunk said.

"Hades!" yelled others.

"Booze and bravery will get you dead, and you know it. Richard Holmes has one leg. How did he lose it? Through stupidity and poor decisions!" Doc yelled back.

Someone hissed.

"Call me a coward all you want, but the revolution you want, the war you want, it isn't time yet."

"Who are you to say?" yelled someone in the crowd.

Doc wanted to tell them he was Hunter Young, the last battlemage of Vineland, who slew Umar and Jezebel Everfall during the Crimson Struggle and killed countless more with fire and disease, which was slowly killing him now, but he didn't say anything. So, he held back and waited.

The two guards burst through the door.

"Listen to the old man. He fought up north. He knows what he says. The blood on his hands speaks for that enough. Man killed thousands using unholy magics and spells,"

The crowd quieted now, having heard from a local confirming the lunatic was a mage who fought in a battle that killed thousands.

A dwarve who helped unload the beer cart last night said, "You fought on the Plains of Ursula. I was there too, saw some heavy shit, a tornado of fire and death, bolts of lightning shattering lines of soldiers, and winds the like of which I never felt."

"I was there too," said another old soldier who coughed up something and spit it out. She had an eye patch and burn marks on her face and arm.

"Aye," said another.

"Me too."

More agreed and stepped forward.

Doc looked around; his gaze and the history written on his face calmed the crowd with understanding and now slight respect.

"We didn't get to bury our comrades after the Battle of the Reaping." Doc waited; the room was hushed. "Yet today, I get to bury a friend and give a son back to a father, and in doing so, I may stop you from getting butchered by the Black Eagles. So, do your best and find me two coffins. The revolution can wait a few days."

Shortly after, a strong-armed woman came by and dropped off two coffins. Doc spoke to the woman for several moments quietly and provided her compensation, and a grave smile passed between them. Doc placed Runt Ashburn, son of General Benedict Ashburn, back into the horse-drawn cart they used to drive into the city, now laying a plain coffin. He put flowers he found at a nearby stall into Runt's hands, attempting to make the corpse presentable. The morning burnt away into the afternoon.

Duncan, a bear of a man, walked up to the cart carrying another of their party, the half-elve Stitch, an ex-slave, thief, and all-around scoundrel, placing him in the other coffin. They were quiet as they maneuvered the bodies safely into their last beds. Two young men's lives were taken late at night at the hands of Holy Imperium Soldiers.

Doc looked at Duncan, the bastard son of a dwarve named Bearfric the Righteous Hand, one of Steelsburg's most famous mercenary warriors. If half-elves were uncommon, half-dwarves were even less so. Doc had only met two half-dwarves in his abnormally long lifetime, and Duncan was one of them. Duncan was an exception to nature as dwarves and the other race orcs could not crossbreed with humans.

The revelation of Duncan's heritage caused chaos in the dwarven capital of Steelsburg, causing a civil war between two rival clans in the city. The war could take years to end. Maynard walked up to the cart.

"They look good, Doc. Thank you for taking the time to make them presentable," he said somberly. He'd grown close to Runt and marked him as a friend. Hades, if Maynard thought about it, he was Maynard's only friend.

"Thanks, Maynard," he took a sip from his whiskey bottle. "Sorry for drinking, but it wouldn't be a funeral without a little booze."

"It's fine, Doc. Duncan and I know you need it to carry on as you do. What we do takes a price."

"What did you give up taking from Runt before he passed?" whispered Doc so Duncan couldn't hear.

Maynard scratched at his face, and Doc watched him do so. Doc noticed none of his fingers held any fingernails.

"That is an awkward price, toes too?"

"No, just the fingers. Hurts like Hades, but they should heal." Maynard said flatly. "And you?

"Another memory of something I loved," said Doc.

"I'm not sure if that is good or bad."

"It's fine until someone reminds you of it. Then it's worse than a knife to the kidney. I still remember my daughter and you, but I'm sure what's done will cause pain sooner or later."

Duncan came back as others gathered around the cart. He was carrying a pewter mug of beer and gave one to Maynard.

"Maynard, you hear from Sorella or Cordial?"

"No, have you?"

"No, haven't heard from Gray Jim either. What about you, Doc."

"Cordial, Gray Jim, no, not either. Duncan, I'm sorry to ask, but who's Sorella?"

"What in the Maker are you talking about, Doc? You know. You introduced me to her years ago. Sorella Silvercrow and her sister, Victoria. It's not even noon yet. Are you that wasted?" Duncan threw his hands in the air. "Don't you have any respect for yourself? Hades, don't you have any respect for Runt and Stitch here."

"We spent the better part of the year getting Runt to Olde Ridgewatch, and he's dead, and now you deny knowing one of your closest friends," said Duncan, exasperated. "So done with you, Doc. Everything we've done in the past, it's over."

Maynard looked at Doc and down at the ground, ashamed and foolish, knowing this was the toll he paid to take power from Stitch as he passed last night.

"Duncan, it's not his fault. He lost the memory this morning. It's due to his condition," he paused and whispered, "Remember, we are apostates. He recently used the high art and lost the memory of Sorella Silvercrow." Maynard said. "So, I guess it was her; she's gone from Doc's mind."

Duncan scratched at his face. "Hades, so, it's like she never existed?"

"Most likely, she will be a new person to him."

"I'm right here, sweet Maker's milk. What or who are you babbling about," yammered Doc.

"Nothing, Doc, nothing," Duncan put his hand on the mage's shoulder. "After we are done here, I need to go look for a friend." Duncan started pulling the horses forward. Nobody rode on the cart. They started walking towards the city. Folks piled out from the tavern and other bars, all wearing dark clothes and mourning. A young boy played the drum for the beat of a military funeral march. Maynard saw several people from last night throwing snowballs and oyster shells at the Holy Imperium guards to join the dark parade.

Dick Holmes and his wife Abigail showed up, the same woman that delivered the two coffins. She wore a thick dress with the same white covering that looked like blood stains. She wore a dark blue ribbon in her hair and another wrapped around her arm. She also held a large cooking pin. Dick had a black eye and his head bandaged, still slightly leaking with blood. He had his wooden foot back on but used a crutch as he joined the march next to the cart carrying the dead. Doc looked around and saw others armed in some fashion. They were not using swords or spears, as they were illegal, but chains, staves, and cudgels were about as if they were hoping for a fight. The horses sniffed and shifted their heads, and the cart moved forward. A dismal parade started, and nobody laughed or smiled.

Alysha - Wolves Beyond the Gates

Alysha looked at the sky above the pine, oak, and maple trees surrounding the stream. The clouds and darkness that came with the rising storm pushed east, making the morning feel more like twilight and less like the start of the day. The storm shifted above her, and the clouds pushed further with a warmer wind as the hand of spring urged winter back to rest. The snow melted, and tufts of wet grass and flowers pulled themselves out from under the cover of winter and the death of fall. She stopped by a stream and looked at herself as she took in the water. Her throat cooled to the water's touch, and she brushed her face for a moment, feeling her scarred right eye and now slightly crooked nose. Her eyes were bloodshot and bruised. She stood feeling the bruises as she moved on toward Counselor City. Wolves howled in the distance, but she felt no fear. They were not for her but for the dead and those with something to lose.

By midday, she came to the palisade walls of Counselor City. She returned to the city without Hob and Bob, and the blood of their murders was still under her fingernails.

The southern gate of Counselor City had a queue near the opening. She needed to grab her few personal essentials from the blacksmith shop. She hoped the Hob and Bob Smithy would have enough supplies to get her out of the city and be safe. Unfortunately, she didn't have a horse, as wolves had eaten Hob and Bob's two draft horses while she recovered in the goblin cave.

"Alysha, is that you? Are you okay?" asked Edwin Flatrock, a gate guard for Counselor City.

Anyone who does not stand with you is against you. Kill them all or make them

41

kneel, a voice whispered deep inside. She pushed the thought away.

"Shit," she swore under her breath and immediately felt awkward. Edwin wasn't a foul person like the creeps that killed Hob and Bob, but he was now a member of the Holy Imperium army, even if he was a local from the city. She looked at his uniform, and sweat formed across her back.

"Was attacked two days back. Bandits. Hob and Bob defended me, and I ran but was chased into the forest." She took a deep breath, trying to calm down.

She stood with a slight hunch and leaned slightly against the gate. Edwin moved toward her, and she allowed him to grab her shoulders even as her forearms shivered from his touch.

"Maker's Luck, you need a healer. I'll fetch a local barber."

Alysha pushed him away more aggressively than she meant.

"I'm sorry, I'm fine, I'm not fine. I need to get inside and feel safe. I need to rest and get away from..."

"How many were there?" he stood still, blocking her path.

"Edwin, are you letting that one through?" hollered the guard on the other side of the gate as they checked people coming in and out.

"Just a second, Brandy. Got a report of bandits south of here," Edwin hollered back.

"I dunno, I don't remember, more than six, maybe ten," she lied. "They came at Hob and Bob. I ran away, and they followed. I hid in the forest and haven't eaten much. There were wolves, too."

Alysha couldn't stop lying. She desperately pulled her hair back from her face, tucked it behind her ear, and looked at him. She knew he saw the scar, her crooked nose, and bruised eyes. "I defended myself and saw people I care for die. Just let me," She let out a sigh, growing frustrated. "Can you let me go inside?"

Edwin looked at her with a concern Alysha had not asked for nor wanted, and her knuckles tightened.

"I'll report this to my captain. Stay at the smithy, Alysha. He may want to talk to you more about what happened." Concern clouded his eyes as he let her pass.

Alysha walked by slowly, feigning a limp, and entered the gate's shadow away from Edwin. She thought he was an honorable man trying to do his job and remembered he was sweet. Yet he now served the Holy Imperium, which was responsible for the destruction of her family and home.

"Brandy, watch the gate. I am going to speak to Captain Steller. He should know about the bandits. Figured Richard's patrol would take care of the bandits in the area," he said as he walked off towards the gatehouse where his captain slept in a chair.

Alysha rounded the corner and ran towards the shop, only slowing to ensure no stitches broke from the effort. She unlocked the door, hoping to find what she needed and get out as fast as possible. She piled up fresh sets of clothes, a blanket, Junior Wolfe's reforged sword, the Wolfe family pipe, and a cooking pot into the corner near the door, taking an extra moment to pack it all as tightly as possible. The sword was put into its sheath and hung on her hip. She didn't care if anyone looked oddly at her anymore and would not let another person try and touch her again. Adrenaline-induced haze gripped her as she lit the coals at the forge and placed candles about as if she were going to work. She wasn't herself. The stress of the past days started to gnaw at her.

As she was grabbing a wineskin, the door opened, and the little bell above gave a ring.

"We're closed. Sorry, the owners are under the weather," she made up quickly.

"I'm sorry to hear," said a rough voice. "I heard wolves outside the city gates this morning and wanted to know if you had any arrowheads?" Alysha recognized the woman named Claudette, who waited for a moment and then smiled. "Ian Shortstride, a scout for General Flint himself, recommended this place. Looks like you didn't make it to the brothel like your friend. Glad your indentured service worked out. Half of those we took this past fall died during the winter. Count yourself lucky. You're blessed."

"By Judith," Alysha whispered.

"Blessed by the Child, Servant, and Maker herself," finished Claudette in her bumpkin draw.

Claudette Leigh was a scout of the Genteel Monks, the group that destroyed Alysha's homestead and murdered Alysha's mother. She stood in the doorway, acting like nothing had happened; her indecency shone through her voice. Claudette's commander, Jared Blackheart, was an enforcer for Robert Flint, General of the Holy Imperium First Army. After her life was destroyed, Alysha had not seen the scout since she led her down to Hob and Bob's Smithy for her indentured service. Indentured service was a polite way to say 'slave' in the Holy Imperium army. The woman was a murderer and arsonist. Alysha remembered seeing her drown babies in the creek when the Genteel Monks attacked her valley last autumn.

The Genteel Monk leaned against the door, staring, her tarnished white robes mocking the morals she supposedly represented. Alysha walked behind the counter where Hob and Bob used to take orders and speak to customers. Her bearded maul, Stormkiss, and sword lay nearby.

"I can take your order and ensure Hob and Bob receive it. Depending on your desired quantity, it shouldn't take more than two days," she said, trying to keep the anger from her voice.

Claudette swayed in the door as if drunk.

"Need two dozen arrowheads. Leave it under my name, Claudette Leigh," she said. "It's dark here. I hope Hob and Bob don't have the pox or Smoldering Plague."

"No, they both had head colds and took too much whiskey last night. Normally, they're right and ready to go, but I think they took too much medicine." Alysha feigned a movement to show someone drinking too much with her hand.

"Well," the Monk said, taking a step closer. "I am sorry to hear that. You look awful. What happened to you? It looks as if you've been in a fight."

"I fell," Alysha responded, thinking fast. "I fell and hit my head coming down from the loft. I can be clumsy. They let me join them for a few drinks last night. I'm cursed with running the shop today while they recover."

"You should go see a barber or, if you can afford one, a doctor. You look out of sorts. That looks to be one heck of a fall."

Alysha firmly put her hand on the table, and her anger rose.

44

"I'll be fine. Worse has happened to me, and I've recovered."

Alysha wrote out a receipt and handed it to her. Then, she wrote up the order in the ledger. "Sign here," she said flatly, pointing at a space on the bottom of the paper.

Claudette took the quill and started signing, leaning down slightly. Alysha watched the soldier sign as she slowly adjusted her weight, moving her hand towards her weapon, the half-bearded maul made of star metal called Stormkiss, which stood against the counter, out of sight.

"Well, I hope they recover quickly. I want this order completed as soon as possible." Claudette finished signing and looked up.

"Of course, we appreciate your business." Alysha tried to steady her tone, but she only spit out sarcasm.

"Alysha. That's your name, right?" Claudette snapped her fingers. Alysha, startled, lost her grip on Stormkiss.

Kill her now.

"Edwin, the guard, said you came back by the gate alone, saying bandits attacked you. You tell me Hob and Bob are unwell and hungover. So, which is it? Gone for two days and attacked by bandits, or hungover and sleeping it off somewhere?"

Claudette slammed her knife down on the table, trying to scare Alysha further, but she was beyond fear and held nothing but contempt.

"Why is one of General Flint's patrols missing? What were you, Hob, and Bob doing in the woods south of Counselor City?"

Alysha knew she had to escape, but her gear was behind the open door. There was only one decision, but it was more of an act of survival. She picked up Stormkiss, swung it overhead, shifting the hammerhead in the down position, and smashed downward. The blow missed Claudette, but that was expected. The hammer's speed, weight, and star stone metal smashed the wooden counter and shattered it into hundreds of pieces, forcing Claudette back from the blast, and they stumbled back into the wall.

"What the Hades!" Claudette drew two blades from her belt. "Stand down, woman!"

Alysha stepped toward Claudette in a slight crouch, like a wolf hungry for prey. A vision of the brown and silver wolf stuck in her mind. She was hungry for death, and Claudette was the prey.

The Genteel Monk approached her, overestimating Alysha, who just smashed a six-foot counter with a bearded maul.

Claudette strived to overwhelm Alysha with the speed of her two short swords lunging at her with half-circle strikes. Alysha blocked the first two with luck and ignorance, but the successive blows left three slices on her forearms and shoulders.

"You filthy blacksmith whore, you're wanted for questioning." Claudette gasped. "The gate captain was right. You were up to something."

Do not trust the Holy Imperium. Kill Claudette and those that taint my Vineland.

Alysha moved against a wall, breathing hard and bleeding. Her jaw clenched, and her thoughts were not all her own.

Her weapon was meant for an aggressive fighter and not built for pure defense. The wall against her back told her she was finished retreating. She shifted her weight and thinned her stance, giving Claudette only her one shoulder as a target. She held onto Stormkiss tightly. Alysha wanted nothing but Claudette dead.

"I protected myself from scum who wanted to hurt me. I figured you would understand, but you're as much to blame as the rest of Blackheart's monks."

She swung her war hammer blade first from below, arching it up and catching Claudette off guard as she expected another overhead blow. She jumped back, and Alysha spun and swung again, exposing her back for a moment but using the weapon's reach to cut toward Claudette. She blocked the blow, but the hammer's strength and speed caused Claudette to lose a blade. Alysha sprung forward and forced the handle into Claudette's stomach, knocking the air out of her.

"Tell me, what would you do if someone killed your family?"

The blow falling into her chest knocked Claudette as if a horse had kicked her, and she fell onto her back. She braced herself, knees bent while her elbows braced her back from the ground. Claudette saw blackness around the corners of her eyes and barely took in air.

Alysha swung Stormkiss from above as if chopping a log, and the blow came across Claudette's chest; the hammer portion of Stormkiss crashed down. Claudette's eyes enlarged and nearly came out of her skull, her chest smashed inward, and she spoke garbled gibberish like a baby.

"You would do exactly what I'm doing, killing everyone that allowed it to happen."

Alysha caught her breath, looking at her work. Then, she walked over, grabbing her backpack as the last remains of Claudette's life left at the bottom of her body.

Austin - Everything is the Enemy

S ir Austin Casting examined his horse's flank, patting its side, and squinted his eyes. The spring season's heat bore down on his face, so he took a swig from a wineskin. It felt refreshing wearing the lighter riding gear, not the heavy plate armor guarding Prince Damon. He took a deep breath of the forest air and was reminded of the strange stories his tutor spoke about night ten summers ago. Professor Leifus from the University of Coldpine wove tales about warhawks, wompus rats, crucible wolves, and the crusades for the Gloomspire. Austin chuckled a bit, looked further into the forest, and watched as the squirrels and chipmunks wrestled with each other over nothing but a blind line of territory neither could see but both felt was theirs by right.

* * *

After Austin had returned from a confession at the Holy Church, he and the captain of the Wildcats, Jasper Pinehard, met with Prince Damon, the leader of the Holy Imperium, and Sir Thomas Casting, Minister of the Armies of the Imperium, inside Trinity Cloudreach, the tallest spire in Vineland. The room was near the top, and they were allowed to use the elevator, which he'd only done while in the presence of Prince Damon. The chains pulled the mechanism up as the slaves deep below the tower labored to guide the two knights to heights few commoners ventured. Only the royal court used the elevator. The rest toiled up the stairs as they spiraled up into the thin air.

He remembered seeing Prince Damon and General Casting looking at a map of the Blightbriar Wilds northwest of Hudson City. The map was old and faded, but it showed a dark tower surrounded by clouds in the mountains. The Blightbriar Mountains were a massive barrier separating the Atlantis Ocean and its coastal city-states, with a handful of city-states to the west before hitting the Grave Reach River and the lands beyond. The myth of the spire carved out of a mountain and its surrounding fortress lurked like a dreary cloud on an otherwise bright day. To those in the Holy Imperium, it was called Gloomspire. The fort was known to many through storybooks detailing the crusades to retake the fortress. The Clearstone and Blitzsteel extended families often sang of battles between themselves, elves, orcs, and goblins around the fortress. Walk into any tavern in Steelsburg or the Iron Valley, and a chorus about a battle on the walls of the Gloomspire could be heard nightly.

The conversation was light, almost casual, from Prince Damon, as if he and Austin were best friends, even though Austin was getting orders from the closest royalty to King Geordie of Great Brightland. Prince Damon anointed in the light of the Maker herself.

"Austin, you, Jasper, and your friends will nip up a mountain trail and check out Featherbottom Lodge. One of my retainers said it has been recently..."

Austin looked at General Thomas Casting, the Minister of the Lords and Minister of the Armies, for a moment and flicked his eyes back to Prince Damon, who controlled the majority of territory this side of the Grave Reach River. He swallowed a small amount of sick down.

"Vandalized." Prince Damon finished.

Austin thought it was odd the prince was acting in such a manner. With the servants and lesser lords, he treated them like garbage on fire. He'd only seen Prince Damon speak like this to less than ten people in his career as a Wildcat. The prince became serious now.

"This matter is important to me, so report your findings to me or your cousin here. Do you understand?" asked Prince Damon.

"Jasper will lead the operation with a company of Wildcats and Blue Templar," interrupted General Casting.

"If you wish to hire mercenaries, do so at my expense, but get good work out of them using my money," said Prince Damon. "I want a victory, an impressive victory, so I can let all of the papers know."

Austin was confused. Were they to investigate a burnt-down hunting lodge or kill bandits on the outskirts of the Blightbriar Wilds? Or both? And if so, the number of knights almost seemed like overkill.

"You're to clear the area and perform further recon around the Blightbriar Mountains edge near the Featherbottom Lodge. The area is Oxfell County, which we all know has excellent farming that feeds into the capital. I've written your orders here, Jasper. Austin will accompany you as an observer; I'll send him ravens so he can report back," General Casting said.

Jasper looked at Austin and smiled slightly, feeling awkward as Prince Damon tried to function as if he was a commander in front of the greatest military commander this side of the Atlantis Ocean. The Redcloak General Casting wore, a military honor bestowed by the King of Great Brightland, King Geordie, was a stark reminder of the type of man and knight Lord Casting was compared to the leader of the Holy Imperium, Prince Damon. As well-known as the Wildcat knights were, when a knight of the Order of the Redcloak appeared, everyone bowed in respect.

"Austin, we expect this to be a three-month campaign," Casting said, trying to supply further details.

"Investigate this incident, it's a nothing. Nothing really, a walk between Trinity Cloudreach and East Village really, it'll be so easy your grandmother could do it," said Prince Damon.

"We have reports that we now can no longer ignore. Jasper and Austin, you're to check the basement of the lodge. You'll find a box holding the deed to the house, a book of gospel verses, a family tree, and a hand ax. If you find these items, they're to be returned to one of us. These are Lord Rotherham's personal family belongings, and the House of Rotherham will reward you handsomely if you were to bring them to myself or Prince Damon," General Casting ordered.

Prince Damon, tired of being interrupted, "I'll not have this or anything else interfere with my Triumphant Masquerade. You know this; I gave you a company to take care of this issue, and the Wildcat's best knights!" He looked at Casting and then at Austin and Jasper with concern. "I trust you to keep what Casting requested between yourselves and nobody else. These matters are done in strict confidence but bring home a victory."

Everyone waited until Prince Damon finished.

"I want a glorious victory over these bandits and hooligans who burnt this hunting lodge down. They are thugs! I want them hung from gibbets and their estates burned to the ground!"

Austin considered that if they were outlaws, they most likely didn't own anything except for what they wore on their backs, but he kept that thought to himself. He'd seen Prince Damon get going like this before.

"No riots in Olde Ridgewatch or propaganda from a bunch of bastards screaming for liberty and an end to taxes will stop me or my party! I won't let the fear of our slaves and servants revolting stop the Holy Imperium celebration of our victory in the Crimson Struggle. It took years to end the stranglehold from the Nation of Stouya and Legion of Carigreed on Vineland. With the Maker's blessing, I won't let some forsaken bullshit stop this party. Get in there make a splashy headline and let us know what you find."

Prince Damon stomped his foot and smashed his hand on the table. "Get this done and I will reward you with high honors, fail me and your careers will be over," his face was reddish orange with rage. He composed himself, smiled, and walked out, his hair slightly askew on his crowned head. Austin watched as the door opened, and two fellow Wildcats followed. He realized he would not be taking the elevator back.

Thomas Casting waited until the door closed. Jasper and Austin waited for their dismissal.

Casting cleared his throat.

"This was not mere vandals. Jasper will take fifty knights and a mercenary company to Lord Rotherham's Featherbottom Lodge to investigate why it and several villages were burnt down. The Holy Church will finance another twenty-five Blue Templar directly under your command, not the churches. I made that clear when Bishop Devon offered their support. We are doing Lord Rotherham a favor, and he, in turn, is helping to fund Prince Damon's party, but there is more to it, as we just spoke about."

Jasper nodded. He understood.

"Establish a foothold near the lodge. And patrol the area until you discover what has occurred there. Austin will provide updates, including your reports and his observations."

"We need numbers, weapons, and intelligence. The Blightbriar Wilds are just that; you'll be outnumbered and unsupported as the Holy Imperium soldiers have pulled back from the fortified compounds along the Kings and Queens roads. Some of the remaining soldiers were picked up by General Flint as he scraped the strongholds for men when he marched toward Grimwood last autumn. We can move in, but it would take some time to come in full force, so take the appropriate precautions. I want a quick win, intelligence, and all of you out of the Blightbriar Wilds before fall." Casting ran his fingers through his hair. "This is not a fucking crusade to the Gloomspire, wherever Gothine hid that shit hole of a fortress."

He took a drink from the prince's goblet and passed it to Austin.

"Drink."

He handed the cup to Jasper.

"Drink."

"You've tasted the prince's best, and so have I. Get us a win, and get back here alive."

They drank the bitter red wine and found tears in their eyes as they swallowed.

* * *

Two days ride to the Featherbottom Lodge. Pap joined the parade of horses as they advanced up the road into the low foothills of Oxfell County, delivering a message directly to Jasper from Prince Damon. Pap looked tired but in good spirits, happy to be in the open country and among soldiers. Everyone loved Pap. He was a true leader, and his war stories were legendary. Austin had drawn drag duty again, was at the tail end of the column, and knew this was a serious combat operation. There were no prostitutes or other column followers so far. Each knight had an archer, squire, and page supporting the knight, while the Blue Templar had a monk in their attendance. The mercenaries tended to their horses and food and camped separately. They were to be the foot soldiers for the excursion. Jasper ordered sentries for the past two nights, and on the last day, he sent four mercenary scouts out to provide recon in case of ambush. Fifteen minutes after Pap passed by Austin, Jasper rode to the back of the column with his squire and page.

"Austin, I received orders. I'm needed back in Hudson City. According to Prince Damon, Pap's in charge."

Austin waited for permission to speak.

"You may speak openly," Jasper sighed.

"You'll be missed."

"I know. I hoped to return to Hudson City with a few scalps and ears." He smiled, not serious. "Sorry, you know I hate that practice. I'm going to leave you my squire, Emma Hopesinger. My archer is joining Pap's lance."

Austin eyed the young woman in her clean new armor. The girl was greener than spring grass. "Hopesinger needs work, but she's respectable with a sword and spear; team her up with Newt Crashbury, your squire. They'll teach each other. Then, in a month, you all will return with a sack full of orc, elves, and goblin ears." He winked. "Just kidding, no scalps or ears. That's an order. We're Wildcats; we have discipline and honor above all."

He looked at Hopesinger. "Austin is a principled man; you can learn a lot from him. Now, squire Hopesinger, what is our oath?"

"*Knowledge, obedience, and duty to Vineland. I bleed for you, and you will bleed for me, and we will bleed for the land,*" she said with a serious face. Austin remembered when he felt the same passion. He still felt the honor of the guard and had pride in his work, but he also knew there was darkness to his position, as well as an understanding of knowing so much and having no ability to change anything. Maybe this mission would give him a better perspective on how campaigns were run and bring further honor to himself and the Wildcats.

"Good! Now, do Vineland proud." Jasper waved his hand and rode off, leaving Emma Hopesinger with Austin, who scratched at the stubble on his face.

"Well, Hopesinger, thanks for joining up. Crashbury is in the middle of the column; go meet up with her."

Austin shook his head. He hoped he would be back in time for the party Prince Damon planned but looked up at a break in the trees and the mountains with darkening clouds and thought better of it. He had orders, and he would follow them. What remained behind the orders was an awkward silence of the unknown.

They broke for camp near sundown. Pap sent the mercenaries known as the Union of Dogs out to forage for food and do any hunting if possible, and they lit the cook fires. Although it was up to his squires to take care of daily tasks, Austin checked over his gear and circled the horse picket to ensure all was well. Then, he walked over to Pap's tent and leaned in.

"Austin, glad to see you. Jasper said his goodbye earlier; figured we would talk today after he left." He offered Austin a horn cup of wine.

"Hot out there today," said Austin.

"It was, it was. Sit. I was going over the company roster here. Jasper did well with the mercenaries. They're killers and murderers, all of them, but loyal and will serve us well. Glad he listened to me when I recommended them."

"They are a bit rough around the edges, sir."

Pap looked Austin in the eyes and saw concern.

"Austin, I was given orders and want to be clear about this. We're to gather intel and get the fuck out of here. Your cousin, General Casting, and Sir Jasper explained that you're to turn back and report your findings as soon as I order you to. Use the birds sparingly for messages before you leave." He took a sip, letting his words sink in.

"The Gloomspire up those mountains is no fucking joke. We're to confirm what shit show happened at the Featherbottom Lodge, make contact, if possible, with the enemy, and then report our findings. Coming into the Blightbriar Wilds with a company of soldiers from mixed squads is a shit idea. They should drop a whole fucking army on this place and weed out the orcs, goblins, and knife ears to remind them who's in charge."

"Sir, I will not abandon my fellow soldiers. Maybe it's a few goblins and an orc or two," Austin said freely, thinking they were on flexible terms.

"Your cousin is sharp as they come. I am sure the prince had something to do with it, but they sent me to this forsaken place because I served up here during the Crimson Struggle." He tapped his wine cup gently on the tabletop, thoughts of that time flashing through his mind. "Austin, you ever see a goblin up close?"

"At my dad's manor. We saw a traveling troop come through, and they made sport of two of them with some wild dogs." Austin looked away, remembering the carnage, and met Pap's eye.

"They looked ragged, green, skinny, and skittish, right?" said Pap.

"Yes, sir."

"Well, I came across a dozen ripping into a farmer's family, using stone, steel, tooth, and nail to maim and eat about twenty years back. I will never forget the sight." The shudder Pap repressed played out in his shoulders. "The farmer's daughter was still alive as they took bites from her thighs like fresh-cut chicken drumsticks. Goblins are lean, muscled, and devious buggers, all of them. I can't believe the capital lets them be slaves; no wonder revolts and murders are happening. They rushed some archers, and one got to one of them, even with six arrows sticking out of its chest. When they get blood-hungry, they will tear through a line of soldiers. So do not, I repeat, *do not* underestimate your enemies."

"You expect trouble, sir?"

"I do. I'm making the mercenary leader, Elora Meldguard, my second in command. The Union Dogs are a weathered troop. They've seen action in the Blightbriar Wilds before. More so than the rest of this lot. If I put the Blue Templar in control, they'll call this a crusade, and then we are truly fucked."

"Pap, if you go down, I don't know..." Austin looked around the tent, concern plain on his face. "Will the Order of the Blue Rose and the Holy Imperium soldiers follow this, Elora Meldguard?"

"If they're smart, they will," Pap stated gruffly. "They will hate me soon enough when they see what shit they are about to get into. This camp tonight is as nice as it comes. There will be no staying in a village moving forward. Everything in front of us is an enemy as far as I'm concerned."

"What about the villages on the map?" Austin asked, pointing toward the paper spread out between them.

Pap took a sip of his wine and pulled at his beard. His fifty winters wore on his eyes. He wiped his hand over his bald head.

"If they're still around, you can bet they're aware of outlaws or others in the area. They either work with them or pay tribute to the enemy. There was no way for them to survive without engagement from those that burnt down the lodge."

Austin was slightly put off. He had frolicked with elves at brothels; something lingered and pulled inside him.

"Maybe trading with elves, but surely not orcs and goblins," he said.

Pap looked on. "Come at this assignment with open eyes and write what you observe. Yes, the village will have traded with anyone. It's been days since we saw a tavern or town walls. Orcs and goblins are nasty creatures, but they create products we use. Those creatures make coffee from mushrooms and use healing herbs and other substances used in alchemy. If the goblins and orcs are as organized as I surmise, they are living with elves and dwarves as equals and not as slaves and servants. I'm betting they're taxing just like the Holy Imperium and church. That's the theory, at least, but Prince Damon thinks it's just outlaws. General Casting believes it's something more."

"If they're that organized…" Austin paused, thinking.

"This one hunting lodge and whatever happened, it's a bigger deal than anything that has happened since the Crimson Struggle ended."

He took a deep breath. "We'll need proof," Austin finished.

"That's why you're here."

Austin looked at Pap and nodded dutifully.

"Remember, respect your enemies. Maybe we get lucky, and it's just a gathering of bandits, ex-soldiers from the Crimson Struggle," Pap said, though his disbelief at that thought was plain on his face.

"That would be something not unheard of around the forest," Austin said hopefully, trying not to think about a unified enemy high in the mountains waiting like a coming avalanche.

"We can hope. I'll introduce you to the soldiers." Pap scratched at his face.

They stood and adjusted themselves.

"Walk at my side, for Maker's sake," he hissed as they exited the tent. "No more saluting outside of tents, by the way. I appreciate the acknowledgment that I am a superior on this campaign, but by the next camp, I will advise the entire company to do away with protocols except calling knights' sir'. Anything more will get someone fucking killed. The bastards in the woods, the Night Keeper Gothine, take them, will pick off the group's leaders first to screw up the command structure and sow chaos."

They walked to the fire nearest the horses and found a tall, mean-looking soldier checking her compound bow for cracks. She was standing with a boot on a stone and was taller than Austin, all arms and legs like a grasshopper, red hair flicking in the firelight. She had a scar around her neck her leather vest failed to cover, and she was lean and muscled, the product of hardship and pain. Austin looked on. She squatted down and threw another piece of wood on the fire. Her comrades nodded up at her as Pap approached. All of them looked at her with respect to past battles fought.

"Elora, this is Austin. He's our communications expert. He has the ear of those high up." Pap gestured toward Austin as they stopped in front of the imposing figure.

Austin nodded, unsure how to proceed; he realized he'd spent too much time on duty at court or in a wine sink and not enough actually saying hello to people.

"Glad to join you all on this campaign," he said briskly.

"I'm Elora. This is Leslie Greathane, Parker Hillview, Keyla Dirkbuckle, and Kenneth Coinfell, the best scouts on this side of the Grave Reach River. That aren't elves, at least." She indicated the company gathered around her.

Keyla looked past him and at Pap. "Boy is green as fuck, Pap. They gave you a bunch of milk drinkers and dandies."

Pap let out a quick chuckle.

"You're Jasper's mate, right? Heard you're on the up and up," she said, her face betraying her concerns about him, "but Maker's milk boy, take off that bright cloak of yours and try to conceal yourself, or you'll be full of arrows before you know it. Here, have a drink," Elora passed Austin a horn of ale.

"Tomorrow, we enter the Blightbriar, and none of us will be drinking to drunkenness any time soon."

Austin took the mug, tasting pine and burning as tears filled his eyes.

"Briar stew, don't ask what's in it, but it will give you courage when you need it, and you'll beg for the Maker's forgiveness when you don't." Elora guided Austin toward a pot sitting by the fire.

"Tastes like the Night Keepers' anus Elora. Are there poisonfire seeds in this?" Austin choked as he took his first bite.

"Ha, can't say, can't say," she winked, sticking her tongue out the side of her mouth. "It's not Goblin Panic if that is what's worrying you."

"Elora, letting you know you're second in command if I fall."

Elora stood. "Pap, why would you do something stupid like that?"

"You should say I'm honored."

"Shit, Pap, you know I am, but..."

"Elora, I am too old for this shit, and you and the Union Dogs are weathered and ready to take this shit on. Brother Walder and Sir Pekka will heel once they see what we are in for, or they will die in the briar. The place is a fucking graveyard for soldiers." Pap and Elora made eye contact, the atmosphere in the group settling as the mission's significance sank on them all.

"Well, let's go. You going to write this all down there, Sir Austin?" Elora spat on the ground and looked away.

"I will," he said, trying to commit this conversation to memory.

"Memory like a steel trap?" Kenneth snorted.

"Something like that," Austin tried to hide his embarrassment at the jibe, knowing it didn't mean anything.

"I got thighs like a steel trap," Elora bragged, smacking her tree trunk thighs with her gloved hand.

Keyla, Leslie, Kenneth, and Parker snickered.

"Yeah, she does," said Keyla, smiling dreamily.

"That's enough," Pap said. "Starting tomorrow, we'll start running two separate three-soldier patrols out in separate directions. Mix up the teams and pick soldiers from the Order of the Blue Rose and the Holy Imperium if they have any experience hunting in the Wilds."

"I'll do my best, Pap. Austin here allowed out?" she elbowed Austin like they were school chums. He didn't say anything but hoped for confirmation from Pap.

Pap's gaze lay heavily on Elora. "Yes, but I need him unharmed. I wasn't kidding; Austin is the cousin to General Thomas Casting, our Minister of Arms and the Lords. You're standing next to a noble."

Elora froze momentarily, adjusting her stance to take in the latest information. "Is this some glory trip, Pap? I'm not a babysitter. I don't need this shit?"

"Austin is a Wildcat and can hold his own. Teach him to stay alive out here, Elora; you get him safely back, and the Union Dogs will be up for a promotion. Wildcats are always looking."

"Shit, Pap, thanks for the gift, you're the best father I ever had," She snorted.

"Elora, I'm the only father you've ever had."

Austin caught his breath briefly as he and Pap left Elora and the Union Dogs to their fire.

* * *

The homestead they found During Austin's first scouting trip was a series of buildings and walls before it was taken by the Blightbriar Wild. Now ash and stone lay at their feet. Soot mingled with the mud of a late spring morning. Austin pushed some of the dirt away from a burned piece of wood. He, Elora, and her scouts were looking at the ruins of a five-house homestead. It used to have a light wall and several fenced-in areas, but most had been taken by fire. They had yet to find any bodies, and the few footprints they found all led off to the west, towards the Blightbriar Wilds.

"What do you think happened here?" asked Austin. He stood, rubbing his soot and dirt-coated hands on his trousers, and looked at Elora.

"Our enemy is either kidnapping folk that live on the edge of the border between Oxfell County and the Blightbriar Wilds, or..." she paused, looking around and if to commit the scene to memory.

"Or what?"

"They're recruiting." She stated flatly.

Austin let out a chuckle by accident.

"It's not funny." She locked eyes with Austin, conveying the seriousness of her statement wordlessly. "I've heard rumors, intel as you call it, that a sizable community is living free up in the hills, in the wilds," said Elora.

He took that idea in for a moment.

"We should get back and report to Pap," Elora ordered.

Austin took in the scene again, the burned houses and crumbling fences deliberating with Elora's theory. "What will you tell him?"

"Homestead of five houses, that's a count of say five to six people per house, was burnt, but no bodies were found. We assume the worst, so they have joined the enemy, adding people to their cause. Assume everyone moving forward is unfriendly." The mounting fear and paranoia were creeping into the edges of her face.

Austin looked west towards the foothills, forests, and mountains beyond, overwhelming him with so much uncertainty. The forest and hills were alive with game, and their potential adversaries lingered in the shadows like a nightmare he couldn't shake. They didn't have enough soldiers, arrows, and swords for the possibilities of what lay beyond.

* * *

The night sky lay before Austin as he put out his candle and put away his journal. He stepped out of his tent. The darkness above their camp consumed his thoughts as the stars gazed down on him. Living in a city and now venturing out past its boundaries reminded him of the vastness of Vineland. Campfires and conversations of unease drifted through the night.

Elora had informed Pap of their findings, and he'd solemnly taken in what info they gathered and continued organizing his plans. He'd written notes, had Austin send a bird back to the capital with the latest news of their progress, and given Austin the night off.

Austin had finished his personal notes and walked off into the camp with a cup of tea. He stood on the edge of the camp, away from the fires, and looked out into the darkness of the Blightbriar Wilds, the faint river flowing off in the distance. Wolves howled, and the flutters of bats and owls could be heard as easily as the popping sparks from a campfire.

"Night off for you, Wildcat?"

Austin looked back and smiled, happy to see the silhouette of Elora approaching.

"Your father was charitable."

"He gave us a night off, too, which is odd." She scrunched her face and shrugged as she settled on the bridge beside him. "I'm guessing this may be a quiet night, or maybe he's just resting us for what is to come."

"You have a negative outlook on life, you know that?" Austin offered Elora his cup of tea; she took a sip and returned it.

"Keeps me alive, I guess."

Austin glanced at her and then up at the sky again.

"Out here, in the wilds, I can see the stars of the Maker and feel the touch of her breath on the wind." He stared into the unknown of the west, towards the mountains. "The air here is different, and the stars aren't blotted out by towers or owl lamps. The noise of the city, I became numb to it; and the smells, it constantly smells like shit and piss and people, unless you're in one of the Holy Imperium towers. Even during mass at the Holy Church, well, it's even worse, they try to mask the smell of everyone who doesn't wash their ass, who doesn't take care of themselves with different types of herbs and candles. I love it out here."

Elora took in the young man. "Austin, out here, the wrong bug can nip you in the arm and cause an infection that will kill you in less than two days, or a ruin bear will stalk you for half a day and kill you while you take a piss. Out here, you aren't the top hunter. You're another appetizer on the menu."

Austin looked at Elora.

"If humans aren't the wild's peak hunters, what is? A ruin bear, a warhawk? They don't even exist anymore."

"Aside from the dangers presented by the black willow trees and their poisonfire fog, or the hardwoods of the oakthorn trees, there are briar boars as big as ponies, crucible wolves that goblins ride like we ride horses, ruin bears do exist, wompus rats, and warhawks, fine maybe they aren't around anymore but who knows."

"I've seen a few ruin bear and crucible wolf pelts in a few towers, but not many." Austin shook his head.

"What do you think guards the skies on the Grave Reach River? Why hasn't anyone conquered the Hazefire Confederacy? The bog monsters, skunk apes, chupacabra, and, of course, the queen of the hunters, the wyvern, all exist or existed, so why not warhawks?" Elora's years of experience scouting made her words lay heavily on Austin. "All these ideas, although myth to most, have a basis. There's too much unconquered land, too much unknown and un-mapped territory to say these myths don't exist."

"You really believe in all those monsters, harpies, vampires, and fucking dragons?" Austin asked, turning toward her.

"You know of the world's majestic oceans, even spent time on them, right? What is the most dangerous animal in the ocean."

"I dunno, a whale or a kraken, or leviathan. The oceans are untamed and unsafe. There are vast areas nobody travels because of sea monsters. Never seen one, though," he shrugged.

"It's a shark; the most dangerous animal in the ocean is a shark; they breathe to kill and kill to breathe. Ask yourself because you believe in the Maker." She snickered for a moment. "The Maker believes in symmetry, right and wrong. If she would put sharks in waters, what would be the equivalent to that animal in the sky?"

"Warhawks." Austin shivered.

"And a kraken or leviathan, they exist, or existed but we only think of them when bards sing and stories are written," Elora finished.

Austin looked to the sky, not saying anything.

"Your head is spinning, isn't it," Elora said confidently. She vibrated confidence, and swagger slipped from her mouth with every word as she spoke. "Why do you think humans don't control any lands past the Stagger Wall?"

"King Christopher and Erica, the Red created the wall to separate the wild tribes of elves, orcs, and goblins from the rest of civilization."

Elora laughed a little and shifted her stance. Austin could tell his answer was wrong, stripped directly from the Holy Church, from a book at university. All that he had done to become a Wildcat, and it felt as if he still wasn't soldier enough. Training and education could only take him so far.

"Here, I thought you were a winter-born man, but you are nothing but a summer-born child. All the monsters you think are tales and legends. They are alive in the Blightbriar Wilds. More so past the Stagger Wall. All the animals, the monsters, and magic didn't go away because some fucking shit-licking king built some roads, castles, and a magical wall." She paused, glancing at the young man. "He didn't, by the way; the Stagger Wall was created by the first peoples long before we humans set foot on the sacred land of Vineland."

Austin looked at Elora with wonder and the attraction of the unknown and lusted for more.

Elora waved her hands toward the mountains in the distance. "We can barely unite a few castles and lands in this vast wilderness. The slim foothold we have in Vineland is a bunch of castles and the slight areas they control around them. At night, we creep back into our fortified compounds. And we don't have control of one-fourth of Vineland. Sure, the sky is quiet above the great cities, but why and for how long?"

"I never thought about this, and I'm privy to many a political conversation regarding the Holy Imperium."

"Now that you are out of the fog of the city breathe in the air of the rest of Vineland. And be mindful that everything in the Blightbriar Wilds can kill you."

Elora stepped away into the night shadows, leaving Austin to his thoughts and unfamiliar fears.

Alysha - Desperate Lives

Out of breath and bleeding, Alysha stumbled to the door and shut it, putting up a board to block it from opening. She looked at Claudette's corpse and realized the challenge she had created. The smell of the body immediately started to fill the room.

Claudette was one of Jared Blackheart's Genteel Monks, and Alysha knew her death could raise warnings to Jared Blackheart and General Flint himself. Alysha had not thought enough about her plans and what she wanted to do. She gathered her belongings, shouldered the backpack over Stormkiss, and walked over to Claudette, checking her body for money. Alysha thought that if she could make it to a different city gate, she had a chance of leaving without notice. Her adrenaline was up, and her mind was still sharp from the fight. She looked at the candle, tossed it against some cloth in the corner, opened the door, and walked out as the inside started to smolder, hoping the fire would drive people toward the area and away from her as she attempted to escape.

The back alleys off the main streets in the city smelled of piss and despair. Alysha still hoped to catch her friend Helena soliciting drunks for money at the Broom and Bustle tavern she frequented. Her best friend wasn't the same person she grew up with after the Wolf Hills massacre, and they were forced into servitude. The last time she had seen her friend, Alysha had promised herself to get them out of Counselor City, if possible.

She created these little promises, like prayers, to give herself a reason to live. She thought those responsible for her mother's passing deserved nothing less than death and struggled to reign in a voice inside, begging her to kill every

Holy Imperium soldier she saw.

She continued to push the narrative inside her head; if she could help her friend, deliver the Wolfe family sword and pipe, and tell someone inside Grimwood about the threat of the Holy Imperium army, maybe this would stop these darker thoughts. Would these goals be worth the air she now breathed since the lightning strike at the altar?

You are more than a sacrifice.

Alysha worried her thoughts and actions were not always her own; for a moment, self-doubt mixed with confusion and anger over everything that had been done to her.

My land, my Vineland.

Would soldiers of the Holy Imperium be on the lookout for a girl who killed an entire scout party near the altar of a goddess banned in worship? Would they find Claudette murdered? Or would they consider the fire a freak accident? It still would not account for Edwin Flatrock and his captain investigating her whereabouts after Claudette did not appear. She thought she would have enough time to leave the city gates and hoped Helena would join her. She didn't have enough money to buy Helena out, but she thought her friend deserved a choice before she left. Alysha had nothing to live for anymore except escape and revenge.

The Broom and Bustle sat on the northern edge of Counselor City between the docks of the Erie Sea and the slums of the city. It was part of a row of taverns, key clubs, and brothels visited by the middle and lower classes of the town. The upper-class-attended bars and brothels found on the city's eastern end as they outpriced the lower-end clientele.

Alysha did her best to wipe down the cuts and slices she received from Claudette, but she would need to clean and stitch them soon. Indeed, a bath and a night's rest would be a gift, but doing so at the Broom and Bustle would be costly and dangerous. Snatching Helena from the grips of her owner was concern enough.

Alysha put her hood up and walked into the tavern through a side door. The place was busy with a lunch crowd of sailors and merchants eating and spitting gossip.

She walked to the bar.

"Well, you look like dog shit on a stick. What can I do for you," asked the bartender.

"Wine, red, not white," she said, knowing that manners in a place like this got one nowhere but taken advantage of.

"Sure thing, sure thing," said the bartender as he looked at Alysha up and down.

"How much to safely store my pack for a few hours?"

"Doesn't look like much. I can toss it back here until after the lunch rush. So, five shills will do. Any longer, and it's ten shills to get it back."

"Bit steep, don't you think?"

"Looks of you, I think you want the no-questions-asked package, aye?

"Fine, throw something in to eat, and you got yourself a deal," she commented. "Here's six shills up front. I'll be in the corner over there," she pointed and walked away with her cup of wine, leaving her backpack with the bartender.

Alysha watched the crowd as she ate, looking at the double front doors, the kitchen door to which she thought there would be a back door for refuge, the stairs leading up to the baths and flop rooms, and the side door she entered. She took a rag out and wiped her arm and leg cuts down, realizing what miserable shape she was in. Exhaustion seeped into her body.

As it was only lunchtime, and the interior of the building was shaded and filled with smoke.

Alysha saw no sign of Helena. The barkeep dropped a half sandwich and a fourth of an onion. She tipped him another shill, and he walked away without a word. She finished the sandwich and ate the rest of the onion.

A newspaper carrier burst through the front door as she was halfway through her wine.

"Fire at the edge of town. Some smith shop went up quickly, lit part of the wall, and another house caught fire!"

Patrons moved chairs and peered outside the windows. Alysha sucked down her wine, pushed to the bar, and grabbed her pack, knowing this would be her best chance to leave. She left an extra shill on the counter and looked at the bartender for a moment. He nodded, swiping the coin and looking out the window.

Her gear was safely on her back as she stepped into the alley and headed north towards the piers of the Erie Sea, thawed from winter. The only traffic in and out would be trade from merchants as the fish remained sunk deep from winter's deep breath. She wasn't sure what to do, but a boat out would be quicker than a hike across to Grimwood.

The boardwalk was slick with rainfall, and every pier looked guarded. She watched as guards questioned everyone leaving and coming in from each boat and felt the strangle of the Holy Imperium everywhere. Either they were looking for her or trying to keep any rumors of the impending siege of Grimwood quiet. The town was alive with gossip about the fire. Alysha turned around, headed to the town's west gate, and found it guarded by Holy Imperium soldiers and not the typical town guards like Edwin Flatrock. Either would have been concerning, but she felt less worried by the town guards.

"Shit," she said as she turned away from the gate, her options to leave dwindling as the sun crept closer to twilight.

"Murder at the southern gate!" a merchant at a stall yelled to another merchant.

Fear and paranoia were creeping closer to her now. The eastern gate housed the majority of General Flint's First Army inside and outside the gate, and she didn't feel she could leave it without getting harassed, caught for murder, or picked out for further servitude. She didn't care much about capture or death but felt she should return the pipe and sword to Felix Wolfe and warn the Grimwood city officials of the coming attack; her life would have meant anything. Maybe if she could kill one more Holy Imperium soldier, she considered.

This is my land.

Counselor City seemed to take in much trade but did not allow anything out, and she was amazed Hob, Bob, and herself could slip out before Holy Imperium guards attacked them. She walked back to the western gate and took a position to see who could leave without harassment. She observed soldiers coming and going easily, but any traders who attempted to escape were pushed back or arrested. The siege of Grimwood was imminent, she thought to herself. She felt hopeless to stop it.

A rider barreled through the gate without thought or care, pushing through the crowd. It was an army messenger, marked as such by the wildcats with wings on the saddlebags and light riding gear they wore. Alysha followed the messenger on foot, but they quickly moved east into the city, intent on delivering their business.

Another came through slower and with less purpose, looking tired and slightly unkempt. This was her chance, Alysha thought. She just needed to get them alone. They curiously walked their horse after leaving the gate and worked their way past Alysha, heading to the tavern she had visited earlier. After securing their horse, she watched the messenger enter the front door. She entered through the side door again, nodding to the barkeep and looking through the smoke as the towns folk talk overlapped each other through dark pints of ale and cheap stew from a large kettle.

The sun was setting, and she needed to leave the city before the gates closed for the night, or she would be trapped in town while soldiers looked for her likeness.

Alysha stood beside the bar with her hood up and watched, the tavern busy with laughing patrons. A minstrel sang in the corner, and Alysha felt glad as it drew attention away. She looked around and failed to see the messenger. He wasn't near the door, sitting at the bar or any tables. Prostitutes were working the tavern. Alysha looked in both directions and decided to walk upstairs quietly. She knew there were rooms used for personal entertainment. The hallway had four doors on each side and one at the end, each closed, and Alysha could hear various forms of laughter and grunting coming from each. Alysha felt embarrassed and disgusted as she opened the first door slightly and peered inside. She saw a dwarve and a shorter woman and slowly closed the door. The next door didn't have a messenger either. She tried another but found it locked, the stress of capture weighing her shoulders. The following door was unlocked, and the couple at the other end of the room were engaged and oblivious to anything other than their current activities.

Alysha looked at the clothes on the floor and found the messenger cape, shirt, and striped pants. She quietly held her breath and slipped her hand towards the lump of clothes. Alysha heard a heaving moan from a woman and then a slight giggle and grunt. The woman exaggerated the "fun" she had to help finish her work quickly and produce more of a tip. Alysha knew her time was short and needed to get the clothes and leave immediately. She thought she could promptly throw the clothes on in the stable, steal the horse, and escape Counselor City without issue. Alysha knew she was taking huge chances, but nothing else mattered. She was frustrated she couldn't find her friend Helena and knew it was a long shot to have even tried. Her backpack nudged the door too far and hit a compact wooden dresser. A breeze came through and interrupted the messenger mid-stroke, and they stopped their coupling and looked back at the door.

"Alysha, what are you doing here, and why do you look as if someone hit your face with a hammer?"

She stood up quickly, holding the messenger's clothes, but said nothing.

"What the fuck is happening here? I didn't pay for two girls, and I definitely am not into role-playing with back-alley pieces of garbage. What are you doing with-"

The messenger didn't finish his sentence as Helena grabbed the man by his privates and twisted. He gagged and squealed.

"Don't you dare move or talk," said Helena.

"I can explain," Alysha said.

"Quickly," Helena said.

"I'm leaving using this man's clothes and getting out, Helena. If you want to come with me, we can figure out how to get you out, too."

The man, still naked and red-faced, looked at Helena and Alysha in pain.

"And what of him," Helena said.

"I was going to steal his gear, but he knows too much. He either helps us, or he's a casualty of war," said Alysha. She moved a stray hair from her face and looked ready to kill this man and leave.

Helena hesitated and looked at the messenger. She slowly blinked at him, which made the messenger catch his breath. Or it was that she was gripping him much tighter than he had been hoping for just a few minutes ago.

"So, what will it be, help damsels in distress or become flower food?"

The Bastards - Black Parade

T he city of Olde Ridgewatch held twenty-five thousand people on the shoulders of a peninsula, including Doc, Duncan, and Angus. They waited for their comrades, Gray Jim and Cordial, but neither reached their meeting point. Maynard could feel the history of Olde Ridgewatch, one of the first cities founded in Vineland, a city filled with violence, betrayal, and death that gave its inhabitants a firm sense of independence and respect for individuality unless forced to act together.

The city was surrounded on three sides by water connected by a walled road called the Neck, with gates on both sides. The bay and ocean supplied natural obstacles to invaders, the tides allowed only a portion of the city to port ships, and a stronghold, Bawstone Keep, on top of a cliff, provided further protection. The town also contained towers on the edges of the water and in the bay. Guards occupied the towers, and Bawstone Keep was on a revolving shift, offering protection to those in the city. Since the military occupation by General Benedict Ashburn and his Holy Imperium Army and a contingent of mercenaries called the Black Eagles, it felt more like those towers were keeping everyone in, like a prison.

Inside the city, the Olde Ridgewatch common area was a park and public garden, but now soldiers from the Holy Imperium were stationed after several threats and riots over recent taxes imposed by Prince Damon. The rest of the army was in townhomes or the nearby city of Roxburrow. Originally a farming town with a port used for trading between locals making their way up and down the Atlantis Ocean, it grew in fits and spurts through raids by pirates or attacks by natives until the keep was built on the cliff overlooking the town. Eventually, the city called Ridgewatch, "Olde," fell under the protection of a clan of dwarves called the Razorbacks, who helped build Bawstone Keep on a cliff above the port of Ridgewatch. After years of control, the Razorback family joined a crusade into the Blightbriar Wilds to wrestle control of the Castle of the Mists from a tribe of orcs, but only a few returned, and humans claimed the town, leaving only slums to the remaining dwarves.

Now hundreds of years later, Maynard and a group of townsfolk slowly moved towards the mayor's house in Olde Ridgewatch as a drummer and piper played a lifeless funeral hymn. The warmth of the spring sun soaked up snow from the previous night, leaving a glaze of shine throughout the parade that moved through the streets. The townsfolk encircled the cart, guarding the occupant to his final resting place. Nobody was sure what would occur when they finally came to the mayor's house, where General Benedict Ashburn held command of the city. It was a somber march, and many carried weapons. Doc soothed the commoners mostly, but the situation remained tense. They walked blocks, and the party was well over a thousand people as they moved through the city, with more joining every few feet. Doc, Duncan, and Maynard led the way, accompanied by Dick Holmes and the strong-armed Abigail and others who fought the Holy Imperium soldiers in the alley riot last night.

"Maynard, as we get closer, fold into the sides of this group and get me, my staff; return it to me, and I'll repay you soon."

Maynard looked at Doc, nodded, and smiled lightly.

"Not a time to smile," said Doc.

"You trust me to hold the staff of the greatest mage ever and give it back to you?"

"Gaston's Beard isn't a toy, Maynard. Besides, you already carry your chosen weapon."

Maynard scowled and knew Doc was right. He loved his staff. It felt like it was a part of him. Gaston's Beard was a staff of immense power, a Paragon of Vineland, a weapon unparalleled in make and might. Maynard's lust for it would be the same for any other mage, witch, or apostate in the land. It was the first of all staffs, as the war sword Twilight was first among swords or the black shield Midnight's Veil was a shield of legend. Imposing warriors would name their weapons in a mocking display, indicating they were a Paragon of Vineland, but only a few were known to be such marvels, while others were lost in antiquity. Doc knew of six but speculated of others. He counted. The sword Twilight and Midnight's Veil, weapons held by the Blackheart family, a wand called Maker's Quill was carried by a peer of his, Olivia Franklin, the Holy Truth held by Lord Washcreek, and Doc's staff were some of the Paragons of Vineland. His staff, named Gaston's Beard, was now in the hands of General Benedict Ashburn of the Holy Imperium Second Army.

Doc had traveled west months ago looking for the knife named Dawn's Breath, hearing a rumor the Ashburn family last held it years ago. Doc knew the Ashburn family was connected to a premonition from one of the Wightland sisters, a trio of women who influenced Vineland for years from the shadows. The Ashburn family would be at the heart of creating a new Vineland, a new country. This is how he met Runt, as his family was splintered due to circumstances beyond Doc's control.

He'd hoped Alysha, the middle sibling, was still near the Erie Sea, but the rest of her path was unknown, and Benjamin was stationed with his father in Olde Ridgewatch. Doc had gambled based on mysticism, guessing which family member carried Dawn's Breath and failed. In doing so, he lost his staff as well.

"Fine, but the price for its return will be higher than you expect, Doc. Don't forget that you can't twist out of it."

Doc nodded to Maynard. "You have my word, Maynard. You bastard, I will arrange a boon of its equal."

Maynard acknowledged Doc and disappeared into the crowd.

"Your speech was truthful. Kept the hot-blooded folk under control. What will you do when we get to the mayor's mansion?" asked Dick Holmes. They marched on, not in lockstep but the shuffle of a mass of people fed on grief and sustained through the tensions of living under martial law.

"We're all going to sing 'Vineland the Last Mistress,' and I'll figure it out from there," said Doc. He was dressed in his tattered and patched-up Holy

Imperium coat. He pushed up his shaded glasses that constantly changed color. "I said I would take care of the body. Runt will meet his father as I promised he would." He looked at Duncan, who nodded and turned away from Doc.

"Nobody raises arms today. It is a day of peace and mourning for those that didn't deserve to die."

They were a block away from the mansion. Maynard slipped out of the crowd towards the right side, where a giant hedged fence blocked the sight of the house. A line of Bitterleak soldiers lined the road, a row of shields and spears blocking the way.

The crowd continued forward. Rows of houses were on their left, with only two narrow alleys allowing escape if the moment escalated further. The mob moved closer, circling the wagon as it led the way, the crush of people pushing closer to each other.

The Brotherhood of Bitterleak, known as the Black Eagles, held the road in front of the mayor's house, while Holy Imperium soldiers held two rows behind them. The Black Eagles coat of arms was yellow and red with black eagle wings spread out. A mass of shields and spears was backed by another shield wall. They would have been intimidating if they were not so outnumbered by the commoners.

"Stand down," the leader of the mercenaries yelled. "Disperse this illegal crowd, or we will be forced to disperse you!"

The crowd slowed, yet nobody yelled back. Doc stepped forward and took off his glasses.

"Soldiers from across the Atlantis Ocean and those of the Holy Imperium behind, we come on a solemn occasion," commanded Doc with an unreal voice. Even Duncan was stunned at his tone and volume. "General Benedict Ashburn's son, Rhett Ashburn, known to his friends and family as Runt, has joined us and wishes to return to his father. Please let the general know his son has returned."

There was commotion from the Bitterleak soldiers as someone left the line behind them, running toward the mansion.

"Now what?" asked Duncan.

"Now we sing," said Doc, and he started on the song 'Vineland the Last Mistress.' Doc took a swig from a whiskey bottle, placed it on the ground, cleared his voice, and joined in. He performed the first part alone; his voice was a mixture of thunder and weakness as it echoed through the streets. The crowd joined in on the chorus, "*Always a Maiden and never the Maker, Always the Maiden and never the Maker,*" the moment surged above their heads as the sea hawks and seagulls took flight.

Duncan looked on as Doc sang an illegal gospel in a desperate moment, thinking this event was madness and would get them all killed. Doc was a lunatic and played everything as if it was a game. He watched as the well-trained mercenaries at first jeered, then quieted as Doc and the crowd moved into the second verse.

He chose a song everyone knew and could sing that was slow enough and filled with enough lonesome moments that felt right for a funeral, yet rebellious in its tone and story, mocking the Maker as a new god and naming the pagan gods as the creators of not only Vineland but all of Midgard.

The soldiers shook their heads. Duncan thought he saw one or two at the end moving their lips slightly to the singing. Duncan pulled at his beard and nudged Angus to follow as he went to the back of the wagon and opened its gate. The crowd rounded on the third verse; it almost felt like they were attending a Holy Church mass and singing gospel to the Maker, Child, and Servant but in defiance of their fidelity as gods. Duncan grabbed the box holding the remains of Runt and pulled them to the edge of the cart. Angus stood to the side, waiting to help. Other hands grabbed the coffin as well, and they pulled it off the ledge, leaving the other coffin containing the remains of Stitch where it lay. Duncan would personally take care of those remains himself.

They bore Runt's coffin on their shoulders as Angus moved the crowd away and passed Doc as the singing stopped.

"Make way! Make way," yelled Angus now. He didn't know why or what he should feel and say, but it felt right and carried authority. He was closer to the boy in the coffin than Runt's father had ever been.

"Make way, make way," he bellowed towards the line of troops. They strode without fear of reprisals past the first line of soldiers and toward the second.

"Make way for General Benedict Ashburn's youngest son! Make way," echoed through the streets, tears streaming down Angus's cheeks and into his combed beard.

The troop's shoulders sagged, and the two soldiers closest to Duncan, as he led the bearers and Angus in front of him, stepped to the side and opened the line as if they were a door. The group followed through, the coffin on their shoulders, bringing Runt to a father who barely knew him.

They stopped at the hedge gates, and Duncan rapped on the door but let Angus speak. The dwarve knew the words now. Duncan, Doc, and Maynard knew Runt, but Angus had watched the boy grow up. He knew the family; he was part of the family.

"General Benedict Ashburn of the Holy Imperium Second Army, I, Angus of the free city of Wolf Hills, bring you the remains of your son and my friend, Rhett Runt Ashburn, dead at the hands of Holy Imperium Soldiers!"

Tears draped his furious eyes.

"Pay your respects and bring us justice for his murder!" Doc finished. The front double door of the mansion opened and out stepped two knights. Frederick Burrow, leader of the Bitterleak Black Eagles, and Sir Donald Williamson of the Holy Imperium. They split off and stood at the door.

General Benedict Ashburn, followed by his young squire, Alfie Von Dyke, stepped outside.

* * *

Maynard made his way to the crowd's edge and watched his companions walk through the Bitterleak soldiers, carrying the coffin of Runt on their shoulders. Maynard squeezed through the hedge and past the fence; his friend's loss followed him like a shadow. He broke into a squared courtyard with the back door of the mayor's house on his left a short distance away. A guard stood near the door. Maynard could make himself less conspicuous but not invisible, and not enough to slip past a guard at full attention guarding a door using a tick Doc had taught him.

Suddenly, the guard at the back door moved his head and heard the commotion on the other side of the house. It was the group carrying the coffin. They must have made it to the manor, Maynard thought.

Disregarding his duty, the guard jogged to the other side of the house. Maynard took his chance, said old, unused words, held his breath, and ran toward the back door. His robe jostled softly. The charm he placed gave a camouflage best used in shadows and the dark. Unfortunately, the charm only lasted as long as Maynard held his breath. He jimmied the door open and looked around, letting out his breath. The house was a closed farmhouse building plan with a waiting room to his left, a dining room to the right, a hallway, and stairs descending near the hallway. Figuring Doc's staff would be in the general's bedroom or study, Maynard headed to the stairs. He held his breath again, his charm kicking in, and ran up the stairs as another soldier in the waiting room appeared, having heard the door open.

* * *

Benjamin Ashburn heard a door open and wondered what the commotion was at the front of the house, and why the back door stood open. He looked around and didn't see or hear anything. Ben guessed it was the house cat his father's squire Alfie Von Dyke favored. He ground his teeth, clenching his jaw, knowing he should be his father's squire and not a lower guard in another knight's company. His thoughts changed again, and the stress and lack of sleep from guard duty and the riot last night came over him. He'd been roughed up by townspeople the previous night and may have killed someone with his crossbow. He and several soldiers with him were beaten and bloodied during a confrontation in a back alley near a tavern. They were chased and harried several blocks until a platoon of Black Eagle mercenaries appeared, breaking up the townsfolk and chasing them off. Blocks later, the first fight in the alley and follow-up fight left four Holy Imperium soldiers in the infirmary. There were rumors of two townsfolk had died.

Benjamin Ashburn's commanding officer ordered him to report the incident directly to his father, thus his appearance at the general's headquarters in the city's center. Benjamin, an archer in Donald Williamson's lance, forced himself to not to think of the general as his father when in uniform. It helped him better maintain his duty and honor as a soldier of the Holy Imperium. He absently brushed his uniform as he closed the door. He noticed the blood splatters on it, unsure if it was from the guards he worked with last night or the townsfolk harassing them with snowballs, broken bottles, and oyster shells.

The riot left him shaken. His skin was pale, and his mind was foggy after his father dressed him down for his light beard growth and poor uniform and didn't comment further during Ben's report of the incidents. He was dismissed, and Ben heard his father start to speak to the captain of the Black Eagles, Frederick Burrow, and Sir Donald Williamson, his commanding officer in his study, but that was hours ago.

* * *

Maynard let his breath go and looked about the second floor. Each time he worked the camouflage spell, he became weaker, but Maynard was amazed he could pull it off more quickly than he had. Gratefulness washed over him as he thought about Runt giving him a part of his soul to Maynard before passing. Maynard saw a decorated door, took a wild guess, and shoved in, hoping a housekeeper would not be present. He was hinging on the commotion outside, drawing everyone's attention.

Maynard looked around and realized this was a well-stocked library housing an assortment of books, with a chair near a fireplace. He needed to find an area where the staff would be stored or displayed. The gathered tomes beckoned him to stay there to see what they had to offer, but he could not weigh himself down further as he passed an ornate book with a black cover and highlighted gold title.

He moved to the next room, finding a bedroom with a cleaning kit, a crisply made bed, and other implements. This was a modest room, and Maynard did not see a staff, only an assortment of armor sets in various states of polish.

Maynard heard movement downstairs, a series of pacing steps, and held his breath, casting the charm again. He thought he could cast it twice more without thoroughly exhausting himself.

There was further excitement outside as Maynard could only guess that the party carrying Runt in a coffin had met his father, General Ashburn.

He opened the next door and found a large bedroom, writing table, closet, and a lounge chair with the leftovers of tea and breakfast. Maynard wondered why the pieces were still there and if the upper portions of the army needed help getting quality service from their servants.

He looked at the table but didn't see the staff and glanced at the edge of the bed. Near a nightstand sat the pamphlet *Ordinary Wit*, and the ink-black staff, Gaston's Beard, stood there like a walking stick with its obsidian blade facing down. He trotted over, let out his breath, seized the staff, and gasped. The power that surged through him felt like nothing he'd ever witnessed in his short life.

Footsteps echoed, and cold sweat dripped off Maynard's back.

* * *

General Benedict Ashburn walked down the sidewalk to the gate where Doc stood next to Angus. Duncan and the other pallbearers held the casket on their shoulders behind them. The sun shined down its warmth, spreading across all it touched, pushing the last dredges of the storm last night away.

"The only reason you're not hanging from chains from a tree is that you dared to bring my family name to your lips. So, tell me, why do you think my son is dead, you disgraced apostate?"

Doc's face jerked with a sneer. Reaching into a pocket, he opened a worn piece of parchment. It showed the likeness of Runt Ashburn, 'wanted dead or alive' written above the sketch. He showed it around to the crowd that marched with them and toward Runt's father and those who followed him.

"I knew I would see you again, general. We have more in common than you think." Doc briefly let a smile creep to the side of his face, and then it slipped back into a scowl. "Benedict, it's not Benjamin that passed away. It's Rhett. He was felled by a Holy Imperium crossbow bolt last night and went to the Maker early this morning. My friend Duncan and I tried to save him, doing everything we could to keep him alive."

"Tis true, general, tis true. He traveled all the way to see you, to be with you, only to be killed," said Angus.

General Ashburn stood there silently.

"That riot you heard about last night had casualties. We were caught in the middle, trying to get out of the way," Duncan finished.

"Alfie, fetch Benjamin from inside. Now," The general snapped. His squire sped away at once. "Doc, Angus, how did you get here? I don't understand."

The crowd around them, both soldier and citizen, were silent. The moment was crisp, the air full of tension yet layered with remorse and guilt like walking home from a bad drunk after arguing with a loved one. The sun's spring heat sapped the chill out of the air.

Angus looked at Doc, unsure what to say, so he tried to give as much truth as possible. "Your homestead was decimated by soldiers wearing the sigil of the Holy Church. We believe them to be the Genteel Monks of Jared Blackheart. The entire town of Wolf Hills was razed to the ground. Survivors were taken as slaves north to the Erie Sea. Runt was blamed by those same soldiers for the burning of his homestead, and Wolf Hills and wanted posters placed everywhere by the Genteel Monks."

"I was in the area, having left Grimwood University, and we saved Runt with the help of Angus and some friends," said Doc. "You didn't listen to me before. Maybe now you will understand I seek what's best for Vineland and your family."

"Marie didn't make it, Benedict, I'm sorry," whispered Angus.

Benedict Ashburn stood straighter. The pallbearers lowered the casket to the ground.

Doc looked back at the people who helped carry Runt home. "Thank you, all of you," he said in earnest.

"So, you brought his corpse all the way here. That is preposterous," Benedict scoffed.

"He was killed last night as we unloaded beer and wine barrels at the Empty Gauntlet. Holy Imperium guards harassed us, an argument and brawl broke out, and we were caught in the crossbow melee. The snowstorm that passed through, the low light from the torches and bonfires in the alley, and the crowd's anger and ignorance of the soldiers led to a massacre in Olde Ridgewatch," Duncan said.

"Some will call it murder. Others will call it a massacre. I suggest you bury your son and make an inquisition before a crowd like the one you see before you come back armed," Doc finished.

Duncan felt the situation turn. He looked at the closed coffin and opened it up, showing the father, his deceased son. The weapons the crowd carried were in plain sight, along with everyone's sentiments on their faces. Legs shifted, and hands tightened on staves, clubs, and farm rakes, months of being pent up inside and tormented by soldiers ready to be unleashed.

"You didn't believe it when we last met, and now a close family friend confirmed what I spoke of. Your son Runt needed you, and now he's gone," said Doc. "All done by the hands of the government of the Holy Imperium led by Prince Damon." He looked down at Runt and back at General Benedict Ashburn. "He deserved a better life. Hopefully, you will give him honor in death."

Doc straightened his jacket and walked away. Angus looked on momentarily and followed, then Duncan and the rest of the pallbearers left a father with his son one last time.

Hudson City - Reports of Unrest

"I have a report here, sir, that Lackmore Port is having some problems?" General Casting's servant, Victor Parish, passed the note to him. "A sizable shipment of tea and molasses is coming in any day now. It may even be in port waiting under quarantine as we speak. We have also had word that specific dignitaries accompany the shipment, so we have further cause for safety concerns."

"What news is this to me?" Casting stood reading another message, holding the one with news of Lackmore Port in his other hand. The table, usually clean, held scattered papers and rolled-up scrolls. Victor could usually stir the general's attention to the matters he needed to address quickly and easily, but General Casting's mind was elsewhere.

"What's taking your attention today?" asked Victoria Parish, her long leg showing out from her skirt like a younger university student. The liaison to the Silver Ivy Leagues and Minister of Education sat on one end of the table, writing and watching General Casting, her haunting eyes, and sharp, cold features taking in every twitch and quirk the general presented.

Victor Parish nodded toward her, and she looked at Madam Thompson, the Minister of the Treasury, silently raising an eyebrow and asking for help.

"Sir, this Lackmore business is concerning," Thompson said gravely. "Those ships carry news, tea, and people of importance from Thamesbridge, including the potential bride, Princess Candice Saltdrift. This port has dignitaries conducting business before making their way to the capital for The Triumphant Masquerade."

Casting looked back at Victor, his servant. "How bad is it?" he asked as he read the news on the riot in Lackmore Port, setting aside another letter that had the royal seal of King Geordie of Thamesbridge broken on it.

"Next to Hudson City and Olde Ridgewatch, it's the largest port, so if this report is accurate, it could devastate commerce for months," said Minister Thompson. She was reading another missive. "We must do something about this immediately. Who do we have in the area to help? Isn't Prince Damon's Second Army, controlled by Benedict Ashburn and supported by Fredrick Burrow, nearby?"

"I'll send orders by bird to have General Ashburn's army depart from Olde Ridgewatch. The report says the Lackmore mayor and his family are missing and presumed dead, and the wealthier parts of the city were looted or burnt. How accurate is this; is this the latest news?" General Casting asked, flustered.

Victor Parish had steady hands and eyes that always looked tense and watery. As General Casting's footman and assistant, he was to be prepared for any event. He'd already sent the orders to have the main force of the first army led by General Benedict Ashburn take back control of Lackmore Port. If Princess Candice Saltdrift was on the ship, her handler and brother Aleister Saltdrift was, too. He hoped to gain Princess Candice as Prince Damon's wife, ensuring Aleister became the Holy Imperium's very own battlemage. This would neutralize the threat of that madman Hunter Young and Olivia Franklin, both powerful mages. The supposed Minister of Letters, Stephanie Shannon, continued playing games and used her little magic to steal secrets and plot against Victor and General Casting. Victor needed someone other than himself and his lover to combat the subversive plots Stephanie planned. This riot of slaves, this revolt was fucking up General Casting's plans and fucking up Victor's, as well.

"This is abridged, sir. I will make sure we have further updates. One moment while I get the orders sent out." He walked out of the room.

"My contacts have been silent about this, and I always get news from my shipping partners. This isn't comforting. Damn elves, it's always the fucking elves," said Madam Thompson, standing, reading a report from Waterhurst, another port city under the control of the Holy Imperium. "Not as bad, but a few letters from friends and relatives noted some of their slaves have gone missing off their tobacco and cotton plantations in the southern city-states." She sighed. "They use goblins stolen from mountain caves that barely last five years before they shrivel up and die in the heat and sun in the Rosewood Dominion and Magnoliafield. I told them to raid the elven tribes. They last longer and work harder. Hades, if they can buy a few casteless dwarves, they are worth the money. There's no need to wait for slave ships across the Atlantis. There are plenty of warm bodies here in the Holy Imperium. The cotton and tobacco trade has taken off, as the amount of giant beaver skins has diminished since the end of the Crimson Struggle. That loss of the city-state of Ursula as a main trade hub really stopped that. Most merchants either fear the Smoldering Plague or the orc tribes from the Burnside Alliance. The echoes of the Battle of the Reaping continue to ripple throughout the economy even if it's been years." She sighed, frustrated.

Victor returned as General Casting and Sir Leadwall discussed further news with Madam Thompson. Victor handed him other messages, letters, and newspapers, including The *Post Enquirer, Hudson City Journal*, and *The Plain Herald*.

"It seems this revolt was coordinated," Madam Thompson said, reading.

"Slaves, servants, and the like have murdered their caretakers, left their homes, and stopped working in several parts of the Holy Imperium," Sir Leadwall continued. "That is from Colehampton, and I have the same tidings from Cinderpool, although neither appears to be as dire as what Lackmore Port is reporting."

The crows moaned and whispered before the official start of Prince Damon's Council, which ran the Holy Imperium. High Judge Sternball, Madam Dianna Thompson, and Sir Leadwall were sifting through notes and missives, trying to bring to terms what was happening in the Holy Imperium.

"Victor, call the rest of the council up," said General Casting.

"Admiral Howl is meeting dignitaries coming into Hudson City Port with Prince Damon as we speak. Joseph Blackheart is training a platoon of knights, readying himself to become a queen's guard for Prince Damon's soon-to-be wife. He advised that there was no news from his father in the west other than the normal tidings from Honey Break. The news of the Republic of

Wind has been silent for some time, though."

"What of Bishop Devon?" stated General Casting.

"Bishop Devon and his Order of the Blue Rose are in attendance with the admiral," Victor answered crisply. "Should I get Brother Hewitt or Sister Temperance to join us?"

Victoria Parish, the Minister of Education, spoke up. "Dear, no, we don't want that riffraff near the Trinity Cloudreach Spire. Let them fester in their so-called Holy Church."

Everyone looked up with raised eyebrows as Victoria criticized the Holy Church.

"It's too late for that, Victoria; the Wildcats are spread thin; some of the Templar are taking over guard duty for Prince Damon's personal guards, the Wildcats are split in half, and the ones that remain are now dealing with further duties in the capital. Prince Damon calls Vineland the Holy Imperium for a reason," said Casting. "Joseph Blackheart, the queen's guard, is very new to the order and is stepping in as well, but I don't want them protecting Prince Damon, so they are training and running other duties."

Victoria looked at General Casting as he read the newspapers and letters reporting a vast amount of news about elves leaving farms and plantations, orcs and goblins setting mines on fire, and servants of all kinds causing mayhem and mischief from Olde Ridgewatch to Crescent City, the most southern city now under control by General Hammer Clinton.

"Maker's long legs, even my hometown reports these vulgarities." Casting gripped the paper as he read.

"We have reports in Steelsburg that our allies, the Blitzsteel family, lost grip of a consequential portion of their underground city as some of the casteless dwarves joined against them, along with several mercenary companies," said Judge Sternball. "The mercenary companies we have employed previously are the Bent Plow Company and the Union Dogs. I believe the Union Dogs are split in two. One group is in Steelsburg backing the Bent Plow Company and loosely supporting the Clearstone family, and we employ the other half of the Union Dogs in our little, what did we call it, expeditionary force in the Blightbriar Wilds north of the city. If this were to get out, it would surely upset our allies in Steelsburg."

Victor poured tea for everyone as the meeting started, finding that Judge Sternball leaned towards the Minister Shannon faction of the council meeting.

"The Minister of Letters shall be here shortly," Victor said as he poured for Victoria and whispered, "We grow weak as plans change; we meet later tonight with Casting and the others."

"Thank you, Victor," she smiled and nodded. "General Casting used to be on top of everything."

"He is, he is." General Casting said. Victoria's voice was sweet and strong like the Thamesbridge tea they all drank now. Casting's shoulders slumped slightly at her voice, his heartbeat slowed, and his brain began to clear.

Minister Shannon walked through the door. She was a strong-shouldered yet slightly pudgy woman, the same build as the well-fed Bishop Devon but sharper in definition. Stephanie Shannon had strength in her bones even as the wealth of conspiracies weighed on her, putting lines and creases on her face. She played with the anchor ring on her finger, showing everyone that she was adept at using magic but chained as well.

"Minister Shannon, can you tell us what the fuck is happening in the Holy Imperium?" Casting sighed.

"I heard rumors, but this conspiracy runs deep in the city-states. I've tried to push for more, but I only hear circumstance gossip, not enough to report to the council as truth." Her answer was taut with emphasis.

Shannon was troubled. Victor looked on. He and Victoria had ways of getting knowledge and controlling Prince Damon. Through the Silver Ivy League Universities, Victoria's control spread throughout Vineland's territories and city-states, bringing in the news while Victor used his birds, massive ravens and crows, to gather information. The postal system fell under Minister Shannon, but Victor had people at every rookery in every city, well bribed to get him information fast and accurately. Most people used doves, pigeons, and lesser birds, while Victor relied on storm crows and whisper ravens, which were challenging to train but harder to catch with an arrow or net. Their only predators were vultures, eagles, and warhawks, which nobody had seen since the Battle of the Reaping.

"You call this a conspiracy. Who's behind it? Give me names. I want dead bodies soon," General Casting snapped.

"We've captured and tortured the slave leaders. Most died crying and pissing themselves, not giving us anything from their bleeding lips." Minister of Letters Stephanie paused, fingering the ring that anchored and controlled her magic powers. "We've already taken action against them, but I fear long fingers from the Gloomspire stretch out across the Holy Imperium."

"They are called the Wrathfall." Victor sided.

Leaning over a map and pointing at where the Gloomspire potentially existed, Stephanie looked up along with the rest of the council. Victor stood out behind these powerful men and women of the Holy Imperium as they grasped at the news of veiled threats from servants, slaves, and those below their station.

General Casting turned, putting his hand on his sword for comfort. Others put down the tea just served to them.

Victor stood tall inside a shadow of the tower's sunlight. Candles and owl lamps lit the inside of the top floor of the Trinity Cloudreach Spire. The air was thin, and the room thick with tension.

"You all forget about me and acknowledge me only when needed. That's ok. I'm always here." Victor paused as he stood crisply in his suit jacket, flexing his arms slightly as he walked into the light, his pale skin brightening even as he slightly smiled in pain.

"The Wrathfall are based in the Gloomspire, where you recently sent a company of soldiers. They are a threat, as presented by the papers and Minister Shannon's information. Your rumors, Stephanie, are truer than you let on. Do not hold back from General Casting. He was running the Holy Imperium before Prince Damon came over with an army on his father's behalf before it was called the Holy Imperium."

"You're out of line, servant." Minister Shannon stood, "I ought to have you whipped in public for even speaking directly to me."

Victoria shifted in her seat, crossing one leg over the other. Victor did not seem phased by the weakness and anger the Minister of Letters showed but did interrupt to break the tension.

"And how do you know this," she asked.

"The Wrathfall recruited me, and I declined after learning all I could. The slave was dealt with. I left his remains in his quarters where the rest of the staff could witness what happens to traitors. The Wrathfall wants to erase our existence from Vineland. This happened on the same night you received the report about the massacre at Olde Ridgewatch."

"Why didn't you mention this earlier, Victor?" Casting, a member of the Order of the Redcloak, one of the finest knights in the Holy Imperium, was out of step and shocked, yet he ignored Minister Shannon's fleeting attempts to exact punishment onto Victor for speaking out at a meeting.

"I dismissed the effort to recruit me. I am a servant to the Holy Imperium, to Vineland, and to you, General Casting. A child recruited me, and a mere twelve summer-old child at that. I broke his neck and separated it from his body with the most utter tastefulness," he said.

Victor looked up and bowed as the door slammed open, and Prince Damon walked in. His blotchy cheeks held lines like smiles under his eyes; his face was a morose sneer, and he breathed loudly from one nostril and a gaping mouth. His guards, General Casting noticed, were two large Blue Templar in full plate armor. They closed the door forcefully and stood inside with the council.

"Look at me, all of you. I expect loyalty. I want this slave revolt crushed at once." The prince's parted and plastered hair shifted, showing a slight bald spot; he moved it back in place. "Immediately!" He slammed his fist on the table. Everyone sat except for Victor, who stepped back into the shadows. "Key people are coming to the capital, and I'll not be embarrassed by elven and goblin scum crossing our borders. They are filthy mongrels that must be stamped out."

"This plot runs deep. It's not just this Wrathfall; there is a group of like-minded young people. Misfits and rebels based in some of our weaker city-states are causing trouble," added Victoria calmly and with almost a song in her voice. This slightly shattered the tenseness of the situation. Prince Damon was the leader of the Holy Imperium, and after a slight outburst, he was easily manipulated.

"I've heard of them, the Bastards of Liberty and another group, the Harlots of Justice," noted Minister Shannon.

Prince Damon turned to Minister Shannon.

"Thank you for your reports, Minister Shannon. Your loyalty is unwavering." He looked at Casting with a slight sneer.

"They aren't royals or nobles, I say!" Sir Leadwall stood up, looking for a fight. "Root them out."

"Fucking pig-loving goblins and elves. I bet the dwarves are part of this madness, too," said Madam Thompson, the group think sinking into all of them just as Victor had wished.

"Who are their leaders?" asked Casting.

"It's hard to put down," Madam Thompson replied, "but the Wrathfall and the Bastards of Liberty, if they were to connect or combine forces, we would be looking at an insurgency inside the Holy Imperium and a potential standing army of unknown numbers lurking in forests unchecked and uncontrolled. The Wrathfall lives on the outskirts, recruiting everyone to join them. Their leaders are a goblin shaman and a large female orc who commands their soldiers. They wish to create a council of one goblin, human, dwarve, and orc, like how the Grimwood city-state attempted to run itself years ago. The Bastards of Liberty may have connections to the Society of Shadows, Olivia Franklin, and the escaped Hunter Young."

Prince Damon straightened his blouse and walked toward the giant window in the tower to look down on the commoners. His slight pooch of a stomach showed, and his smell, as if he hadn't adequately wiped, lingered. "We must deal with Young now; he's too dangerous to live. Place a bounty on his head. I want him dead." Prince Damon turned and stared at the table as if he'd only heard the last part of what was said recently. "The same for this Olivia Franklin. I have no time for mages, witches, or any who use the old ways. All magic users who are nobles should be bound by two rings on each hand. Those not of noble blood will be burnt at the stake after their hands are removed. Any royal family found to have the ability to use power I will deal with personally. Is that clear? Purge all mages, witches, and warlocks. Their existence is a curse on all of us. Unleash the Order of the Blue Rose."

Prince Damon looked at Stephanie Shannon and the binding ring on her finger. "Is that clear, Stephanie?" She nodded her head in silence. The movement of her head held contempt and a slight amount of fear.

"That will keep them out of the fucking capital until we can get ourselves more secure. These elves and goblins revolting; any caught are to be crucified on the road, and their children will be separated from the criminal slaves and shipped to another city where we will work them to death. Fill the factories with these vermin children and make their parents toil the ground. They are all animals. Our economy will spring to life and make us all very, very," he paused and sniffed loudly, wiping his nose as if he had just taken some wizard salt. "Very rich."

Austin - Too Peaceful To Be Dangerous

Austin wrote to General Casting and Prince Damon explaining the last two villages they passed in Oxfell County, Leefside and Foxpine, were barely inhabited and hostile towards a company of soldiers marching through. In Leefside, one of Lucius Walder's Templar found crudely written pieces of bark stating, "Death to Damon!" and "Freedom from Tyranny." Behind the village leader's house, they found a small hand printing press and a stack of pamphlets called *Ordinary Wit*. Brother Walder set the village on fire without asking and put every villager to the sword. Babies were torn from their mothers and smothered, children were speared through the chest, and all resistance was stamped out as throats were slit. Brother Walder personally crucified the village leaders, cutting them open and pouring honey on their wounds to invite pests while they slowly suffocated under the weight of their own bodies.

Pap returned from taking a shit and nearly lost his temper on Brother Walder. He waited until the massacre ended, drew Walder away from the carnage, and asked Elora to clean up the mess the Templar made. Austin observed, as Pap explained in not so many words, that Brother Walder had let everyone in the forest know of their presence. He also reminded Brother Walder that his soldiers were there for support and not to purge villages for the Maker. When the company made their way to Foxpine, they found the town empty and stripped of anything useful. Pap cursed Brother Walder, giving his monk's latrine duty for the next few nights.

Austin looked up through a canopy of trees and saw the start of the mountains, thinking the next village of Hawkhallow would be the last point of civilization on this side of the Razorshine River he would see. The Razorshine River ran south to north into the Erie Sea. Somewhere, he thought, deep through the mountains and hills, was the Gloomspire, a fortress stronghold fought over for generations. A tower and two gates at a mountain pass separated the west side of the Blightbriar Mountains to the east without another pass for hundreds of miles. It was said that whoever controls Gloomspire controls the trade between Hudson City and the Commonwealth of Erieland. Most folk found other ways, using the Erie Sea to bring trade to the city-states on the other side of the mountains. Local hill folk walked deer paths, which carts and caravans could not use for fear of ambush and robbery. Rivers were used for trade as well. It was why the dwarven city of Steelsburg commanded such power. Once the Dwarves lost control of the Gloomspire to a combined group of orcs, elven, and goblin forces, the dwarves founded the Grindstone Citadel along another mountain pass, whose river lifeline fed into Steelsburg.

The Blightbriar Mountains and the woodlands, often called "The Wilds," stretched north from the shores of the Erie Sea south, down the eastern side of the continent, separating the port towns and cities from the interior of Vineland before the hilly farmlands and forests butted up to the Stagger Wall. The abyss of the wilderness held scores of elves, goblins, and orcs. Austin wondered if they had started to intermingle after years of plague, war, and the threat of slavery from humans.

"You know you should be watching our backs, not writing in your journal, Austin," said a familiar voice.

Austin looked up from his stopped horse, journal bent in his hand.

"Elora, good to see you. I was trying to write a bit more about the history of this place; besides, I'll watch your back anytime; you know that."

She smiled at him. "Watching my behind now, are you?"

"What no, I, I, I —" he stuttered.

"Wow, calm down, Wildcat, calm down. Set your second squire on drag; you're joining my dogs on a little recon of the Hawkhallow area. For now, Pap isn't going to let the Templar stumble around on point anymore. He's fixing we may see action soon."

"You believe him?" Austin asked, slightly nervous.

"Buckle up your gear tight and run light with me; we're off the chains and hunting," Elora responded. "We'll check out Hawkhallow and the surrounding area and report back. If they seem peaceful, we'll use it as a first base of operations until we move towards the lodge. If it's abandoned like Foxpine, we could be in some deep shit."

"Place seems too peaceful to be dangerous sometimes," he said as they approached the middle of the caravan. The soldiers were stirring in the morning air. Austin saw monks and soldiers laughing and drinking wine as they passed. Brother Walder, gave them a hard stare when they rode by. Austin made a note to speak to Brother Walder and Sir Pekka Deeran on his return and get their make. Pap had ordered a light morning for the soldiers to let his scouts recon the area and wanted to move on the village late in the afternoon. It was early morning, and the sun was barely awake.

"Austin, don't kid yourself. Prince Damon and the commander of his armies sent several of his guard and members of the Holy Church to investigate a hunting lodge," she said. "Something isn't right about that. I've done some shit contracts, but this smells of something else entirely."

Austin nodded but didn't respond. His unease settling past his ignorance in the given circumstances created a steaming pile of anxiety deep in his bowels. He looked out into the morning horizon and saw pine trees, groves of black willow, and oakthorn trees as the Blightbriar Mountains lay ahead. Up the road, they found Keyla, Parker, and Leslie prepping for their recon mission, their faces painted to help conceal them. They carried short compound bows, often used by elves and orcs in combat, and short swords or tomahawks. Elora handed Austin a biscuit with a piece of dense meat.

"Chew quickly. We'll paint. Hawkhallow Village is in front of us some ways; along with the Razorshine River, there should also be a crossing into the Blightbriar Wilds," Elora said as she finished her preparations. "You keep quiet and use hand signals. As I know you like my behind, follow us. We are looking for signs of anything- the village or potential danger. Thanks to the shit for brains Templar, they know we're coming."

"Unfortunately, we don't know who they are," said Parker.

"Could be bandits or old soldiers looking for a profit. I'd love for that and not a nest of forsaken goblins. I am sick of getting their blood in my hair," Keyla complained.

Keyla wore a green-dyed short hair strip on her head and shaved sides. She smeared something dark on Austin's face, her breath smelling of meat and honey.

"Careful with him. Remember, he's a prince's boy, reporting to our commander-in-chief himself."

"You shittin' me, Elora," Leslie said. "The prince's very own bootlicker himself. He's going to get us killed!"

"Remember, Pap said to get him some action," said Parker.

"Not here to babysit some cake eater's son."

"Pap said he's dependable," defended Elora.

"Shit," Leslie sighed. "Okay, okay. When we slow down, step heel-toe and watch for dead wood. If we run, you run on your toes and zigzag to avoid bolts and arrows. You get me, Wildcat?"

Austin nodded, realizing the seriousness of the situation.

"Anything past the river is an enemy, but try not to engage."

"We're going across the river?" asked Austin.

"If the village looks passive, yes, we push to the crossing and investigate further," said Elora. She grabbed Austin by the chin in surprise and moved close. "Anything past the river is an enemy. We do our best not to kill innocents. We ain't going to be raping and pillaging places, but if I give the word, you will fucking burn a village down and put a nun to the fucking sword; you get it, prince's boy?"

Austin did get Elora; he was given an order.

"Yes, ma'am"

Elora snickered, along with the others.

"You know those heavy horses won't do shit once we get in the Blightbriar Wilds."

"Leslie's right. We need another hundred or so of the Union Dogs," said Keyla. "Too bad the other half are in Steelsburg."

"We have what we have; for now, we scout and teach these soldiers how to deal with the Blightbriar Wilds." Elora shouldered her pack and began forward. "Hawkhallow should be straight ahead, and the crossing somewhere past that. Now let's move."

* * *

The village of Hawkhallow wasn't hard to find. Elora, Austin, Keyla, and Parker took horses off the road and into the woods, following deer paths until they found the fields the village used during summer. Parker stayed with the horses on the edge of the field, and the rest followed around the fields. They soon came to the village.

"Hawkhallow," Leslie whispered. "Circle and report back no contact."

All three left, leaving Austin in his spot to observe. He quietly waited as he watched a ragged man pull water from a well in the middle of the village. He heard laughter from children and saw drying garlic and herbs on a cabin wall. Overall, the homestead - that's what he would call it, not a village - looked as it should. The wood from their homes looked sturdy, a mixture of oak and ash. He saw no orcs or goblins but did note an altar on the edge of the village. It was for one of the pagan gods, but Austin couldn't tell which. It didn't matter to him; they were all false and wicked in his mind. Austin thought of Elora and shifted his stance as he crouched on the ground near a tree. He checked his surroundings behind and to his left and right and felt truly alone. When he returned from this recon, he would remind his squires and page to work together for the rest of the campaign. Getting lost in the wilds would get you dead quickly.

Austin tried to keep his mind steady as sweat dripped off his back. He squatted between a stone and a large pine tree; the forest floor was damp enough that shifting didn't make noise. The village residents moved about, cleaning fish from the river and mending baskets. Sometimes, villages like this had no central leader, and the town barber, smith, or oldest person took charge of any problems. Mob rule worked in small communities, Austin thought, *but it also burnt books and murdered people for witchcraft.*

The forest around the Blightbriar Mountains presented excellent hunting as the river seemed to stop some of the beasts from crossing into territory controlled by the Holy Imperium. Even so, most folk knew better than to be outside once the sun drifted past the horizon. It was Lord Rotherham who built the lodge just inside the Blightbriar Wilds over ruins of an older manor; he wanted to walk out on a balcony and kill a fox the size of a pony. Everything in the Blightbriar Wilds was meaner and more dangerous than their counterparts on this side of the Razorshine River.

"You still alive, beautiful?" Elora whispered. She looked tired and worried. Austin nodded.

Keyla and Leslie returned as well.

He watched as Leslie and Keyla backed away from the village, keeping their faces forward, and shifted towards the river crossing. Elora grabbed Austin's hand and showed him how to do the same. He felt the warmth of her touch as the sun broke through the leaves and branches above him. He breathed in the aroma of pine trees and fires from the village.

"So far, so good; village seemed fine."

"Agree, although that means they have a working relationship with whoever is in charge of the area, right?" Austin asked.

"Yeah, Pap has his work cut out for him; either take over the whole place or offer some assistance to get them on our side."

"You trust any of those villagers?" Leslie asked.

Austin countered quietly, "Isn't trust all we have out here?"

They moved toward the river pass.

* * *

They jogged and ran, pushing past the village. Austin felt well enough when they stopped but held Elora, Keyla, and Leslie in higher regard. He was formally trained and continued to stay in shape even through endless shifts guarding Prince Damon, but to witness three others wearing a mixture of armor and arms run and not be winded was impressive. If all of the Union Dogs were as dependable as their scouts, they were a force to be reckoned with.

The Razorshine River was in sight of them. Elora stopped and commanded Keyla left and Leslie right off the path the caravan would take to check the opening ford's area and mouth. They waited near large stones braced up against an older oak tree.

"Notice trees on this side are now much older from when we started a few days ago, and the ford of the river there, it's almost a gate, pine trees on both sides like a tall fence and creating that big canopy again, and the two oakthorn trees, one on each side of the trail like gates." Elora pointed ahead as Austin got his bearings.

Austin looked at the trees, their gnarled bark, twisting trunks, and large branches like blades and thorns sharp as knives where leaves should grow.

"When one grows, normally more follow. You rarely see two by themselves like this; they grow like large briar patches, only trees."

"True, I've seen them before, but they're to be avoided. They don't burn, and it's too hard to cut one down without hurting yourself or others," Austin said.

Impressed, Elora nodded. "This path shows the start of the Blightbriar Wilds; look to the other side."

Across the river, the trees were primarily oakthorn, black willows, and other much older trees, like white spruce and purple maple.

Leslie came back first, reporting this side was clear.

"I did see a series of tracks, some human, some not, but they were covered up well, no telling if they were coming or going. Maybe they were heading upriver. Saw them as I was about to turn back."

"That's not great news. Anything else?"

"Just some big shit, couldn't really tell who's shit it was, too big for a human, big fuckin' bear, or crucible wolf maybe?"

"Children stories," chided Austin but was uncertain of his remark so he smiled.

Elora was severe and unfazed. "What, how large?"

"It was broken up from falling from the canopy, but the size of horse shit only, you know, from a bird or something."

"Fuck me," Austin said. "Okay, so you're serious."

"Right, fucking hate this job."

Keyla returned shortly after, reporting the same thing: large pieces of feces around the broken canopy of the river.

"Okay," Elora nodded, absorbing the information from the two scouts. "We cross quickly, do another circle, and get our asses back fast. We need to tell Pap what you two saw. Let's cross and hope for the best."

The river's passing was low, in places only ankle deep as the stone shell was worn down from the chilly waters of the mountains. There were deep pools of dark water where fireflies danced across. Austin did not relish stumbling and falling into those as he went. He looked again and realized they were not fireflies but faint pixies, creatures of magic and fables, bright and tiny in the sunlight. They spirited away and stared at them longer. He shook his head and moved into the Blightbriar. Tales of pixies said only the dead could hear their tiny voices.

They crossed the oakthorn tree gate into the Blightbriar Wilds and into a distinct and dense environment not their own. Compared to the woods they had traveled through previously, the wilds felt of another time and another world. Austin heard and saw squirrels and chipmunks the size of house cats, birds, and bugs he'd scarcely imagined. Thoughts of giant warhawks lingered in his mind, as did animals the size of horses with a thirst for flesh. Sun came through enough of the canopy to breathe life throughout the forest but left enough shadow to shed the anxiety of the unknown over all that moved below.

They walked a deer trail, a slight upgrade, surrounded by mostly pine trees. The canopy of the long pine needles allowed sun rays to the path. Old needles lay on the forest floor, keeping vegetation down except for a batch of ferns and briar bushes, whose thorns protected the sweet red and black berries birds and squirrels argued over.

They moved off the trail, keeping it to their right, and quickly came upon tracks again, another well-used footpath. After a brief time, they saw cabins in an opening between a thicket with no defensive walls. There was no movement around the buildings, and Austin had noticed no animals in sight. Elora held up all of them, thumbing her tomahawk, and left the group where they squatted. She gave a sign that she would get closer herself and follow up shortly.

Austin watched as she moved quickly and quietly in the undergrowth towards the building, peeked inside, and then moved back.

She returned quickly.

"Grain storage is more than a village needs. Let's get back across the river," she said.

Austin was tense as they moved, only feeling relief after the river crossing and skirting the village as they returned to Parker and the horses.

* * *

"The vanguard of the caravan shouldn't be that far along," Leslie said. After an hour, they heard commotion ahead of them as birds circled the sky.

"They've been hit."

"What, how?"

"Make sure they know it's us; I don't want a javelin or arrow in my throat by our own soldiers."

An arrow sped by Austin's head.

"It's us, you twitchy fools!"

"Password," a soldier yelled.

"Prince's Crown, now don't take my tits off with that arrow and tell me what happened."

"Caravan's been stopped. Looks like bandits or someone hit the tail end of us, killed a foot soldier, and hobbled wagon wheel and ran," said a Holy Imperial soldier on sentry duty.

"Captain moved all the gear off the wagon and gave us a heightened sense of security."

"Where is Pap now?"

The soldier, still on edge, pointed behind him, "You'll find him easy enough."

Pap was in the middle of the column as Austin and the rest of the Union Dog scouts walked up.

"What you find?" he ordered.

Elora acknowledged Brother Lucious Walder and Sir Pekka Deeran before beginning.

"Small homestead of locals; they don't look like a threat but are peaceful enough where they are tight with whoever controls that side of the area. Pap, we found a lot of grain storage, enough to feed a larger force on the other side," said Elora. Parker, Keyla, and Leslie lingered behind Elora and Austin.

"Sire, the crossing is perfect for an ambush. We found tracks near the opening on either side but can't confirm the number count. They walked in sync with each other. Who'd we lose?" Austin asked.

"Came close to losing your squires, but they fought hard. It was a quick burst of about fifteen enemies. We killed two goblins and two orcs but no bodies. They dragged them back under a stream of arrows into the cover of the trees. One of ours, Wilfred, I think, took one to the throat."

"You scouts were supposed to stop this type of thing," said Brother Walder.

"We saw no contact other than the village and what Austin reported. It could have been them who made those tracks, but they seemed to have just stopped and disappeared," Elora said.

"Little goblin shit holes," said Sir Pekka Deeran. "Some were up in the trees, loosing down at us as the others retreated. Those buggers are fast."

"That solves that mystery," said Elora. "We found shit on the path leading up to the crossing and on the other side. Human-sized and other groupings were much bigger."

"You think orcs then?" questioned Pap. "Orcs don't climb trees that I know."

"Orcs, sure, and goblins can be expected at this point, but some were bears and the like. The Blightbriar Wilds hold perilous creatures," Elora finished.

"Right," Pap looked at each of the groups in turn. "We learned some information and gained more questions. Let's contain the town, take those living there as part of our camp, set up a home base behind the river's opening, control this side of the Razorshine River, and make a foray across to check on the lodge. We'll fortify the gap and go from there. "

"More digging, sir?" asked Brother Walder.

"Unless we hit the water. We got stone, too, so we can build some good fortifications. Yes, more digging."

"Horse won't work well in the wilds other than on the shabby roads, too thick in the brush; we need to be mindful of that when we cross on the other side," said Elora.

"You're telling me. Let's get moving," said Pap. "Fucking prince didn't give me enough tools to cook with."

Alysha - Three's Company

"Can't you just let go of me," whimpered the messenger.

"If I let go, you try to escape. Right now, I have you in complete control now, Edgar." Helena twisted the man's privates tight in her grip, and the messenger squirmed through fear and pain. "Which a moment ago you liked."

"I promise I'll help. We could leave together tonight. I could take you as a prostitute and this fine person as your guard, and," he paused, thinking as clearly as he could give the ow, he found himself in. "Say Jared Blackheart ordered to bring you out of town for a special service."

Helena was naked with her hand on the Holy Imperium messenger's crotch, and she squeezed harshly. He yipped and moaned so she loosened her grip.

"Could work," Helena said.

Alysha drew Junior Wolfe's sword and put it to the messenger's throat. "Both of you, dress. Edgar, all we are asking is to get away from this town, free and clear, and then you can do what you wish. Helena, he a reputable man?"

She snickered a little. "He never hits me when he comes by and tips. So sure, yeah, he's alright. I hoped he'd buy out my contract and make me a wife." Helena let go of the man as she stood to dress.

Edgar looked at Helena and Alysha. He was naked as the Maker humbled him and smiled his crooked teeth, hoping to make an impression. It was less than a remarkable sight Helena or any other woman wanted to see.

"I got off shift, needed to relax, and been thinking about coming here for a week. I can help. It's just a job delivering messages; I don't want any trouble and don't care for the army. I like riding horses."

"It's true. He does like horse riding," Helena said, smiling as she slipped into her clothes. She grabbed his saddlebag and opened it. "What do we have here?" she thumbed through it, and Edgar grabbed the bag.

"No, no, you forget you're not in charge here," said Alysha. She sliced at his arm, cutting him.

"Ow," Edgar howled, "that hurt you-"

"You what? Say it, and I'll cut your manhood right off!" Alysha's thin face held back an irritation that simmered behind it.

"Edgar, did you stop to see me before you finish your route?" Helena inquired.

"Told you I was thinking about you for days," he looked at her.

"That's sweet. Ain't that sweet, Alysha?" she handed Alysha the letters.

"Shit, I need those. They're to be delivered to General Flint's command unit on the other side of town before midnight," said Edgar.

"Better find two horses and get us out of here before then so we give you these back." Alysha waved a handful of letters in the messenger's face. "Wouldn't want you caught with your pants down like this now, would you?"

"I should have just gotten drunk," he mumbled to himself.

Alysha allowed Edgar to dress, and the three made their way out of the tavern and out the side door. They moved around to his horse, and Alysha grabbed its reins. Edgar walked them to a barn where he commandeered three horses, ordering the groom to prep the saddles under the command of a message of the Holy Imperium. Once saddled, the three moved towards the closed eastern gate as the sun dipped below the edge of the town's newly constructed walls.

Alysha was unsure of herself, but Helena sat on her new horse and smiled away, laughing and making a joke with Edgar. She had no idea how Helena, who had been frolicking in a room with this man thirty minutes ago, was now extorting him into fleeing, unsure where their next stop or next meal would be. The idea of death scared Helena less than staying as a woman forced into prostitution.

Edgar led Helena and Alysha toward the gate.

"Are you leaving with this woman, Helena?" he said. "I mean, will I see you again?"

Helena smirked. "Oh, honey, we're just making sure Alysha is safely out of town. Don't worry, your pretty little head. Once I know she's safe, I'll come back with you, and we'll have a fun time all night after you drop off these messages." She patted her breast where she had tucked the letters from his messenger bag.

Edgar smiled, dreaming of a sordid night with his favorite plaything, oblivious to his current position. He forgot they had stolen three horses. Other than breaking curfew and sneaking out of a town under Holy Imperium military control, the one offense of stealing a horse could get the three of them hanged without trial. They moved forward, and he straightened himself. That didn't include the woman with the sword and the missing messages he no longer had in his possession.

"You there, strike the gate so that we can leave. I have direct orders to deliver these two to the palisade guard captain," he called out to the gate guard.

"Closed for the night," said the rough-looking city guard. "Can't break my orders."

Edgar looked back and sighed.

"I understand your orders, you farmer's bastard. My orders," and he gripped a set of papers with a stamp. "My orders trump your orders. See this sigil, Wildcat with Wings? It means I can fuckin' go where I please as I must deliver my messages. Whether it's military orders, messages or," and he pointed, "these packages."

The guard looked as if thinking would burn the last living thought inside his egg-shaped head and looked behind Edgar towards Helena on a horse with a long cloak on and her breasts heaving out from it.

"Been an odd night. Maker's breath, whatever; half my team is fighting a fire near the southern gate. Blacksmith shop set some new walls aflame and several houses nearby. They are looking for the owners, two old soldiers, and their apprentice," he mumbled, struck the gate, and raised it enough for them to get out.

Alysha flicked the man a shill and nodded, while Helena raised her eyebrow at the last news but didn't say anything, only winked at the guard.

The guard stepped back and closed the gate.

"Find another gate if you want back in. I won't lose my head for this."

The eastern gate of Counselor City drifted behind them as they headed east at a tense trot. The fire at the southern end hovered on the horizon as the black smoke blotted out the stars in the sky. Alysha tried to act calm and continued forward. She turned to look back at the braziers burning around the palisade walls, hoping soldiers wouldn't feather their backs with arrows, finding they were escaping and not delivering messages or goods.

"We go until we can't see the city, and you can have your documents back," Alysha mentioned, trying to figure out the next step in her escape and hoping Helena would join her. Alysha nodded to Edgar and nudged her horse, watching Helena lead. He was over the moon for her and would have made a proper suitor if times were different if soldiers from the Holy Imperium hadn't shattered Alysha and Helena's lives last fall when they destroyed their homes and sold them into servitude, forcing them to live in Counselor City on the shores of the Erie Sea.

"I'd like to get back as soon as possible, slip through the south gate, and give out these reports, but I don't," he paused. I don't know what to say about being late when I return the messages. I shouldn't have stopped off to see you to begin with."

"You'll think of something," Helena said and looked back. "You're a bright boy, aren't you." She talked to him like he was a dog, and he half smiled at her.

"I just had to see you," he said quietly. He was older than Alysha and Helena and not a poor catch if Helena were into the soldier type, and if they had not left, Helena may have done okay with Edgar. Well, Alysha was done with soldiers, done with men in general. She had liked being around them; they were simple and treated her nicely, but the kissing and groping always felt wrong, and she would go numb to the slightest touch from any boy who tried. She changed her thoughts and concentrated on the next breath, moment, and escape.

She hoped the House of Wolfe's tobacco pipe and family sword would get her and Helena into Grimwood before the Holy Imperium attacked the city. She thought the Wolfe name was known to some folk in the city. If she could warn someone in power at Grimwood, maybe they could repel the planned attack on the city, or maybe she was being a completely foolish little girl. And then another thought drifted in.

From what she could remember, her father, General Benedict Ashburn, said the city of Grimwood was a challenging city-state to attack, and he wouldn't want to try. *If Grimwood could kill as many soldiers as General Flint and Jared Blackheart brought to its walls, so much the better as long as Holy Imperium soldiers die.*

They picked up their pace on the muddy road, and Alysha didn't look back at Counselor City.

"Well, Edgar, you want to join us? We are going on a little adventure. We could burn those messages and leave the Holy Imperium behind," Alysha tempted the man.

The three stopped at a crossroads. Smoldering stakes lined up the road. The bodies long deceased.

"What stinks?" asked Alysha, waving away from her nose.

"Jared Blackheart's Monks burnt a family of heretics here. Worshipers of the Profane," said Edgar quietly. "I watched. They weren't mages or witches; our soldiers found a minor altar in their back shed. I couldn't stop them. I don't like to see peasants killed like this. We should whip those pagans until they repented their sins against the Maker, Child, and Servant, not burn them at the stakes. You know, if they catch you two, they'll crucify you both, murderers, escaped slaves, and the like; they crucify on two crossed stakes or on tall poles. I don't want that to happen. Let's get moving."

"Maybe you shouldn't join us," said Alysha to Helena as she moved her horse and shifted her hand slightly to the sword at her hip.

"Honey, let's head back then. I think you can weasel me back in," Helena said, looking at Edgar and smiling with her eyes. She moved her horse closer and leaned in. "I'll make it worth your while. It's been a rough day. Let's get a nice bath in after you deliver those messages." Helena smiled with her chest pushing up towards him.

Edgar's eyes betrayed him, and he looked down at her chest as Helena's knife smashed into his windpipe.

"From now on, I'm only a whore when I want to be, you sick bastard," she said, taking the blade from his neck.

He gasped for breath, but Helena pulled him, shifting him horizontally between the horses, letting the blood drip onto the ground.

"I don't want too much blood on his clothes. I need to change out of this horrid dress into his clothes as best I can," informed Helena.

"Shit, I thought you would let him go," said Alysha. "I was about to take his head."

"We're horse thieves at best now, sweetie," Helena laughed, pulling the dead man from his horse. She started stripping him and changing in the shadow of the burnt family.

It smelled like a roasted hog and made Alysha want to throw up, but she commanded herself and started acting. "I'll search his bags and take anything worth coin or will help us get along. Then, we take the best horse, push the other off in another direction, and hope anyone who may track us follows that one."

"You start that fire back there, Alysha?"

"What, yeah, I did. I was attacked, and Hob and Bob were killed. I returned and started packing to leave, and one of the Genteel Monks visited. We fought, and I burnt the place, hoping to hide her corpse. I didn't think it would go much further. Been trying to figure out one thing at a time."

Helena nodded, taking in her friend's story. "It's near twilight; we can follow the road briefly. We best keep the Erie Sea to our right and hope we don't hit any patrols."

"I want to get to Grimwood," Alysha stated. "I hope to warn the city about the Holy Imperium First Army here, but I would think they know what's coming," said Alysha. "I have Junior Wolfe's pipe; want to give it to his brother Felix."

"You got goals like some knight out of a story, Alysha."

"Not much is left in my life; it seems like the right thing to do."

Helena looked at Alysha, and her bravado slipped slightly.

"Shit, okay, can't believe you got that thing still. All my possessions are back in the city, which wasn't much. Guess I have all Edgar's belongings now: a nice knife, a better dagger, flint, a compass, and messenger packs. He has two maps here, too. Those are worth a fortune," said Helena.

"You don't have to come to Grimwood, Helena. If I could, I wanted to help you. Not sure you want to go to a city that may be under siege soon."

"How do I look?" Helena asked.

She walked out of the shadow wearing Edgar's riding boots and striped pants, her short corset pushing her chest out, and his jacket with the sleeves rolled up. She pressed his cloak into the back saddle pack on her horse.

"You look just right," said Alysha. Helena looked stunning, but she kept that thought to herself.

"Right, so towards Grimwood?"

"Stay on the road and turn south when we can. Might be best to come in from the south before the Litchbury Mire starts," Alysha said.

"That seems right. Something my mom always said. About Grimwood's gates," Helena said.

"Four gates of Grimwood beckon, on the night of the damned, grim meaning, dim meaning, howling wind west, raven sky north, dark eyes seek south, grim watches east," Alysha whispered as they got on their horses.

"I remember now, yeah, Mom said a graveyard like a moat surrounds the entire city, and the one on the eastern side facing us is the one nobody uses because of the black willow trees and the poisonfire fog. Remember playing ghouls in the graveyard back home? I wonder if that's where stories came from?" She chuckled as if this was still an adventure, showing her a bit of her old self. Alysha had to remember that Helena had been through her own Hades and dealt with her nightmarish life in her own way after they were separated last Autumn.

"My mom said the city was cursed, the cemetery was known as Black Willow Falls, and followers of the Maker never used it, but my father said it was all bunk," added Alysha.

"Shit, that could be the safest place for us with Jared back behind us. Man's got a hard-on for the Maker, Servant, and Child. The giant psycho pervert."

Alysha moved her horse forward, away from the city's grip, and Helena followed.

"You're a sick woman, Helena. Let's get out of here. We can sleep once it feels safer."

They moved off into the darkness of the night, letting the road keep them safe as the openness of the fields surrounding Counselor City disappeared behind them, and the trees of the Grimwood forest awaited them. Behind them, a gate from Counselor City opened again, letting out a group of soldiers searching for a messenger, and two women wanted for questions concerning a missing scout unit, arson, and horse theft.

Austin - Howls and Horns

Hawkhallow Village was empty as the Holy Imperium Expeditionary Force marched into the area, with no birds, farmers, or fires burning. The villagers had taken anything of use, leaving huts and a well with drinking water. An archer found tracks leading down a path into a small open grove and across the river. By late afternoon, the company made it to the mouth of the river. They were commanded to dig in at the grove's edge before the river crossing, creating a defensive trench and wall. The ground was a mixture of stone, forest decay, and clay. The soldiers grumbled under their breath as the knights and Templar ordered their servants to work until Pap and Elora commanded everyone to dig. The soldiers built a shallower pit and a palisade wall braced by stone and clay until dark. Pap requested outer fires built outside the defense to make their force look larger in the dark. Austin heard screeches and animal cries he'd never witnessed in the wilderness—mixtures of a lion and a bear roaring up in the mountains. Pap set up sentries, switching their posts every two hours on each corner of their squared-out camp. Because of the time, the spiked fencing wasn't perfect, but it was a start.

Austin watched as Brother Walder, partially drunk, walked into Pap's tent, irate over the order to force his soldiers to perform manual labor with the rest of the company.

He couldn't hear everything, but something broke inside the tent, and Brother Walder walked out red in the face, rubbing the side of his jaw. Austin watched as he walked back to a small circle of his Templar and gave them the order to start digging and putting up picket fences. Then, he walked into his

110

smaller tent.

Austin walked toward the tent after putting his shovel down. He knocked loudly on the post outside the tent.

"Brother Walder, it's Sir Austin Casting."

"Enter, enter," said Brother Walder.

Austin saw the Templar putting a bottle behind a large rectangular shield called a scutum. The shield bared the insignia of the Holy Flame, a sword pointed up with the blade, eventually becoming the tip of a flame. When he was younger, Austin wished to become a Blue Templar like most boys, but his cousin groomed him into knighthood. Eventually, he became one of the youngest knights raised to a Wildcat and a member of the royal family's guard.

Brother Walder was a stouter man, around four notches shorter than six foot and nearly two hundred pounds. His beard was unkempt like a silver miner's, and his hair was long on the back and sides and swooped over the right eye, reminding Austin of a wild horse's dark mane. His fingernails were dirty, and his beard glistened like a gift from the bottle hidden behind his scutum. The shield looked well kept, either never seen action or repaired and painted to hide scars and blemishes. Compared to the Templar, it looked better of the two. The man's eyes were gray, cold, and off-putting; Austin thought of Elora's eyes for a second and pushed the thought away.

"The youngest Wildcat ever; that puts you at fourteen, fifteen springs, young man?"

"I'm nineteen winters past now, Brother Walder."

"It's Okay, Sir Austin; it's fine; I'm thirty-two summers past. Blessed be the Maker." Brother Walder put his hands up to mean no offense.

"I've come to let you know if I have time. I can finish some of the work assigned to you before I go out on my security duty tonight. I don't mind."

Brother Walder raised his eyebrows and reached for his bottle.

"Well, thank you, Sir Austin, but I've already assigned that work out. Drink?"

"No sir, not while on duty."

Brother Walder stared at him.

"Well, it helps my joints, you see. Sir Austin, you technically outrank me and have me at my best. What can I do you for."

"No rank here, brother; we've met formally in the command tent, as I took notes during the briefings with Pap," he paused. "And the others." He didn't want to mention Elora as it would anger Walder. "But I wanted to take a moment to say hello, and if I could offer any assistance during our campaign, please let me know."

"Assistance. That's interesting," Walder stopped himself.

"Sorry, sir. Yes, well, I guess I have access to people in high authority; I may be able to help," Austin said, realizing he was going in a direction he did not wish to go.

"How about you not mentioning the argument," he burped, "or you finding me wallowing in my tent here in your reports back to the capital?"

"The report is already written, Brother Walder; I noted aggressive negotiations with the command structure on where to place the camp. No names, no further details."

He was half correct. Austin would send formal letters back but keep a personal journal, writing finer details about the campaign and how the mission unfolded.

"How do you see the orders being carried out here for this campaign?"

"Not too difficult; we get across the river, burn that village, and verify nobody's alive at the lodge. We see any heathen goblins or elves, massacre them, bring some ears and noses back to our superiors in the civilized world," said Brother Walder.

Austin nodded slightly, but he didn't want to reaffirm too much of Brother Walder's idea of collecting intelligence.

"Our Maker put humans above the elves, goblins, orcs, and even the dwarves. They are all heathens and need to walk the Path of the Blessed or perish, here or when they die, and the Maker judges them unworthy," the Templar proselytized.

Austin felt sick thinking of using his religion as a weapon, an excuse to murder and burn. He made the sign of the Maker so he wouldn't have to acknowledge what Brother Walder just said. Walder did the same, nodding at Austin's fake approval.

"What are your thoughts on Sir Pekka Deeran, captain of the Holy Imperium soldiers?" Austin asked. "I haven't met him and want to provide Lord Casting and Prince Damon a fair take on how we started the campaign and who will be responsible for our success."

"Sir Pekka is no Redcloak like Lord Casting. He's Vineland-born but comes from an old family, nonetheless. Better soldier than that Elora Meldguard, tell you that. She's a mercenary bastard in over her head and not fit to be Pap's second in command. Heard Sir Pekka was part of General Hammer Clinton's 3rd army that split apart."

Austin's ears turned red in anger, and he shifted his silhouette so as not to show his emotions to Brother Walder. The Templar snapped his fingers, his voice slightly slurring as his mind tried to keep up with his lips.

"Sir Leadwall's man, that's it. Sir Pekka came from Castle Greenleaf and picked up Elora, the bastard, and her Union Dogs along the way. More like fleas, you ask me."

"I did, thank you. I'll be on my way," Austin finished more abruptly than he wished. He winced to himself, glad Walder could not see his face as he walked out of the tent.

"Brother Walder," Austin said as he left, turning his head back. "Pap is considering Elora for a position on the Wildcats and others on this campaign. He'll also ask my thoughts, as we're soldiers in blood and spirit. Keep that in mind, specifically how you and yours present yourselves. We need honest soldiers in the Wildcats, and Pap thinks Elora fits the mark. I wonder who else he'll choose."

He left without further thought or comment, the warm summer air hitting his face.

* * *

"Fuck this place," Jaden, an archer from Sir Pekka's soldiers, said to her left as she walked outside the fence with Austin; the sun had set two hours ago; he and Jaden had drawn one of the four shifts of security duty after sunset.

"Keep your eyes away from the fire and out into the darkness, Jaden. We see something, we report it, and if we see danger, I blow the horn."

"You ever been inside the Blightbriar Wilds, Sir Austin?"

"Just yesterday, Jaden."

"I heard there are owls as big as dogs that swoop down and steal children from their beds," said Jaden, shaking her shoulders anxiously.

"Didn't see any owls on the other side of the river when I was out scouting, just some big damn flies. Make sure you stay together with someone after guard duty. It's unsafe to piss alone out there, you hear me?"

Austin felt like a fraud, acting as if he had already served in combat in the Blightbriar Wilds, but he thought that anything he could tell this scared archer would help.

"What's with that giant arch made of oakthorn trees, Sir Austin?"

"From what I understand, it shows a difference. Here is the end of civilization, and over there, with the arch made of pine trees and surrounded by the black willow and oakthorn trees, the start of the Blightbriar Wilds, and the mountains follow behind them."

Jaden said nothing, just examined the darkness, and shivered when a creature moaned out on the other side of the river.

Austin shivered involuntarily, too.

"No need to get too rustled up; if you can hear their breathing, then you know they are close," Austin said mockingly to Jaden, trying to use bluster to give himself courage. He knew he'd hardly speak like this if Elora, Keyla, or Leslie were around. Austin wondered if any scouts would still be up when he got off sentry duty.

"Not many orcs down south, mostly arrow ears and swamp goblins. We got the short end of it when Sir Pekka got his command. Sir Leadwall split up with General Hammer Clinton and came up north, bringing me with him. Prince Damon called for troops, and now I'm in Gothine's taint cause some rich man's hunting lodge got torched," said Jaden. She spoke freely as if Austin were her equal and not a knight. At least Austin was getting the truth of the Ow from someone other than a commander.

"How long have you signed up for Jaden?"

"Me? Five years, and I become a citizen of the Holy Imperium; they're giving me a piece of land to farm if I make it. Most of the soldiers I started with are gone. I got two years and a wake-up, and I'm done."

"What do you mean by gone?"

"Either they left or got dead. Think about fifty signed up; I say less than ten are left out of the original group. The rest we got are recruits signed up over the winter."

"Well, I'm glad to count you among us, Jaden, just a little longer."

Jaden smiled as the torchlight shadowed her face. Howls, from crucible wolves and others from animals no soldier had ever seen, responded.

"Just want to go over there, check on that lodge, and get us out of this forest, Sir Austin. The wilds give me the creeps. Give me the swamps and swamp goblins to prick with my arrows. They screech, but they don't howl like that."

"How many swamp goblins you pick off with that bow?"

"Sir Austin, I can drop an arrow through a goblin's eye at a thousand paces. I got well over twenty when I was younger."

"Thousand paces?" Austin questioned a soldier's brag but didn't challenge it.

"Yes sir, no lying here. If I'm lying, I'm dying."

"Let's hope not, and I hope you get your citizen papers here soon, Jaden. Here comes our reprieve."

The night's breeze ended, and Austin wiped his face, trying to keep the mosquitoes away.

"Why are you on guard duty, anyway, Sir Austin? I don't see any knights doing so," Jaden asked.

"Pap thinks it's best to have a mixture of sentries; as we go into the wilds now, you'll see other knights joining and performing duties. That's why you're seeing them dig in and help make camp. Besides, I'm here to observe and give notes to Lord Casting himself, and he wants all the details possible about the area, so getting an archer's perspective along with a high knight's perspective is just as important."

Jaden spat out a bit of chewing tobacco.

"Shit, well, thank you, Sir Austin, for including me in your report."

Austin heard the forest quiet, a short yelp in the middle of the camp, and then a scream.

"Down, now!" Austin ducked. He grabbed Jaden, shoving her to the ground. Three arrows feathered the air and landed behind them.

"Jaden, blow the horn, ambush."

"You saved me," Jaden mumbled.

"Blow the fucking horn!"

Another horn from behind the camp blew and stopped abruptly.

Jaden let a wale off from the horn, sounding like a deer dying mid-climax.

"To arms, to arms!" a voice yelled.

"Ambush! Shields, shields!"

"Stay low and hope they don't hit us from either side; keep blowing! Let's get back to the camp." Austin hauled Jaden behind him as they scrambled toward the camp.

Arrows feathered around them, but Austin felt they were coming from a long distance. He could see the extra braziers around the camp light up, giving the base further visibility.

Another arrow sliced toward them from their camp.

"Friendly, friendly!" He yelled over Jaden's horn.

"Thought you was one of them goblins," a Holy Imperium archer said.

Austin and Jaden climbed up the mounded clay and stone through one of the picket-fenced doors. As they made their way through the palisade door, he saw nasty-looking long arrows sticking out of the walls of their camp.

"Have some discipline, you fool. If you can't see your enemy, you can't hit them," Austin shouted at the archer who nearly killed him and Jaden.

"Jaden, when day breaks, collect all enemy arrows, don't touch the tips, and leave them at my tent; I want to inspect them. Stay at the door in case a sentry from one of the other sides comes through here. I'll find the captain." Jaden assented with a curt nod.

Austin jogged to the command post, worried another barrage of arrows would fall onto the camp.

Pap was with Elora, Sir Pekka Deeran, and Brother Lucious Walder.

"Austin, welcome," said Pap. "Looks like the enemy is assessing our defenses."

"Indeed, filthy savages," said Brother Walder.

"We should make a foray out with the cavalry," said Deeran.

Pap looked at Brother Walder and Deeran, and Elora turned and rolled her eyes at them, looking at Austin.

"Putting calvary out at night will lead to more deaths on our part through accident. The ground is rocky and unstable; an elvish or orc arrow or a random tree branch will unhorse your soldiers. Brother Walder, they may be savages, but they're smart and cunning. Don't underestimate them. They do exactly what I would do if the places were switched."

"The rest of the sentries return?" Pap asked.

"We had eight out situated on the corners of the fences; so far, six returned," Elora replied tightly.

"Who's out there?"

"Two of my lads, good sports; they are just being safe getting back," said Sir Pekka.

"Let's hope so," said Elora. "Those arrows falling are a variety of shafts. Some look like they are from black willow and oakthorn trees. It takes forever to make, but with the right archer, it can slice through armor like cheese."

"I've heard of those but never seen one," said Brother Walder. "Always thought it was an old whore's tale," he finished mockingly.

"My dogs brought me two of them; they are worth a pretty penny. I can bring you one if you wish, Brother Walder."

He shook his head as if he didn't want to believe her. "Not necessary."

"No more sentries tonight. Guards are doubled at the doors. We'll wait for the other two, and if they don't come back, we'll look for them at first light," Pap said sternly. "For the next several days, we'll build up our defenses here and do the same at Hawkhallow Village. Is that clear? We'll also need a base to fall back if we get overwhelmed. We've no idea how many enemies we face."

Deeran nodded, as did Elora. Brother Walder, hesitating, nodded as well.

"You will have my best, sir, no matter what you order," said Brother Walder.

"Alright, now get some rest. Send word if the sentries come back."

Crickets and toads frolicked in the night as the fires snapped and burned down. The soldiers on guard duty remained on edge as the darkness carried on into the unknown.

The Bastards - Shattered Family

Maynard felt power and desire as he grasped the legendary staff, Gaston's Beard.

"Servant's cock," he swore. Downstairs, a commotion ensued. The front door to the mayor's mansion banged open, and feet clomped on the wooden floors. He remembered that if caught, they'd kill him for theft at the least. He gripped the staff and crept to the open door, sliding behind it to listen. Mages like himself and Doc were outlawed in the lands of Vineland. Maynard wore no binding ring and was not part of the Holy Imperium Army. He could see it now. After a short fight, he would be caught as a thief and found to be a mage, and a Blue Templar would be sent for, and then the torture would begin until a binding was placed on him, and then he'd be burnt at the stake in full display in a public square like so many before him. True, he had more power now, but he could only do so much before overwhelming numbers took him.

* * *

Benjamin walked upstairs, investigating what he thought were footsteps in his father's quarters. He tried to creep. At the top of the stairs, Ben turned and walked into the open door of his father's study. He scratched at his eyes and, Maker's beautiful breasts, he was tired. Ben looked around and didn't see anything out of the ordinary. He turned and heard a slight whisper.

"Here," it said.

Ben turned around. "Hello?" he asked to nobody in particular.

Maynard continued to hold his breath, back against the wall. He was trying to figure out if Ben was talking to him, but nobody else was in the room.

Ben walked past Maynard and stopped at his father's desk. A large, heavy box sat on top of it. He'd seen it under his parent's bed years ago when he, Alysha, and Runt had played ghosts in the Grimwood graveyard around the house. He was looking for his brother, Runt, who had always been the best at the game. Ben had been curious before. He opened it and looked long at the knife, touching it once before quickly shutting it and moving on to find his brother. Now, he did the same, knowing what was inside. The blade was sheathed in dark leather, well-kept and well-made. He pulled the knife out and felt pride in it, his father's blade, his family's blade. It was called Dawn's Breath, a symbolic knife used by each Ashburn child after their first kill during a hunt. He'd taken it when he left Wolf Hills, but his father demanded it back after the odd meeting with the two mages. It always felt like he should have it.

The knife, a mixture of silver and black metals, was sharpened on one side. The dark silver metal gleamed like light through a dirty window seven inches long with a small, hooked notch near the handle, allowing the knife to block another blade before meeting the handle. Ben looked at it for a moment and, without thinking, took the blade, shoved it back into its sheath, stuck it in his belt, and walked out.

* * *

Maynard watched this moment unfold and felt the air around him still, and he breathed again, feeling dizzy and unsure of himself. He listened as Ben walked down the stairs quickly, and he heard the front door open to the mansion.

"Archer Ashburn, the General has requested your appearance outside on the double," Maynard heard. He held his breath, casting the charm again. This time, it felt manageable, and he thought he could hold the charm for much longer than previously. The name Ashburn rang in his ears. Was the soldier Runt's older brother?

Footsteps drifted away from his presence and outside to the front of the manor. Maynard waited another moment, then glided down the stairs in utter silence, slipping out the backdoor, sticking to the side of the house and the foliage of the back garden as camouflage.

The guard did not return, and Maynard could only guess that whatever Doc, Angus, and Duncan were up to, had drawn everyone's attention away. Maynard slipped through the hedge and fence into the crowd as it slowly dispersed in all directions.

* * *

Benjamin Ashburn walked behind Squire Alfie Von Dyke, seething that this upstart was his father's squire, not him.

"Archer Ashburn, what you told me about last night didn't involve this," he said to his son. "Explain yourself?"

"Permission to speak freely, sir," requested Benjamin Ashburn. He stared at his father, a coffin behind him, and his squire. His father's eyes were seething but also filled with pain and frustration. He was on the verge of tears.

"Drunkards attacked us near a bar. We tried to remain calm. The crowd used bottles, snowballs, and wooden staves, and someone stabbed our captain. We loosed our crossbows and kept the crowd back with sword and spear until we could back out of the alley and retreat to safety, as I wrote in my report and spoke to my captain and you last night." Benjamin hadn't slept at all since the events from last night, a near riot. "We carried our captain's body to safety and called for reinforcements. Upon their return, they found nothing but blood, the rest covered by snow, now melted as of this afternoon."

His father walked in a half circle. Next to the coffin, Benjamin saw an old family friend, Angus, the cook from Wayward Inn, a thin man next to him was dressed in a patched-up Holy Imperium soldier's coat, which Ben swore bore badges of high office. There was another brute of a man with a beard behind. Angus caught Ben's eye and nodded. Benjamin saw a hint of melancholy there.

"Who ordered the attack, soldier?" his father asked.

"There was no order," Ben replied. "The rules of war say a soldier may protect themselves and their comrades when set upon by aggressors. It was our right. We feared for our lives." *What in the Hades was Angus doing here in Olde Ridgewatch?* Ben's mind twisted with questions.

"Did you see any weapons? What threatened you, a snowball, a busted bottle?"

"The snow was blinding. We were outnumbered, sir."

"Either the snow was blinding, or you were outnumbered. It can't be both now, can it," General Ashburn said sharply.

Sir Frederick Burrow and Sir Donald Williamson looked on, slightly disgusted, and Alfie, the snake, placed his hand on Ben's father's shoulder as if consoling him and prayed, "May the Maker, Child, and Servant be with him now and forever as he followed the Path of the Blessed to the beyond."

"Thank you, Alfie," he patted his hand and looked back at his son. "So, you couldn't see and verify your threat," General Benedict Ashburn waited, letting this ferment. "Next time, you'll verify your targets before reacting." He pushed the lid of the coffin over, exposing the body. "After you view the body, you are to see me afterward, and we'll prepare him for burial. Good day, soldier."

He briskly walked away, and Alfie walked behind him, faintly hiding a smile. Sir Burrow, Sir Donald, and a string of manor guards followed, leaving Ben with the coffin.

Ben, not understanding, watched his father walk away, the other soldiers following. He looked back at the coffin and stepped forward, realizing the body inside was his brother, Runt Ashburn.

He fell to one knee, using the coffin to keep him steady to ease his shaking anger, and tried to understand what he was seeing, what had happened last night. He hadn't seen Runt. He saw the previous night's large snowflakes, bottles hitting the brick walls, and rocks and snowballs hitting them as the crowd disobeyed direct orders from himself and the other Holy Imperium soldiers. They were to disburse and return home. He released his crossbow and dropped it, or did he aim towards the crowd or the air? Nothing. He couldn't remember; it was a haze.

"Oh, Maker, what-" he choked, "what have I done."

He remembered a crowd of drunks, snow, and not enough light in the alley by the Empty Gauntlet Beer Hall. Snowballs and oyster shells were thrown at him, along with loud jeers and taunts levied toward the soldiers on patrol. Benjamin didn't know Runt was in the crowd. Someone had stabbed his captain. How could he know? How could he know?! Tears blinded him now as the snow blinded him last night. Two crows circled overhead, echoing sorrow and frustration as if knowing of Ben's loss.

* * *

He knelt by Runt for an hour until soldiers, archers he didn't know, came up to Ben and took the body. "General's orders, he said you had enough time to grieve, go see your pap son, he's in his office." Ben hadn't realized he was on his knees, and his legs wobbled from the pain of use, feeling the shocks and needles strike him as he stood. Sir Donald looked at him. "You have some new orders coming, boy; having you serve under me was a pleasure. Now head inside, we'll take care of your dear brother," said Sir Donald with more emotion than he'd ever seen the man show. He didn't even realize he was being spoken to; his head was awash in despair and anger.

Ben came to the door of his father's den. His father, General Benedict Ashburn, sat in a cushioned chair, glass in hand filled with tea. The same room Ben had been in before his world changed before he found he'd killed his brother and stolen his father's knife. Ben didn't salute or knock; he was done with all of it; discipline, torture, or kill him, he didn't care. He knew this day, these last hours were the lowest he'd ever get, and somehow in the depths of his despair, looking at the man, his father, he realized he didn't give one shit about becoming a knight, being an obedient son, or anything else. His hand grazed the handle of the knife, Dawn's Breath and felt better, felt slightly less dead inside, and wanted something more than to follow a chivalry code, to be a proud Ashburn, to be more than a general's son; he wanted to be more than the shadow of a glorious general, and if he couldn't, maybe he'd live in the shadows themselves after all, some knights served the

123

Holy Imperium while others were orders of the Holy Church and others served their city-states and families. *Why not be a knight of the shadows, a shade knight, a knight of reckoning.* Let the crows conspire in their towers, gambling lives with policies they don't follow and force everyone beneath them into chains and poverty. Benjamin would become a knight of reckoning, crushing those who would harm the innocent and starve the poor.

The light danced around the room, keeping the shadows at bay. It wasn't twilight outside yet, but the house was dark, and his father hadn't let the servants light a candle. Someone whispered, *"Yes."*

His father looked up and back at him.

"Sit, Ben."

Ben stood at relaxed attention.

"Sit, I will order you if I have to."

"I'm done with this dad. Done with trying to be a knight, trying to be," he paused. "Trying to be your son. All of this, I no longer serve under General Donald."

His father interrupted, "I know, Ben. I know, I ordered that. You aren't fit to serve as an archer, but I haven't given up on you being a man at arms, a knight yet. I have been rough with you, trying to teach you and let you become a knight independent of my name. Our name. The politics of court and life are too much, and they've ruined your brother, your mother, and your sister."

Ben came over to his father and looked down at him. He'd been crying, mourning, and writing in a journal.

"You may speak freely; I've asked Alfie to take the night off. The servants are at rest in their quarters but speak quietly still; there are always those who may listen." The words said were not those of General Benedict Ashburn but those of his father, and he looked broken. Ben looked at him; his age wore on him, the battles, schemes, and stress of military life more than Ben realized.

"There are now only two Ashburn alive. We are an old family with no cousins, aunts, or uncles; nobody except you and me is left." He stood and offered Ben a seat, but he declined again, touching the knife. His father looked at him and half smiled.

"So, it's yours now. I'm relieved and sorry," Benedict pointed to the knife. "It's powerful and will call to you. Do not listen; only use it as a last resort. Take the box with you when you leave and the messages I have on the table." He looked at his son, wearing defeat on his face. "I disgraced myself at court, as the rumors state. I fell for another woman, Victoria, who played with my infatuation between myself and General Flint, and I didn't know how wrong I was, but many others in court knew. I thought it was a chivalric love, but when I was near her, it became more, and I embarrassed myself, and General Flint and I were exiled."

Ben stood straighter and listened, realizing the rumors and gossip were more truth than lies.

"I served the Holy Imperium more than I served our family, and it ruined us, and my arrogance and selfishness did the rest, so now I wish to remedy that. If you want to be a knight, give these letters and the knife on your belt to General Casting. He will make you a better man than I ever could." His father looked him in the eye and showed the redness from crying.

"And if I don't want to be a knight of the Holy Imperium, and I no longer want to be your son?"

There was a long pause, and Benedict Ashburn looked at his son Benjamin. He took a deep breath, sipped his tea, and walked over to the fire, jabbing it with a stove poker his back to his son, knowing Benjamin awaited his answer.

"Then kill him and Prince Damon with Dawn's Breath and let the court of the Holy Imperium burn."

Ben took a step back. His father spoke of treason, of regicide.

"The letters on the table will give you knighthood upon delivery," Benedict said. "The price is the knife, the Ashburn family blade Dawns Breath." He gave his son another letter and money. "Take your friend Stu with you; he may join you. If you choose the shadows, you may have to bloody your hands of the last person that trusts you." He smiled as the firelight cast light onto his eyes, and the rest of his face darkened. "This letter will give you the agents you need to accomplish your goals. Either way, I will remove myself from the games of court moving forward. The Ashburn family is dead. It's up to you and what legacy you leave now."

"What do you mean?" Ben couldn't call him father anymore or ever again.

"I cannot say I'm sorry for what's done, just as you cannot. They were unintentional accidents, but we can learn from them or let them kill us. You have choices now to be better than I ever was."

Ben took all the letters, walked over, grabbed a bottle of dwarven vodka, looked back at his father, General Benedict Ashburn, and walked out to leave him with his thoughts and grief.

* * *

"Maker, that feels better," said Benjamin after he buttoned up his trousers. His hands shook slightly. His friend Stu had light duty for a few hours, leaving Ben to grieve alone. The smell of urine in the alley drifted over the other refuse in the gutter of Olde Ridgewatch. He picked up a bottle of dwarven vodka. It still had three-fifths left, but Benjamin was clearly on his way to a worse place. He looked at the wooden wall of the building he'd just soiled and grasped at his face, smacking it once to sober up, and then took another sip from the bottle. The only remaining feelings sunk down deep into his stomach. He'd returned to the alley where the riot had occurred and looked around. The broken glass, blood stains, wood staves, and half-burnt torches lay on the ground. Ben tried to place where he was, and if he'd done it, if he'd killed his brother on purpose or on accident. He searched for clues, but somewhere deep down, he knew he'd done it. He'd put a bolt from a crossbow into Runt Ashburn, his youngest brother, killing him.

Ben stumbled out of the alley into a street and looked right, watching as folk quickly went about their business as the day drifted past the afternoon. He lamented how cheap life was and how quickly everyone moved on. He was Benjamin Ashburn, the son of General Benedict Ashburn, his brother's death lay before him, and nobody gave a shit.

"Hey, there you are. I've been looking all over for you," a familiar voice said. Stu, his tent mate, one of the soldiers involved in the 'Massacre at Olde Ridgewatch', had found him. "I heard. Uh, is there anything I can do for you?"

Ben took a sip and looked at Stu in his uniform, wearing the Holy Imperium colors, navy blue, gold and white, and felt despair and anger at what they represented.

"You off duty?"

"Yeah, just finished my report. I'm sorry, the whole camp is talking about your dad dressing you down in front of your brother's corpse, plus the papers are calling it the Olde Ridgewatch Massacre, at least some of them. I guess some are calling it the Riot at Olde Ridgewatch."

"Yeah, what are the guards saying?"

Stu paused. "It's not great either way, some soldiers expressed sorrow, and some said shit luck. You know how soldiers are. Many old-timers lost plenty of friends and family; the younger ones, who aren't as kind, said it served the dead bastard right. The town's on edge now. Black Eagle mercenaries are patrolling everywhere in groups of at least four or five. They found two barrels from last night full of swords, maces, and the like. Someone's smuggling weapons into Olde Ridgewatch. The stocks are full at the public square. There is a rumor of a public protest or another funeral like your brother's. Maker, take him on the Path of the Blessed."

"My father decided to bury him in the city. I was getting him ready to take him and bury him in the forest outside the city limits. This city is a curse." He took another sip from the bottle. "I have new orders and permission to take you with me if you'll join. I'm no longer an archer under Sir Donald's lance. You want to come to the capital to help me deliver a message to General Casting?"

Stu looked at Ben, not sure what to say.

"I have messages from my father to deliver directly to General Casting. I'm to leave now," Ben hiccuped. "Actually, a few hours ago."

Benjamin looked at Stu in his uniform and felt disgusted at seeing it. He or his friend may have killed his brother. "Get changed and meet me at the Wild Goose. I'm getting supper, and then I'll finish getting drunk nice and proper."

* * *

Duncan, Angus, and Doc pushed a small raft into the water and said prayers.

Stitch's body was lashed to it with stones on top of the corpse, and oil spilled over them. It made its way out, and Duncan aimed.

"Wish Cordial, Sorella, and Gray Jim were here," said Angus.

"Me too, Angus. Me too," said Doc.

Duncan let go, and the arrow struck true, its flaming top setting the raft and Stitch's remains aflame.

"What's done is done; we must find Cordial and Sorella, ensure they are safe, and leave this cursed city. It's about to turn into more than a back-alley argument. This place smells of revolution," Duncan said.

"Well, we fostered it and are part of it whether we like it or not," Doc interrupted.

"I've had enough war. Fighting the Holy Imperium is a death wish. Hades fighting for the Holy Imperium is a death wish," Duncan countered.

"Your thoughts keep you from becoming a knight, squire," Doc parried.

Duncan was unarmed, but years of frustration showed as his fingers clenched into fists and his veins pumped with blood and passion.

"You need your gear back. We should head back out of the city. Let's check a few bars to see if there is any rumor of Cordial about it. Maybe we'll get lucky." Doc took a nip from a flask, and his eyes flashed. A slight figure appeared behind them, stepping out of the shadows; he wore glasses and a sense of pride now, and Doc felt power where there was only simplicity and hunger for knowledge. Maynard continued to wear the robes of college students, yet he looked more of a man now, after such a journey from Wolf Hills to Olde Ridgewatch, with one of the most powerful weapons in Vineland in his hands.

"Maynard, you're back," said Doc happily. He looked at his student, no, his peer, and realized he felt pride in the man he'd become. Doc also took in Maynard as he carried his staff, and a pang of loss and jealousy arose above the voices in his head. He mumbled the voices away.

Maynard walked toward Duncan, Angus, Doc, and others during Stitch's funeral gathering. He felt powerful and alive. "Give me a second, everyone," Maynard walked to the water and watched as Stitch's body burned in the ocean and slipped into the dark water. He spoke a few words, cradling the staff, and turned back to Angus, Duncan, and Doc with a sense of stillness and confidence.

"Doc." He held onto Gaston's Beard. His hand shook. Maynard ached to keep it, use it, and let himself become part of it as whispers and laughter resonated from its core.

Doc stared at him and knew the struggle Maynard was going through. He wasn't going to ask for the staff back but was willing to get it from Maynard, hoping for its return. He'd personally taken it from the mausoleum of Gaston, the first magic user hundreds of years before.

The staff and its obsidian blade sang to Doc as they spoke to Maynard. They could feel the pull like two lovers after the same prize.

Angus and Duncan looked at the two of them as they felt the air lift and pressure build, and Duncan took a step back, having known Doc for too long to not take precautions.

"You two going to stare at each other all day?" Angus croaked, shattering the silence. "It's getting dark; I need a drink. You coming, Duncan?"

Angus walked between the two mages as if nothing were happening, and they weren't mentally resisting each other's lust for Gaston's Beard. As Angus walked, he bumped into Maynard, who had lost grip on the staff. It clattered onto the stone ground between Doc and Maynard. It was the length of a great sword, made of murky wood with signs of a foreign metal, maybe star metal, woven through the seams of the wood. One end held a dark obsidian blade that felt like it took the life out of anyone who stared too long. The other end was a white rounded stone held by the roots of the murky wood wrapped around it. Maynard remembered having it, the balance it provided, and the confidence that radiated through him when he held it. He missed it already. He thirsted for it.

"Yeah, I'm coming," said Duncan. He walked between the two mages and picked up the staff, not feeling or noticing anything. "Maynard, Doc won't say anything, but thank you for returning this. I'm sure if something befalls him, he'd like you to have it, but after spending time with him, he'd like it back for now."

Maynard grabbed the staff from the big man and handed it to Doc. Doc's hand, sweaty and trembling, took it, feeling relief even as he saw a touch of remorse in Maynard's eye.

Doc nodded, "Thank you, Maynard. As I promised, you will be rewarded. Duncan, if I don't see you again, I appreciate all you've done."

"You not joining us, Doc?" said Duncan.

"No, I'm off to see the Gray General and some new friends."

Maynard stood there for a minute longer.

"Duncan, you and Angus, take care. I'm going to stick with Doc for a bit."

"You sure about that boy? Sure, that's wise?"

"He has more to teach me yet."

"Doc doesn't teach, Maynard; you may learn from him, but he doesn't teach. He takes," Duncan finished. He spat on the ground.

"I can take as much as him now, Duncan."

"Sure thing, Maynard, we'll be around until we find Cordial and Sorella. If we leave town, I'll leave word at Windmill Pub near Crimson Yard." The big man and the dwarve waved.

Maynard saluted with two fingers, pulling away from his head, and walked, catching up to Doc, who had lit his pipe. Neon green and red smoke poured out, causing an unnatural fog. "Wait up, Doc, wait up," said Maynard.

Duncan sighed and looked back at where Stitch's body drifted down into the dark bay and scratched at his beard. He'd seen enough friends and soldiers go the same way, not even as pleasant as getting a funeral. Some were fed to the crows and scavenger goblins that picked at the corpses after a battle, and some were lucky enough to be laid in an unmarked pit.

"Let's get that drink, Angus. Maybe we can figure out where the Hades Sorella and Cordial got off, too. Where is a good place to go?"

"Near the dwarven quarter is the Wild Goose; we might hear some news there, and they have some decent food, too."

"Show me the way, Angus. Show me the way."

Alysha - Poisonfire Fog

They rode until the darkness overtook them and pushed on further until Alysha found brush cover away from the edge of the road. Helena fell asleep as soon as she got off her horse. Alysha could barely see the road and hoped the same for anyone passing by. Before collapsing from exhaustion, Alysha rubbed down the horses and tried to ensure they had grass to eat. When she returned, Helena was asleep against the tree, so Alysha took both cloaks and sat beside her. When she awoke, it was early morning, and she was dimly aware of the smell of Helena's hair which held a slight scent of strawberry and cigar smoke. The smell lingered. She smiled briefly, and the rest of her thoughts returned as she started thinking about the day ahead. Alysha didn't hear the spring birds singing in the early morning. Horses galloped past them on the road from where they sheltered. She slowly moved away from Helena, who awoke as Alysha shifted.

"Riders," Alysha whispered, "can't tell if they're passing by or searching," she whispered to Helena. "Let's get the horses saddled. If we need to flee, we head south and circle north toward Grimwood. I think we may be halfway there."

"Ok, I'll follow you," Helena said. They readied their horses, and Alysha slinked off to see if the riders had moved on. She walked away from Helena and peered out into a thicket of bushes. Against the backdrop of the early morning, she saw a group of six riders standing on the road. Four were dressed in the garb of the Genteel Monks wearing tarnished white, well-fitted robes with the Maker's emblem of a black sword with a burning candle for the blade facing up, the same group who killed her mother and burnt

Helena's and Alysha's homesteads this past autumn. The other soldier wore a mockery of elvish and Holy Imperium leather armor, bearing General Flint's house sigil of a black bear against a green background. The one non-Genteel Monk was giving orders, but a loud argument broke out between the two Holy Imperium Soldiers and the Genteel Monks. No swords were drawn, but Alysha felt it could occur at any time. She thought it was Ian Shortstride, but she was too far away to know.

Alysha watched as the argument ended, and four soldiers continued down the road, which started to veer south as the Grimwood forest loomed ahead.

The two other soldiers steered their horses toward Alysha and Helena, hidden in a thicket of overgrown bushes.

"Shit," Alysha said to herself.

There was a whistle up the road. The one dressed in elvish gear spun his horse around and followed the other soldiers south on the road, swearing loudly.

Alysha hurried back to Helena.

"We don't have many choices now," she warned, trying not to panic. "They headed southwest on the road, blocking our exit. We could follow slowly behind them and hope we don't catch up, but I feel they may have been looking for someone, and they would question two women oddly dressed on the road. Especially one half dressed as a messenger of the Holy Imperium."

"You're right; they most likely found my dress. I left it in the bushes last night," Helena frowned.

"I don't want to, but I'd rather face the unknown than six soldiers; we could head directly into Grimwood forest, at least keeping slightly inside it, and hope to hit the Erie Sea and then take beach paths into the city?" Alysha's brows creased as she tried to think of another plan.

Helena looked unsure but nodded her head. The woodland itself lurked in front of them. The Grimwood forest was a wall of oakthorn trees with blotches of black willow trees mixed in, and because the oakthorn was nearly impossible to cut down, it created a barrier defense on the eastern portion of the city-state of Grimwood. These trees were massive, and they grew thorns instead of leaves, blooming blood-red flowers during late spring and early summer. Their beauty gave way to the rigidity of their thorns, which were jagged enough to cut cloth and pierce flesh. Another property of the trees was their ability to withstand flame. Since King Christopher Goldthorn and Erica, the Red armies had tried to burn down the Grimwood forest, failing due to the oakthorn tree's resistance to natural and unnatural flames. There were gaps in the forest created by black willow trees bunched between the stout oakthorn trees, allowing animals into the woods, yet stories and lore showed that humans often did not make it out once they entered its depths.

"Ok, worst-case scenario, we get separated, head north until you hit the sea, and break east. Let's go. Let's hope we make it, but we can meet up where the Erie Sea meets the walls of Grimwood." Helena nodded as she listened to Alysha's instructions.

Helena ate hard biscuits from the messenger bag they found on a saddle. Alysha tried to eat, but her stomach felt like it was rejecting the food. The grass and leaves had spring dew on them, and she breathed in the air and felt better from it. She drank cool water from a water skin and quickly crossed the field past the road where the soldiers had been. They walked down a ravine and followed a deer path into darkening woods. Alysha noted the oakthorn trees as they moved closer, finding the thorns to vary in size, some as small as a knife and others large enough to impale her if given a moment.

* * *

There was a natural light-gray fog to the forest floor swishing and creeping around their feet, but it did not obscure the women's vision. Squirrels danced about with chipmunks scurrying in the underbrush of fresh grass shoots and aged, tired leaves from last autumn. The sun slipped through the forest's canopy for now, but Alysha could tell it would darken as they veered further west. They attempted to keep the main section of Grimwood forest to their left as they headed north. Or what they thought was north.

Helena stopped her horse for a minute.

"We aren't going to die here, are we?" she asked, forehead wrinkling with nerves.

"Your bravado is gone now after the initial rush?" Alysha asked, mocking Helena slightly.

"Yeah, well, the harsh reality of not having a roof over my head settled in," Helena countered. "I felt safe last night next to you, but I have a horrible kink in my neck, and I'm sore from riding already. The only riding I was used to was on a cheap mattress."

"There is no going back now, only forward Helena. You've got me, a horse to travel with, and a goal to get into Grimwood. That's what is keeping us going."

Voices echoed from behind them.

"Over here, I picked up their trail," someone shouted.

"You fool, they could hear you," said another.

"Go into the woods there." Alysha moved her horse into a thinning trail deeper into Grimwood. Helena followed as quickly as she could. They road silently for an hour, their pursuers not visible behind them, but they could occasionally hear them in the distance. The sunlight above was no longer the bright yellow and green hues from earlier, but a pale blue as the canopy above grew thicker, and the fog at their feet rose further, now hitting the horse's thighs.

Alysha stopped for a moment and tossed a rope to Helena.

"So, we don't get separated in the fog; tie it to your saddle; if we get into open ground, untie it in case we need to run."

"Good thinking." They continued what they believed to be north and west towards Grimwood and, hopefully, safety. Alysha passed a splintered tree struck by lightning sometime in the past. It was one of the few bright spots they saw in their travels in the forest. She leaned over and snapped off a piece of the wood. The sun shone down where they had not seen any sun previously.

She noticed the absence of woodland creatures and birds. *It is time.* Alysha felt hungry and unstrapped Stormkiss.

Helena raised her eye brown and moved closer.

"Someone's near," Alysha said. There are two trails that lead out from here," she thought aloud. I wonder how far we are into the woods. There is a green tint in that direction; best not head that way, the trail next to it," she nodded. "You first. I will follow shortly."

Helena moved her horse forward, "I'll go a few hundred feet and wait."

The trauma of the past year bonded them closer, even if their experiences were separate, different versions of pain and sorrow. Worry filled Helena's eyes as she parted from Alysha. The rope that held them together was now untied and put away.

"For Wolf Hills," Helena said, and she nodded to Alysha quietly as she moved her horse past Alysha. She reached out and touched the hardened shoulder of her friend in parting.

"For each other," said the woman holding her axe hammer, and Helena slid into the woods and down the trail.

Alysha turned her horse around and neared the path with the fog that held a slightly greenish tint. Runt would have called it pea green; her mother would call it chartreuse. It looked vile, and she didn't want to touch the fog. She felt this path would lead her, or whoever followed, into trouble. She wrapped a shawl around her neck so that she could pull it over her mouth and nose as a precaution. On the other side of the glen ambled a horse with a Holy Imperium soldier on top of it. The soldier wore light chain mail and a faded sigil of the Maker's sword with the candle as the blade. They looked excited yet worn.

"You lost, lass? We're looking for someone like you." The soldier was wintered older than Alysha, with forehead-length bang-cut hair and a trimmed blond mustache.

"You look lost; what are you doing in my woods? Best be careful, or you'll get into trouble yourself." She said back, slowly moving away from him. In the distance, they heard people yelling for a man named Rook.

"Blasted fog," he said, his horse skidding away from the vile green-yellow fog below. "Why couldn't you be a defenseless, scared milkmaid like in the books."

He moved forward, his hand on a short, multi-spiked, one-handed mace.

"My boss wants to talk to you. The Blackheart has questions. We are to bring you in alive if we can. We think you might know about some problems in Counselor City recently at a blacksmith's shop."

"Where are the other monks?" Alysha asked as she continued down the path, leading the soldier away from Helena.

The soldier didn't answer but steered his horse around the shattered tree in the center of the glen. Alysha slowly moved her horse back onto the path, the greenish fog looming at its feet.

Alysha grabbed her horse's reins and spurred the horse forward, the smell of decay lingering in the air. She screamed, "Hades with this," and pushed further as the rot and decay closed in around her. Thorn, pricker bushes, and dead-fall lined the track along with the mist. She remembered tales of the black willow poisonfire fog and its dangers. If she stayed on the path, the fog would remain away, but she feared for herself and her horse if she were to slip off to one side. Her horse became nervous, and she slowed and patted its neck. It kicked and danced away from the poisonfire fog. Alysha knew to trust her instincts and that the fog was far from a pleasant experience.

She hoped to lead this man further into the woods, circle around, lose him, and meet Helena on another path. Alysha urged her horse faster now, struggling to lead and escape the soldier following her.

"You're a sweet thing! Just stop so we can talk!" Rook yelled, his breathing forceful as the trees rushed past. "Damned fog."

Alysha saw another grove and leaned into her horse, pulling her scarf to her mouth and nose tighter. Alysha knew she would fare better off fighting this soldier on foot than on a horse, even if it put her at a disadvantage. *An axe favors solid ground to fell a tree.*

The soldier gained on her as she slid off, and the swing of his mace missed, the inertia of the swing and speed of his horse taking him further into the new glen. The fog and acrid stench made Rook cough. Alysha fell on the path; the poisonfire fog surrounded the entire grove, leaving only a small area open and not covered in pea-green-tinted fog. The smell of decay seeped from the black willow tree in the center of the grove she stood nearby.

Tall, knee-length grass surrounded the tree. The black willow was identical to the last grove; only this tree proved alive and thriving. She watched the more confident Rook turn his horse, and she held Stormkiss in front of her.

She veered toward the tree in the center, hoping it could offer protection.

He spurred his horse toward her, and as it neared, she rolled toward the black willow, its long roots poking out of the ground in spots. Her shoulder and back cracked against the roots, and she followed the roll, pushing against the tree. Rook failed to accommodate the uneven ground, and his attack floundered as the horse stumbled. Alysha recovered and now had her back to the tree. Having trapped herself against the tree, she hoped this would make Rook overconfident as she prepared to go on the offensive.

Rook gained control of his mare and pushed it forward toward Alysha.

"You got nowhere to go, girl. Stand down, or I'll run you down."

"Never!" She lunged at the horse with the spiked tip of Stormkiss, and the horse pushed back against Rook's commands, kicking its forelegs to defend itself. Alysha screamed to scare it more; she pulled the weapon back and shifted to her right. Rook pushed forward and swung his mace, leaning down; Alysha caught the mace and tied up Rook's hand by hooking the axe head into his horse's reigns. She pulled down as he pulled up, and the axe blade dug into the horse's neck. The horse kicked and hit Alysha and Stormkiss, partially throwing the rider away and Alysha and Stormkiss back into the black willow. The horse stumbled into the roots and fell, breaking one of its legs. Alysha's horse spooked, circled, and ran back where they initially started. Alysha lost her weapon as she hit the tree but still had her sword at her hip, the reforged Wolfe family sword. She got up, dazed, and searched for Rook.

The horse with the broken leg tried to get up and stumbled, flipping and wailing toward the grove's edge. Once it hit the fog, it screamed as if on fire, bucking its legs as part of its head and body submerged into the green mist. Its fur fell away, and flesh blistered and twisted in pain. It suffocated while its lungs melted as if burnt alive. Alysha found Rook on the ground, half-standing, holding his hip. Without a thought, Alysha rushed him and swung. He put his hands up to defend himself, but her blade met his hands and fell directly into his face. He made a muffled cry as the blade sunk in, his fingers falling to the ground and his body convulsing. It was a messy cut and messy kill. Alysha felt strength return to her body.

She breathed, cleaned the gore from her sword, and picked up Stormkiss, hoping to find her horse and Helena.

The Bastards - Goblin Panic

The Wild Goose, a cellar bar on the northern side of Olde Ridgewatch, was frequented by sailors, off-duty servants, and other folk who needed to get out but didn't wish to be seen. It found its odd niche of attracting a variety of townsfolk from different tracks of life, all of whom came for the food, stayed for the drink, and always felt safe. The door guards hardly took bribes, unheard of in a town entire of folk that did. Duncan walked in. Angus followed behind, but the two-door guards stopped him. He still carried a knife, hatchet, and large intimidating dwarven cast pan on his back like a shield.

"You really want to give him a hard time? He just got off work and needs to relax like the rest of us," Duncan said to the strong-armed woman. She looked at her compatriot and nodded.

"Any trouble from him, and it's your asses thrown in the streets, and we'll watch as the Black Eagle guards stomp your heads in and make sure all the papers know."

"Noted," said Duncan.

"Never had trouble before, and the place has been around for years -the entire town is filled to the brim with anger and deceit," scoffed Angus as they made their way to a table.

Smoke from hand-rolled cigarettes and pipes spewed elvish tobacco as laughter mixed with a harpist playing in the corner. Angus and Duncan shared two rounds of Olde Ridgewatch ale and went into the back alley to piss on the wall. The music wasn't loud enough to drown out the despair inside their heads.

"Excuse me, kind folk," a young man said as he held the door for Angus and Duncan as he exited. Duncan twisted his face, recognizing the young man.

"You, how do I know you?" said Benjamin Ashburn in a slight haze.

"Don't know, lad, but you smell like my dwarven friend's mother after taking too much medicine."

The young man laughed and then hiccuped.

"I saw you the other night, I think. You were with my brother."

"Ben, let's go," Stu said, pushing him into the door.

Angus scratched at his beard. "Benjamin Ashburn, as I live and breathe, is that you, boy?"

Ben took a moment to consider and try to clear his thoughts. He touched the knife inside his light jacket and felt a little more at ease when his hand neared the blade.

"Angus, from Wolf Hills, it can't be." He held onto the door for support.

"You know this dwarve and this brute?" asked Stewart Slickback, known to most as Stu.

"Watch it, lad, or you'll find out how much of a brute I am," said Duncan.

"Sorry, sorry, we've had a few drinks. We are mourning my friend's brother's passing."

"Hades, you *are* Runt's brother," Duncan said under his breath.

"Yeah, you got a problem with that?" Ben questioned, liquid courage bubbling up. Duncan looked down at the boy and saw his grief mixed with courage from drink well up inside the arrogance of youth. Ben was going to get himself into trouble if someone didn't intervene. Or maybe he was looking at a mirrored image of how he felt inside.

"Sorry, we were supposed to be traveling south to the capital, but Ben's had a wee bit to drink. I guess we both have," said Stu. He hiccuped and swayed. They looked as if they were on a ship in a storm.

"Ben, this here is Duncan. He and others helped bring Runt to Olde Ridgewatch after your mother passed and Wolf Hills burnt to the ground." Angus pulled at his beard slightly.

"Wait, my mother. I had forgotten about her and Alysha," he stumbled, hit his head on the corner of the door, and fell unconscious into the piss-filled ground. Stu laughed at Ben, himself, and the state of the entire moment before throwing up in the corner, his eyes bulging and the vomit searing his throat as it came up, but he held it back.

"I shouldn't have laughed. You said his mother is dead too," Stu slurred. The alcohol had not helped Stu or Ben one bit. Ben thought he'd killed his brother, but he wasn't even sure. Stu could have done it, too. They were the only ones with crossbows during the melee that night. "Didn't he have a sister? What the fuck is happening here? I think I'm going to…"

"Go outside, you fool," Angus said, pushing Stu out the door to throw up. "Nothing to see here; we'll take care of it." The bartender looked at the mess and walked away, shaking his head.

Duncan looked at Ben Ashburn, the older brother of Runt Ashburn, the kid he'd worked so hard to do a little right in the world and failed.

"Let's get them cleaned up," Angus said as he picked Ben up.

* * *

"Listen, boys, I'm older than most, and I've seen plenty close to me die: the woman I loved, my brother, and knights I swore to protect, each taking a piece of me with them as they passed into Nirvana." Duncan looked up for a moment and then down at his drink. "The one thing I learned is that everything is futile when you see someone you love and can't help them; all that is left is hope. In the end, atheists seek hope through a god they ignored before, and the religious seek hope through science, and we all become the base of who we are, grasping onto anything to keep our head above the waters of despair," he said. He sipped a cup of whiskey, thumbing the edge, lost in a moment. He looked at Ben and Stu. One sat nursing a beer, the other still passed out, leaning on the table. "But we carry on for their memories and for those still living, to make sure their stories are not forgotten."

Duncan looked at his aged hands and then the tavern in discomfort, lost in his thoughts. He was the only half dwarve he knew of who should have been shorter, but he was as big as a bear and healed better and aged slower; it's how he came to know Doc, who confirmed his father was Bearfric the Righteous

Hand, a famed warrior and dwarve. Elves and humans had crossbred, whether by love or violence, but humans and dwarves couldn't conceive except for him.

"Or anger," Angus said, "or you grasp onto anger and righteous wrath to fill the hole left after everything you cared for turns to mud and shit." He looked at Benjamin, his eyes glazed over, slightly lost in his thoughts. Ben shifted a knife he'd carried to the inside of his jacket, and his hand seemed to move there often.

"Wake up, you idiot," Angus yelled.

Ben opened his eyes to see a table before him, along with Stu sitting uncomfortably, Angus, and the large brute that was Duncan. His thoughts were muzzy yet clarified quickly.

"I need tea or watered wine."

"The best you can do is this light beer. We also grabbed a bottle of whiskey," said Duncan. "City is boycotting East Thamesbridge tea on the account of the taxes."

"You said my mom is dead," said Ben; he scratched at his eyes, trying to find clarity. "Father said it was a lie, and then he said we were the only ones left."

Angus looked at Ben with pity in his eyes. Turning away for a second, he took a deep breath and turned back, having gained the needed composure. "Yes, I'm sorry. Mia Ashburn, your mother, died when a group known as the Genteel Monks burnt your homestead. We think they may have a vendetta against your family," Angus said.

"My dad never said anything until recently, but there were rumors before," said Ben. "I traveled with him near the city of Affectus to a meeting. It was the only time in the past few years my father treated me like a son he cared about; I was his guard, or squire, something at least. There were a bunch of important people there. Someone called the Gray General, a crazy man saying he was a battlemage, another striking person, she or he, was very sharp-tongued, quick with wit." Ben stopped. "Maker, they were radiant."

Angus looked at Duncan for a moment. "Go on, Ben. Anyone else there?"

"There was a struggle, but before, there was an orc and goblin, and the general Wash -something or other he had a guard with him, and another,

Olivia Franklin, I think; I swear I heard the name before in a newspaper. Anyway, this crazy mage character wore glasses and said my mom was dead or hurt and something about my sister, but my dad blew it off and said he was lying. And there was trouble with the Order of the Blue Rose."

"The Blue Templar? They are always bad news, son," Duncan said and winced. "Sorry, Benjamin."

Ben looked at Duncan and nodded slightly. He was feeling better now, more awake. His mind was still muddled, but talking felt right. He was feeling better now that he wasn't around military personnel. He looked at Stu for a second with slight disgust.

"We think the Blue Templar are lining up behind Prince Damon; your dad may have pissed someone off, causing your home and the rest of the village-" Angus paused. "Your mother's gone lad." He paused again and looked away. "I loved her as much as you, and she's gone, and Vineland is worse for it, and after losing Runt, well, maybe it's time someone pays for the crimes against the innocent."

Ben looked at Angus, sorrow creasing his eyes. A voice deep inside whispered *Your time to move into the shadows has come.*

Stu perked up, thumbing the pewter cup full of whiskey. "Yeah, the other soldiers talk about it when Ben isn't around. They say that General Ashburn, Ben's dad, got mixed up at Prince Damon's court with General Flint's mistress."

Ben glanced at Stu, a touch of revulsion welling as his friend spoke.

"They were exiled from court. We know the Genteel Monks are part of General Flint's troops in the First Army. I bet Jared Blackheart's Genteel Monks were ordered to visit your hometown to settle the argument that occurred at court," said Stu. "My old man said that the Blackheart family always strives for more power. They'd take the crown if they could." Stu looked around as if people gave a shit about the Holy Imperium in a place like this. "I bet Jared Blackheart wants to become a Blue Templar."

"This is all too much." Ben took a long pull of his beer. "Pour me a slug of the whiskey. Fucken' dad. Did you know half the army left the city? Left Bawstone Keep with only a few Black Eagles and a local militia inside," he stopped, and memories bubbled above the alcohol, numbing his thoughts. "I killed my brother," Ben breathed.

Stu looked at him. They were tired, eyes red and barely open. "No, you didn't. If anything, it could have been me."

"I'd never been in a situation like that. I didn't know."

"How could you, how could any of us? They weren't supposed to be there," Stu muttered. His ears felt red and warm.

"He was supposed to be at home. What was he doing here?"

Duncan watched the young man through the shroud of grief he knew too well. He watched Ben sip whiskey, not feeling it go down. His eyes were full of pain as he talked through what had happened in the past few days.

"It's hard to say, but the man who spoke to your father with Angus tried to save your family in Wolf Hills; he's trying to save Vineland. At least I believed him before all this. We go back, way back, fought together, fought against each other," Duncan said, trying to comfort the lad. "He's insane, sure, but also a person you want on your side. He's Hunter Young, a battlemage and the one that brought an end to the Crimson Struggle. He killed Umar and Jezebel Everfall and slaughtered thousands using fire, wind, and all sorts of evil shit on the plains of Ursula."

"Folk called it the Battle of the Reaping as Gothine himself reigned death that day. Sir Hunter Young cut down hundreds like reaping grain. Believe what Duncan is saying, boys," advised Angus.

"I always heard the Brokenhearted One killed those two mages, and the Maker brought down a great wind to change the tide of battle," Stu interrupted.

"No, the Redcloak Sir Hunter Young killed those two and saved the day for the Holy Imperium, and then Prince Damon threw him into an asylum for it. He escaped and later hired me and my friends to take your brother Runt from Steelsburg to Olde Ridgewatch to be with your dad and try to explain to him what's happening, how his family-" Duncan stopped. "How you and your father - and if your sister is alive - are in trouble." He looked down at his whiskey. "We were trying to reunite your brother with your father; we were trying to do something right for a change." He breathed in. "The words are meaningless but should be said. I'm sorry, I don't think you killed your brother. I think all of us did. I think some dick of a prince, some general high up, wanted your family to suffer, and it cascaded like a waterfall."

"We don't know where Alysha is, Ben." Angus reached over and placed a hand on the weary man's shoulder. "We briefly searched for her around the homestead, but she wasn't among the fallen. That's the best we got. She may be near Counselor City or Grimwood if she's alive."

"This is a lot to take in," he breathed in deeply and looked at Duncan and his old friend Angus, his face lined and aged. Angus probably loved his mother more than his father did. He laughed slightly; the poor dwarve was always around during the holidays, more so when his dad had left and before he'd traveled to join the army.

Angus looked on and said, "Take it from someone who drinks too much. You should stop now, sober up, and grab a cup of tea or two."

Ben snorted, "Haven't you heard about the taxes? Tea is on its way out. Most folk drink coffee now. It's not taxed here."

"Fine, it's time for coffee then, you little shit." Angus and Ben smiled, but tears remained on the edges of their eyes.

"Pretty sure I'm done with this soldiering thing, man." He tossed the whiskey back in one go. "All of this after a near riot that ended in Runt's death. Fuck all of this. I just found out my mom's dead, and I killed my brother. Fuck the Holy Imperium and the Blue Templar."

Duncan and Angus looked at Ben and Stu and poured more whiskey, so much for coffee and sobering up.

"Cheers to lost family," one of the four said. It didn't matter who, as all of them had lost a family member due to tragedy.

They threw down the whiskey and poured another.

The door opened, and a young girl, twelve winters old, ran inside and yelled.

"We march tonight, join us for Prince Damon's tea party!" and left as soon as she came. The door creaked shut before Ben saw people walking past the Wild Goose. Someone threw a bottle at the door. It shattered, and the drunks laughed. The door opened again, and an older woman came in. "We march on Bawstone Keep. Join us for justice and free those arrested during the Olde Ridgewatch Massacre."

"Shut up, you ass clown!" someone yelled, followed by mirth as the drunks spiraled into their cups.

Chairs scraped against the floor, and Duncan saw people walk out the door. Ben felt energized.

"Stu, let's see what the other side is doing." He got up without waiting for an answer, walked up the stairs of the cellar bar, and out into the street.

Duncan and Angus looked on and then stood and followed. "Best keep an eye on Ben," he said to Stu.

"Right, I don't think I could take it if he were to get into trouble," said Angus.

They opened the door, and a river of townsfolk crowded through the streets. They carried torches and wore primarily black or their best church clothes. A group of hooligans wore cheap imitations of native elves not seen in the area for years. They carried oaken barrels of Thamesbridge tea.

"What's going on?" Angus asked an older man walking by with a pitchfork.

Duncan, Ben, and Stu stood behind him as they watched much of the people of Olde Ridgewatch move past them. Someone was handing out mugs of what Duncan thought was beer. Angus took one and sniffed it, taking a sip.

"We march on Bawstone Keep to free our family and to ask for justice for those murdered during the riot. The town's church leaders and city council are walking to demand the end of a military curfew and return those arrested during the riot," said a mother carrying her child in a sling on her chest. She marched on.

"This is watered-down goblin panic; this shit is extremely dangerous. I've seen a dwarve charge a pack of wild rats naked and kill them all with his hands on this shit," Angus mumbled.

Ben took Angus's cup, drank deeply, gave the rest to Stu, and walked into the crowd.

"We're going to toss the tea that came in from Great Brightland and all of the rest of those Black Eagle mercenaries back into the Atlantis Ocean," said a young man with feathers twisted into his hair. He hollered and moved on with the townspeople with the barrel of goblin panic tucked under an arm, offering anyone who wanted a drink. The crowd indulged, resentment in their eyes and anxiety in their thoughts.

"Oh shit, where's Ben," said Stu. "There he is." He pointed and ran off towards him.

"Let's go," grumbled Angus. Duncan moved with Angus through the crowd, following Stu. "Goblin panic is a war drink goblins use for battles; it drives them into a frenzy. This could get bad quickly."

They yelled for Ben, but the townspeople sang hymns, drowning out anything else. As everyone moved toward Bawstone, Duncan's fear and Angus's worry rose.

Duncan grabbed a wooden stave from a barrel and lit it from a brazier in the town square. The atmosphere was intoxicating, and people passed around jugs of whiskey and skins of wine as they marched through the town. The parade of people grew as it moved west towards the Neck's gate, which should have been closed as twilight. The Neck was the only land route out through the city as it was nearly surrounded by water, creating the Bawstone Bay and an excellent port for ships. The Bawstone Keep stood on a cliff side overlooking the town and bay.

Once the guards saw the massive crowd, they left the gates open, knowing they would be torn to pieces if they didn't. The verbal exchange with the guards was quick, but the crowd grew anxious as they crossed the path.

Everyone squeezed through, and Angus, Duncan, and Stu were soon on the other side. They found Ben singing along with other townsfolk as a ceramic bottle of hard cider was passed around.

"What you think is going to happen once this mob gets to Bawstone Keep?" Angus said.

"Let's hope it's not a repeat of a few nights ago," Stu mumbled, and Duncan and Angus remained quiet. They were unsure, just as Stu was, having taken part in a near riot, but they were caught up now and part of the crowd. The entire group's momentum was their own.

"Duncan! Angus!" a smooth voice raised out.

Someone grabbed at Duncan's coat.

Duncan whipped around to see who grabbed him. "Cordial! It's good to see you! Where's Sorella?" he asked, relieved to see his friend.

"That's why we're marching. She, along with a bunch of townsfolk, was rounded up and was caught after dark with no papers and weapons on her. I heard others were arrested for participating in a riot."

"Ah, Vulcan's beard. It's all our fault, then," Angus said.

"Wait, where's Maynard and Runt? Where's my buddy Stitch?" asked Cordial.

"We-" Duncan sighed, running his thick hands through his hair. "This is not turning out how we thought it would," he said.

"Free our friends!" someone yelled as they walked. The crowd pushed on, and Angus, Duncan, and Cordial, three old friends, also moved along. Stu and Ben were in front of them as people weaved in and out of the group, shouting and singing.

The crowd stopped and tossed the barrels of stolen tea over the side of the cliff into the water. The gathering exploded into cheers.

"Down with Damon's taxes!" several yelled.

"No more massacres," said an older man carrying a torch.

"Leave Olde Ridgewatch," another said; she was holding a young child's hand.

"Did Runt meet his dad? I heard there was a dust-up with Holy Imperium soldiers," Cordial said. "They passed through town early in the morning, and I was caught up. They started bashing heads and arresting people down in the city's lower section. Sorella and I split up in an alley; they arrested her. I'm sorry, Duncan. I couldn't stop it; they outnumbered us. They would have killed both of us. It was those Black Eagle goons from Bitterleak."

"We saw them too. They mean trouble," Angus replied.

Ben pipped in, having overheard, "My brother's dead, mate. He's fuckin' dead. There was a mix-up between Holy Imperium soldiers and a crowd at the Empty Gauntlet, and people got hurt. Bunch got beat up, and three, including my brother, were killed."

He passed a bottle of vodka to Cordial and stumbled slightly.

"Drink for him and seek justice," Ben said. "Or drink to dull the guilt of killing your friends and family."

Cordial took the bottle and looked at Ben.

Angus waited until Cordial drank, and they kept wandering with the crowd. Duncan put his hand on his shoulder. "Cordial, I'm sorry, but Stitch and Runt died in that riot. They took bolts to the chest. We couldn't save them, even with Doc and Maynard helping."

Duncan, who stood over Cordial, grabbed him and hugged him. Not used to such affection, Cordial let him, and the crowd moved around them. Angus stood and waited as shadows from the torches moved across them. Cordial pushed his head into the big man's chest and prayed, not for serenity but revenge. He went through various emotions quickly; his shoulders slumped, and he pushed away from Duncan, tears in his eyes, and drank deeply from the bottle. Tears welled from the burn and pain of the vodka and the loss of a friend who was more than a brother.

"Fuck me, I think," Cordial coughed, "I think we're in the right place. Let's get Sorella back."

"Free our friends!" the crowd shouted.

The walled fortress of Bawstone Keep, a curtain wall built upon a cliff, gave a line of sight down into the city and the surrounding bay. Initially, it was a light house, but the area was reinforced by a group of humans and dwarves and gradually built up over time. The fortress's main entrance was a winding road up to the cliffside curtain wall. The path was two carts wide, with one side leading to a dead drop into the ocean and the other butted up against the cliff. The curtain wall was a mixture of poured dwarven cement and red brick that withstood multiple forays during the Crimson Struggle. Bawstone Keep was the base for control of Olde Ridgewatch, a prison, and a seat of power for the rulers of the given area.

The fortress was staffed by the local townsfolk militia and backed by a force of Bitterleak mercenaries. The lighthouse now lay retrofitted with a ballistic scorpion. The inside held three separate catapults that could rotate at hundred-and-eighty-degree angles to provide coverage throughout the area. The prison sat below the fort near the water level deep inside the cliff walls, with cells filling with water from the pipe drains in the prison floors. The worse the crime, the lower the cell and the more danger of drowning before trial if a prisoner was lucky enough to call for a trial.

"No justice, no peace!" The crowd cheered again. "Prince Damon wears a hollow crown of tin and glass!"

"The Makers will be upon you," a loud voice said above the others.

* * *

After her capture in Olde Ridgewatch, in a blurry haze of pain and numbing cold, Sorella came to, shivering through her legs and arms, chained to the ceiling and floor. She lifted her head and smelled urine, tasted the metallic copper of blood, and listened to the Atlantis Ocean attempt to break through the granite walls of her cell in a chamber deep below Bawstone Keep. Her hair lay against her face, and her leg twitched, not touching anything other than the binding chain. She couldn't feel her other leg, recalling she had caught a crossbow bolt in that leg earlier. She gripped the chains suspended from the ceiling and lifted them to relieve the pain in her wrists as her toes barely brushed the ground.

She'd been in some awful positions before, but hanging from a ceiling naked and bleeding was pretty close to the worst she could think of. She reached out to her two familiars, a pair of black crows, hoping to get more answers as to where she was and what was happening.

"They won't answer you, Silvercrow," said a voice.

Sorella turned to see another naked form, an orc chained up diagonally from her, breaking her attempt to connect to her familiars.

"Shit. Where's the torturer then?"

"Above, having dinner; then they will come down to ask us questions. Ask you questions, and they will hurt me for fun."

"You already confess?" asked Sorella.

"Yes, an orc killing his master is confession enough."

"I see," Sorella spat. "Fuck them, orc. Fuck them."

"I'd kill every one of those bastards that beat me and cut my horns from my head," said the orc through busted lips and a bruised face.

"I'm-" Sorella began.

"Silvercrow, my clan knows of your stories, knows of your man," said the orc. "The failed squire who will be your knight commander."

Sorella laughed, and her ribs hurt. She realized they roughed her up before chaining her to the ceiling.

"What's so funny, Silvercrow, my queen?"

"We're in the dungeon of Bawstone Keep with no hope of escape, and I can't escape my dead husband's ghost."

"We know of your dead husband, and I speak of what you and Sir Duncan will do in the future for us all. For all of Vineland."

"Sure, sure," said Sorella. "We just need to escape a prison dungeon surrounded by cliff walls and ocean water."

"Name's Taug, daughter of the sorcerer Falstaer Vicorm, but let us not tell our torturers. Ahh, not until we have knives to their throats," Taug said, laughing to herself.

Sorella's eyes rolled back into her head, the tingling in her wrists from the shackles causing pain followed by numbness.

The darkness broke as a door opened.

"Hope you ladies are ready for fun. I brought another professional to join us just in from the wilderness." A brutish yet thin man walked in carrying a torch. He wore robes of the Holy Church and carried the Path of the Blessed symbol, a torch shaped like a sword, with the flame end as part of the tip, the mark of the Holy Church, and the righteousness it represented to harm without care or worry of the consequences.

"Wake up, you filthy wrenches, and welcome the Hangman of Steelsburg, Gray Jim."

A large man wearing a jacket made of cowhide walked in carrying a case full of torture instruments and a dwarven lantern.

"Let's get to work, Mr. Smoothhorn. Let's get to work."

Sorella - Dungeon Crows

Blood dripped from their bodies as they hung like butcher's meat. Gray Jim moved a table near him and unrolled a leather cloth with mortar hammers, pliers, vices, doctor's implements, and a small bone saw. Taug shifted in her chains, and she looked at the other man in the Holy Imperium robes and spat.

"Fuck you and your Church; your Maker's been around for a few hundred years, while my gods have been here before man even existed," Taug said threw broken lips and chipped teeth. She knew what she was, but nothing further could be done. A broken slave cannot be split further.

Mr. Smoothhorn moved quickly, grasped Taug's face tightly, and looked into her eyes.

"I do the Servant's work, as I'm advised, and enjoy it like the Child. This is all for the glory of the Maker." He smiled, his mouth full of decay and rot. Mr. Smoothhorn's eyes were bloodshot and blue, his hair blond and parted, a middle-aged and underwhelming man, yet his robes gave him power and confidence over people chained before him. He pushed his finger close to Taug's eye, and she shifted and swung from her chains in pain and fear, but he stopped quickly and moved toward Sorella, gazing up and down, and deep inside, he lusted and was disgusted by his passions for what he considered a lesser race.

"You're to tell me why you are in Olde Ridgewatch and everything you know about the riots here and the slave revolt in Lackmore. Maker's will, please make it hard so that I can cure your heathen soul with the fiery pain of my faith."

Mr. Smoothhorn pushed her cheeks in so her lips squeezed like a fish, and a snot bubble appeared in her nose. He let go and turned to grab a small pair of pliers and a doctor's scalpel.

"Shh, shh, quiet now, but only for a moment. Understand the only people you cared about are gone now. Dead. The only person that cares about you is me. It's funny; the only real connection you have left in life is the person who wants to see you die in the most painful way possible. The only love you will ever feel now is the love I'll give you as I slowly carve your life out. So, struggle all you want, strain against your chains, and know I am here until you are nothing but meat in the ground." Mr. Smoothhorn took a breath. "But I am tasked with knowing what purpose you have here and who you serve. The commander of the Black Eagles demands answers, and Prince Damon and his council demand answers. All I seek is your breath and blood."

"What is your name, please?" asked Gray Jim. Sorella eyed him and spat on the ground.

Gray Jim looked on. He looked at Mr. Smoothhorn, nodded slightly, and moved toward the table, picking up a blade used for surgery.

"I'm of the Silvercrow family, one of the first families of Vineland; we lived in the Gloomspire for generations before the crusades made a mess of Vineland before King Christopher and Erica the Red were even born."

Mr. Smoothhorn raised an eyebrow at this. He took his hand and sliced slowly down her arm. Sorella looked at the blood and realized her arms had gone numb because of how long she'd hung from the chains.

"It won't hurt for a bit, but give it time. The nerves need to catch up. Good Sorella. May I call you that?"

"You should call her queen," said Taug. "Queen of the Wrathfall."

"Oh, we know that is not true. You are only half Silvercrow, aren't you? Your blood, the blood dripping from your arm, and the wound on your leg, it's tainted, isn't it."

She looked at him. Gray Jim stepped toward Mr. Smoothhorn, turning toward Taug slightly.

"Yes."

"Liar!" He sliced. "The human blood in you isn't tainted. It's a gift, you elven swine."

He smashed her face, breaking her nose with the palm of his hand. Her head snapped back, and all four chains went taught as her body shifted slightly back and forth, utterly helpless. Smoothhorn licked at the blood.

"Now, why were you in Olde Ridgewatch, you pig? Why?" he demanded, focused on the answer, his righteousness radiating from his rotten smile.

"We were there to save," she said, catching herself.

"Yes. Yes, speak." Smoothhorn waited impatiently.

"To save Vineland from the Holy Imperium, to start a revolution."

"Excellent. Gray Jim, please bring this news to Sir Burrow of the Bitterleak Brotherhood. He is going to want to hear."

Mr. Smoothhorn stopped mid-sentence.

"He is going to," he mumbled, breath seeping from his lips.

Mr. Smoothhorn stopped again, unable to speak, his lips trembling and eyes shifting back and forth.

"He's going to find your body dead on the floor, you sack of shit," said Gray Jim, and he finished his final blow from the knife, slicing right across Mr. Smoothhorn's throat.

"You could have done that quicker," said Sorella.

"Well, I had to pick what I wanted to use, Sorella. You know I'm a meticulous man. I need to get you out of those chains quickly. You're lucky I got hired here. Where is everyone else?"

"Get Taug as well. We'll need all the help we can get trying to escape."

Gray Jim started working on the chains.

"My queen, you know this man?" Taug asked.

"Yeah," said Sorella. "He's a right bastard, the kind you want in a fight on your side." She smiled slightly. Pain shot through her arms as she slumped to the ground, hopping on her less wounded leg. "I'm in a bad way here."

There was noise above them, loud footfalls, and chanting.

"What's happening? It sounds like a party is going on above us," asked Taug.

"The townsfolk of Olde Ridgewatch are protesting at the gate of the keep. The entire jail is full of townspeople arrested because of a riot. Must have pissed off the wrong people."

"Good. Good," she shook her head. Gray Jim unchained Taug.

"Did he take your horns?" Gray Jim asked. He helped Sorella into her clothes and armor that lay in a heap near the door. He bound up the wound on her leg, but it needed further attention soon.

"My master did when he first bought me. I killed him two days ago," said Taug.

Gray Jim bowed slightly, "I'm sorry for the loss of your horns."

Taug smiled, "Never heard a human apologize. This Bawstone Keep is a strange place."

Gray Jim looked at them. "Sorella, come here and stand still," Gray Jim lifted her head. "Duncan is going to hate me for doing this," he said.

"What?" Sorella asked.

He took his fingers and smashed her nose back into place. Sorella gave a slight scream and lost weight on her leg. Gray Jim caught her. She threw up, relieving her head and face pain.

"That hurt, fuck that hurt," Sorella mumbled.

"Sorry, had to do it, or it wouldn't heal right."

"That's if we get out of here," Sorella barked.

Taug walked up to Mr. Smoothhorn's corpse and kicked it furiously until she got tired. She then started taking his clothes off and dressed. Next, she rooted around the table and gathered knives and other implements, walking with a limp. Gray Jim didn't say anything, even if some of the tools may have been his.

Taug moved quickly for how injured she was, a ball of meaty bruises and open wounds. She put a knife to Gray Jim's throat.

"You trust this man, Silvercrow?"

"Taug, yes, we traveled together; after we got into town, we split up. I've broken bread with him and fought at his side. We can trust him."

Taug nodded.

"Sorry, Gray Man," she said.

"You can call me Gray Jim."

"I am Taug Vicorm. I am indebted to you."

"Funny way to show it," Gray Jim said.

Taug bumped her hornless head into Gray Jim so they were as close as lovers. Her eyes were full of pain, her face bruised, and she pushed her hips closer to his. "Says a man who was about to torture me."

"True, true," he said. They shared the same breath. And he took a step back and put out his hand.

She spat on it and slapped it.

"Well, that is out of the way. I'll check the other room and start letting the prisoners out. They'll move up to the cells to the next dungeon. I'll give the keys to whoever is the strongest. We'll move in the other direction and hope to escape without them. I don't know this keep well enough, so we could be guessing in the dark," said Gray Jim.

"We're close to the Atlantis Ocean and a river. We might get lucky and find an outlet that way," said Sorella.

"That would be a high drop, Sorella, and most likely barred up."

"I agree, Silvercrow. You may be able to fly, but Gray Jim and I'll drop like eggs onto a pan," finished Taug.

Sorella laughed a little, thinking that she had met another crazy stranger, one like Doc.

"The fortress doesn't hold many guards. They were called away after the riot. I heard Benedict Ashburn took his force to Lackmore," said Gray Jim. "We have a chance of getting out of here."

"The Wrathfall have started their revolution; they are to take back what is rightfully theirs. Vineland will be free," Taug said. She looked manic yet happy, her eyes in the shadows, yellow and powerful. Sorella and Gray Jim looked at her.

"We worry about getting out of this fortress alive before we start any revolutions."

"You cannot start what has already begun."

"What riot, Gray Jim," Sorella interrupted.

"I forgot you were taken early," he said.

They reached a door and peered out.

"There was a riot in Olde Ridgewatch a few nights ago. Several were killed, and I heard a slave revolt occurred at Lackmore," said Gray Jim in a loud whisper. They carried no torches and stayed in the shadows made by the light sources perched on the walls.

"My people and the elves planned to break free for months. It was supposed to happen here too, we were to rise, break our chains, kill our masters, and escape to the Gloomspire," Taug said.

"Something like that, but it was only a few hundred I heard. Not many slaves rose up in Olde Ridgewatch," said Gray Jim.

Taug huffed. "Those that stayed are all cowards, too used to drinking milk and being warm inside, forgetting that chains and ropes are unnatural. They forgot what fresh mountain air, the blood of your enemies, and the spark of a fire outside feel like."

"Well, to get out, we either fight our way out or quietly escape," said Gray Jim as they moved forward.

"Fight until our last breath," said Taug.

"Taug, I don't know you, and you can barely stand. We need to be resourceful here. Do you want to live out this night? "Sorella asked.

Taug looked at her. "Yes."

"Ok, let's think this through," said Sorella.

"We push the rest of the prisoners up to the right stairs, take the back chamber, and use Smoothhorn's office stairs to make it to the next few floors. I hope we meet nobody else. I lead the way, considering I'm allowed to walk around," said Gray Jim.

Taug put her arm around Sorella to keep her from stumbling.

He opened the door and walked out, moving to the right of the room to a jailer sitting on a bench playing a game of cards. Gray Jim now carried his long executor sword on his back and a short sword at his hip.

"Jailer, have you seen Smoothhorn? He left me his keys."

"Keys? Mr. Smoothhorn never leaves his keys to someone else. Thought he was in the room with you torturing those two prisoners," said the jailer.

"I finished up with them." He wiped his hands and cleaned off Mr. Smoothhorn's blood. "Where are the rest of the guards? Maybe they know."

"Servants pointed tail. They were ordered to the gate. I guess there's some protest." the jailer sighed. "They went up to investigate. Left me here to ensure the locals down here don't make a fuss in the dungeon. Playing cards with myself now."

Gray Jim gripped his chin.

"That's sad news. We're already short-staffed. I wonder where Smoothhorn could be, unsure what to do with the bodies."

"Bodies? You were supposed to torture them, not kill them," said the jailer.

"Tell you what, you go see if they're still breathing. I need a drink." Gray Jim sighed.

"You're worthless. Wait until I tell Mr. Smoothhorn. He's a professional and doesn't put up with your rank-ass artistry," said the jailer as he stood, looking up at Gray Jim. He returned to the door, and Taug stood near the other side.

Gray Jim turned and put his arm around the jailer's head, snuffing the life out of him. He walked up to the first jail cell and opened it.

"To the right and up is freedom. Fight, and you can escape. Wait, and you're surely dead. Get the others out quietly."

Eyes and hands peeked from the cells when the first one opened. Soon, the room was full of newly freed prisoners; "Go, the first room should have clubs and blades, then up the stairs, veer to the right. You heard the guard. They are understaffed. Squeeze the pigs now and let them squeal on your way to freedom," instructed Gray Jim.

The prisoners moved up and away from Gray Jim. Taug opened the door, and they moved in the opposite direction into the shadows of Bawstone Keep.

Alysha - A Cause for Pain

Alysha's side ached from the horse kick, and she was lucky to have deflected a portion of the blow with Stormkiss. Her earlier wounds throbbed and leaked blood, but she felt vigorous now after the soldier's death. A clean river and sleep for a day or two would be exactly what she needed. She considered laying down at the foot of the lightning-struck black willow that now appeared in her vision and letting the goddess of spring, Judith, take her and Hades to her enemies. She was starting not to care anymore.

There's more retribution to give.

"Rook, where are you?" A soldier screamed, and immediately Alysha snapped out of her delirium. Alysha ran and stumbled, tracing her steps back. She felt drunk as her head spun and her legs failed to take safe and accurate steps forward. If she fell, the fog could overwhelm her. Her vision blurred. She couldn't use Stormkiss as a crutch. Its spiked head and blade were too dangerous, so she left it strapped onto her back, and the blood weeping from a series of wounds was starting to take a toll. The fog in the grove turned from green to white and gray, and Alysha felt better, the sense of doom and despair diminished as she left the green-fogged path behind her.

She heard horses to her right, took off her scarf, and breathed in, attempting to be as quiet as possible. She knew there were more Genteel Monks and Holy Imperium soldiers searching for their lost comrade and potentially two people wanted for a series of crimes. Alysha felt her strength begin to return.

"Thank you, Judith," she whispered and moved down the other path, knowing one wrong decision could kill her.

* * *

"Where the Hades did Rook get off to?"

"I could have sworn I heard a horse."

"Ian, you're Flint's best scout. What say you? Where could Rook and these two criminals gone?" said the female Genteel Monk, Sister Softfellow. Her lined face and stark hair were pulled back like a strong-willed raven with years of challenging times behind her. She carried a short sword and buckler, along with a bow.

"If you had listened to me at the crossroads, we'd have those criminals hanging from a tree or captured. They saw us cross their path at the crossroads and circled behind us, hoping to go north and get to the Erie Sea instead of going south as you took us."

"Watch your tone, you Blightbriar Rat," she warned. "I asked where we should go, the left or right path?" She pointed with her short sword.

"I recommend not yelling for Rook. We'll find him eventually. And let me lead the search so you don't ruin the hunt."

She was moving her horse around where Alysha had walked through, covering her escape. The other three monks who watched the argument were also not standing still on their horses but circling the glen.

"My last name, Shortstride, is based on the Blightbriar ghost cat you and your kind have hunted to near extinction, Softfellow."

"It's Sister Softfellow, scout, and remember, I am in charge. I asked for your opinion on this hunt, not a history lesson. General Flint is the only thing keeping you from purification by the Path of the Blessed. Remember that."

"We go left, and we find the criminals; we go right, and we find death," Scout Shortstride confidently advised.

"I trust you like I trusted all of the Profane who lived in those villages we burnt last fall," Sister Softfellow said. "Hear that, boys? Ian thinks we'll find death to the right, where two sets of horse tracks exist. The Servant, Child, and Maker's blessing are upon us. Fear no evil, and none will come to us," She nudged her horse behind the other three as they stomped down the right path, and the green fog nipped at their horse's ankles.

Ian waited and looked at the grass around the other path, knowing his quarry was going in another direction.

"Move it Shortstride! That's an order," he heard echo down the path with the green fog. "There are horse tracks this way, I bet Rook has them cornered."

"They won't make it out of here alive if they keep this up," he mumbled to nobody, but the gods, but the gods didn't pay attention and hadn't cared for the elves for ages. The path Alysha walked grew tighter from the foliage. Glancing behind her, she didn't feel directly followed, but it would be a matter of time until the corpse of Rook was found. The trail led north and, at times, towards Grimwood, nothing but capture and her death waited behind her.

Alysha roamed for an hour until she saw birds in the distance behind her fly up from a break in the tree canopy; the sudden urge to move faster took hold of her. The fir trees towered over the rest of the other trees, creating a darker umbrella-like feeling. Hunger, thirst, and exhaustion gnawed at her thoughts as she approached a crude signpost at a break in the trail. She looked at the sign, as it showed pictures, one of water pointing off to the right, a skull pointing to the left, and a tower straight on. She looked at the start of each of the paths and saw fresh horse tracks on two of them.

Behind her, she felt her pursuers even if she could not see them yet. The forest was getting quieter.

She couldn't explain it, but the two paths with tracks felt like the wrong choices. She wanted to find Helena but going further north or east seemed counterproductive. She hoped that if Helena were to hit the Erie Sea, she'd trade her horse for a boat ride. Although it went against common sense, she headed onto the trail that seemed the worse choice, the one with the skull and tombstones, trying to not to leave any tracks behind her.

* * *

The Genteel Monks, led by Sister Softfellow, followed the new path, watching the horse tracks. They slowed their horses at a light trot as the way thinned, and the forest from both sides closed in on the group. Ian, the lead scout, remained at the back of the group with Rook's body tied to the back of his

161

horse.

They stopped as the path broke into three separate areas. "Two of us take the one with the watermark; two more take the one with the tower; Ian, you and your dead friend take the one with the tombstone marker. If you find a cemetery, leave the body at the gate. Pray to the Maker, Child, and Servant, and leave him to rest," Sister Softfellow commanded.

Ian looked at her and nodded, not wishing to speak as her ignorance astonished him, and he would be more than impolite if he did.

"Travel for maybe an hour; if we don't find them, we'll report back that we lost them, and they most likely died in these forsaken woods."

"Ahh, that grass is sharp," yipped one of the monks as he sucked his finger. "This place seeps of evil and despair," he mumbled, finger in his mouth.

"Meet back here in one hour," ordered Sister Softfellow.

Ian watched them go and wondered if anyone could tell how long an hour even was. He knew that whoever had killed Rook had looted his corpse, taking a quill, ink, a map of the area, and a coin pouch. He dismounted and guided his horse down the track towards the oldest cemetery in the city-state of Grimwood, the Garden of Sorrow, known to most as Black Willow Falls.

* * *

Alysha approached a damaged gate with two large tomb markers securing each side. Past the gate was a steep drop-off into a deep ravine. She walked to the edge and realized there had been a bridge, but it now lay broken and impassable. Far below the remains of the bridge, tombstones and obelisks grew like the poorly maintained teeth of an orc. She looked left and right, taking in the trees, vines, tall grass, and years of leaves and brush on the ledges that led down to the bottom of the ravine where tombstones and mausoleums dotted the landscape shadowed by tall black willow trees. This was Black Willow Falls, the cursed cemetery of Grimwood.

She remembered her mother telling her stories of Grimwood's Black Willow Falls and the moat that never came to be. How the lords and ladies of the city took the slaves who dug the great moat around the acropolis and buried them under their work, separating the dwarves, humans, and, lastly, the elves to their plots. Old stories of ancient times were told to warn children about the dangers of noble power and betrayal.

* * *

"The Golden Age held tarnish and decay under its veneer. The Goldthorn family built monuments on the bones of the oppressed and filled their cups with their blood," Maria Ashburn said.

"Now Maria, don't scare the child," her father interpreted as they sat near the fire in their home.

Her father, Benedict would sigh as he read *The Plain Herald*. "They killed the slaves who made the moat, fewer mouths to feed in the harsh Grimwood winters, Maria; you know that, and the moat doesn't work because the dwarves and elves argued about how the mechanism to fill it with the Erie Sea should work so they sabotaged the lock, and nobody has ever been able to fix it."

"They called the place Black Willow Falls," her father said. "Those black willow trees grew up in the pit after a while, giving off a green fog that kept wildlife away, and when it rained, the sides of the moat looked black with specks of green light reflecting on its surface. The other parts of the cemetery are still used today and can be reached by stone stairs near each of the remaining bridges. The poisonfire fog makes the eastern unsafe nothing more, no curses no ghosts.

* * *

Now, Alysha looked down on Black Willow Falls, searching for the stairs she recalled her parents talking about. "This is no place to play ghouls in the graveyard," she said. The winds shifted, coming from the east. She saw the greenish fog linger and drift in patches up and down the uneven rows of the tombstones. She smelled decay and a sense of hopelessness, like in the grove with the green fog surrounding its edges.

163

"Psst," she heard.

"Psst." she looked to her right and saw Helena peaking behind one of the mausoleums on top of the ravine. Alysha looked back and hobbled over to her.

Alysha said Helena's name, and tears drifted down. She touched her face, and then her face was touched. Their foreheads drew together. She felt a short relief and a surge of energy as Alysha's dirty blond hair and Helena's darker brown hair mingled together, and it almost felt like home.

"The horses are gone. I took what I could carry and pushed them off towards the Erie Sea," Helena whispered. "Why do you look worse every time I see you?" Helena said, smiling painfully.

Alysha grinned through her tears. She was glad to hear of Helena's worry and delighted to know someone cared for her, even if it was just for a moment.

"There are only five left now."

She smiled, but it held anger. "One less bastard," said Helena.

They heard the noise of a horse and moved up against the mausoleum wall covered in rotting vines to hide in the shadows. The cliff's edge was only feet away from the side of the mausoleum. The stone was dark and cold to the touch.

"You've already moved inside the gates of Black Willow Falls. Any further, and you can count yourself as dead as the rest of my family below," warned Ian from the other side.

Alysha looked down and across the edge, hoping to find the stairs.

"If you are looking for the stairs, I know they are on the other side. I've read my history. Elves bled to make those stairs, and the city of Grimwood betrayed my brothers and sisters for their work."

Helena gritted her teeth as frustration grew. She hated it when men were so confident that they talked, as if every breath they took was more important than hers. Alysha shifted next to Helena tensely as they stood against the wall, unseen for the moment even as the man spoke.

"It's why I joined General Flint. This entire land shall bathe in the blood of descendants of Grimwood for what they have done to my people. Now come out, both of you. You may gain amnesty if you know something important."

Alysha squeezed Helena's hand, pushed her back, and stepped out, grasping at Stormkiss.

Ian stood on his horse and looked at her. He was fresh, while Alysha was exhausted, beaten, and bleeding from multiple wounds.

"The blacksmith's servant, is it not? Alysha Wolfthorn, I recall, or is it Alysha Ashburn?" he smiled slightly.

"How did you-"

"It took me the entire winter to tie the two together. The Ashburn family is wanted, and there are posters of your brother everywhere. Your father is well-known in the circles I keep with General Flint and his pet, Jared Blackheart. When we met at the blacksmith shop, it was your strength and the look in your eyes. I helped scout Wolf Hills before General Flint had Blackheart burn it down."

"You'll die for that," she said.

"Given better circumstances, I think it would be an interesting fight, but you can barely stand." He raised his compound elvish hunting bow at her. "Remember making these arrowheads for me?"

Helena rushed from the side and tackled Alysha as Ian released his arrow. They tumbled down the cliff, spinning and falling through brush, pricker bushes, and saplings. Alysha lost grip of Stormkiss, and Helena swore and flipped down and away, turning and jolting to a stop.

Ian swore and slid off his horse, dragging Rook's body to the edge. He walked to the other mausoleum and snapped off a series of mushrooms in assorted colors, holding his breath. He quickly opened the corpse's mouth and shoved it in, pushing it down its throat the best he could, mimicking a chewing motion with Rook's jaw. Ian walked over to the horse, took his canteen, washed his hands carefully, grabbed a wineskin, brought it over to the corpse, and poured the draft down Rook's throat. The corpse didn't move because it was dead.

Ian said a prayer, picked up the corpse, and threw it over the side of the cliff, where Alysha and Helena fell.

"Good luck, Alysha Ashburn. May Judith be with you in the end."

The Bastards - Liberation

T he townspeople of Olde Ridgewatch carried torches, pitchforks, and other implements as they marched up the twisting road to the main gate of Bawstone Keep. With each step, the crowd grew, gathering students and faculty from Crimson Yard University, shopkeepers, other merchants,h servant,s and apprentices from all the trades. Duncan lost Benjamin and his friend Stu in the crowd. The parade had begun with a sense of euphoria and celebration, yet anger rippled through their voices as they sang and indulged in wine, beer, and the foul drink called goblin panic. They chanted for the freedom of loved ones stuck inside the dungeons of one of Vineland's oldest walled fortresses and against Prince Damon's taxes. The dread of this crowd turning into a mob crept closer with every step they took toward the gates of the keep, the riot where Runt and Stitch had died still fresh in everyone's mind.

A long winter of harassment from the Bitterleak mercenaries and Holy Imperium soldiers had fed the mob's cause. The change in taxes and the arrest of their friends and loved ones after the Olde Ridgewatch massacre were the excuses everyone needed to demand change.

A mixture of local militia and mercenary soldiers looked down on the protesters from the keep's walls. No one spoke for their side.

"Freedom from the Black Eagles! Freedom from the Bitterleak! They carry no justice in Vineland. The Maker grants us freedom in Olde Ridgewatch. Give our loved one's freedom, or we give you death," one of the loudest protesters yelled.

The crowd cheered the most at the last part of the speech. The leader, who looked to be a minister, tried to keep the mob from turning violent but only fueled the crowd with righteous energy through her demands.

"Down with your taxes and a pox on the house of Farover!" a voice yelled.

Duncan and Angus watched the crowd from the side, struggling to stay out of sight of the archers staring down the arrow slits from above. Usually, there was a metal steel gate, a chained gate behind it, and a reinforced plated gate made of wood and metal behind that gate. Two gates were up, and the multitude pushed the last gate. It visibly shook.

The gathering was jolly and cheerful as if it were a party, but there were sights of blades under cloaks, and the commoners continued to drink from wine jugs or bottles passed around. The goblin panic barrel lay empty behind them, the elixir churning in the crowd's veins.

"This could turn ugly if someone does something wrong here," Duncan said to Angus. Angus now stood on a large stone to see what was going on. "That goblin panic has been given out to a lot of people."

"Aye, people could be crushed. And if they decide to break this protest up, a lot will die," said Angus. "Arrows and bolts don't care about the innocent; they kill everyone equally."

"Cordial!" Screamed Duncan. "Cordial!" Duncan watched as Cordial approached the gate, following Ben and Stu.

"Angus, get Cordial. Stay with him. He's not right. He could get himself hurt; or someone else." Duncan commands the dwarve. "We need to get Sorella out of this place. There's another gate. I'm going to try to get in that way. We have a man on the inside."

"No justice, no peace!" someone screamed in the crowd. Then, a student from the university started to sing a hymn from the Holy Church. The group shifted and moved, hundreds of people acting as one and yet acting independently, their emotions syncing up at that moment. They knew they were there for something, but the thought, the moment, had not yet come.

"Meet back at the pub from earlier by the university if we don't talk again. We'll get our gear and figure out what to do next. But, first, I need to get Sorella out."

Angus looked at Duncan, his eyes bloodshot from drink and tears.

"Ah, sure thing, Duncan, I'll stop Cordial from seeking revenge." He touched Duncan's arm briefly and pushed off into the crowd.

"Just like I can stop an owl from flying or dwarve from drinking, I'll stop Cordial from killing," he finished, but Duncan didn't hear as each of them was lost in grief and pain.

* * *

"Who commands Bawstone Keep and these gates!" the protest leader demanded.

She stood on a barrel, waving a flag of Olde Ridgewatch, red, white, and gray with a bear as its main symbol. Hundreds of people from Olde Ridgewatch were in the crowd. Duncan took stock and saw men, women, and children in attendance. He felt uneasy, realizing how poorly this adventure could turn if the guard captain were to rain arrows down.

The crowd waited for a reply from the two towers that controlled the front gate of the keep.

The leader, Lesia Suremount, stood on the barrel singing a hymn. Others caught in the moment joined the hymn. Duncan had heard the song before, at funeral marches.

"Amazing Maker, how sweet her heart," they started. Angus scowled as he grabbed Cordial's arm.

"How are we going to get inside?" Cordial asked. Angus didn't answer; he just monitored the top of the walls for movement. No shields were presented, nor orders were given.

The hymn ended.

"We demand a trial by jury for the prisoners inside this keep or their immediate release," yelled Lesia Suremount, her clean robes a beacon in a sea of merchants and townsfolk.

"Says who!" someone yelled from the tower.

"Minister Lesia Suremount of the Holy Church of Olde Ridgewatch," the minister shouted back. "The mayor always provided a fair and just system, and we expect no less from you. We demand justice for our loved ones. If not, the Maker herself will take you as heathen who do not follow the Path of the Blessed."

The soldiers and guards looked at each other. One of the guards on the ramparts yelled, "We don't want any trouble!" He wore local militia colors of red, white, and gray, like the Olde Ridgewatch flag, and was shoved by the other soldiers who wore Black Eagle colors on their surcoats.

"No, you just don't want resistance," Angus yelled back in a bellow, and the crowd agreed with laughter and cheers.

Suddenly, screams echoed behind the gate, and a large shutter of metal grinding started.

The guards' leader at the wall stepped away from the crowd's sight.

"Open the gate!" Benjamin yelled with authority. "General Ashburn demands you open the gate!" Stu laughed as Ben attempted to sound like his father. They stood five feet away from Angus and Cordial. Cordial stared at the back of Stu's head, anger funneling towards his hand where a stiletto sat sheathed.

Stu followed. "Open the gate. Let it be the Maker's will!"

"She is righteous and just," finished Benjamin. Cordial caught Ben's silhouette as he yelled and moved towards him, looking down at Stu's boots. The boots of a Holy Imperium soldier.

* * *

The crowd screamed as the leader of the Bitterleak Black Eagles, Fredrick Burrow, appeared. He looked down upon the public with disdain and opened his mouth to address the gathering. This was the moment when they would all know the terror and evilness of the Black Eagles, and then, instead of a scream coming from the crowd, screams came from behind the walls and gates. Ben looked up at the wall and then through the iron-barred gate, seeing a large group of people enter the courtyard.

"The prisoners have escaped," said the handsome man named Cordial, whom Ben had met minutes ago. He smiled at Ben, putting his hand on Ben's shoulder. "They're armed. This is about to get interesting."

More screams and soldiers were running into the prisoners, a melee ensuing. The gates clunked loudly and slowly started grating up; the crowd surged, and Ben, Stu, Angus, and Cordial pushed forward into the gate.

Ben adjusted, got low, and put his hands under the gate, bracing it with his legs and back, lifting it up. Others followed behind him.

"Lift it up, lift!"

The crowd shoved and slid under the gate, rushing into the courtyard.

"Freedom!" Ben yelled with all his might for the crowd, and he and the gate continued to move up. Cordial looked at him and nodded with a smile.

"You Ashburn kids are something else," he said, but Ben didn't hear; he was still yelling into the night.

* * *

Duncan watched as more guards moved away from the top of the gate. There was a pause, a quick silence in the crowd, and a scream from behind the gate.

"Something is happening," Duncan said loud enough for others to hear.

The iron gate shifted and slowly moved up.

The crowd cheered and rushed forward. Minister Lesia Suremount fell from her barrel, lost in the mob, as it shoved the gate and started banging on it. Duncan could feel the shift in the crowd. This would be the moment of slaughter for all of them.

The gate gave as someone released it from inside, and everyone rushed in, pushing a guard to the side, grabbing their arms, and pinning them to a wall. They beat his head into the stone, stunning him. He dropped his sword, and they dropped him, stomping on him without remorse.

The tide changed; thoughts of the Maker, righteousness, and freedom stayed at the gate, and the base instinct of the mob took over. Arrows fell into the crowd but had no effect as the crowd replied with rock and stone. Duncan was hemmed into the courtyard as the mob rushed the few soldiers inside, who were bludgeoned and beaten, their swords and spears taking a few townsfolk before the rest of the crowd's rage tore them to pieces. The local militia soldiers turned and started killing the Bitterleak mercenaries.

170

The booze and goblin panic fueled the unrest inside the courtyard, and morals and sensibility were left behind. Duncan pushed his way toward Angus as they moved inside. He saw a group of people coming out from stairs on the other side of the courtyard, armed and killing anyone in uniform. Someone had released the prisoners below.

"Meet back at the Windmill Pub!" Duncan yelled when he saw Angus momentarily before losing him as the crowd shifted and shoved each other. People braced each other's backs with hands and arms pushing forward where the few guards left attempted to defend themselves. Cheers erupted every time a guard died. Their clothes and armor were ripped from their bodies. Duncan saw mercenaries dead, naked, and thrown from the walls. Barrels of tea were cracked open and smashed, leaving their expensive contents on the ground to mirth and shouts.

It was hard to keep from standing. There were so many people. Duncan shoved off to the left, using his size and strength to make his way as he searched the inside of the keep. He pushed open a door and saw a young guard hiding in the shadow like a lost kitten. The boy was maybe sixteen summers old and looked scared. "Where are the cells," Duncan barked. The boy was barely old enough to hold a sword. He pointed behind him. "Careful, the steps are slick," the guard warned.

Duncan took the guard's sword. "Take off your uniform, or you're not gonna make it home tonight." He said as he jogged into the darkness. After minutes, he slowed and listened as he neared a torch on the wall. A steel gate stood open, and a jailer lay dead, throat slit. Duncan crept, slower now, around a corner and met an angry-looking orc and Gray Jim near a smaller second gate. Behind them, Sorella barely stood. "May the Profane smile upon all of us today," he said. He walked up to Sorella and brought her inside his toned arms. "My gods, you look like shit; how do we keep ending up in dungeons and darkness," he said to her.

"It's the only place I can get you to show your true feelings for me," she mumbled into his chest, giving in to a slight bit of weakness as she breathed him in.

Duncan kissed her head. "Let's get the fuck out of here."

Taug bowed.

"Sir Duncan Silvercrow, knight of the Gloomspire, an honor."

"Don't mind Taug. She's one of us now," said the tall hangman, Gray Jim.

"Gray Jim, glad to see you."

"Where's the rest? Maynard and Runt, Cordial and Stitch," Gray Jim asked.

"They're gone. We need to get out of here and fast."

Gray Jim nodded. The crowd floors above them cheered, shaking the stone foundations below.

"The common folk have taken the keep and are hanging the guard's bodies on the walls by now. We aren't part of this, whatever it is," said Duncan. "Angus is grabbing Cordial, and hopefully Ben, Runt's brother, and we'll meet back at the Windmill Pub."

"The revolution has begun now; there's no stopping it; the Holy Imperium will face our wrath," said Taug as she rubbed one of her ruined horns on her head.

"Back to the Crimson Yard University and the Windmill Pub, get your weapons, and get the Hades out of here," agreed Gray Jim.

"We can't outrun the future, Mr. Gray Jim," Taug said to herself. "We get resources and move to the Blightbriar Forest and mountains. I know where it's safe," Taug commanded.

"It sounds crazy, but we should listen. Taug's been right so far," Sorella nodded.

Lightning lit up the night as they made their way above ground.

The bastards moved up and into the edges of the courtyard, and Duncan looked on as bodies hung on the walls; bonfires were piled with broken crates, barrels of tea, and paperwork from offices. Two crows cackled above the bodies. The entire keep smelled of the blood lust still high in everyone's thoughts.

Taug pointed and laughed.

"Sorella, your comrades have returned. What do they see," said Taug.

Sorella looked up at the crows and smiled, holding Duncan to stand. "We need to leave this place. Many lives will be lost here, and I don't want my friends to be among them."

They moved towards a smaller separate door and left as quickly as possible. Duncan hoped he'd soon see Angus, Cordial, and their new companions, Ben and Stu. Sorella had passed out after she looked through her two birds. Duncan had seen this before. He carried her for as long as possible, and Gray Jim took over.

They returned to Crimson Yard University and looked back towards the keep as laughter and merry-making echoed between thunder and lightning in the sky.

* * *

The keep's local militia had joined the mob, and the few soldiers who attempted to withstand the mob were killed. The crowd moved over them like hungry ants, full of righteousness and the bliss of blamelessness only a large group of people can bring as their emotions fed on each other. Ben lost himself in the crowd. When someone bumped him in uniform, he unleashed the anger of grief on the soldier without thought. The soldier scratched and grabbed at Ben's arms, but life gave way as he was choked, leaving nothing but soiled trousers and the look of nothingness that the dead gave after passing. Ben didn't even see the dead soldier; he just moved on as a local slapped him on the back and congratulated him as if he had won a prize at a town fair for strangling a soldier so quickly.

Ben's emotions twisted between resentment at the Holy Imperium for what happened to his family and sorrow for having been complicit in his brother's death. The weight of the Olde Ridgewatch Massacre pressed on his shoulders, and now he'd been on the other side of a riot helping to rid Bawstone Keep of Holy Imperium soldiers and the Bitterleak mercenaries, people he'd have called comrades a few days before.

Murderer, traitor, insolent son, he thought to himself. He looked at his hands, trembling, one slid towards Dawn's Breath stroking the handle, feeling calmer, he smiled. Another thought twisted inside his veins; *we celebrate death.*

A townswoman Ben had seen working a merchant's cart previously walked up to him and kissed him hard on the mouth. She tasted like dwarven vodka and onions, and he unexpectedly kissed the elderly lady back. His head spun, and she danced away. There was a bonfire in the middle of the courtyard, and dancing as the blood of the Bitterleak Black Eagle soldiers dripped from their bodies hanging on the walls. They had been sliced, bashed, and broken by farm instruments and their own swords and axes. The dead townspeople were forgotten in the orgy of the moment.

Ben had lost Stu, taken a sword, and killed one of the Bitterleak soldiers himself, and he'd done it with such ease that now smoke, laughter, and euphoria drifted around with cups of ale, the taste of liberation on everyone's lips.

He walked towards a barrel, poured himself a cup of ale, and drank it. Bitterness and a metallic taste lingered as he swallowed, cooling his chest and numbing his thoughts.

"So, you're Runt's older brother," said a voice behind him.

Ben turned and put the cup down, putting his hand on his newly acquired sword and sliding his other hand to the knife on the other side.

"Is there an issue?" Ben asked.

"No, I see the resemblance. You look more like your father, though, I think; Runt, from what he said, looked more like his mother. Never met the woman, though," Cordial said. "How did he die? How did my friend Stitch die?"

Ben took another cup and gave it to Cordial.

"I killed my brother, I think; I'm a soldier for the Holy Imperium. I was, I guess," he looked at his hands with stains of dirt, soot, and blood on them. "We were on patrol, and there was a scuffle; it was snowing, and I couldn't see very well." Ben looked away from Cordial and into the firelight. "Something hit me in the face, an oyster shell, I think. Six soldiers were trying to keep a curfew, but the tavern patrons outnumbered us and drew a crowd surrounding us. The snow, and all the screams and yelling. I can't remember what happened except for my friend Stu, who came along tonight. We were the only ones with crossbows; we fired, and your friend Stitch and my brother were hit." Ben hung his head. "I didn't even know Runt was in the city. They both died."

Angus came up carrying a bottle of something dark.

"It's true, Cordial. It's true," he said as he passed the bottle. It's best we get out of this place now before more soldiers show up. Duncan told a similar story. It was an argument that got out of control."

Ben looked at Cordial and took a drink. "Stu or I killed people important to you and me. It was a mistake, an accident. I'll live with it for the rest of my short life, and the only thing I can do now," he looked to the sky, "is make amends. I must make this place, Vineland, better for those that come after me."

Ben looked away, "I am going to put a stop to all of this, all of the plotting against my family, all these royals making people's lives miserable."

Cordial laughed, and Angus shook his head.

"How are you going to do that lad?"

"I have paperwork indicating a plot against my family. I am to deliver it to General Casting in Hudson City personally," said Ben.

"How are you going to do that?" Angus was trying to dissuade him.

"My father, who's barely spoken to me, gave me orders and messages I will deliver to General Casting in person. I don't know what they say, but if I give them to him and place this knife in his hand, he'll make me a knight and end all of this. He also gave me a separate letter and said to find and hire a member of the society of the moon." He pinched his nose for a second. "No, the Society of Shadows said they would help me." *They would help me get revenge, he thought. Maybe I should kill General Casting and Prince Damon instead, he considered.*

Cordial looked at Ben. "Are you serious? You want to hire someone from the Society of Shadows to get you to Hudson City and get the messages to General Casting?"

"I know I need to go to Hudson City and deliver the messages to General Casting, along with this knife," Ben said quieter yet out loud. "I haven't decided to leave the knife sheathed or unsheathed upon delivery."

"Are you ready to die trying?" Cordial asked.

Ben looked at them and said, "I'm already dead, so what does it matter?"

Alysha - Burnt Graves

After tumbling down the ravine into Black Willow Falls, rot and decay assaulted Alysha's sense of smell. Brackish water seeped into her clothes; she opened her eyes to an overgrown maze of decaying trees and grave markers draped in vines and ground cover. As she came to, the pain of dozens of cuts and bruises reminded her of her frail state and need for days of rest. She questioned the strength she felt immediately after receiving a cut or scrape, noting it would dissipate after the thrill of the fight, which left her weak and vulnerable. She moved those thoughts to the back of her mind and concentrated on finding Stormkiss and Helena. No birds sang inside Black Willow Falls, nor did a breeze shift the leaves or sun breaks through the canopy of trees. Patches of gray and green fog drifted around the area, marking territory where no living thing could survive. Alysha didn't hear mice or squirrels as she did in other parts of Grimwood and knew this place masked danger in every crevasse and wrong turn. The ground grew tombstones like teeth, with moldy wooden markers revealing the poor, and mausoleums celebrated the rich. All could be seen between trees and bushes marked by a fence, gate, or obelisk from a time long forgotten. Puddles of repugnant water and broken paths were separated by overgrown briar bushes. There were too many trees and grave markers to call it a bog or swamp, but this was not a place anyone wished to linger. The agony of tumbling hundreds of feet down a ravine sang inside Alysha's ribs.

"Helena," she said hoarsely as she rolled onto her back and assessed her arms and legs. She felt her ribs and found her right side painful to touch, but her toes and fingers wiggled as she assessed an assortment of cuts and scrapes. "Are you here?" Alysha's voice echoed off the trees and tombstones nearest her. She heard a groaning near a group of black oak saplings pushing through a pricker bush. "Did you break anything?" she voiced in the groan's direction.

Alysha reached behind her, searching for Stormkiss. Pain radiated from her side, forcing a sharp bolt to shoot up into her shoulder and through her neck. Stormkiss and her backpack were missing, lost during the fall, both of which she felt were essential to her survival. She still had the Wolfe family sword reforged with the same starstone used to make her bearded maul, Stormkiss. The sword was double-bladed, and she felt safer with it in her hand. She spat out a gooey and coarse bit of blackish liquid, unsure if it was blood or the mud from her fall.

Another moan, but it sounded more animal-like or male than what Helena would make. Alysha stood, hearing her knees pop and crack. It could have been her back. She really couldn't tell anymore with so much distress in every part of her body. A bush moved and parted, and Alysha saw the shadow of someone moving toward her. She swayed on her legs like a drunk, shifting to a shorter hill and out of water. The entire area smelled as if a heavy rain had pushed through earlier, leaving large clouds of insects seeking shelter and feeding on anything that managed to live in the basin between the city of Grimwood and the forest after which it was named.

The shadow moved in jerks and hitches towards Alysha, and she held her breath as it came into view.

"You can't be alive," she said as her voice shook. "I killed you and your horse."

Yet the corpse of Rook, a soldier of the Holy Imperium, shook and jolted towards Alysha. It leaked greenish-dark blood from its wounds, bound by an elven incantation, tainted mushrooms, and whatever curse lay on Black Willow Falls. Her arm was weak, and her vision blurred. The acrid stench of the place was making her dizzy.

The corpse moved forward as she plunged the sword deep into its flesh, and it gave way with ease, the flesh melting to the touch of star metal but not enough to stop it from swiping at Alysha. Its strength and speed were quicker than Alysha expected as she tried to pull her sword back, but it refused to leave the thing's stomach. The corpse's hand grasped onto her, and it screamed a moan, spitting worms, blood, and rotting skin toward Alysha. She kicked at its knee and slammed her hand down onto the arm that held her, breaking bones. A blur of a body slammed into the corpse, and the thing's hand separated from its wrist. Alysha fell as she pulled the dismembered hand's fingers from her shoulder.

Helena brushed herself off as the corpse struggled and moaned on the ground. She swung Stormkiss down awkwardly, cutting the body into two pieces. More worms and putrid green and black blood burst from its body. Helena stood back from the gore and vomited from the stench.

Alysha smiled at Helena when she finished. They were both barely standing but alive and together.

"Trade you this bloody axe thing for that sword," said Helena.

Alysha looked down in a daze, picked up the blade, and staggered to her.

"Take it, and give my baby back," she twisted in pain.

"We need to get to the other side, climb the stairs, and get out of here, or this place will kill us."

"Lost our backpack and food," Alysha said and kneeled on the ground, spitting up blood.

"Get up, girl. We aren't going to die here," Helena said.

Alysha's eyes rolled back into her head, yet she held onto Helena and Stormkiss. Her skin was hot to the touch yet near white in color. Helena half dragged half walked Alysha towards a hill and a mausoleum.

After several steps, Helena heard the corpse festering and sinking into the ground and hoped it was the last of it. She'd never seen sorcery before and never wished to speak of what she witnessed.

"You'll go no further, you two," said a voice.

Helena turned, and Alysha raised her head, attempting to reach her senses.

Four Genteel Monks, soldiers of Jared Blackheart, stood where Rook's corpse decomposed. The ground still shifted and bubbled, but they were transfixed on Helena, who had her arm around Alysha, propping her up. Helena had one hand on her sword, and Alysha stood, dizziness encroaching, her vision blurring as she gripped Stormkiss tightly.

"You three take those two, alive if you can, or at least able to speak," said Sister Softfellow.

"I'd rather die than be chained again by the likes of you and your kind," said Helena as she gripped her sword.

"Oh, I heard whips and chains excite you, girly," said one of the Genteel Monks. He padded a large club with his empty hand and gripped its leather handle tighter with the other. The other two carried spears.

Alysha stumbled, and Helena glanced at her.

"Alysha, if you are the praying type, might be the time."

"No prayers needed, Helena. We are in Judith's hands now,"

The three monks moved forward over grave sites. Sister Softfellow remained at the back, nudging the area where Rook's remains bubbled and rotted on the ground.

"What happened here, girls, is something from Hades itself. This place is filled with your profane magic curse, I say. Once the general is done with you, I promise, Jared Blackheart will torture you and burn you like the witches you are. Now get them, boys!"

They moved on the girls quickly, and Helena and Alysha scrambled back, searching for more solid ground. They stepped out of the poisonfire fog and moved onto a stone path leading up to the mausoleum. As the three monks advanced, a mixture of damp leaves and overgrown grass gripped them.

"Guess it's as good a place as any to die," finished Alysha. Helena chuckled mirthlessly at this.

The first monk came at Helena and swung his club down. Helena tried to block it with her sword, whose star metal blade helped blunt the blow, but the monk's swing was forceful, and she nearly dropped the sword.

With what little strength she could muster, Alysha swung her axe toward the monk attacking Helena, but he deftly dodged away and back into line with the other two monks.

"Careful boys, she may be a hurt little thing, but she has claws,"

"Looks like a sad beat-up alley cat to me, Jeff."

"True words. Put your weapons down, witches," said the monk named Jeff.

"No need for further violence."

Alysha swung Stormkiss in a long arch to keep the monks away, and they trod lightly as the blade cut through the air. Alysha's swing was all drama with no real power behind it. She feared she would not have enough strength to do any damage if she made contact. The fall from the ravine and the poisonfire fog dulled her senses and made her nauseated. Helena seemed to be faring better.

Alysha finished the axe swing, and the other two monks pushed their spears forward, causing another gash on Alysha's forearm and striking Helena's shoulder. The first Monk, Jeff, jerked in quickly, hitting Helena's wrist and backhanding Alysha with the same stroke, knocking both weapons onto the ground. The green fog encircled the monk's legs. The cuts on Alysha helped clear her mind slightly.

"Got them, Sister, blessed is the light."

"Quality work, Jeff. Tie them up. Let's get out of this fog."

Alysha jumped onto Jeff's back and bit into his ear. Helena scratched at his face. The other two monks bashed each of their heads with the blunt end of their spears. Helena fell with pieces of skin and blood dripping from her fingers. Alysha released Jeff, tearing a part of his ear. "Ugh, my ear, she bit my ear!"

"You'll be fine, Jeff," said Sister Softfellow. "Keep quiet, you'll wake the dead," she snickered. "Touch any of us again, and I'll cut your thumbs and tits off, you whores," said Sister Softfellow. "You get me?"

Helena was grasping her head, tears of pain and anger blurring her vision. She sat looking through the gray fog at her knees. The mausoleum door stood open before her.

"We told you, Sister," said Alysha. "Not going back in chains." She grabbed Stormkiss from the ground and dragged it against the stone, causing sparks.

She looked up, eyes bloodshot and blood dripping from her mouth and nose. Helena tried to focus but could only see a living scarecrow with a large bird-beak-like nose running towards her from the mausoleum door.

"Maker, Servant, and Child protect us," one of the monks said and backed away, falling onto the other. The third monk stood still, spear in hand, and

Sister Softfellow drew her sword.

"Maker's grace will protect us; Path of the Blessed is with us," she said, holding onto her faith as if it were a shield.

Alysha, dazed, turned her head to see a creature with large glass-like eyes and a long tube-like nose staring at her. It wore a hooded cape and cowl draped in shadows except for the green gas it pushed out from its hands. The gas floated past the girls, and Helena and Alysha were barely conscious and bewildered to say anything audible. The creature moved past the girls. She watched. The fog around Alysha and Helena turned gray.

"Leave here!" the monstrous scarecrow screeched as poisonfire gas pushed out of its hands further.

Helena and Alysha crawled toward the mausoleum from the monks and the creature.

"Die, you fiend," screamed Sister Softfellow as she swung her sword, the other Monks cowering behind her.

The monster stepped back from the swing. It stood taller than Sister Softfellow and clapped its hands, creating a large spark. The spark fell to the ground, igniting the green poisonfire fog and creating flames. The monster's fingers lit and spewed toward Sister Softfellow. She stepped back and pushed one of the other monks before her.

"No, no, no!"

They screamed as the poisonfire gas lit her robes and the green fog below them. The other monks caught fire, their robes ablaze, melting their armor and the flesh underneath. Their screams and pain did not stop until their hearts gave or tongues twitched. Sister Softfellow made the sign of the Holy Church and ran away in the other direction.

The fire spread among the graves, clearing any living matter the fog covered. Grass, bugs, and mosquitoes burnt, while the other animals sought refuge as the fire spread.

Alysha watched in a daze inside the mausoleum with Helena's back against a stone-encased coffin. She smiled, not caring if the creature that stood before her was a saint or sinner; she smiled through bloodied teeth, one hand on Stormkiss and the other gripped by Helena.

181

The monster grasped its hands, and the gas stopped pumping through its gloves; as the bodies of the monks stopped screaming and fell to ash and bone, it turned and walked toward Alysha and Helena. They were sitting now, exhausted, bruised, cut up, and barely able to walk.

The monster grasped its face and pulled up at an angle, releasing what Alysha saw as clips and buckles.

"It's not a black willow monster. It's a human. A man." Helena gripped the Wolfe family sword and stood.

Alysha, grasping Helena's hand, stood and held Stormkiss in front of her as the delirium of the poisonfire gas numbed her thoughts of desperation and survival.

"I thank you for saving us; give us your name and purpose so that we may know if you wish to harm or that you may bring pride to your family and aid two ladies needing safety and rest," Helena sputtered as if she were noble. She spat at the ground for proper effect.

"Well spoken, but first, tell me why you have my family's sigil on that sword?"

The man of a mere twenty summers pushed his hair back.

"Never mind, I have no time; if either of you wish to live, please follow me," He walked toward them. "You are the first people I have seen in some time, and although bleeding and beaten, you don't look as if you have the Smoldering Plague. If you wish to live, put your weapons down and follow me, or the poisonfire gas will return. Stay in it long enough, and those wounds will fester and infect, and if that does not kill you, your thoughts will muddle, and the voices inside your head will argue until you drive yourself to harm others or yourself."

Helena looked at Alysha. Alysha thumbed the cross of the sword Helena held and pushed it down.

"Tell us what to do."

The man walked toward them quickly, pulling two vials from his belt, shaking them, and popping the corked caps.

"Drink these at once," he handed them each a small vile. He fumbled to his side and lifted a lamp, opening two windows. An owl lamp light appeared, brightening the opening of the crypt they now stood in.

Alysha breathed in the looming death, the light from the lamp, and the burnt ash from outside and felt the pain of Grimwood, its history, and the lingering moments of today seep into her.

"Name?" Helena asked.

"Felix," he said. "Drink now." He cleaned the glass eyes of the mask with a portion of his cape. He grabbed another vial, shook it, and drank.

"It tastes of unripe berries and cider with bubbles, cleans up a muzzy head, and stops some of the effects of the fog down here. We'll need it to make it back to my lab."

She looked at this man who had saved her, unsure but unwilling to return outside, and drank and smiled at Helena.

Helena said, "Felix, nice to meet you, and cheers," and threw back the vile. "An enemy of the Genteel Monks is a friend of mine.

Felix pushed past both, walked behind the dwarven cement coffin, and pushed on a stone flower pedestal; with effort, the coffin shifted, and a trap door opened.

"Both of you, go down the stairs and wait at the bottom. I must close the mausoleum door, then I'll follow. Don't light any lamps or create any flames, or the poisonfire that lingers at your feet will alight and melt you."

Alysha felt better pushing on the side of the wall for balance in the darkness. Helena followed.

"What tales we shall tell when we make it out of this," she said, and Alysha laughed like one does when they see a hanging. The laugh was full of mirth and wrongfulness of the entire situation. Felix followed down.

"I'll lead with the light, hold hands, and keep my pace; if I give you this mask, place it against your face and breathe in. It supplies clean air."

He placed it on each of their faces once, and they tried it, feeling better but slightly lightheaded during each breath. Felix shifted the trap door above them back into place, leaving darkness and the owl lamp as their only light source.

"Come. We go to my lab," he said. "There, you can tell me why monks from the Order of the Blue Rose tried to kill you both," and he moved forward into a vast cavern made of arched brick. The smell of toxic fog, decay, and darkness lingered at their knees, and they moved toward the underside of Grimwood.

Hudson City - Shifting Knights and Pawns

Sir Leadwalls looked out across the city into the night. No, not the city; it was the capital, he thought, the very capital of the Holy Imperium, and he secretly wished to supplant General Hammer as Lord Protector of the South but needed to be patient and learn more. *Maybe one day*, he would even become as powerful as Sir Thomas Casting, the Minister of Lords and Minister of Prince Damon's Armies. He'd attended meetings before at the Council of Crows, Prince Damon's internal council for the affairs of the Holy Imperium, but he wasn't ready for the speed of politics. A whirlwind of exchanges and adjustments affected thousands in Hudson City and other city-states and territories. He could wipe out an entire village with an arrogant remark. The power of his voice now was more potent than the sword. How far he'd risen, he still felt like a fake and unworthy to stand next to a man like the Redcloak General Casting. This was his first time meeting after dinner to discuss military manners. He was of barely noble birth, and he was conversing with General Casting, who was close to Prince Damon and his father, King Geordie, across the Atlantis Ocean in Great Brightland. He laughed at himself, slightly giddy, and then returned to running the Holy Imperium.

They were in the same room where the council meetings occurred, and he had arrived early. Victor Parish, General Ashburn's servant, let him into the room. The window inside the tower was magnificent, and he walked up and down it, looking out into the darkness. The cook fires, braziers lit outside of homes, and the owl lamps created by deft dwarven hands dotted the twilight landscape like stars across the capital. It was a wonder. The owl lamps were incredible; smokeless light held in crystal form. The secret to making the lamps was known only to dwarven mages born every other generation, so the historians said.

"General Casting will be with you shortly; he's attending to matters in his office. Can I offer a refreshment? We have dwarven vodka from Steelsburg just in," said Victor Parish, offering a glass to Sir Leadwalls. "The last of the Clearstone vintage." He smiled. "These bottles will be hard to find soon."

"Wine would be fine, anything from the west if you have it; if not, something from near Counselor City would do, Victor."

"I will see what I can do, sir." Victor gave a bow.

"Thank you, Victor," Sir Leadwalls was unsure if he should thank Victor. If he were just a servant or even a well-trained slave, it would be unnecessary, but if he were something more, then providing respect would go a long way in his time at the Council of Crows. His recent outburst about the threat of slaves recruiting high-up servants in the capital had shaken the Council of Crows, but Casting had given the man his support, and the matter was ended.

Victor disappeared, and minutes later, a side door opened. General Casting walked in, fit and ready to work. He carried a sizable rolled-up map.

"I appreciate you meeting me during the later hours, Sir Leadwalls. There are no formalities tonight. We are discussing tactics and the next steps; I need your thoughts on military matters," said General Casting. "I receive all communications from our forces in the field. You know General Robert Flint, Jacob Blackheart, Clinton, and Ashburn. As you saw in our last meeting, our Minister of Letters doesn't give us all the necessary details."

Sir Leadwalls nodded.

Victoria Parish, Minister of Education, walked into the door, holding a glass of red wine. "Oh, our guest has arrived. Excellent. Have you started?" she said. She wore a man's trousers and school shirt unbuttoned to reveal enough."

"Yes and no," said Casting.

Sir Leadwalls looked on.

"You look uncomfortable. Please sit," Casting said and pointed, so Sir Leadwalls sat. "Madam Thompson will not join us but trusts that we will make the right decisions in her absence if it makes East Thamesbridge Company money."

"This revolt started in an estate in Lackmore, spreading out like the Smoldering Plague if we're making metaphors. The slaves were primarily elves, but heavy labor orcs and goblin miners joined. They burnt the mayor's estate to the ground and killed villagers. There are reports of pillaging and burning any building haphazardly. It was a blight on the Holy Imperium as foreign dignitaries arrived at the port. General Ashburn has his second army spread out from Olde Ridgewatch to Lackmore now."

"It feels as if all these threads are coming undone," counseled Victoria.

"It can sometimes feel that way, but we have news that Robert Flint and the first army will have Grimwood in their grasp soon. We also have a signed treaty with the Blitzsteel family, which is now in control of at least the top portion of Steelsburg. Their alliance with the Holy Imperium will be solidified when we marry one of Rodric Blitzsteel's daughters to a royal family member. She will join our council as well."

"They will allow such a match. Will the Holy Church agree to this?" Leadwalls said with concern.

"Prince Damon is the Holy Church, and the Holy Imperium is him. Yes, both sides have agreed. It is not a match to allow them into the royal lineage per se; it's one of his daughters to a lesser royal, some third cousin of Prince Damon. We know that most relationships between dwarve and humans lead to no children, so it's for political purposes. She'll be a hostage and ally for us and give us insights we previously lacked. Nevertheless, as they finish mopping their civil war underground, we now have an opportune supply of their steel and other works."

They looked at the map of Vineland, which showed the Stagger Wall across the Blightbriar Mountains and the wilds to the Atlantis Ocean.

"As we pulled resources from Olde Ridgewatch to put down the slave revolt before it spreads too far, the garrison at Bawstone Keep fell under protest from the townsfolk."

Sir Leadwalls stifled his smirk. "This feels like we can't put the fire out. If it isn't one thing, it's another; how is Benedict Ashburn back in Prince Damon's good graces?"

"You're right. If it were one or the other, it would be a trifle, nothing, but…"
Victor Parish cleared his throat loudly.

"Victor, do not interrupt," advised Sir Leadwalls.

"Sir Leadwalls, it's allowed in such meetings. Victor is privy to my discussions and advises me when most are not around to speak. I'm sure we'd be interested in what you wish to convey. He is in my trust and thus in yours."

Sir Leadwalls took his breath in for a moment, realizing that Victor was more than a servant; he was a counselor and confidant to General Casting, although quiet. He was well placed to learn, listen, and be forgotten.

Victor placed the tray he used to bring the wine down and looked at the map. General Casting and Sir Leadwalls sat at a large table, looking over a paper map with troop markers and flags for cities under Holy Imperium control and other banners for either neutral areas or aggressors against the Holy Imperium.

"You have sent a company towards the upper Blightbriar Wilds, and I don't think the force will be large enough for what you hope to accomplish. That area is tumultuous with elven tribes, orcs, goblins, beasts, and monsters not seen since Erica the Red and King Christopher. The revolt at Lackmore and other city-states where slaves rose against their betters was coordinated. It may now be calmer, but a spark could set it off again. Prince Damon's hard hand will do a job to a point, but more may be needed."

"You must be joking, Victor. That is absurd," piped in Sir Leadwalls.

"My lover is not joking, Sir Leadwalls. The Parish family used to be something more," Victoria said.

"The Parish estate used to run the border near Castle Gloomspire. I don't make light of the situation. The Blightbriar Wilds took the estate and our farmlands, leaving only Victoria Parish and me out of our bloodline. We were wiped from the nobility's bloodlines and thus pressed into our current position. The property was sold to pay off my family's debts to a distant royal family relation. The slave revolts trouble me as they could ignite something more with these tribes in the Blightbriar Wilds," he whispered quietly. "The Wrathfall are a problem on their own. If they were in communication with these loose gangs like the Bastards of Liberty and Harlots of Justice or coordinated large contracts with the Society of Shadows, it would be civil unrest for all of Holy Imperium. It would be like the Crimson Struggle all over again. "

What is he bloody talking about, Wrathfall, Sir Leadwall thought. "You talk as if Castle Gloomspire is real, and what of this Wrathfall?" asked Sir Leadwalls. "You made your point in front of your betters already, Victor. Know your place."

Casting took a large drink of vodka. "Prince Damon and this party have taken too many resources, even with the extra mercenaries he hired, which we can barely afford," General Casting stood up, knocking his chair over. "This is madness."

Sir Leadwalls watched as Victor Parish confidently walked over to Casting and brought Casting another glass of vodka. Victor whispered into General Casting's ear for a moment only the two could have heard, and Casting walked back over to the table, placing his hands on the surface.

"We leave Olde Ridgewatch to the locals. For now, force all commerce to Lackmore and Hudson City and lower our taxes on each port. It will suck the business dry from Olde Ridgewatch and punish the so-called merchants. I will have Minister Shannon start a rumor about the Smoldering Plague reaching down into the city to cause more pain. Hades, if the rumors of that vileness coming from the Plains of Ursula are even half true, this will be the smart thing to do. Call the city under quarantine for the next two months. Nobody gets in, nobody gets out. Have soldiers put quarantine flags on the Kings and Queens Road signs pointing towards Olde Ridgewatch." General Casting was feeling more like himself now, calm and calculated. "That will let General Benedict Ashburn clean up the slave revolt in Lackmore, crucify those that rebel, and return and take Olde Ridgewatch by force again if he must." General Casting now stood straighter.

"Victor. I understand your concerns about Gloomspire, but we have too many parts in the field. I will await what our messengers say about the villages by the Frothclear and Razorshine rivers and send as many Wildcats as we can to support the force there. Sir Leadwalls, send word to your soldiers outside Waterhurst to prepare for a long march. The Holy Imperium will need them to support Olde Ridgewatch or into the Blightbriar Wilds to back our expeditionary force there. Do research on both areas until a decision is made. Victoria, I presume Staghollow University will allow Sir Leadwall access to its library.

"Of course, my lord, the Silver Ivy League's books are always open to our nobles and royals," Victoria said with a sharp smile. She looked at Sir Leadwalls, who shifted in his seat.

"I will prepare our soldiers for anything, sir," advised Sir Leadwall. His eyes shifted back and forth between Olde Ridgewatch and where supposedly the Gloomspire was located, calculating the march his soldiers, mostly born in the south, would make. Either position would have them in a spot fit for glory, but they would not be familiar with the populace or the terrain. He looked up at Victoria and then Victor and settled back onto General Casting as the other two left him uncomfortable, their pale skin almost seeming lifeless.

"Victor, I'd like to know more about what Sir Jacob Blackheart is doing out west. I want the city-state of Honeybreak to bow its knee to Prince Damon by the end of Summer. He's been piddling too long and trying to play politics instead of conquering in the name of the Holy Imperium. The same is true for the so-called Republic of Wind. Why have they not sent more than one emissary praising Prince Damon's win on the Plains of Ursula? News from them has been scant of late. Can we even count them as allies at this time?"

"You're right, of course, sir; the rumors from that far come from ships that make it through the Erie Sea. There are reports of pirates on both the sea and horse clans of elves and goblins raiding the Republic up and down the Grave Reach River. General Jacob can only concentrate his force on one thing: taming the Republic of Wind and its vast farms and fields, or Honeybreak and the twin city of Dawnworth that it trades and supports."

"The pirate rumors are a non-issue around the Erie Sea; we have that well in hand," Casting said, dismissing the comment like a whiff of smoke.

Sir Leadwalls twitched, "We should ensure the Republic of Wind sends delegates to Prince Damon's Masquerade to verify their loyalty and keep a few members of their delegates as wards."

General Casting nodded, "Yes, and then we could concentrate on Honey-break and either conquering it by siege or pulling it down into the fucking river."

Victoria looked at Victor for a moment while the two soldiers made decisions that would kill thousands. She raised an eyebrow slightly and wrote down notes. The history of Vineland continued to grow.

"Your strategy is sound; just remember the Republic of Wind and its knights have always had a complicated relationship with the knights of Grimwood."

Casting laughed slightly. "Victor, you know much history, but just remember, if I'm not worried about pirates on the Erie Sea and Grimwood, then neither should you. We will have Grimwood well in hand soon enough."

Victor stood straighter and nodded, pouring more wine for Sir Leadwalls.

General Casting watched as Sir Leadwalls peered at the map. The man was practical, but he needed to ensure Sir Leadwalls stayed within his station. He considered sending him and his soldiers into the Blightbriar Wilds to chase ghosts and monsters.

Gloomspire Gate - The Chaos of the Moment

"Do you know where we are, Knight Commander Nirinath Sladestone?"

They stood on the side of a large stone cliff with a gap that opened below in the middle, letting the Frothclear River push through each side of the soft shale stone from west to east. High cliff walkways lined each side of the Frothclear River, allowing groups of hunters to run easily on each side from the Gloomspire fortress to where the Frothclear and the Razorshine rivers met. The soft shale mixed with harder sandstone and limestone creating hues of dark gray, green, and brown throughout the cliff walls. Wind and storms could whip through the area and, if caught in the open, push a person into the river and feed the gods another soul.

Sladestone knew where she was and hated when spoken down to, so she waited patiently and did not answer, not to contemplate the question but to upset her compatriot. She looked across the gap of the cliff where her soldiers waited quietly. Goblins, dwarves, elves, and orcs united for the first time in generations to push back their adversaries who waited across a forest on the other side of the Razorshine River, which ran south to north.

The Frothclear River was loud enough to cover any noise created by her army. She took a deep breath and enjoyed the pride of seeing the mass of warriors before her. They were ready and hungry for blood and the hearts of their enemies. The Gloomspire was one of the few passes across the Blightbriar Mountains. Other passes and gaps were hundreds of miles away, like the Grindstone Citadel controlled by the dwarves, the Shrewtuff's Pass, and Rooksgate Hold. The Gloomspire Gate, where Knight Commander Sladestone stood, was sacred to all before it, and behind it lay the Gloomspire, a fortress bathed in honor, mysticism, and blood. She had made it something more, unifying a community with a goal of land where all were equal. The people were now the Wrathfall, and their goal was to push back the human tide that washed away their culture, sold friends and families into slavery, and made them sick with disease and rot. She waited because the mage repulsed her with his rituals and constant singing. The goblin stood, if she could call it that - more like hunched over - holding a staff, wearing a warhawk's beak like a mask carved down to give it an even more menacing look.

Falstaer Vicorm, known as Falstaer the Rain Miser, the mage that stopped the battle for the Gloomspire, lightly hummed a calming song to the four first gods, Sif, Stribog, Judith, and Jupitor.

"The times bring forth growth. Judith and her maidens are among the flowers that bloom this year," Falstaer whispered. "The history of this land changes now." Bones and feathers rattled on the goblin's body, hung from pieces of leather on his belt, and across his shoulders over the tattered clothes the mystic wore.

The Gloomspire Gate was a stone cliff with steps carved into each side, high above where the Frothclear and Razorshine rivers met. Judith's winds weathered the peaks of the gap herself years before anyone existed. Each side of the ridge provided a view above the tree line of the Blightbriar Wilds. A simple push, Sladestone thought, and she would watch Falstaer fall to his death and all his magic he professes, and that blasted singing would not stop him from landing and scattering his guts all over the gap that led to the Gloomspire.

She breathed in deeply, shifted her weight, and decided against it. Falstaer would land on top of her soldiers, and their lives were worth more than his. "We are at the Gloomspire Gap, the only gap in the Blightbriar Mountains controlled by the Wrathfall."

"Yes, that is true; for one that does not read, you know much," said Falstaer as he flicked a tick off his shoulder.

"I read my books, study our maps, and listen to the songs and whispers that dance on the winds. You still think less of me after what I've done. I just don't read your holy texts; they mean nothing to me," Sladestone looked down at the river, almost as if the waters below gave her life and energy.

"Yes, I'm sorry, I assume too much. Our gift of the printing press from the mage Olivia Franklin was a boon for the people. We were beasts in the wilderness before. Now we create art, the written word, and instruct our children so they can become more than what we were."

"I mistrust her, this Olivia Franklin," cautioned Sladestone.

"She's a powerful ally; if we slip, she would be a vengeful enemy. Olivia was taught by Gaston, the first mage who had long learned the secrets from the gods themselves. I am a child compared to her power."

"That's why I don't trust her or you."

Falstaer laughed. "That is ok, my friend; I wouldn't bathe with you in a clear pool of Jupitor's tears."

Sladestone even smirked at this.

"We walked up these stairs carved by the winds of Judith to pause for what we are about to do, to give thanks to the four seasons, and ask for their blessing."

The air felt serene; the mists of the river mixed against the touches of the sky as wisps of fog drifted about. Sladestone knew if she continued towards the cliff's edge, she would see the wrecked hunting lodge cut out through the forest and the Razorshine River some distance away. She may even see the campfires of the Holy Imperium fools off in the distance.

"Get on with it. Those Holy Imperium fools wait for us," Sladestone ordered.

"You want to roll over them like a storm, and you could, but that is not the way. They have armies of thousands, and they are well-armed and armored. We have just one army and need to forge better weapons and thrive. The tomahawk you took from the hunting lodge can only do so much. The Servant's Guide is one of a kind, but we would do better to have more Paragons of Vineland at hand for what is to come. Wait until dark and harass them until they don't know how many or who attacks them."

"This is our land, our home, and they hunt our food and kill us for sport. I will bathe this ground with their blood," Sladestone hissed.

Falstaer grasped at the chain jerkin Sladestone wore. Sladestone looked down on Falstaer as if he were a disease.

"Do not ever…" she began to snarl.

"You are a better warrior and strategic mind than I have ever known," Falstaer said quietly but with power singing in his words. "Do not needlessly let anger, bitterness, and honor kill your friends and family. Our enemy don't know the land or understand our people. We should give to those humans, orcs, goblins, and dwarves that need our help, and those that do not wish for our help, we'll destroy. This group of soldiers across the river will die, but we don't need to shed blood while they are in a fortified position."

Sladestone took a deep breath, knowing the goblin was right. She knew she should wait.

"We'll harass them when they try to sleep and attack them as they are halfway across the river, and the holy river will wash their blood clean and away from the Gloomspire, and the fear we provide from the skies will guide the rest of this war. They will know our wrath," Falstaer demanded. "This war will last a long time, but we fight for our homes while they fight to conquer. Now, let me begin the ritual."

Sladestone stepped away from Falstaer as he began to sing and shake his arms to the sky. The fog around the cliff wrapped itself around the edges, creating a clear space. She stood among stones, the grass chewed down by mountain goats. The rocks stuck out of the ground like ill-formed rectangular teeth in a circular formation. In the center stood stones built into an arch she could walk through if she wished, watching Falstaer now as he sang, moving in a counterclockwise motion inside the stone circles, grasping at several of the goats and slitting their throats, letting the blood fall into the grass as their bodies jerked and stilled. The wind pushed out, and Sladestone felt her skin prickle as the unseen forces she could not comprehend gathered. Rain fell but did not touch them inside the circle, and Falstaer Vicorm the Rain Miser continued to chant and sing with fever and passion.

He crossed around the arch, and Sladestone thought she should have seen him through the other side. Yet she saw another place, not even in the same area—the inside of a home, shack, or cellar. Sladestone blinked, unsure of what she had seen, and it disappeared just as Falstaer stopped singing and appeared on the other side of the arch.

"You do not believe, and that is ok, but you feel and see, and now you understand some of what is possible," said Falstaer. "What I do is attempt to touch beyond flesh and blood, and sometimes it works, but there is always a price. I have lost a year of my life to show you what this arch and the blood of sacrifice can do. We have opportunities to strike at our enemy's hearts, but it will take much more than goats to complete."

Falstaer took an ancient yet exceptionally clean knife from a sheath. It was the same knife he'd used to kill the goats.

"What would you give to keep the Gloomspire safe and for your people to thrive?" Falstaer looked up into the eyes of Nirinath Sladestone.

She looked at the goblin's yellow eyes and saw sincerity and hope.

"Everything." Nirinath breathed. "I would give up everything I am to keep my people safe; it is why there is no fear when I attack."

Falstaer took her hand and sliced down from the tip of the palm to the elbow quickly and quietly.

"So you say, so you do."

He took the blood from her and smeared it on all the stones inside the circle and as much as he could in the doorway.

"We are done, and you may attack as you wish. We will wash it at the river tonight before you wake the Holy Imperium soldiers."

Sladestone looked at her left arm and the cut as they walked back towards her army. It was healed, but there was already a deep white scar. It reminded her of some of her tattoos across her gray body, some the color of a deep crimson red, others dark as the pupil of an eye, and this blade cut a white slash from palm to elbow. She looked back at the gate, knowing the importance of what occurred may be bigger than anything she could imagine.

"Come now, Knight Commander, you don't believe in religion, but your soldiers do; let them know the sacrifice you made to the Profane so they feel that they fight for their homes but also for their gods."

Falstaer and Sladestone created a community of orcs, goblins, elves, and dwarves at the stronghold after a dwarven crusade pressed the community at the Gloomspire fortress. Sladestone had defeated the assault in the tunnels through ambush and guile against a large dwarven force from both the city-states of Steelsburg and the Grindstone Citadel. Falstaer appeared and appeased the attacking groups, brokering a peace with the company of dwarves under a truce flag while the two sides traded their dead for proper burial. He'd given the dwarves access to the holy sites inside of Gloomspire under the condition the fortress would be a neutral city for all that entered, governed by himself and a representative of the dwarven, elvish, goblin, and human cultures. Currently the group numbered four as they had yet to find a suitable human leader for fifth seat in their congress of leaders.

There were still tensions between the distinct groups, but Falstaer had started to incorporate a mingling of the races not often seen. Their fortress was massive both above and below ground, and although each group favored parts of the city-state, Falstaer did his best to ensure a specific section was not overrun by one culture.

"We wipe out these soldiers; they are on our land; this isn't one of their cities or farms; this is our land they want to take, so we wipe them out and take back what is ours," Sladestone said.

Falstaer nodded, knowing this was just the beginning as the journey towards a new country had only just begun.

* * *

Austin sat on the edge of the tree line in tall grass, his feet cold and wet, and tried to dry his bowstring. He waded across the Razorshine River before the sun even considered cresting the horizon, along with three other Union Dogs mercenaries. He was supposed to be just observing but wanted to be more than a glorified guard to the celebrity of Prince Damon. Today, he was acting as a scout, pushing across the Razorshine River before the main force crossed. He'd done enough work to become a knight through his skill in tournaments, and his family name helped him become a Wildcat, but he never felt he earned it. In this campaign, he could at least gain respect from those around him.

Pap wanted to move half the soldiers over the river early this morning and sent Austin and the other three Union Dogs over as scouts, checking for traps or potential ambush. They had found no signs on the ground and sat and waited as the soldiers across the river readied themselves. The waters were low, and the horses would be able to traverse with ease. Elora would lead the rest of the Union Dogs first, leaving their mounts on the other side and taking the river on foot to move better in the Blightbriar Wilds. Leslie was near him, and two others, a hedge mage named Milo and Silva, who carried an elvish compound bow, were spread across the riverbank's opening, looking for trouble. Milo specialized in creating fog and smoke cover and could occasionally heal folk. Austin thought he looked like a fraud, but Leslie and Elora said he was on the up and up. The hedge mage twitched, and Austin thought he'd piss himself at the first sign of trouble.

Leslie said he's the only mage they had, so there was that. A fog pushed in from the Holy Imperium side of the camp, rolling down the banks, across the rocky shore, and over the river. Austin felt it before it came and noticed the wildlife around him stilled. Even the mosquitoes had disappeared. He took a moment and looked behind him, seeing movement on the other side of the river as the Union Dogs broke out of the tree line and crept towards the rocky shore. Austin checked the tree line again on his side and scanned the area. Not even squirrels danced in the underbrush, but he heard crows cackling in the trees. Leslie made a sign to start the crossing to the company of soldiers.

The Union Dog mercenaries moved into the water, separating themselves so if one fell to archers or got hurt, the group wouldn't stop the crossing.

Austin heard something and looked up at the crows in the pine tree above him. They cackled and lifted their wings in warning, but the noise came from the other side of the river. Mounted Templar separated the remaining Union Dog mercenaries on foot, taking the lead as they crossed. Austin knew they were to wait until the mercenaries had established a firm hold on the other side of the river but had disobeyed. The Templar and accompanying monks started to push their way onto the shore and split the line of soldiers on foot, loudly. All the birds left for the sky, laughing as they took to wing. Leslie shook her head and mouthed the word "fuck."

The Razorshine River gurgled as the horse's hooves plunged into the water angrily. Brother Lucius Wilder was in the middle of his soldiers as they walked through the water. Austin heard the whistle of the shaft before he saw the arrow strike the first horse full in the head. More bolts and arrows followed. Certain elvish and orc tribes would hollow out their arrows, so they whistled, hoping to strike fear into their enemies. Austin searched the forest cover to see where the shafts came from. A monk screamed and fell from his horse face down into the river. The few Union Dog soldiers took cover near larger stones as the lead horse kicked and screamed on its side, spreading blood and fear among the rest of the animals involved in the crossing. The other Templar behind the lead horse was caught in the hysteria of the dying horse and the knight drowning in the Razorshine River. Austin gambled, took aim, and loosed on a large crow laughing high in a tree. His aim was off, and it fell into the tree's bark. He heard a slight moan as the tree bark fell to the ground. The enemy was covered so well they blended into the natural cover of the trees and brush. *They fight like heathens*, he thought to himself, *no honor, no pride.*

"In the trees," he yelled. "They're in the trees!" He hoped someone could hear him, but the rush of water, the screams of horses, the war cries of the monks, mercenaries, and Templar knights all stuck in the middle of the river just added to the moment's chaos. Austin notched another arrow and looked back as he heard another flight whistle through the air and fall on the confused soldiers caught in the open between river crossings. Pap appeared on the other side and made a sign for the scouts to take cover as best they could, and he sent volleys of arrows overhead and down into the canopy where the suspected enemy was hiding. Hundreds of shafts fell, several of which came down near Austin and Leslie; Leslie made a sign towards Milo, who produced a horn which he blew out, and acrid smoke poured out of the horn, filling the crossing. Austin, Leslie, Milo, and Silva each grabbed a wounded soldier and carried them back across the river along with Union Dog Mercenaries. They left the dead in the river. Pap unleashed another three volleys of the heavy arrows into the canopy, but they heard no screams of pain, no yells of despair. The whistling arrows stopped.

Leslie was panting from the crossing and carrying a heavy knight with Austin.

"That went terribly," Leslie said with mirth. The knight moaned. "Unhook his cover." The knight's eyes blinked, and blood smeared from his lips. "Where are you hit?" Austin looked at the knight but didn't see anything. The knight moved her left arm slightly, and Austin found a large crossbow bolt under the arm.

"We'll get you help, but we have to get you off the shore here," he said. "Leslie, you ready? I'll grab under the armor here; you get the feet."

They pulled and carried the knight as she bled out and died.

* * *

"What the fuck happened out there? I explicitly ordered the scouts to verify the landing before we crossed," Pap yelled. "Maker's tits, you fucked this up, Elora! And Austin, what the fuck was that? I told you to observe, not play hero, not get in the action. You're the cousin to Vineland's most powerful general."

Elora, Austin, Sir Pekka Deeran, and Brother Lucious Walder stood at attention inside Pap's tent. Austin knew he would be hardest on Elora's Union Dogs and Austin as they were at the front of the crossing. Elora had recommended strike teams move across the waters at night in groups of five to supply better coverage and to put at least a blunting force across the river before the rest of the main party crossed. Still, Pap had rejected the idea due to the forceful requests from Sir Pekka and Bother Walder, who felt their professional forces deserved to be at the front of the line and to cross with the strength of their body as a sign of their respect and prestige. Pap had relented by performing a standard crossing of a handful of scouts first and then those on foot next, followed by the armor at the end. He knew it was wrong but didn't want to lose knights in a crossing where an ambush was possible. The Templar force disobeyed orders and crossed too early, causing the mess in the river where Templar knights fell to crossbow bolts and arrow shafts, with one drowning in their armor. They had lost foot soldiers and two of Elora's scouts, including Milo, the only mage the entire company had, along with three knights and four horses. Milo was struck by a bolt in his stomach and had died in camp after the battle.

Pap set a small table with maps in front of him while they all stood. At the tent opening, he had two Wildcat Guards and two regular soldiers, all loyal to his command, with him as backup as he dressed down the group in a show of force.

"Elora, your scouts are on night patrol for the campaign. When we attempt a crossing, I will give the initial push-through to Pekka's men. You are dismissed." He waited until she left. "Austin, you will stay put as your orders have been, and continue to be, to observe as the eyes and ears of the Royal Council."

Pap stood and looked at Brother Walder.

"Brother Walder, you disobeyed a direct order as I requested your knights to wait until our foot soldiers made the crossing safe for the heavy horse," Pap shouted.

"With all do respe-," Brother Walder started and was silenced by a slap in the face from Pap.

"I did *not* ask you to speak nor were you ordered to speak, soldier. You disrespect my authority again, and you will sit in stocks outside of camp for the goblins to flail at night. You get me, Brother Walder?"

Brother Walder put his hand to his mouth to check for blood but said nothing.

Pap pulled out a lovely handkerchief and presented it to Brother Walder, who took it.

"That was given to me by Prince Damon himself. For your mouth," Pap looked at the man he had just humiliated. Austin watched on.

"I'm upset and frustrated. We have limited resources and are potentially outnumbered in a hostile environment. Brother Walder, Captain Pekka, this is a serious situation, not a campaign for glory and honor. Any soldiers lost will be buried at the back of the camp; we cannot lose a soldier to bring the bodies back to the capital. As of now, you may speak."

"But commander, this goes against our standard protocols," Sir Pekka said.

"Also, against the Holy Church's wishes, this is not sacred ground nor of the Maker's design."

"I understand, but the bodies will be returned once our mission is complete. Remember, if possible, our mission is to verify what happened to the lodge, neutralize any threats, and return."

He tapped the scroll with General Casting's orders on the table and returned to his seat.

"We have three knights who need burying that carried weapons, armor, and personal family effects, along with other soldiers. Write your letters and secure the effects. Do you have anyone suitable to be knighted and can take up arms?"

Walder and Pekka said nothing, unsure of what Pap was asking. "Knighted or not, I fear we may be at this for the long haul. Our scouts should be able to confirm what happened to the lodge. I expect Elora to confirm this in the next few days, but the second part of these orders puts us, until relieved, here for an extended stay. Consider who can fill that armor until the knight's family claims it."

Alysha - Dark Fever

Alysha wasn't a dead weight on Helen's shoulder, but she wasn't a bunch of flowers either. The stench of urine and feces burnt their nostrils as they waded through a tunnel filled with the gray water from Grimwood's sewers above. Human refuse, rats, pieces of garbage, and fluids flowed in the opposite direction via a sloping grade as they pulled against it and toward Grimwood City. Felix led the way with his mask on, which piped in clean air through a leather tube and a concoction placed on his back, which included a large jar with multiple plants and moss inside, giving off a hued glow. One side of Felix's mask occasionally pushed out a slight green fog Helena and Alysha saw back in Black Willow Falls.

"I don't think Alysha and I can make it much longer. How much farther?"

"Just a little more, and we'll be at my lab," breathed Felix through his mask.

Helena wasn't sure how much trust she could put into this person, but he'd saved them from the Genteel Monks and, if she understood correctly, may have killed them. Both Helena and Alysha needed to stay by Felix, as he had the only light, a lantern of dwarven make, and without it, they would be lost in utter darkness.

"Helena, you stink. You could really use a bath," mumbled Alysha.

Helena smiled, "At least you're well enough to joke. Gods, you're heavy, you cow."

"Rude, give me a second. I should be able to walk," Alysha staggered for a second and stood, pushing herself up using Stormkiss, before she coughed and threw up into the gray water as it trickled past. Helena noted the liquid was black, which could mean blood.

Felix turned back and moved toward them. "Keep moving, or the effects of the gas could be permanent." Helena and Alysha didn't understand but also wanted to get out of the lower sewer of Grimwood, so they moved forward. After fifteen minutes of trudging, Felix pushed out of the gray water into another catacomb. The damp air brought a mildew-like taste to Alysha's mouth. Her head still spun, and she felt like she had drunk an entire bottle of the dwarven vodka her old caretakers Hob and Bob used to drink. She spat again, placed the scarf back over her mouth, and closed her eyes to steady herself from dizziness. When she opened them, she didn't see anyone.

"Hello," she half said, only to hear an echo.

"Wait, don't move," said a voice. Alysha stood still in the dark, only to hear the rhythmic beat of water dropping from afar. The despair surrounded her, and she could feel the acrid stench of shit and piss drift past her scarf. Her eyes watered, and she fell against a wall filled with corpses held inside its long shelves.

"Judith, this is awful. I hope Helena is safe," she whispered to herself.

Something scurried over her feet and past Stormkiss. She gripped the handle, and it reassured her. The catacomb was circular, with shelved openings where wrapped bodies lay. She could see as her eyes adjusted to the shades of black and gray. A shadow inside a shadow moved towards her, and she tensed up, hoping it was Felix and not something else.

"Here, walk quietly now until I say it's safe. We are crossing an unsafe passage. No noise. Your friend awaits on the other side," whispered Felix.

"If you are tricking us, I will-" Alysha began.

"No tricks," Felix cut her off. "Just unsafe above and near. We pass a dungeon and rooms of torture." He twisted off his mask. "Breathe in, and then we move." He said in the darkness and pushed his fowl mask onto her head. "Breathe. It's clean; it'll give you energy."

She gasped inside the mask, tasting the air, savoring it like a spring morning with cool sunshine and storm clouds. He pulled it off.

"Now quietly," he grasped her hand in his gloved fist and then moved. His hand felt like leather and metal, with gaps where rivets lay deep inside.

They moved in the shadows and heard others breathing, muttering to themselves. Alysha heard a cup rattling against a bar and someone gnawing on a bone, and they were bigger than rats.

She felt a hand grasp her, and she looked back into the darkness.

I see you both, a monster and a goddess, the darkness said, or so Alysha thought.

Felix pulled her on and forward, moving along quietly. After ten minutes, they stopped; he turned his lantern on again by opening a small door, letting light out. Helena stood in the light, shaking. "I never want to do that again, waiting alone in unending darkness," Alysha and Helena hugged, giving comfort and courage back to each other. Felix looked away and pushed against a rounded wall, opening another deep passage. They moved inside it and pushed the stone door closed. "We're safe, but best to be quiet for a while longer," said Felix.

Helena and Alysha pulled away from each other and stood unsteadily.

"We moved past old catacombs and a dungeon used by the council of Grimwood, but those below are long forgotten. Only a while longer."

After the catacombs and dungeons, they moved on and upwards, finally climbing a carved-out ladder of bricks and holds that led into a cellar. Felix lit another lantern and closed a significant sewer drain, snapping a lock in place where they had just climbed out. He locked it shut, and Alysha watched as he placed the key in his right pocket.

"Alysha and I offer our thanks. Where are we?"

"We're in a cellar near the eastern gate of Grimwood. My makeshift laboratory. I assume you aren't from Grimwood because you wouldn't have ventured into Black Willow Falls cemetery if you were. Your friend lay her down there on my bed."

"I'm Helena, and this is Alysha." Helena helped move Alysha to the bed as Felix moved around the room. "We're from Wolf Hills originally, by way of Counselor City."

"Yes, well, why did you come to this forsaken place? Have you not heard of the quarantine? Did your parents never tell you the stories of Black Willow Cemetery? You'd be dead if I weren't gathering samples for my work and performing a poisonfire fog burn-off."

Felix walked over to the two women on the bed carrying a doctor's satchel and looked down at them. "I assume neither of you has the Smoldering Plague, but I must check each of you. I need to take a sample."

"A sample of what?" Alysha sat up, gripping her weapon. Her vision muddied, but she pushed through the pain and nausea. Helena grabbed a knife.

"You will not be searching my body for anything."

"I will get my sample from you, Alysha, when I fix your wounds if you don't bleed out first. You, Helena, have several cuts as well. Take the knife you are grasping and drag it over the one on your shoulder. The sooner I confirm you are both clean, the sooner I can sew you up like your little dolls." He turned and walked away.

"If I wanted you dead, I would have left you two to the soldiers in the cemetery," he flung over his shoulder.

Felix stood over an instrument and started fixing its knobs. It had cylinders attached, lenses from spectacles cleaned and purified. "Bring me your knife, Helena," he said. "And don't stick it in my back."

Helena walked over and handed it to him. He shook it onto a piece of glass, put it into the instrument, and peered into a cylinder. Helena waited for a long time while Felix investigated her blood.

"Helena, take your knife and scrape one of Alysha's wounds, please. I think you're safe. My bag has clean bandages. Please staunch your wounds. I'll sew you up shortly," he said, snapping his fingers, still looking at the instrument.

"If I'm fine, why do you keep looking at my blood," she said, glancing toward Alysha, who was lying on the bed, eyes closed, bleeding onto Felix's blanket. "Please hurry. Alysha's pretty pale."

"Yes, yes, science takes time."

Helena walked away and started to tend to Alysha. She was grateful they made it this far. They could have, should have, died so many times now, but it felt even worse if they were to get into the city only to die by a wacko in a cellar who wanted to dissect them.

"You're both clean of the plague, but I'd like to study your samples more, if possible." He walked to the bag. "I will do my best to be modest, Alysha, but this is science. I'll need to see the extent of each wound." Alysha's eyes rolled into the back of her head, showing only the whites of her eyes. She started mumbling slightly in another language.

Felix looked at Helena. "She has a fever. Put this in her mouth and grab my mask and the glass cylinder." He ordered. "She's in awful shape."

He walked over to a shelf of jars, grabbed one, and started mixing ingredients. He replaced the moss from his glass cylinder backpack with fresh herbs and new moss and put the old ones into a large container that smelled like rotting dead skunks, capping it quickly. Helena nearly threw up at the stench. Felix washed his hands quickly and placed the mask on Alysha.

"This should help, I think. Your friend Alysha will need to rest after we close these wounds. And she has broken ribs that need to be wrapped tightly after I push the bones back together. I've seen worse but only really done this with cadavers before the plague."

Felix walked over to another shelf and moved books around, grabbing vials and pouring liquids into two wooden cups. Helena thought she saw a powdery substance, which could have been wizard salt, a powerful drug used for both pleasure and in medicines but was also highly addictive.

"Here, going to be up for a while; need to stay awake," said Felix.

"I thought you were mixing up something to help Alysha?"

"This bubbly substance should give us enough energy to get us through the surgery and work I must do on Alysha and you. Bottoms up," and he sucked down a tub of reddish liquid.

"Tastes like lantern fuel and sugar," Helena gagged.

"So gross yet slightly addictive. Now let's get to work."

Felix set Alysha's bones while she was passed out and breathing through the scarecrow mask he placed on her. He cauterized her wounds and sewed up others.

"She's lost a lot of blood. It will be three or four hours before we know if she will pull through. She's pale, but I think she'll make it. The bleeding stopped as I worked on her," he was washing up before working on Helena. "If infection occurs, and it may, she will have to fight it."

Helena looked at her friend lying on the bed, beaten, cut up, and sewed back together, looking like a monster with an odd mask.

"I'll take the mask off her now. Come over, and let's get you fixed up."

"How did you end up in one of the most cursed places in the city-state of Grimwood?" Felix asked. "Oh yeah, this is going to hurt. That vile we drank may give us energy, but it doesn't take the pain away. The only booze I have is not for drinking but cleaning my instruments."

Helena winced but did not scream, and Felix worked on cleaning and closing Helena's minor injuries.

"We escaped servitude from Counselor City, which is under Holy Imperium control, and traveled here to warn about a Holy Imperium army coming to take over Grimwood."

Felix frowned and looked at Helena. "I'm afraid to say it may be best that the Holy Imperium comes to the city, not to sack it, but to save it."

Helena's shoulders slumped.

"The Council no longer controls the city. They fled to their estates and don't dare return." Felix scowled. "The Smoldering Plague above the Erie Sea has spread to Grimwood, toppling the economy and those who once ruled here. The city's quarantine closed off different corridors and gave gang leaders or merchants power. The plague still lurks in the shadows while criminals and murderers walk the streets."

"Is that why no trade passed into Counselor City on the roads from Grimwood?"

"The winter was brutal, and there was suffering the likes of which I have never seen. The bodies were burnt, and family names that lived before King Christopher's arrival died out," he sighed and ran his fingers through his greasy hair. "We're in the Grimwood University corridor; I've kept the poisonfire gas at bay until I'm replaced. If a burn-off doesn't occur every month, the entire mote will fill with the poisonfire fog, rendering the cemetery unusable. I don't know what the mote would look like or how dangerous it would be if I wasn't here. Students in the College of Science have been performing burn-offs for generations, but with all that has happened, that could be over soon. You are the first two people I've seen without a mask in over a month. Well, and those monks trying to kill you."

"What of the Grim Vultures, the knights of Grimwood?"

"I heard a few went with each city leader when they left, but most stayed here to keep law and order. Two detachments of soldiers left the southern and western gates when the Smoldering Plague wreaked havoc on the city, but neither returned. For all I know, they may all be dead. Most in the town didn't survive the first or second wave of the plague," the scientist recounted.

"This is going to burn some," and he pushed a red-hot knife onto one of her wounds.

"Wait, ah shit, that hurts!" Helena gasped, trying to contain herself.

"Best not to dwell on it," he said. "You're all finished."

He walked away, removed the mask placed on Alysha, and checked her breathing and pulse. "It's light and steady. We'll wait the night out and see how she is in the morning. She's on my bed; I'm afraid we don't have a say on the matter. You can take the chair or floor. When we wake, you can tell me why you carry my brother's sword." Felix threw two blankets at her.

"This, it's yours? I didn't know. Alysha gave it to me when we escaped," she said, putting her palm on the blade's handle.

"I haven't seen him in years, and you said you were from Wolf Hills. I can only assume the worst. Your friend can tell me more when she wakes up. Her fever is low. She should be able to talk to us in the morning. I have research papers to clean up and notes to take, but rest your head near your friend. I'll try to be quiet as I clean."

Helena sat next to the bed Alysha rested on, putting her hand on Alysha's leg and pushing a blanket against her head. Half lying down on the bed's frame, she wanted to stay awake, but soon, sleep took her as Felix cleaned up his laboratory, preparing for another tomorrow.

Sorella - Separate Choices

After two hours of walking, Gray Jim, Taug, Duncan, and Sorella returned to Windmill Pub. Duncan pushed the door open and walked up to the bar. Mitt, the owner, stood serving a few younger students but moved them along upon seeing Duncan.

"Mitt, we need rooms and our stored gear. How fast can you start a hot bath?"

"Water is already warming for another client, but I can move you up the line."

"Good, I want my sword and shield now, and you warn me of any trouble coming through the doors."

The pub owner nodded.

"You know I want no trouble," he said under his breath.

Duncan considered that thought, letting it settle over coals of anger and resentment, and ensured Sorella and Taug could get cleaned up and a bath. Then, Duncan left to speak to Mitt, leaving Gray Jim to guard his friends.

Duncan grabbed Mitt by his shirt and pushed him against the wall.

"You fenced in weapons without telling me, and it got two people killed, so everything you do for me is free now, you piece of shit," Duncan spoke through his teeth, rage widening his eyes.

"I'm sorry, Duncan, I heard there was trouble. Let me down. I'll get the rest of your belongings.

He hurried off, and the server dropped off beer and medical supplies in the washroom, where Taug and Sorella cleaned up.

"I heard there is trouble in Olde Ridgewatch, a riot or something near it, and the locals took over Bawstone Keep. Any truth to that?" Mitt poured himself a large stein of beer and passed another to Duncan.

"We were just there. Someone let out the prisoners, and they took it from inside while people from the city came through the front gates. The Bitterleak mercenaries didn't fare well against the common folk."

"So, it's happening already," said Mitt.

"What's happening, Mitt." Duncan looked on, tired and strained with anxiety and wrath.

"We've been. Those in Olde Ridgewatch want control back of the city-state."

"I don't want to be part of some bullshit revolution Mitt."

"Well, it's too late. Your dear friend Doc started something that can't be stopped. You're in it one way or the other. You can't be neutral on a moving caravan. Acting to protect it, siding with bandits, or not doing anything are all choices with consequences."

"Shit metaphor Mitt. Get us a pack of provisions. We are leaving as soon as my two friends can walk."

"Sure, that's the least I can do," Mitt said, shaking his head and walking away.

"Jennifer," he said to his head server, "mind our guests washing up. I must update our friends in Affectus."

* * *

Taug and Sorella bathed and sutured their wounds. Duncan had taken over guarding the door, oiling and sharpening his sword, trying to think of where to go next. He knew Doc and Maynard were off towards Affectus, the so-called city of neighbors, to meet with General Washcreek and others. He should have seen this sooner. Doc and his friend Olivia Franklin had been making waves after the Battle of the Reaping, calling for fairer taxes and a more unified country with every major city-state getting a say in the affairs of the Holy Imperium. They both submitted newspaper articles and pamphlets throughout the capital under false names until Doc was cast out of court and jailed in an asylum for "provocations while at court." The newspaper articles slowed but reappeared a year ago when Doc hired Duncan, Sorella, and others to secure items and money. His crew hit banks and town manners, stealing documents, money, and jewelry from which they all received a cut. Duncan realized Doc's cut was to fund something big, like a revolution.

Duncan heard footsteps up the stairs and stood up, moving into a shadow. His friends were safe behind the door, resting.

"Relax, Duncan, it's me. Brought a peace offering," said Mitt. "You're right. I shouldn't have involved you and your friends."

"They killed a kid and someone I've known for years, Mitt."

"I can't fix that, Duncan, but I can help. I have horse tack and gear for you all in the stalls out back for situations like this. It's the least I can do. Also," Mitt handed Duncan several pieces of paper. "Letters and news for you. Once you've read it, burn it. Have the ladies rest up. I noted a few safe houses for your travels. Drop my name and ask them how they make a tree grow,"

"What you said earlier when we first met," Duncan thought aloud.

"Blood and freedom. Give it room to grow and water it; sometimes, you spill a little blood to get it to grow," said Mitt with tired yet determined eyes.

Duncan didn't thank him; he just nodded. Mitt walked back down the hall.

"Mitt, did you know Doc? Did you know what he was up to?"

"It's not some grand conspiracy of crows. Everyone is born with the right to become something more than their parents. The right to an education, to do as they please in their own home, the right to worship who they want, the right to read what they want, and the right to have a say in their government. Those fucks in Hudson City think their shit doesn't stink. The war ended, and Vineland was supposed to get better, but it's just getting worse," he said. "It's time we try something else." Mitt paused. "Doc agreed with me and others and paid for the weapons; he's helped before when we needed money." He walked away from the shadow and into the light as he disappeared downstairs.

"Shit, we need to get out of here; this whole fucking place is going to be at war in less than a month," Duncan said to himself.

Duncan knocked lightly to check on Sorella and the new addition to his crew, Taug. They were both asleep, wounds wrapped. He closed the door softly, reading the documents and pamphlets. One was news about a

Triumphant Masquerade celebrating the end of the Crimson Struggle on the Battle of the Reaping anniversary. Many nobles and foreign dignitaries would be in attendance. Another smaller piece of paper was a short story about sickness sweeping villages, wiping out families and homesteads, and causing entire remains to quarantine in the north. Duncan had gotten sick after the Battle of the Reaping from the Smoldering Plague but recovered quickly. Finally, another pamphlet described a series of missing children and animals near the forests of the Blightbriar Wilds. It spoke about a large predator who snatched the children or animals away, leaving no trace or tracks.

Duncan squinted at the next one as the type was tiny and worn down. It said *Grimwood burns, and we'll rally to our trustworthy neighbors.*

The last one was a short letter sent explicitly to Duncan. *Duncan, I'm off to sever the head of the lead wildcat, and Angus is with me. We'll keep an eye on the second son. He's with us now, and he's a right proper bastard. Cordial~*

Duncan folded the messages into his pocket to let Sorella read. He wasn't sure where to go next. Cordial and Angus are going to the capital, he suspected, which was insane. Taug and Sorella needed to flee Olde Ridgewatch as they were escaped prisoners. There were too many choices. He was torn between his friends heading south to Hudson City or leaving the whole chessboard and finding a place to regroup and stay out of the political fray unfolding across Vineland.

If Duncan read everything right, he guessed emissaries would meet in Affectus to discuss Prince Damon's rule of the Holy Imperium. He wasn't sure how many city-states would join Olde Ridgewatch in their outright rebellion, but the sentiment that many had enough of the egotistical despot was easily found among the common folk. All Duncan knew was he'd had enough death and war for now. Decisions needed to be made sooner rather than later, and he wanted the smartest person he knew to help with his muddled thoughts.

Duncan ran his tongue over his teeth and stood. He'd saved Sorella and this orc, Taug, but lost Cordial and Angus, maybe for good. He nodded, waited a moment, and walked into the room where Sorella and Taug lay.

"I have news," he said, looking at his friends.

"Cordial and Angus aren't coming back. I think if I read the message correctly," he handed the messages to Sorella. "They may have a go at hurting someone with a high profile in Prince Damon's court."

Sorella read the missive and turned back to Duncan, concern on her face.

Taug said the words nobody else dared to whisper. "Kill the Prince," she smiled. "You can't stop the inevitable; the Society of Shadows never fails. I bet your friend Cordial took a job as an excuse, but either way, their minds are set."

"They're taking the boy, Benjamin Ashburn, with them," Duncan said.

"You mean Runt's brother?" Sorella sighed.

Taug scratched at her stub of a horn and cleaned her nose. "They aren't taking him along. He hired them, Duncan."

"What, how do you know these matters? What are you talking about?" Duncan said.

"She's a mage and kind of mad like Doc. She sees and dreams events that have yet to occur," Sorella explained.

"Shit, another crazy mage. I can't get away from you people." Duncan scratched at his beard.

"You're stuck with me, Knight Commander Duncan; we head to the Gloomspire. It's where freedom lives," Taug nodded.

"Yeah, and where is that at? It's the tales of superstitions and hunting stories. I fought a siege at a mountain keep once and wasted seven months at the first gate by a river long ago; it's not worth it."

Like Sorella, Taug stood and put her hand on Duncan's shoulder.

"Taug and I decided we're riding for Gloomspire. It's a place where the dwarves, orcs, humans, and even goblins live with each other and have more freedom than any other place I've heard of. I spoke to a few tribes of my people over the winter. They mentioned it when we were wintering at Mount Nittany University. My people traveled there through dwarven tunnels to seek refuge. Think about that," she paused. "Elves traveling through dwarven tunnels in the winter to a place where they can be free and be themselves."

"Sounds too good to be true," he looked at both, their minds already made up.

"Choose to save Cordial, Angus, and Benjamin, or become something more than a squire," Taug said and looked on, judging the situation.

Duncan looked at both and sighed deeply. "Which one will let me kill Jacob Blackheart?"

Sorella laughed, but the laughter was from sadness and not joy. Taug smiled because she couldn't even guess what Duncan could do.

They spent two days at the Windmill Pub. Mitt provided them with food and news about what was happening. The Holy Imperium's grip on Olde Ridgewatch diminished as soldiers were seen leaving the city on a forced march, leaving only the local militia guarding the city's towers. Rumors of a slave revolt in another port drifted through pubs and whore houses like reefer smoke on a weekend night.

* * *

"What's your stake on all of this, Gray Jim?" Duncan asked the executioner.

They stood at the bar nursing a spring ale full of notes of pine and elder flower, bitter at first, burning going down, and soft buzz after each sip.

"I've got no profession anymore; that's two hangman jobs in less than a year, all because I met you and Sorella."

"Cordial and Angus are heading to Hudson City to get into who knows what. I fear I may never see them again. Sorella and Taug are heading into the Blightbriar Wilds."

Gray Jim gripped his mug as they sat at the bar. "What are they looking to do?"

"Start over, start something more than scraping by, I guess."

"Scraping by in the city or scraping by in the wilderness." Grey Jim scratched at his face, lost in a thought. "Two sides of the same coin. What will you do, be with the woman who has been your companion since I met you, or go after Cordial and Angus?"

Duncan looked over at Gray Jim. "Everything I touch, put hope in, and pour my love in ends up six feet in the ground. I owe it to Runt to try and save his brother."

Grey Jim sighed. "You told me before you don't age the same as the rest of us, that dwarven blood pumping through your veins. You also heal up differently and can't have kids. What the fuck are we doing here, man? We stay here; this place is going to burn. There are a lot of pissed-off people around. We either join this revolt or leave and try to start something better." Gray Jim looked at Duncan. "I've got nothing here, no honor, love, or family on the coast. I'm heading with Sorella and Taug into the Blightbriar Wilds."

Duncan's stubborn mind was already made up before he started the conversation. "I saved Sorella. She understands. I'll see her again. I need to at least try and do something for Benjamin and stop Angus and fucking Cordial from whatever they're planning."

"You aren't saving shit, Duncan. They are going to end up dead, and so will you. Take it from a failed hangman. I know death, and I know idiots looking for it. They all end up on the butcher's block or at the end of a noose."

Duncan nodded but didn't say anything further. Like the truth Grey Jim had just spoken, he just drank the last of his bitter ale down.

∗ ∗ ∗

Sorella, Gray Jim, and Taug walked their horses on the edge of Roxburrow, Crimson Yard University behind them. The humid morning mists drifted against the grass. Sheep and goats roamed around a field, relishing their breakfast.

Sorella wore her floppy hat to keep the sun off her face, and even Gray Jim doffed a tricorne hat. Taug put up a light hood of her cloak to conceal her features and rode between them. Sorella and Taug donned chains, and each of the three had access to a key, playing the role of slaves to Gray Jim. Sorella's two crows, her familiars, rode the waves of wind above them, watching for danger and roadkill.

Duncan was absent and had left his room without leaving word of where he was going. Sorella turned around, looking back at the Crimson Yard University.

"He's coming; just relax," said Taug.

"Not until he feels he's done the right thing," said Sorella.

"That's a stubborn man," said Gray Jim. "Will he be able to find us after he's done what needs doing?" Their horses moved toward the west and the Blightbriar Wilds.

"He always finds his way back to me," said Sorella Silvercrow.

Hudson City - Burn the Books

P rince Damon stood in the ballroom of The Nightingale Theater. Victoria Parish was present at his request and had become his self-imposed biographer and secretary. She'd evaded his advances so far, so he demanded she attend events he wished to place into his biography for "posterity's" sake. Today, the executive chef Oloff Burnstew steward Vladimir Richpike and other members of Prince Damon's inner council discussed business and political manners in hushed tones while the chef and his steward collaborated with Prince Damon on The Triumphant Masquerade details.

"I want a large chocolate fountain here, Oloff," demanded Prince Damon. He was on his second glass of slim soda and vodka. The Nation of Stouya, a bitter enemy of the Holy Imperium, had sent four cases of slim soda to Prince Damon as a sign of warming relations between the two powers. Stouya and Carigreed had fought for years over their holdings in Vineland. Their war finally ended in the north on the Plains of Ursula when three mages, each representing a nation, fought, and their armies were decimated. The last mage standing bore the standard of the Redcloaks, a society of knights originated in Great Brightland long before Vineland across the Atlantis Ocean was even founded.

"I've been lusting after mushrooms as well; let's have several plates of mushrooms and Bitterleak Burgers; of course, I have one of those nearly every day along with those slim sodas," advised Prince Damon.

"I know a specialist for your mushroom request, Prince Damon. She is a miracle worker with them; you could almost call her an alchemist," noted Oloff Burnstew.

"Excellent," Prince Damon remarked. "You may be ugly as a hung over orc, but your advice on food is always spot on." He turned and snorted a mixture of ground-up tobacco and wizard salt to help his focus as he made decisions, a habit that was all the rage of his court. He closed his snuff box with a sharp click. "This party will be tremendous; many beautiful people will come."

"I am a peaceful man. I'm the most peaceful man ever to live. The Triumphant Masquerade is a celebration of unification and our victory over the losers, the Nation of Stouya and Legion of Carigreed," he said and drank from his cup, his stubby hands circling around both sides. "Shit, this is a terrific slim soda. Richpike, has the Nation of Stouya advised who will attend the party yet? I'd love to at least know the name of my potential wife."

"My grace, the Queen of Stouya has sent a large group of guests, including Princess Grizel Vickers from Stouya and her close friend Princess Gabriela Clawford of the city of Bitterleak, who now commands the lands of Greatmaw. Also, Kara Giannini, a renowned ballet dancer, has joined their party," advised steward Richpike.

"I have heard wonderful tales about Kara and her legs. Bards sing wonderful songs about her," Prince Damon looked far off, caught in his perverted thoughts. He twisted slightly as if he was trying to quiet a fart building up inside of him. "Who else may be attending? This party will be magnificent." He didn't wait for an answer. "The papers say Princess Gabriela Clawford has a very voluptuous figure, but I'll be the judge of that; I'm a great judge; everyone knows that."

"Mae Bloomhood, a poet and actress from the far lands of the Four Queendoms, will be in attendance, but she comes with complications," Richpike overstepped.

"Wadda yah mean? I need to know as much as possible here. This Bloomhood, what kind of name is that? By the way, Bloomhood? See, it doesn't even sound good; she probably has a horse face."

"Her bodyguard is a renowned warrior, and they both have strong ties in the Four Queendoms. Getting involved with her could cause issues we're unprepared for."

The chef had stepped back while steward Richpike stepped closer. Other members of Prince Damon's Council of Crows noticed and moved closer.

Prince Damon pushed the thought away. "Four Queendoms, I have four massive armies that serve at my whim. Real winners, you know. We kicked the shit out of those losers, the Nation of Stouya and the Legion of Carigreed. Four Queendoms, more like four whoredoms. Who else?" Prince Damon rubbed his hands together.

"Laura Speers, the entertainer from Cinderpool, will attend. She's in the city promoting her latest work, and the Legion of Carigreed has sent Princess Charity Mapleton, and, of course, your father sends his regards along with Princess Candice Saltdrift."

Prince Damon's eyes shifted from Richpike to lusting after Victoria. "Victoria, what are your thoughts on these potential matches?" He looked at her, baiting to see if she would show any slight emotion.

She picked up her quill and pushed up her glasses, moving a piece of her hair away from her chiseled face. She was a shadow today, but it always felt like she could erupt with violence even though she wore no armor and carried no weapon.

"All would be grand choices, your grace. It depends on what type of princess you wish by your side."

"And you, what of you?" he probed quietly as he moved closer. She continued to write. "What of you by my side?"

She felt his breath smelling of desperation and sticky, sugary soda water.

"How can you take notes so far away and in the dark, Victoria? Hmm," he said, wanting to press into her. "How can you hear what I say?"

"Your grace." She moved the paperwork away from her chest so she no longer blocked the distance between Prince Damon and herself. "In the shadows, I can hear everything." She looked Prince Damon directly in the eye, raising her chin. Her pupils flickered too red and back to normal. Prince Damon blinked. "And you know I am already spoken for. Now get back to the party plans, or you'll piss yourself in public," she whispered.

Prince Damon cleared his throat.

"Yes, well, thank you for getting that down, Victoria. Steward, who is the Legion of Carigreed sending?" He walked away from Victoria and back into the light of the windows and in the court.

"Your grace, we believe there's a problem." said a voice from behind. Two men started walking toward Prince Damon, who turned toward the comment. Oloff Burnstew, the executive chef, and the steward Vladimir Richpike now stood behind Prince Damon, waiting for dismissal.

Bishop Devon and Minister Shannon walked toward Prince Damon, mumbling and plotting in whispers and bitter chuckles. Bishop Devon held a book, while Minister Shannon held multiple pamphlets. Minister Shannon, the Minister of Letters, did not speak and waited as Bishop Devon blustered forward, spewing the gossip.

"What is it, Bishop Devon? Can't you see I'm working here? You know it isn't easy creating the biggest party Vineland has ever seen. I'm the one doing all this work while you cackle and gossip like children. If we were in proper court, I would have you flogged for interrupting me." Prince Damon stopped and waited for the threat to land. "You hear me, stripped of your shirt and whipped with a cat of nine tails like a sailor. Are you a pretty little sailor, Bishop Devon?" He waited, and Bishop Devon said nothing. "Fine, what is it, my pretty little sailor. What can be so troubling that you are interrupting my party planning?"

"I know since you've taken an interest in newspapers. You now own the *Post Enquirer* and outlawed the *Hudson City Journal*," started Bishop Devon.

Prince Damon interrupted the elderly man. "That reminds me, Stephanie, why hasn't *Hudson City Journal* stopped publishing? I continue to hear that rag is still active among commoners. I'm surprised the knuckle-dragging common folk can read, yet hear it is that the paper continues to publish."

"Your grace, we are working on it; every issue we find gets destroyed. Burnt as it were, but it's like a disease we can't cure yet. But if you let Bishop Devon go on, he'll explain."

Prince Damon took another drink from his goblet. "Fine, go on. Oh, and I want a castle made of champagne glasses for the party. Do you hear that, Richpike?"

"As you wish your grace," he commented behind Prince Damon.

"Make it one of the centerpieces," the prince pointed. "Here."

"Your grace, a book we believe about you, is making its way around the court and in the commons. I dare say, if a commoner can read, it may be in their hands. It's cheaply made, not something from the court printing presses. It's from the same press that prints *Hudson City Journal*."

"You know I don't have time to read. What is this all about, Devon? I have matters to attend to."

Bishop Devon shrunk back, bumping into Minister Shannon, who pushed him toward the prince.

"You see your grace in the book." stopped Bishop.

"Your grace, did you ever read *The Lonely Nights of the Milkmaid* or its follow-up, *The Early Mornings of the Lonely Milkmaid*, while at university." Stephanie interrupted.

Prince Damon was initially annoyed and slowly registered what Minister Shannon had said.

"I may have flipped a few pages."

"It's hardcore erotica, your grace," she paused. "Read by young people while at university and passed along."

"Go on, Stephanie."

"There is a new book out now, and everyone is reading it. It's like the others, a lonely milkmaid and her salacious adventures in wanton sex with everyone from orcs, elves, slaves, commoners, dwarves, and even with a prince."

She paused. "The book details her adventures with the prince and his inability to get up his appendage until he sees two dogs eating a pile of burning refuse."

Prince Damon stood quietly for a moment and took a long breath.

Stephanie was surprised Prince Damon was so calm. She wondered if he didn't understand the significance of what she was telling him.

"Your grace, this is one of the most popular books in all of Vineland. We don't understand why there are so many copies, how they were distributed, and who put them out."

"Are you saying there is a hardcore erotic book in the public stating I have a tiny dick, and I can't get stiff until I see two dogs eating burning shit?"

"Your grace, that, I know this may sound difficult, is not the worst of it.

Inside each book, there are pamphlets. One is called *Ordinary Wit*. They call for the overthrow of the Holy Imperium using words like liberty, free speech, and tyranny, and they talk about your new taxes."

"Tyranny of what? From me? We have the Council of Crows; the merchants and nobles have spokespeople in the House of Lords. I know how to run a country, and these heathens have representation. I tax because of the needs of the people, not to hurt them!" Prince Damon ran his fingers through his thinning hair. Sir Thomas Casting walked up as the situation tumbled out of control. Prince Damon, the man child in charge of the Holy Imperium, and Sir Thomas Casting, Minister of the Lords and Minister of the Armies, stood tall, strong-armed, and strong-willed. He *ran* the Holy Imperium while Prince Damon played party thrower. The two men were complete opposites of each other.

"My Lord, the House of Lords has not met since before the Battle of the Reaping. You dismissed them during the war and saw fit to have the people's demands brought to court monthly," reminded General Casting. He stood taller than the prince, holding more of a stately figure. His secretary, Victor Parish, slipped over to Victoria Parish, who stood off to the side, taking notes and nodded, whispering something inaudible to each other. They both had attached themselves to the council without being asked directly by anyone.

"I hate those complainers. Can't they mind their betters? I mean, I am a man of the people; I know what the commoners need, and they need this fucking party. I'm throwing it for them. We will have so many guests in the ballroom, and I've asked for the public squares to have music and clothing houses making masks for the public to buy. We get profits, and they get some profits."

"My prince," and General Casting bowed and returned up. "I agree; this printing press must be found, confiscated, and destroyed. The books are just books; if you react aggressively, more people will read them. The pamphlets are more of an issue. I suggest..."

"No, no, no! They are children, and if they wish to act as such, a firm hand and a strong father are what they need. Collect every book and every pamphlet, stack them in public squares, and burn them. Burn every single last one of them."

"My prince, your Wildcats are busy guarding you and the visiting dignitaries before the party, and the Copperheads are already over-stressed with security duties; who will you get to round up books and pamphlets all over Hudson City and the other city-states you control?"

"Bishop Devon, get your Blue Templar out in the streets, rounding up these texts and burning them in the town squares for all to see. If anyone struggles, burn them too; I'll not have this blasphemy read anywhere in my country!"

Bishop Devon nodded with a stern smile and dismissed himself.

Knowing he lost this debate, General Casting frowned and excused himself to speak to Madam Diana Thompson, who represented the guilds and merchants about the budget and deficit Prince Damon was creating.

Doc - History Written by Losers

Maynard led the two horses Doc had procured, giving each of the animals rest as they journeyed from Olde Ridgewatch south, past the port of Lackmore, to the city of Affectus. Doc had obtained different copies of the *Post Enquirer* and the *Hudson City Journal* and was catching up on the news of Vineland as they slowly walked the horses down the road. Maynard knew he had plenty to learn, but Doc felt changed after what the papers were calling the Olde Ridgewatch Massacre and started treating Maynard more as an equal or at least with more respect.

"Do we have my medicines, Maynard, for the rest of the trip? I'm doing fine; I just want to make sure, trying to be more mindful of the creeping fear that plagues me," Doc said through gritted teeth, his pipe full of reefer mixed with southern tobacco from the fields of the Rosewood Dominion. The smoke a mixture of yellow, white and jade puffed out and melted into the air.

"Yes, we should be sufficiently stocked unless we're robbed, sir," said Maynard.

"Let's hope it doesn't come to that. I'd rather not have to kill anyone ever again directly. Who knows what would happen to them," Doc said.

"And to us," Maynard finished mumbling to himself.

Maynard was very aware of the use of his power and what it could do to him. He wondered if his fingernails would ever grow back. Doc had advised him that with every use of his power, it would have a cost. A true expert could push the price in a specific direction. Most trained magic users who mastered this technique traded time and used a piece of themselves to cast. This caused most users of power to age quickly and have their bodies break down. It's why stories show mages and witches looking old and haggard. Doc had shown Maynard how to prepare defensive and offensive workings for trips. Doc ran his fingers over his smooth head remembering how he'd given up all his hair because a highwayman attempted to kill him while he traveled on a trip similar to this.

Maynard had often wondered how old Doc was but had failed to find out. The staff he carried was one of the oldest items he'd ever seen, and the thought of it echoed every time he looked at it. Previously, in drunken stupors, Doc had let on that he'd expanded his age and had lived longer than most people around him but had not explained the process or the price. *What would the cost be to live an extended life*, Maynard pondered.

Maynard gently pushed Doc in the right direction as their feet tapped up and down on the brick-lined road. The newspaper Doc read was blocking his eyesight.

Doc coughed. "It's funny. How many city-states does Prince Damon hold?"

"There's over ten major city-states in Vineland. The big ones: Hudson City and the surrounding territories, Olde Ridgewatch, Grimwood, The Republic of Wind in all its vastness, Lackmore, which we passed," Maynard said, naming off the city-states.

Doc mumbled to himself while Maynard spoke as his own thoughts battled with voices he could only hear. He stopped Maynard from continuing. "Thank you for sending those letters, by the way. I didn't need to deal with any Holy Imperium Soldiers back there and it was important we get those off to the right people."

"You're welcome," and Maynard continued. "Well, there's Affectus and its open borders, Waterhurst and Cinderpool; the Rosewood Dominion isn't a city but a series of fortified plantations and strongholds like Wheathold and Liathland."

"You're correct, but it's best to collect them under the name of The Rosewood Dominion. There's also the Crescent City. Do you know you can't bury the dead there? They either burn them or put them in crypts and the lovely Magnoliafield where we get our illegal reefer." Doc pulled on his pipe as if oxygen only came from that device and nowhere else, and the tiny bit of reefer lit inside glowed and calmed him. He continued gripping the pipe in his teeth. Smoke the color of bright purple filtered out of the pipe. Doc laughed quietly; the ease of his burden diminished.

"That doesn't even count the dwarven strongholds like Steelsburg and Colehampton or the city-states near the Grave Reach River constantly under siege like Honeybreak." Maynard interrupted. "There was the city of Ursula, but nothing lives there now except birds of prey and sickness."

Doc turned and Maynard opened his mouth, but he stopped for a moment, guilt bubbling up inside of Maynard for mentioning it. Doc's power had made the town of Ursula a destitute plague-filled metropolis, slowly decaying from the Smoldering Plague, which started after he'd killed his two friends, Umar and Jezebel Everfall, and countless other warriors during the Battle of the Reaping. His twisted storms filled with toxic winds swept the plains of Ursula, and he'd tossed lightning like a child tosses stones into a pond, leaving nothing but decay and death, all for a hollow thought that the fledgling Holy Imperium was superior to the Nation of Stouya and the Legion of Carigreed. Doc concentrated and pushed the voices away, mumbling to himself. He took a flask out from his faded military jacket and took a swig. The burning barely doused the voices deep inside. He handed the bottle to Maynard, who took a sip of guilt and remorse with Doc.

"Prince Damon and his nobles say we now live in a grand time, but all is not well, is it? The nobles live on the high, but their slaves, goblins, orcs, and elves work their fingers to the bone and drop dead trying. Their children are sold like cattle and pigs, and the rest, if their spirits aren't snapped by the yoke of the Holy Imperium, are hunted like wild game." He cleared his eyes of dust or tears, Maynard wasn't sure. "Blue Templar are burning books," He stopped for a second, lost in his own fury. "Burning books at the prince's request because they don't like what people are reading, more like they're scared people will think differently or learn something," Doc said with anger lining his face.

Maynard held back a sigh. He'd heard these comments before in a drunken stupor, but this time, it felt different. After the Olde Ridgewatch Massacre, everything felt different.

227

"The prince makes demands of the royals, the royals push those demands on the nobles, who piss on the merchant class who shit on the commoners all while a slave class holds up the economy without being recognized, and when it gets bad, Prince Damon blames it on the anyone but himself."

Maynard looked at him, this worn-down mage still full of righteous fury. *He genuinely loved Vineland.* Liberty and freedom were not just words thrown around to make him look principled or worn on a tricorne hat like he was in a religious cult like the Red Sashes. That group of followers had taken the words of the Maker and twisted them. They worshiped the Templar like proud boys and girls in grammar school and, more importantly, their leader, Prince Damon, like he was a god equal to the Maker herself.

"Book burners," Doc spat, reading a headline in the paper. "They're the worst, weasels and cowards, the lot of them. Prince Damon and his peers can't stand the thought of someone lower than them, someone they don't know, finding a little joy in their lives or learning a different viewpoint," said Doc as he slightly choked. He shook the paper he was reading as they walked and folded it. He took a quick nip of the flask and handed it back to Maynard.

"Prince Damon is lord and commands the city-states under the control of the Holy Imperium. His word is law backed by the Maker in all her glory, and his actions are pure and just in many people's eyes, Doc." Maynard said, stoking Doc's rage through debate, "At least that's how the commoners see it. The majority of people in Vineland worship the Maker and see Prince Damon, the bastard son of King Geordie of Great Brightland, as the rightful ruler."

Doc looked at Maynard. "We must show them the truth, dam it all, that he's a bankrupt, morally corrupt fool of a man-child that only wants what's best for him and couldn't care less about anyone else."

Doc thought on Maynard's statement. "Ahh, here is a teaching lesson. What do you think of dwarves Maynard?"

"From what I know, the dwarves were here before humans came to Vineland, along with the elves, goblins, and orcs; they work hard, are superb craftspeople, are wary of magic, make a impressive beer, and invented vodka, the printing press, and owl lamps. They put family first and are strong in battle; some say a dwarven shield wall is the best defense against a cavalry charge. Obviously, there is more to them as a culture. Would you like me to carry on?" asked Maynard.

"No, no, that is fine. Do you know who made the first printing press? You mentioned it. The dwarves take credit, but do you know who it was?" Doc asked.

"I always heard it was a dwarve. They presented it as a gift to King Christopher and Queen Erica the Red," said Maynard.

"A dwarve presented it to the King and Queen. Yeah, sure. But his apprentice was the one who thought it up and built it, printed off the first copies of a pamphlet spreading it around an underground dwarven kingdom."

"You're saying his apprentice wasn't a dwarve?" asked Maynard.

"I'm saying the dwarve who presented the first printing press was an outcast, and in so much, the only person who would be his apprentice was a teenage goblin. The dwarve taught the goblin to read, write, and mold steel with her hands. The goblin invented the press, and the dwarve took the credit."

Maynard pushed up his glasses.

"History is written by the winners, but with the printing press, that changes everything, that puts the power to educate, the power to read into the hands of not just the royals and the nobles but everywhere, and as we have seen from the smoke that billows outside of churches in Hudson City and the city squares, it threatens the very foundations of government," Doc stated. He took a massive inhale off his pipe and offered it to Maynard.

"The Gray General is recruiting a militia now to protect Affectus and some of the other areas against what he's calling highwaymen and gangs of thieves," Doc exhaled as he spoke.

"What does that mean?" Maynard asked.

"War, I hate the prince and what I helped create," Doc stopped and looked to the sky. "Maker's luscious ass, thousands will die. I may not survive all those voices." His stance weaved slightly. He changed the subject, like a scholar flipping through book pages. "Do you know how dwarves make their owl lamps?"

"No, it's a closely held secret."

Doc spat on his fingers and put out his pipe.

"You said we're equals now. You have power within you; the only difference is you were humble enough to give me Gaston's staff back, and I have years of experience. Frankly, I'm stingier than you, but do you know why? Do you know why I'm mean, bitter, and always angry?"

Maynard sighed and looked away from Doc, feeling this conversation was useless. "You took what remained of your daughter's life force and consumed it as power, as we did to Runt and Stitch, and used it to kill thousands of people, cursing you to hear their screams and pleas as they died for the rest of your unnaturally long life?" He left out a breath of air.

"Yes. But not just that. The drugs and the drinking help me with the voices; it's the unease of which I have too much knowledge. Dwarven owl lamps, the ones the rich use to light the way at night, flameless light that never goes out. Only dwarves can make the lamps. No human has ever been able to figure out how except me. And knowing that makes me bitter and angry, you see. To much knowledge."

"How would knowing that make you bitter?" asked Maynard.

"Because nothing is virtuous, or proper or how it should be. There are no heroes, and dwarves are not morally good people as they should be, just as orcs and goblins are not inherently evil." Doc stopped and moved closer. "I want Vineland to be free from itself." He breathed on Maynard. It smelled of onions and reefer, and Maynard held his breath. "Dwarves and humans are no better than elves, goblins, and orcs; that is what I want Vineland to be, all of us equal in our sins against each other. Humans are awful and far from noble, but humans still hold dwarves in high regard. They build and make strong walls for all of us, but not all power is what it seems. It takes a soul to light an owl lamp, my friend, a soul. Each color, each light represents a soul." Doc sighed. "The brighter the light, the younger the soul."

"How does nobody know this?"

"Dwarves keep their secrets deep within," Doc said. "And now, you know, and that knowledge will make you bitter inside because when you look around a big city like this, you realize they don't care how they get their owl lamps because it doesn't matter. Nothing changes until it affects a person individually."

"How do we change them?"

"We shake the foundations of the Holy Imperium and create a society based on a living and breathing document that withstands the tyranny and greed that we all hold in our hearts. We get those who keep this land together and bind them to the foundation of a new country, a united Vineland," said Doc.

Maynard wondered if the reefer and wizard salt that Doc had sniffed made him talk, as if anything he said made any sense.

"We tell them the truth until they can't ignore the cruelty in front of them any longer."

Alysha - Streets of Despair

Hold onto the oblivion, she whispered to everyone and no one all at once.

Alysha woke to the smell of the East Thamesbridge tea wafting through the air. "Where are we?"

"You're safe, but not for long." Helena smiled. "You look like shit, sweetie."

"I just woke up, and that's the first thing you say to me?"

"After mumbling about oblivion and the maidens of Judith. Yeah, I figured you would want to know the current circumstances of our situation and how you look."

Alysha scratched at her eyes, smiling lightly, feeling the weight of the last few days fold in on her all over again. She ached but felt the air in her lungs and her best friend by her side.

"Glad you're back, Alysha."

"Glad you're with me, Helena. Where's my-" she grasped around for Stormkiss.

"On the other side of the bed. Your axe is safe next to you. I moved it a bit so you wouldn't slice yourself open as you fought the fever. You passed out and have been recovering for some time. Felix, the student who saved us in the swamp, confirmed we didn't have the Smoldering Plague and bandaged us up. He said to drink this tea after I mix some of this crushed fungus into it." Helena placed a white and pink powder into some dark tea.

"He said it will help fight, what was the word. Infliction, flexion," she paused and snapped her fingers. "Infection! That's it. He told me weird tales about little animals we can't see getting into our wounds and blood and making us sick. I don't really get it."

"Tastes like shit, but cheers." Alysha pounded the warm tea down. "Head feels like garbage; garbage caught fire."

"You said I said something about oblivion and the three graces or maidens of Judith?" Alysha asked as she swung her legs off the bed.

"Yeah, I dunno. I didn't write down what you mumbled. It was just a fever dream, I'm sure," Helena shrugged.

"Three graces," Alysha grasped at her dream, its threads slipping away. "I remember three witches or wise women." She sat up, head foggy, and her hand touched Stormkiss, and she gripped the handle. "The three graces of Judith were Rowan, Blacklace, and Grapeseed. Remember, we had a neighbor named Rowan. She lived across the river, Rowan Wightland was her name."

"The crazy hag that lightning struck when she tried to escape?"

"Yeah, after Jared Blackheart and his monks burnt our homesteads, they enslaved us and marched us to Counselor City. For whatever reason, Rowan managed to survive the onslaught and then spoke to me as we walked. Those two kids that ran away..." Alysha paused. Helena glanced at her as they both remembered the tearing of flesh and the war dogs. Alysha pushed past that memory. "It was more than that, her escape and the lightning hitting her. She followed Judith, and she didn't die when that happened."

"Sure, as shit looked like she wanted to kill herself, at least I can remember; I wasn't all there after what happened to my family." Helena visibly shook. "Bastards, all of those monks should die."

Alysha's mind spun as she got up, holding onto her bandaged wounds. She wasn't ready to fight, not totally recovered. She felt the weakness inside her veins. Yet she knew they weren't safe where they rested. *The followers of the Maker beckon the gates of this grim city.*

"Where's this Felix? The Holy Imperium is already here. It's too late to do anything to save this city. We need to escape. Go to another city-state, go to the woods, anywhere but here. We came to warn them, but it's too late."

"He went out and said he wanted to talk to his professor about what you said. He'll be back soon. It's late afternoon. You were out for some time."

Alysha put her feet on the ground and stood. She was shaky and weak.

"Feel like I've had too much to drink."

"You look it. I don't know how much you remember, but Grimwood is chaos, according to Felix." Helena relayed what Felix had informed her of. "The city council left due to the plague, and the few remaining city guards are weak and can barely guard the walls of the city. Felix said rival gangs rule the streets, and the university, what's left of it, is one of the only safe spaces. When the Holy Imperium comes, this city can't withstand it. There's nobody to warn because there's nobody to care about anyone here. We made a mistake coming here."

"Shit."

Alysha looked into Helena's eyes, and giving each other a moment of calm before reality crashed in.

"I'm in no state to travel yet, but we need to leave," said Alysha.

"Any idea where we could go? This city is done for," agreed Helena.

"There are farms to the west and south, until the Litchbury Mire begins. Only a few choices, there's the Erie Sea Lane that hugs the shores of the Erie Sea, a few questionable swamp roads, which most don't take because of the looming tower in the middle of the mire. Or we head south, which the Holy Imperium Army is patrolling, same could be said west of the city as well. We are stuck unless we go into the swamp but somehow avoid the army that is about to surround the city," said Alysha.

"Right, this is awful. I wish we could just go back home."

"That's not a bad idea. We could go back to Wolf Hills, start over and rebuild a house," Alysha said hopefully lost in the fantasy of the thought.

"Some of the farmland must be usable still."

Alysha took a deep breath looking up and tried to focus. *You betray yourself and Judith returning home before your work is complete. Nothing can grow from ruins without the blood of vengeance to water the roots of Vineland's foundation.*

"I mean, we could do it. We could do it together," Helena shrugged. "We could see what Felix thinks. I wonder what the university is going to do. I doubt the religious zealots would want this university to teach the way they do now. I bet they get firm and start burning texts and scrolls that don't align with the Maker."

"Helena, you, and I don't need a man to save us. We aren't princesses," Alysha remarked. "We're survivors, fighters. Let's gather what we have in case we need to leave quickly. Grab what we can, but don't make it too obvious. You think he has drinkable water we can take?"

"Yeah, I'll fill up a few skins and make sure I have more fungus snot for you." Helena began to move around the lab, then stopped, thinking. "Alysha, he asked about the sword. I didn't know what to tell him, how to tell him."

She looked at Helena and buried memories returned quickly. She was there when Junior Wolfe died. It was so quick. When the Genteel Monks attacked out of the woods by their bonfire in autumn, Jared Blackheart came out of the shadows and killed Junior with a spiked mace and his dark shield. He murdered Alysha's mother, Marie, and Helena's parents. Moments later, the Genteel Monks drowned Helena's younger siblings in the river. Those strong enough to work were chained and taken to Counselor City and pressed into servitude and slavery.

"Helena, do you think we could ever go back after what happened down by the water's edge?"

She looked at Alysha and then stared past her as the memories swept over her. Alysha saw sorrow and mourning, and her fury, and a lust for retribution grew.

"No, there is no going back."

The door to the front of the office opened, and Felix walked through in his monstrous form, looking like a half-raven half-goblin in his dark cloak, gloves, and mask to filter out the bad air. He pulled off his face mask.

"You're awake," he blurted. "I have questions and answers. Helena, Alysha, tell me of my brother and why you have my family sword."

Felix Wolf entered his laboratory, tossing his mask off.

"Talk, I must pack up what I can carry on my back. The city will fall in the coming days. The last boats are leaving the city; so far, only a few know, but it will be hysteria before too long."

"Thank you for saving Helena and me."

"I was just gathering materials for my experiments; I'm no soldier like my brother. I don't rescue maidens but hate the intolerance of those who prey

235

on the weak." He stopped and pushed his receding hairline back. "I'm sorry, my mind and mouth don't work simultaneously. I'm sure you would have done the same for me if the situation had been reversed. This city, at least what it used to mean, didn't stand for the ignorance possessed by those that attacked you."

Alysha braced herself before dropping the news to Felix. "Your brother was killed defending our valley's homesteads by the Genteel Monks led by Jared of the Blackheart family. He carries his shield, Midnight's Veil, and he shattered our lives, and your brother's, using that shield and his war mace," said Alysha as she looked at Felix, a doctor's bag in his hand. He stopped packing and looked at the ground.

"He gave me this," and she pulled out an ornate pipe. "His last moments were of you and your family's legacy." She walked toward the scientist and pressed the pipe into his twitchy hands. He smelled of sweat, cinnamon, and ash.

"He had his sword with him, but we were taken as captives. Later I came across it in my work as a smith in Counselor City. It was reforged with star metal into what Helena has now. It's shorter but just as good."

Helena walked up and unsheathed the sword, presenting the blade to Felix. "Our thanks for saving us. This is the only thing we can give, and it was yours." She bowed. Alysha had not seen Helena act with reverence in a long time.

"He was a kind man, wove a fine story, and kept our town at ease until the soldiers came, but by then, it was too late. They burnt the town and most homesteads in the hills and valleys."

"'Tis true, Felix."

He looked at the sword, took a deep breath, pocketed the pipe, and walked away, turning his back on the two women. Alysha knew he was going through a series of emotions as Felix's academic mind tried to process his brother's loss.

"We'll smoke the Wolfe family pipe when we are safe together and hopefully free of war and this bloody plague," the man said stiffly. "Helena, keep the sword. Use it to kill those that would harm you. I bet you are better at it than me. I'm a bit more of a thinker and tinkerer."

Felix began to move around the lab again. "I need my journals, clothes, a mask, and a microscope. You're welcome to change into my clothes if you wish to make your travel better. I hope to get all three of us on a boat heading west. Grimwood University was given one of the towers at Pinelight Island to house their library and potentially to create a new university on the island itself by the Republic of the Wind."

Helena and Alysha changed into a medley of clothes, replacing anything ruined, ripped, or ill-fitting.

Alysha laughed even as it hurt her chest. "Bruised ribs or not, we look a mess."

"It's fine. We don't have a choice, and the city is in a place where nobody will care. I think I have enough to bribe our way on; plus, I have journals that belong in the library."

Felix shoved laboratory equipment into the underground portion of the laboratory. "Help me move this stone." Helena gathered dust and threw it down on the ground. "Try to hide what I can. Possibly in a year or two, I can retrieve the rest if the place isn't found during the ransacking of the city."

He took a deep breath as the stone moved. Alysha grunted and the stone slipped into place.

"Felix, we have no money to get on this boat."

"It's fine. I'm sure they'll take you. I'll say you're my assistants."

"Felix, we're both armed. We look far from scholarly assistants."

The women followed Felix out of his laboratory and moved east and north along the city wall, away from the open, unused eastern gate. The city was alive, but the movement and noise came from other portions of the town.

"There wasn't much staff left at the university and less so students. Most left before the quarantine started." Felix sniffed. "Now that I think about it, it may have caused more harm than good, as those who did not wish to quarantine spread the sickness to those they escaped." He stopped for a second from the fast-paced walk they started. "There were reports of homes and manors falling silent as constables or family members found those inside all dead from sickness. They were either boarded up or burnt across the city's outskirts."

"They should close that gate. Aren't they worried an army or something else would come through it?"

"You were down there; nobody wants to be down there if they can manage it. The forest is too thick, the poisonfire fog too dangerous even for an army to try against." Felix shouldered his bag. "We're moving out of the university's neighborhoods, into the Crile Street gang territory. If something happens, let me talk. If I say run, you run, make for the port, or if not, back to the gate, it may be shitty inside the graveyard, but you don't want the Crile gang capturing you."

"What's so bad about them?" Helena asked.

"The Crile gang is into extortion, security for local businesses, and sneak thievery. They own brothels and gambling halls frequented by students," Felix whispered as he walked quickly down the street, the road's brick top coming up to meet him. "I used to make booze for them on the cheap. It helped me pay for essentials before we had a misunderstanding." He stopped and pushed them into an alley as three tough-looking young hooligans walked by a stout, scared female and two sinister fellows. They waited silently in the shadow of the door ajar, the smell of rotting food and death pouring out of the hovel. "They like to cut off people's ears and hang them in the Crile Street public square about a block away. They've spread into other areas since the quarantine. I don't think they would sell out to the Holy Imperium, but what do I know."

Alysha loosened Stormkiss and kept it at the ready. She felt pain spiral up her leg and arm, her wounds still fresh. She felt a bit dizzy from her fever.

"We need to keep moving. I'll need to rest soon; I'm still not recovered."

"You know those three?" asked Helena.

"Yeah, the girl is known as Corporal Chunk. She used to be the leader of a poorly trained group of mercenaries; she has orange hair and is pretty stout in body, and the youngest, dressed in grays and black with stark white hair, is Manchester. He has blue eyes and yellow ones. They say he sees ghosts, can cast curses, and is quick with a blade. The one in the shadows is Beastie, with dark, shaggy hair slicked back and yellow eyes. It may be part goblin. He's always around, listening and learning. A nimble-fingered thief, I hear.

All three together are a team of trouble in a broken city. Best we stay away from them."

Felix had forgone his mask and had it stuck in his satchel; he said he had two others, but those wouldn't work awfully long as he only had a minor portion of moss left, one large canister, and three other canisters much smaller. He mentioned he wasn't too worried about the plague now that the Holy Imperium was attacking. Before they left his laboratory, he wondered if the quarantine was being used by whoever was left in charge to give cover to agents inside the city before it was seized.

"Let's go two more blocks than right and left and down steep stairs, then onto the boardwalk and out through a wall door and another boardwalk. There should be a dingy we can use to row out to the ship. My professor is waiting for us." Felix said to Helena and Alysha.

"Waiting for who, Felix?" Helena asked briskly.

He started walking and turned back. "I said I have my journals, a student, and an apprentice who needed out of the city. I advised them you were both clean from the Smoldering Plague."

"This professor, you trust them?" Helena asked.

Alysha looked back. She was carrying Stormkiss, ready for any problems but still in great pain.

Felix took out three vials of bubbly pink liquid. He drank one and handed the other two back. "This witch pepper will help perk you up for two or three hours. We'll be wide awake. After that, we'll crash hard and will need to eat and rest."

There were shouts and screams at a distance and a low rumbling.

Helena took the vial. "I could use the pick me up. Gonna die sooner rather than later."

They both downed them and tossed the vial. The glass shattered on the stone walkway. The witch pepper was a sugary, bubbly mixture that burned on the way down with a faint lick of strawberry flavor.

They rounded the corner, and Alysha immediately felt more awake, as if she could open her eyes further and sense more.

"What is that drink?"

"Mixture of carbonated sugar water, herbs, and vodka. Found the herbs in an apothecary by the wharf in the summertime. Amazing elixir, but in pure form, not like this, can be highly addictive. I saw it make a rat's heart explode if they got too much of it." He took a breath and stood up straighter. "That was very diluted." He smiled back. "If my measurements were correct."

Felix ducked into an alcove and pushed Alysha and Helena into it, covering them both in a large cloak, hoping to look like a shadow. Several rough-looking hoodlums ran by.

"This way, this way, to the south gate."

"Something must be up," Helena whispered.

"I think it's everyone for themselves," Alysha said.

"Me too."

"If this doesn't work, I don't know what to do," said Felix, looking at the women. He shouldered his pack and gestures for them to follow again.

* * *

The night march of General Flints army had gone well, and the column of Holy Imperium soldiers was in competent order as dawn broke. The vanguard had taken a small village near the city before townsfolk had woken up to work their fields, and they found no ghosts on the edge of the eastern Grimwood forest.

General Flint waited at the middle of the column as they edged the woods, pushing his men on. He watched as his favorite scout, Ian Shortstride, worked his horse toward him.

"What news?"

"The forest will not burn, even with oil. The gases are too dangerous and could wreak more havoc on the army if we tried that way," Ian answered curtly. "Once you get close to the forest, the winds shift as if-" the elf paused. "I've spent time inside, sir, and made my way to the city's edge searching for the two murderers. I saw the gas take one of the Genteel Monks myself. It's folly to test those boundaries. You command the army, sir. Posting two platoons to travel up and down the forest line would be safer to ensure none escape the city. You may find a few here and there but nothing to break your flank or mount a feasible attack as you approach from the south and west."

"Blackheart's men said they could burn it, and you suggest not to. I know the history of this place. The massacre occurred near the edge of the city of your kind and others."

"That was years before my existence. The forest is large, but with twenty or so mounted scouts, they could provide intelligence to your command post to stop any flanking. You won't see any cavalry from the Gray Vultures come from eastern Grimwood. The eastern gate's bridge is destroyed, and there is nothing but death that lingers in the unfinished mote."

"So be it. Get your men on it. I'll have Ridgesnake send the other platoon. I'm disappointed you didn't find the murderers. Two females, you said."

"Yes, sir, they took out several of the Genteel Monk's soldiers during our investigation near the city. We believe they had help getting through the forest, by a local."

"Yet you feel there is no immediate threat?"

"Absolutely not. Black Willow Falls, the eastern mote where the Grimwood gate bridge remains shattered, nothing lives down there. The poisonfire gas will kill any that linger on the mote floor. Besides any group of soldiers would get lost or have an accident. We have been lucky so far on the night march. It was easier with Jared Blackheart away."

"We shall see what the rest of the monks say upon their return. You know what I plan Ian, Jared will be back and will eventually oversee Grimwood, unless I send him back to the capital after the attack. I don't see a reason I would linger at this husk of a city after I have purified it of its sinners."

Ian Shortstride bowed in silence.

Flint grabbed his horse. "Patrol the eastern portion of the area, capture, and kill any that try to escape. Now I have a city to take."

"As you wish," Ian said.

Flint looked on at Grimwood in the morning light. Ian took in a breath and hoped that those strong enough would survive the rising tide as Flints Army came to the southern and western gates of the city of Grimwood. The outer portion of the city not protected by the mote would burn. Everyone

241

not leaving before the sight of the army would be put to death. The large siege engines moved slowly up the roads as the sight of a lone tower deep on the horizon peaked from the first rays of the sun. The smell of milkweed, hill mint, and primrose rode the wind.

Hudson City - Selling Tomorrow

"This plan of ours, this order 1776, will make governing the Holy Imperium easier?"

Prince Damon looked at the stack of papers written by Bishop Devon, Admiral Howl, and Minister Shannon with bored concern.

"Yes, we believe so. We wanted to know your thoughts after reading these past few nights," said Minister Shannon.

The prince thumbed the pages in front of him. Jasper stood behind him with Brock Rustblade at his other shoulder. They were the two primary guards for Prince Damon today. Jasper thumbed his sword and occasionally tapped it to keep his attention. Maker's round tits, he hated lunch meetings. The prince had been taking them more often lately, with only a portion of his council, and they ended up discussing and making judgments without including enough sane people to stop the prince from making shit decisions, and he could do nothing but stand and watch. Sir Rustblade witnessed it as well.

Jasper breathed in at the thought of Prince Damon reading the massive parchment before him, knowing he had not read more than the first few paragraphs. The last few nights, the prince had binged on wizard salt and imported wine from Great Brightland with Laura Speers and her valet, a tall blond woman named Pearl Daniels with a sharp nose and wit. This was Jasper's third day in a row on guard duty. He'd escalated Brock Rustblade to the status of Wildcat to help him run personal guard duty as he'd become a trusted confidant, and they ran the nights when Prince Damon wanted to be something other than royalty. This was at the suggestion of General Casting.

It strengthened the Wildcats but weakened the city guards as Rustblade was still transitioning into his new position. He would spend his off days training his replacement in the guards. The only tricky part was that Rustblade was not of noble birth, and this grated on Joseph Blackheart, so he ensured the two were never around each other. He had Prince Damon raise Rustblade using falsified papers to get around to it when he was knighted with the backing of General Casting and Sir Leadwalls.

Prince Damon took a bite of his Bitterleak Burger. The man loved these sandwiches and ate them every other day during the noon hour. He spoke with his mouth open, getting a vinegary, sweet tomato paste on the parchment marked "Order 1776".

"This officially bans the profane religion from existence," he said, asking and telling those who sat at the rectangular table.

"It makes it legal to burn, mutilate, and hang any worshipers of the old religion; it also puts a tax on churches that do not follow your faith," said Bishop Devon. "The religion has been banned by the Holy Church for years. This makes the crime more serious."

"That's interesting. The Holy Church isn't taxed, but followers of the Divine Church and the People's Church will be taxed. This could bring in revenue, help pay our debts with our other taxes, and affect everyone equally," said Prince Damon. He dipped his fried potato sticks in vinegar and slurped from a goblet.

Jasper wondered if General Castings knew about this plan, the tax, although necessary, would cause issues with the Nation of Stouya, whose people mainly worshiped the Divine Church, which was similar to the Holy Church but with more pomp and ceremony and also the Legion of Carigreed whose people worshiped the very open People's Church. Both religions were like the Holy Church but had enough nuances that a holy war could break out at any time if the ruling people decided to discriminate too much. Jasper wondered if he could meet with General Castings in passing soon to inform him of this Order 1776.

The prince yawned, and the others ate. His attention was drifting.

"Your grace, the order is based on the Holy Church's understandings and comes at the," Minister Shannon paused for a moment. She was toying with partially eating Bitterleak Burger. "It has your father's blessing."

Prince Damon put his food down and wiped his mouth, taking another sip from his goblet, his slightly pounced stomach sucked in.

"My father," Prince Damon said his ears turned a light crimson. "He writes to you but not to me."

Minister Shannon swallowed a cup of cool wine and deferred. "My messages do not come directly from King Geordie; they come from his court council; I am your Minister of Letters and Ambassador from Great Brightland, your grace; I receive information from sources, including Great Brightland's Minister of Letters. Any direct communications from King Geordie or other family members are sent directly to you and unopened on pain of death."

She did well there, Jasper thought.

Prince Damon nodded, turned his head away, and stood abruptly, turning his back on those sitting. They sat, unsure whether to stand or sit, and continued eating. He put his hand up to the right, back to them, indicating they were fine.

"Apologies. I thought I may sneeze and did not wish to interrupt your meal," Prince Damon said. Jasper and Joseph looked away slightly as the prince cleared his eyes and turned back to the people sitting.

Bishop Devon interrupted. "Other than raising taxes on other religions, your grace, Order 1776, once you are crowned King of Vineland, would promote families by forcing those women who are unmarried by eighteen to have an arranged marriage through the help of the local government, all be it a sheriff, mayor, or ruling family all through the Providences of the Holy Imperium. This would bring more growth and cohesiveness to all areas of the community. The order also especially outlaws any books, written texts, and pamphlets that do not align with the teachings of the Holy Church unless under direct supervision of the Silver Ivy League's Council. It also gives the Holy Imperium's regulations on those universities by reviewing their finances and educational materials so that they fall in line with the Holy Church and thus your Holy Imperium, your government."

"Excellent, there are too many spinsters about; some of them even attend universities. To many of them, as far as I'm concerned. A woman belongs at home, caring for their family and making babies. I love women, I think all women are strong, and they are strongest when they back their husbands and take care of their children."

Those in attendance nodded along, smiling, and congratulating themselves, which made the prince happy. Jasper felt as if he could vomit.

"And you want me to sign this now before I'm crowned king so that it would take effect upon my crowning?" Prince Damon said. He stood and walked around the table, running his short, stubby fingers through his greasy, thinning hair.

They were sitting inside Prince Damon's chambers, and their mid-day meal was nearly over.

"Tell me more about the universities. Did this order 1776 go through Victoria Parish's hands as well? She is one of my trusted advisors," said Prince Damon as he licked his lips.

"No, it did not," said Admiral Howl quietly.

"Tell me, Prince Damon. I heard the play write, and actor Laura Speers has performed for you recently," Bishop Devon said, changing the subject. Prince Damon's short attention span had left them as he thought about Victoria Parish's long legs, but he shifted back to important matters.

"Yes! These past few nights, she and a friend have been going over lines in my apartments. They've a most invigorating show they will be putting on," said Prince Damon with a smirk.

"Miss Lane and her friend Pearl Daniels are quite talented people. Gorgeously talented people."

The past few nights, Pearl Daniels and Laura Speers got high on wizard salt and vodka, ending last night where Prince Damon dressed up like a journalist, wearing a wig and, barking like a dog while receiving a spanking from both women. Sir Jasper had to ensure Prince Damon was safe, leaving Sir Brock outside. He found the actress and the valet wearing nun habits, standing over the prince in bed as they urinated on him, covered in the wanted posters of Hunter Young and Beneatha Franklin and hundreds of coins. All three were laughing hysterically. Jasper looked around to ensure the room was safe and closed the door to let them continue their debauchery. The prince had not asked him to attend the festivities which disappointed Jasper, but he remained professional throughout his duty. Every day he questioned increasingly if he was still a close friend to the man he grew up with. The prince had once been his best friend and confidant, but the prince had pulled away more as The Triumphant Masquerade neared. In circumstances like this, the pain inside him was deep, and he swallowed it down even further. He still loved the man and thought that Prince Damon had loved him, but he was unsure, and the loss of that love and, even more importantly, the friendship left Jasper hollow.

"This order is important; I like what I've read. Just know as much power as I give to the Holy Church, I am its leader here in Vineland. All of Vineland, is that clear?"

Admiral Howl and Minister Shannon nodded quietly as Prince Damon stabbed his finger directly into Bishop Devon's chest. "Say it for all to hear Bishop, I, Bishop Devon, worship the Maker herself and the ordained Prince Damon of House Farover as the leader of the Holy Church and all of Vineland."

The bishop's mouth trembled and smiled with a shaky self-assurance, "I, Bishop."

"On your knees, bishop. On your knees," Sir Jasper and Sir Brock stepped forward and around each side of the table closer to the bishop who clumsily, moved his chair. "Walk over here and get your knees, Bishop Devon," said Prince Damon. Looking weaker with each step, the bishop quietly shambled over, meek, and humbled. He was a strong man for his age, but with each step, he looked feebler. By the time he reached Prince Damon, Bishop was the dutiful, obeying servant Prince Damon wanted him to be. The prince cupped the old man's chin in his hand. Jasper tensed; he'd loosened his sword from his scabbard, and everyone in attendance was quiet. Every shuffle and movement echoed. The prince smiled. The bishop's guards, Brother Hewitt and Sister Temperance were outside the doors, Jasper thought, as if Prince Damon had heard Jasper think it.

"Brother Hewitt and Sister Temperance, step inside, please," screeched Prince Damon. "Watch your master kneel before me. Witness your prince's greatness."

The door opened, and Templar gasped. Prince Damon smiled. They walked in, and Bishop Devon was kneeling in front of Prince Damon, who stood before him, the man's face held by Prince Damon of House Farover.

"Look at me in the eyes, Bishop, and say it," said Prince Damon. Admiral Howl flinched slightly, and the two bishop guards breathed in deeply.

The bishop, an older man by scores of years, looked up at Prince Damon in visible pain. The prince smiled momentarily, then stopped and looked down, a streak of meanness crossing his lined face.

"I, Bishop Devon, worship the Maker herself and the ordained Prince Damon of House Farover," Prince Damon squeezed the man's chin, and tears welled up in the bishop's eyes. He let go of him. "As the leader of the Holy Church and all of Vineland," said Bishop Devon in a choked voice.

The prince tapped his face slightly and guided him up.

"Good," he said aloud and whispered into the man's ear, smelling warm milk and vodka. "Tonight, you may join me, Laura Speers, and her friend Pearl Daniels."

Prince Damon did not bother to look at the two Blue Templar guards but dismissed them with a gesture, "Return to your posts. Now!"

* * *

"Did you see this trash, Conway?"

Murrow Edward the editor of the *Post Enquirer* was reading the *Hudson City Journal*, now outlawed and illegal by Prince Damon's request.

"This trash- we broke the *Hudson City Journal*, yet it's still getting published and read just as much as before. Even the nobles are quoted in it anonymously. This Olivia Franklin should be jailed and hanged for treason," said Murrow.

They sat in Murrow's office, reading the illegal paper and smoking corncob pipes. Conway poured whiskey into a clay mug. The air was light, and the smoke from the pipe was heavy with rumor and speculation.

They were supposed to review the *Post Enquirer* front-page spread for tomorrow's paper. The paper sold on the corners of streets all over the city. Yet the *Hudson City Journal* and the *Post Enquirer* rivalry lingered around the capital, first making it into the hands of the lower classes and filtering up into noble houses.

"Olivia Franklin has the balls to call Prince Damon, a man with the blood of the Maker in his veins, a liar and whore, like a drunk fishmonger. She has a price on her head now, but she is surely a dead man after today," said Murrow.

"I agree, I agree. But she can write. Bloody witch. Did you know a group of outlaws tarred and feathered tax collectors in Wolvenshire?" said Conway. "That's right outside the capital."

"I heard similar incidents in Affectus by my contacts in the Society of Shadows." Murrow took a pull off his pipe. "Probably was the Society of Shadows who did it themselves. I heard it happened in a few other places, like Affectus."

"I mean, it's Affectus. That's insane, considering the place is known for love and pacifism. It's the most open city in all of Vineland. I say there's not enough rule of law; too much liberty. Of course, we have the situation in Olde Ridgewatch and the riots around Lackmore, but these new taxes are starting to hurt everyone. Pisses off the masses."

"I'd love to see the bloody witch burnt at the stake naked."

Conway shifted in his chair uncomfortably. "Sure, does have guts, though. May not win friends with the nobles, but I mean, lower-class people agree with this story." He took the paper from Murrow and read the front headline.

"Yeah, these taxes hurt, but if we don't pay the soldiers from the last battles of the Crimson Struggle…" Murrow considered lost in thought. "If we let those debts linger, then there are just a bunch of pissed-off soldiers milling about, which could make life worse. More civil unrest. It's the prince's right to do it. It hurts me too, but we pay them it, right?" Murrow said. "Do we have any other story pitches to review?"

"My favorite newspaper carrier said several sails were stolen from one of the admiral's private ships, several deep red sails, which is odd, I'm keeping an eye on that, may lead to nothing." Conway shrugged, then jolted upright in his seat, "Oh! We can do a piece on some of the dignitaries arriving for The Triumphant Masquerade."

"That may be it; everyone loves reading about tarts and debutantes lusting for the royal prince. Who's rumored to be in the mix?" Murrow asked.

"So, we have some of the names the prince will mingle with, but they have no hopes of marriage due to their weak noble or royal bloodline like Kara Giannini, the ballerina," Conway paused for a second. "I saw her last year. She's in a class of her own."

"Go on, Conway, go on."

"There's Mae Bloomhood, the famous poet from the Four Queendoms; I heard her bodyguard, a knight named Lothar Waterguard, is more than a bodyguard." He winked. "Mae's in town to expand her works in the Holy Imperium."

"Miss Bloomhood has a way with words, and the knight is rumored to be the best horseman and archer anyone has ever seen."

"Horseman, sure, sure; I've also heard he's as big as a horse."

"Conway, that's enough." But he was smiling. "Who else can we add to this article you're now writing," Murrow said, pushing up his glasses and sipping whiskey. "Your source, Minister Shannon, we are lucky to have her.

Conway grinned slightly. "You know everyone loves a little tease. It will get more papers sold. I've heard that Kara is out; she has elvish blood, and Miss Bloomhood, the poet, is out. She doesn't bring any alliances, and honestly, Lothar Waterguard would challenge Prince Damon to a duel and crush him with the pole axe he carries. Looks like a giant fucking axe on an eight-foot pole." Conway snapped his fingers. "Laura Speers is coming too- everyone says she's like a character out of the *Lonely Nights of the Milkmaid*."

"She is," Marrow leaned forward. "Luscious figure."

"Yes, she has amazing," Conway snickered, "eyes. But again, she is far from noble blood; they do grow beautiful in Cinderpool, though," finished Conway. "We really should get our hands on some wizard salt; it helps me focus and write faster."

"Shit's illegal," Marrow said, "Sniff enough of that wizard salt up your nose, and your brain will bleed."

"So that leaves Prince Damon with three main choices, Princess Charity Mapleton from the Legion of Carigreed, Princess Grizel Vickers from the

Nation of Stouya, and the dark horse, Princess Candice Saltdrift from Great Brightland who is Prince Damon's distant relation."

"Wait, I heard Grizel posed for elusive nude paintings when she toured the Nation of Stouya with Princess Candice Saltdrift," Murrow said. He looked around and realized his office door was closed.

"That rumor's true. There are likenesses of her floating around art galleries in Stouya and sets of indecent playing cards can be found in taverns and halls. One must love the dwarven printing press, But King Geordie and Prince Damon can blow it off as propaganda as we all know those three nations are constantly at war."

"So, the lead is Charity Mapleton and an alliance with the Legion of Carigreed," Murrow said. "That's an interesting theory."

"It is, and it makes sense because Prince Damon's father is King Geordie, he wouldn't need to marry Princess Candice. And the rumor about Rowanne, if persistent enough, if written about, could cause problems with her. It's more than likely going to be Charity."

Murrow stood and took a drink, "Well, lean into it. I want a straight news story about Triumphant Masquerade and an anonymous editorial or made-up name, giving all those juicy rumors room to breathe by the end of the week.

"Fine, I can get that done. You know every city-state will be sending a potential match for Prince Damon. We could highlight each."

"Yes, let's do that, but as far as sure things, I think he wants someone that will solidify not just Vineland but become a power like his dear old dad in Great Brightland or the Legion of Carigreed. Our Holy Imperium needs to look strong in the face of others like The Hazefire Confederacy."

Murrow hesitated. "You know we need another story about The Gloom-spire, that mountain fortress. Where is it again, somewhere between Grimwood and Hudson City up in the Blightbriar Mountains?" asked Murrow. "I heard Lord Rotherham's hunting cabin was destroyed. Talk with your Blue Templar contact Sister Temperance Wightland and see if they can get us more on what happened there. We'll publish a story on that. With the news stories about the party, the editorials about Prince Damon's potential brides, and stories of goblin mages and orc knights, we'll sell these papers like crazy. The commoners will eat this shit up." Murrow smiled.

Conway took a big swig from his cup. "I mean, we barely have a rumor about that place. No idea who's in control of it, or where it's found," said Conway. "Why not do a few more stories on the Steelsburg civil war?"

"His Grace Prince Damon has personally recommended against further stories about the civil war in Steelsburg. The matter is settled; the Blitzsteel family now controls the city and are allied with Prince Damon and the Holy Imperium. The Clearstone family, if any remain, are terrorists if they continue to claim dominion of the city and exiled from it if they leave." He took another sip as if he ended the war himself, even as dwarves fought each other in dark tunnels deep underground, blood mingling with stone. The fissures created by the war formed blood feuds that may never end between families.

"Get what you can from the Templar, Sister Temperance. They control the mail in and out of Hudson City now," said Murrow. "I know that on good authority."

"What about the witch in the Litchbury Mire?" asked Conway. "I mean, if we are going to write about trashy tales told around campfires."

"Well, there is no sex appeal there. We need sex, need more violence, let's whip something up about that tarring and feathering angle, let's get something going there, make those bastards, those thieving unpatriotic bastards look like the shits they are!" Murrow said. "You get a copy of the new book that's been about?"

Conway laughed, "You mean the saucy milkmaid and her erotic adventures. Knights, and elven orgies, and orcs taking their pleasures? You into that shit?"

"I heard the new one is called *The Milkmaid at Twilight*, and it has some real spice and political metaphors that refer to Prince Damon."

Conway took notice. "Really? Well, I mean as a journalist I think it's our duty to get our hands on one."

"Be quick. Prince Damon banned it along with a lot of other texts. Get your hands on a copy, I will add it to our stash in the cellar of the paper, you know for prosperity." Murrow smirked.

Conway started taking notes. Once Murrow started in on an issue, he rolled through his thoughts aloud. Crude stories came through quickly. Truth be damned as long as it sold papers.

Alysha - Crushed Hopes

Felix waited near a door some distance from the Grimwood northern gate. The gate was three separate closures lined up in a row, including a dwarven-forged solid metal gate, a third black ash gate, and an elven-forged chain net, all closed off since the whisper of the plague occurred. Today, foot traffic continued through sets of doors owned by the guilds and merchants, two on each side. Felix mentioned the university controlled one of the doors itself. When they neared it, they found it unguarded, leaving Alysha, Felix, and Helena unnerved. The other gates had queues of common folk coming and going, and most were going, knowing the city may fall soon.

Alysha felt distress in the wall's stones throughout the Grimwood metropolis. The city was built by enslaved people and servants on the shores of the Erie Sea. She felt the water as it pushed its waves against the stony shore and imagined winters where Stribog's winds would sweep down from the north, freezing the city's gates shut for months on end, only to be opened by force and fire from the Grim Vultures tasked with keeping the town alive through the cruel months. Judith's spring had brought vines back to life on the walls, swarms of insects, and birds singing, but Alysha had heard no birds today. Now, she stood against those walls on the city's northern end, hoping for a safe escape.

Helena scrunched up her nose and whispered. "Always hated the smell of fish when my ma cooked it up."

The crest of the morning sun seeped through the shadows.

Felix knocked on the door twice, waited, and knocked thrice. They waited.

"Who waits this morning?" someone spoke through an opening in the door. The entire setup was more complicated than she imagined, as the wall's thickness created a set of doors controlled by those inside it.

"Nobody's servant but I?" Felix responded, his voice hitching on the passphrase.

"We are nobody's master except our own," The man in the door responded.

The door opened, and a Grimwood University Professor stood at the threshold. They carried a large stave with crisp metal spikes on each end. Behind them stood another door open, and the deep grayish-green Erie Sea was in the distance. Fog rolled in from the stoned beach, and the Grimwood forest met the sea. Alysha saw the large lock separating the sea from the unfilled moat. It stood partially covered by vines and overgrowth. The high tide of waves splashed against the beach stones, bringing in clumps of seaweed, a long-dead fish, and their accompanying natural perfume of decay. An eight-foot boat lashed against the waves.

"There's little time left. Bring your journals, and let's be off."

The professor was older than Felix. Her hair was lush, silver, and white. She was older yet formidable, and Alysha could tell she was used to being in control.

"Who are these two? We have no time for whores, Felix."

Heat flooded Alysha at the harsh words, anger threatening to take over. She had seen jealousy before, and this smacked of it.

"They're not whores." He looked back and winked. Helena put her hand on the sword at her hip with a smile.

Alysha was fairly sure Helena was going to kill Felix.

"We protected each other from my lab to the dock, and they came to warn us of the attack from the Holy Imperium."

"Warn us of something we already know." The professor clucked. She started rushing down a series of stone stairs toward a small boat. A cargo ship remained anchored in the distance from the dock, hoping to provide the city with much-needed food and other stock to trade. Alysha and Helena looked on as two large ships made port near them. Men at the pier were lashing ropes to secure each ship. Rows of folk lined up on the docks, waiting to board, their lives carried on their backs.

"They won't even fit on the boat unless they can row."

"We can row, professor," Alysha said as she swallowed her anger. "We believe the main force of the Holy Imperium will be upon the city within hours."

"How do you know? Where does your information come from."

"We escaped Counselor City and made our way here."

"Helena, Alysha, this is Professor Dorta Benders."

"Professor Benders, if you have room aboard, we can serve the university. I'm a blacksmith by trade, and Helena is an exceptional tailor. We can both read and write and read as well."

Alysha held her breath as Professor Benders untethered the boat.

"Felix, throw your gear and get in." The white fog rolled out from the forest onto the rocky shore. Professor Benders looked at the mist." The library has already moved to Pinelight Island and into the tower. We now have supplies, teachers, and the remaining students on the ship. They await us, and then we leave for the island."

Someone yelled back at the two ships as people lined up to board them. A commotion and argument broke out, and the desperation of a city about to fall took over.

"Can't tell if that is a good omen or not. Get in and get on those oars, both of you. Felix was always a sucker for a smile and skirt."

Alysha noted they looked like shit on a stick, and neither wore a skirt.

Professor Bender tried to push off as Alysha sat at the boat's oar. There was a scream from the two ships docked nearby. Other commotion came from the boat further away. Alysha's head swiveled to see soldiers traveling down the ship's planks.

"Shit, shit, shit, let's move."

Felix looked at the ship they were to row to and saw a body fall from the side. "What the-"

"We've been fooled. The ships are full of soldiers," Benders hissed.

"Professor, get in," Felix said quickly. "We can at least make it out safely and away from the city." She jumped into the boat from her knees in the water, her arms and stomach hitting the side. An arrow feathered her back as she made an 'oaf' sound.

Felix grabbed her, but she sank into the deep green and gray water. The people attempting to get onto the boats fell to arrows and bolts from the ships holding Holy Imperium soldiers. Archers feathered all who tried to escape onto a boat or back into the city. The screams and commotion of panic started and spread on the wind.

Alysha made the decision. "We can't escape in this, back into the woods. Felix, those tunnels you took us through. Do any lead south? Helena, out into the water, follow me. Felix, are you coming?

He looked at where his professor had fallen—her body and silver hair floated in the water, hitting the rocks. Alysha grabbed Felix and slapped him in the face.

"Bury that grief and live now. We must move."

His eyes widened again. "Right tunnels, maybe, but it won't be safe."

"Safer than here," Helena said. The chaos before them had erupted into the slaughtering of the common folk.

He hopped into the water, leaving the boat. People from the city fled to them and met arrows and bolts in their backs. Others moved past the dead bodies onto the rocky shore of the Erie Sea, grabbing the now-empty boat. The docks and rocky shore became a new graveyard for Grimwood.

Alysha shouldered her axe and crawled up the large stone shore, pushing Helena and Felix on and towards the Grimwood forest and Black Willow Falls, hoping it was safer than a conquering army.

"Into the fog. Felix, you know what's hazardous you lead. Go, go, go."

Alysha could hear someone screaming for their baby as water splashed around them and moved into the white fog, rolling out of the forest, knowing death lay behind her as an arrow bounced off her back and hit her axe, Stormkiss.

A stone wall built into the woods around the large lock kept the water out but had weathered over time. Felix found a gap and squeezed through, pushing up against a root the size of a horse. He put his hand through and guided Helena.

Alysha pushed through and saw an immediate difference. The Erie Sea took its fill of the dead behind them as the wall muffled its waves. She looked at the oakthorn, black willow trees, and grave markers below them. The different fogs shifted and pushed against each other like cloudy snakes eating each other's tails.

The forest to her left was separated by a cliff that looked extraordinarily difficult to climb. She stood on a ledge and found that the only way forward was down.

"Alysha, stay against the wall and grab onto where I do," Helena said. They followed a sketchy path against the wall that butted against the right side of the city that led to stairs near the collapsed bridge to the eastern gate.

"Don't fall, and I won't say don't look down. Too late for that."

They stopped halfway to the stairs. Alysha and Helena were shaking at the height they stood.

"What will we find in the tunnels."

"The same poisonfire fog from before, and rats coated in slime, making their bites eat away at your flesh." Felix showed his left arm, blistered black and gray with red streaks. "I was lucky. I've seen folk lose arms or legs from a bite. Oh, there are goblins and giant spiders adapted to the fog."

"You're telling us this now? What about when you saved us," Helena huffed.

"We didn't have time. Aside from the rats, gas, and gutter goblins. They're less intelligent but far more aggressive animals than those throughout eastern Vineland."

"We don't have time now; your city's about to fall to the Holy Imperium; the looting and burning should be our concerns; we can deal with gutter goblins and rats," Alysha pushed them on.

"Aren't all goblins unintelligent?" Helena asked as if they were not surrounded by a conquering army.

"Seriously, am I the only one trying to live here?" Alysha asked.

"No, they aren't scholars, but they're as innovative as humans, dwarves, or elves. It's not the race, ladies. It's how they are raised. I've met goblins in the west and near the Republic of Wind who were fair traders and successful merchants. The only problem goblins encounter is prejudice against them. They usually use a go-between. They're incredibly savvy in their businesses."

Helena laughed as they moved against the side of the cliff again. Alysha couldn't tell if it was from the thought of an intelligent goblin or because they were hundreds of feet high on a cliff's edge, heading for an even more dangerous destination. "Felix, you take us ladies on the most amazing dates."

Felix snorted. His foot slipped. He swore and composed himself after getting a better grip along the cliff path.

"It's slippery there," he finished. "Just a bit longer, and we're at the stairs."

"Joy," said Helena, she glanced back at Alysha and winked.

Helena's sarcasm made Alysha smile even as she broke out in a sweat.

"Felix, how long until we crash from the vial you gave us?"

He moved to a safe area near the top of the stairs toward the front of the eastern gate. He scratched the back of his head. "If we're lucky, it will hit us when we are halfway out of Black Willow Falls."

"Then what?"

He started walking down the stairs, using his hand to guide himself, but he did not answer.

Helena followed, and Alysha looked at the eastern gate open near the broken bridge and the stairs before them. Inside the gate, she saw smoke and no hope. She started down the stairs, noticing they were not the only ones who thought to find escape in Black Willow Falls.

The smell of decay hit first, as did the sound of thousands of bugs ready to bite and nip at any flesh exposed. She looked upon a black willow tree, the bark deep as midnight yet sparkling at times as luminescent bugs settled into the cracks of the bark, as the giant branches hung down them like an overturned umbrella, the leaves as dark green as a day would allow.

"Hate this place," Helena mumbled.

"Hate it, yes, but respect it." Felix pulled out his mask and gave Alysha and Helena two masked as well, not as well made.

"Gothine made this place," Helena swore.

"Gothine didn't make it; humans did, and Path of the Blessed guided them."

"I have to agree with Alysha," Felix smiled and lit his family pipe. "Gothine stole knowledge and is a patron to those at university. He didn't make this place." He stopped and coughed.

259

Helena smiled. "Serves you right. We need to get going, not get high."

"Maybe you're right, but it calms my nerves. I bet the university helped engineer this place, so I was tasked with keeping the poisonfire fog down to a controllable level. Come, we must make it to the wall that blocks the other part of the moat. Step where I step, and if you see a dead body, stay away from it. This place defies even my logic sometimes."

Alysha and Helena nodded, knowing too well what a dead body could do in Black Willow Falls.

* * *

The ships at Grimwood harbor unloaded Jared Blackheart's Genteel Monks unto the shores of the Erie Sea, and they ran to the northern gate of Grimwood. Jared watched as his soldiers killed those who attempted to escape the Holy Imperium's wrath and righteousness.

"Cleanse this place, my brothers and sisters; those that do not bow and submit are yours to smite, for the servant is the first of the Holy Church, the might of the right and the hand that protects the Child and serves the Maker and all of her light."

The crowd on the docks ran back to the gate even though it was closed. The doors they used to exit were shut to stop the invasion of the city. Arrows and bolts took the first group as they fell into the water. Blackheart watched as clubs, swords, and axes smashed those that ran, falling on them. He looked toward the city walls and saw Grimwood City guards above. They discharged arrows down, but he felt no fear as he held his giant black shield, Midnight's Veil.

"Blair, Gail, and Shay, your team is to scale these walls; get lines and rope ladders up there now! Caldwell, where is that half-goblin."

"He partook in the first attack, sir. He is below killing and looting on the shore."

"Thank you, Sister Softfellow."

He paused and looked at her for longer than he felt comfortable.

"Your punishment is that you will need to lead the initial wave. Caldwell is in his blood lust; he and his crew are first through the door after Blair, Gail, and Shay open the gate and the doors to the port and the city."

"As you command, Blackheart."

"Your failure was a disappointment but will be wiped clean today. Cleanse yourself through the sinner's blood. Don't let any escape."

She bowed and gazed at the mighty man, Jared Blackheart, with the pain of regret in her heart.

"General Flint should have the rest of the city gates covered now. We'll meet him in the middle inside—or better yet, he will meet us."

Sister Softfellow smiled and followed the rest of the monks down toward the gates, watching three groups of soldiers scale the walls of Grimwood. Smoke and screams continued to come from inside the city.

* * *

They moved through the moat without comment, taking cover as others from the city descended to shelter from the siege above. They could hear the large stones from the west slamming into the Grimwood walls, stone chips and dust draping them from above.

"The tunnel is at the base of the southern bridge. There are several entrances, including a door sealed long ago."

"How are we going to unseal it?"

"I don't know. Think of that when we get there."

"It's going to get worse from here. There may be soldiers in the moat attempting to get through."

Alysha heard steel meeting flesh, stone breaking bricks, and constant wood bashing against the southern gate. The sounds and violence were the happiness of men feeling free of the constraints of laws and righteousness. The tree line of the Black Willow Falls broke, and they saw the south bridge of Grimwood. It was an immense display of stone columns. As she looked toward it, the bridge was four or five carts wide.

"A fall from that height could kill you two times over."

"Truth Alysha, truth, you would have a long time to think before the end,"

Helena nodded.

The southern part of the cemetery cleaner than the eastern version, as the wall separated the two and kept the poisonfire mist confined near the black willow trees near the east gate.

"If we see soldiers, put our masks on and move close to a black willow tree. The fog should scare them away if they're smart."

A stone the size of a wagon wheel fell from above, smashing headstones and stopping near Felix. He looked up.

"This entire city will be destroyed, all for nothing."

* * *

The great city-state of Grimwood was under siege, and there weren't enough soldiers to protect the villages surrounding the city. The inner keep rumbled as fire and stone fell upon the Grimwood walls. Deep inside the keep, eyes closed in prayer, whispering to gods never seen, babies screamed, and children asked for parents who would never return. A Grimwood city guard at the southern curtain wall aimed his arrow through the side of a battlement and released it, sending an enemy soldier to their death. He looked behind him, and a tower inside the city collapsed. He swore and pulled another arrow, taking aim. A Holy Imperium trebuchet in the distance released another massive stone, and he watched the arch as it fell behind him. Is his wife under that rubble? Is his child safe?

"Look alive, soldier. You can't save them, but we can outlast this. Stay true to your aim." He looked down and took another life, choosing his work over the fear of his family's death.

The Grimwood curtain wall was over ten feet thick, a mixture of mortar and stone with a line of dwarven poured stone down the middle. It stood over forty-five feet high at the two bridges and doubled the height at the foot of the moat, making Grimwood one of the most challenging castles to lay siege to. Below the south and western bridge into the city, the moat walls were pure dwarven poured stone with steel driven deep into the Vineland soil. The soil itself was a mixture of dirt, clay, and rock. Another stone missile smashes the curtain wall, shaking the soldiers on the battlements. Quinn thought about his family, and his mind drifted to his fellow soldier, Michael.

Another stone hit at a distance, shattering the poured cement and causing hundreds of sharp pieces to spin and spit in every direction. Arrows fell haphazardly throughout the city, glancing off roofs and storefronts. Most missed their marks, and others left screams and tears in their victims.

After hundreds of years of journeying to the shore, stones were pulled up and used as ammunition for catapults and trebuchets. Dust and smoke blinded soldiers on the bridge, the parapet walkway on the curtain wall, and the few turrets still standing.

Michael loaded his crossbow and handed Quinn another shaft. "We got these bastards. They can't get a ladder up, Quinn."

"Right, we'll never bow to the Holy Imperium!" The wall shook again.

"It'd be nice if we had more help." Michael looked around at their numbers. They were capable soldiers, but less than half they needed, and half of them were city folk fighting for their family's sake. The Smoldering Plague had cut the population and caused rifts within Grimwood.

"The damn university should be up here fighting, but they left early this morning on three ships for Pinelight Island, where they have been shipping their fucking scrolls and books." Quinn spat.

"Cowards," Michael said.

Quinn took a breath and held it as he ducked. He stood, looked down, released a bolt, and ducked to the ground again but didn't get up. Michael looked down, saw Quinn's leg twitching, his britches turn wet, and looked on. He gasped like a fish, an arrow in his throat.

"For the Reach of Grimwood!" Michael screamed and stood, releasing his crossbow as another stone crashed into the turret above him. The floor at his feet weakened and twisted as the entire structure gave. He shrieked for a moment as stones fell away and tumbled down, bouncing off the side of the bridge and into the empty moat below, filled with graves, where his body landed.

* * *

Kavin, on the other side of the bridge, looked up and moved as a body fell, hitting the side of the bridge on his right and into the moat. The men to his side pushed a battering ram into the gate. "Heave," it bounced against the gate. "Heave! For the Imperium!"

They are trying to kill me. Kavin thought. Maker, he just wanted to be at home reading a book; why was he even here with people trying to kill him? But he had a job today, and the job should be done, and there was money to be made and all that. "Heave!" The battering ram smashed into the gate. Its chain, steel, iron, and wood shook with each shout. The gate didn't move. "Heave!" More arrows fell.

He pushed the shield out of the way and released an arrow into the sky. The arrow went up, but another shield blocked his view. "Heave!" The battering ram hit. Arrows fell, barely missing Kavin.

They're timing the arrow shots to the word. Heave, Kavin thought.

"Heave!" Bill yelled.

"Stop," Kavin ordered. The arrows fell from above, one landing in his hand. "Ow!" He stared at his hand. That was not supposed to be there. It seemed almost unreal.

"Heave!"

The arrows fell in front of him.

"Stop!"

"Heave," and the ram smashed the southern gate again. The arrows stopped falling from above.

Wait, what? Kavin pushed the shield above him away with his good hand. *Were they gone? Was the battle over now?*

Oil spilled from above, falling into his mouth. He gagged and tried to yell stop, but he gasped further as his stomach boiled, his eyes and hair roasted, and he fell onto the soldier who held the shield. They stumbled down into each other, a mass of burning oil, flesh, and deteriorating armor.

* * *

The oil splashed on the man in front of him; Kavin was his name, Bill thought;

good man wanted to start his own bookstore after his time with the army. The man was now squirming on the ground. Bill stepped back, wiping the oil off his arm. A basket arrow hit before him, catching those covered with oil alight. He watched and yelled, "Heave!" Nobody listened; they all screamed and shrieked as they burned. The smell was awful; the soldiers behind him with shields pushed him forward, so he grabbed a handle of the battering ram and pushed a lump of someone out of his way and pushed the ram forward. The work of a captain sometimes led to getting things done himself. "Heave!" he yelled again but didn't finish. A large stone hit his shoulder, and he stumbled to the ground, the air knocked out of him. Soldiers above him walked over him and crushed his stomach. Someone rolled him over.

"I'm still alive," he threatened, but nothing came out of his mouth but blood. He opened his eyes and found a bolt in his chest. They pushed him again, and he fell off the bridge, failing to scream.

* * *

Alysha waited near a black willow tree while they looked for the sewer entrance near the southern bridge. The bridge made of poured stone shook as the soldiers above pressed forward. Stone and arrows fell around the bridge as screams of pain and commands were given. She saw a slight body fall to the ground, making a harsh sound as it hit first a puddle of stale water and then mud below. It would decay there. She thought about how someone should spread flower seeds over the dead after a battle and let nature take over. An odd thought, but not strange. It seemed a sinful idea. Helena stared at the bridge in awe.

"There, by that ivy."

Felix pointed, and Alysha saw a bright patch near the side of the bridge. A thunder of stone streaked through the sky, hitting the curtain wall hundreds of feet off to the left of the southern bridge.

"This city will fall from the port. Once they open the northern gate, they will filter in and take the two main gates from within. After that, the massacre, the burning."

"I hope the Smoldering Plague kills them all," Helena said out loud in a prayer.

"I wouldn't wish that on anyone," Felix yelled above the cries and crash of wood and steel above.

"We go after the next set of arrows fall. On three."

Alysha watched from the darkness of the tree. Soldiers from Grimwood poured black pitch liquid tar onto the battering ram on the southern bridge above them, burning those attempting to break their way in. An arrow with a lit head spun onto the battering ram, setting the pitch on fire. Those under the battering ram not choking from the pitch felt the flames before they burnt.

"Now!"

Felix ran first, followed by Alysha and Helena, as stones and dust floated by them on both sides. Alysha saw bodies burnt and crushed by rocks. Felix started climbing to the ivy. Helena looked up as another gap in the noise above occurred, and something flashed around the corner of her eye. A crash of stone and fire slashed across Alysha's vision, and Helena pulled her hand, jerking Alysha to a halt. A stone burning with pitch bounced off the bridge and tumbled directly into their path, hitting the sewer opening where Felix pried the door open.

Austin - Orders to Follow

T he weeks took their toll on the soldiers stationed at Oxfell Gate. Every bird chirp made sentries jump, every squirrel dancing across tree branches invited fear of the enemy above, and every day, the morale of the Holy Imperium soldiers withered. They sat in an entrenched compound on the Razorshine River's eastern side with another secure encampment further back in a fortified village called Hawkhallow. Pap was smart enough to place the position on higher ground to stop a mild summer flood from washing them out. Scouts were sent across the river, losing one or two at a time. Some were found dead from arrow shafts and traps set by their enemy, and others were eaten by a foul animal from the Blightbriar Wilds. Austin was convinced the animals in the Blightbriar Wilds were controlled by their unknown and unnamed enemy. Twilight brought raids of the silent warhawks who would swoop down and drop stones from above, and early morning arrow shafts would rain down from various positions across the river to remind the Holy Imperium soldiers the enemy was there and waiting for them. Half of the Union Dogs were dead, and the scouts they did have dwindled to five total. The rest of the company consisted of soldiers from the Holy Imperium army or Templar knights and monks. The fighting force dwindled. Pap used Wildcats, including Austin, as guards around the Hawkhallow Village base camp, rotating them in shifts for duty at the Oxfell Gate camp.

The fear of the warhawks grew as the raids increased, leaving any soldier without a crossbow feeling exposed.

Austin sat on a stool at a makeshift desk, taking notes as Elora, Keyla, and

Leslie stood at attention in Hawkhallow Village. Looking around, he took in the recent changes to the camp. They had fortified their camp with a sunken trench and briar bushes and started putting up palisade walls like they had built at the Oxfell Gate. Their enemy haunted the western side of the Razorshine River, unseen and unwavering in their defensive position.

"Our intelligence suggests Featherbottom Lodge, owned by Lord Rotherham, is north of the river crossing. That's our mission: find the lodge, verify what happened, and report back. I would have preferred to take control of the entire area, but that doesn't seem possible," Pap said.

"Sir, we should cross in force and show this weak enemy who we are and let the hand of the Maker wash over this entire cursed forest," said Brother Walder.

"I agree; we have a secure front now; we need to show them who we are as soldiers of the one and only Maker," Sir Pekka Deeran said.

Austin looked at the room and felt the tension in the humid, hazy air. His quill moved sharply and swiftly on the scroll.

"I'm glad you agree." Pap bobbed his head stoically. "We move in force early tomorrow morning to take the other side of the river to establish the crossing. Brother Walder, you will lead the heavy horse. Pekka, your archers will provide support while the first group crosses. I will follow the scouts and two platoons of foot soldiers with a handful of Wildcats. Brother Walder will take our soldiers after, and Pekka will follow with the archers. I'm counting on you, Sir Pekka, to keep us safe as we cross. Brother Walder may have his hands full at the front of the cross. The Union Dogs as a force lack the numbers now. Leslie, Keyla, Kenneth, and the rest of the Union Dogs will mix in with the Templar during the crossing. I want Kenneth at my side, Leslie and Keyla scouting in front."

"Sir, this sounds like it's going to be," Elora said, but Pap interrupted her.

"Elora, you, Parker, and Austin have a separate mission. You're to cross north of the river, find that damn lodge, and report back to us on what the fuck happened. Run light, don't fucking drown, and get back to us. If our crossing is quiet and we control both sides, you meet us on the other side and report back. If you hear the madness of battle, you cross back over and wait at Oxfell Gate camp with your intelligence; it will be lightly guarded. If it's bad, push back to Hawkhallow Village. I don't think it will come to that."

Austin peaked up. Pap was taking a bold stance. The last letter he received from the capital must have been explicit and required further action.

"Before we move, I want your leaders to write letters of regret and leave them with their personal effects. The chain of command will follow as Elora and Austin go out on patrol. Me, Pekka, Walder. Is that clear?"

Brother Walder nodded, scratching at his chin, and Pekka smiled quickly and nodded. Elora gripped a necklace she wore at her neck.

"These orders are all written here, and each of you has a set. Get your soldiers ready. Two platoons of foot soldiers cross first, then the heavy horse, in groups of three, quickly after, establish a perimeter at the mouth and keep it open for the rest of us right before dawn breaks. As the first group crosses, our archers will feather the other side of the river, creating a net of arrows. Elora, Keyla, and Austin will be well gone by then. Go make some coffee, you three. It's going to be a long night. Get your affairs in order."

Pap dismissed them all, and Austin finished writing.

"This is your last mission with us," Pap told Austin, grabbing his arm as he rose from the desk. "After this, I want you back at the capital. You let them know what you've seen. I keep getting orders and reports from Hudson City, but they don't make sense. It's like they aren't even reading what I've sent them." Austin's superior released his hold on him but continued his tirade. "The orders I've written are explicit. You, Elora, and Parker will return to Hudson upon your return from this last mission and report our current situation to them. If this goes well, we'll hold the crossing; if not, we keep a force here on this side, drawing the enemy toward us. If Prince Damon wants this damn lodge, we'll need more bodies and a better idea of what the fuck is happening in the woods across the river."

Pap heard a knock at the post of his tent.

"Enter," he grumbled. "Figured it was you."

"Pap, this mission and crossing," Elora said.

Pap put up his hand. He rose from the table, striding over to the scout. She stood silenced by her father. Austin looked on from his seat and then away as Pap embraced his daughter and whispered into her hair, taking her in momentarily.

"This whole mission is fucked. Get in, get eyes on what the Hades is happening, and get back across the river."

She felt her father's strong arms envelop her, contrasting with the humid evening air, and her fear mingled with his. The moment ended, they both fought back the tears of the future unknown.

"You heard what I told Austin? You're heading back to the capital once you get eyes on the lodge?" asked Pap.

Elora looked at her father, concern, and anger showing on her face, and turned to Austin, who now stood.

"Yes, sir, we'll prep now and complete our mission."

* * *

Sladestone warmed her hands at the fire as her best friend and lover sat beside her, sharpening arrows. She nodded as four sturdy and cocky goblins came near but waited to be acknowledged. They all stood four feet high, dressed in light leather trousers and vests painted for war. Their eyes darted away from the fire, yellow and more accustomed to night than day. The freedom of their lives showed on their bodies and gave them a cockiness few saw in a goblin. They were predators who chose the sky as their hunting grounds.

Sladestone stood, pushing at her knees as she did so, and towered above them. The armor she wore adjusted as she shifted. Always ready for battle, she trained her body to grow strong while at rest.

"How many are ready for the battle?" she asked the goblin standing before the other three.

They all stood tall, unlike most goblins, who tended to hunch. They had molded themselves to stand more often outside and not hunch over in hollowed-out caves.

"We have twelve warhawks ready to ride; ten of them are large enough to drop stone, and the other two are to be used for reconnaissance and can be used to drop other surprises."

"How many shall we use for the battle to come?"

"Two, one attacking and the other to sow fear while our forces stymie them at the crossing," the goblin said. "And the two birds will rotate attacks so they do not get tired."

"Cloudstrike, I thank you for the report. Keep the others in reserve and ready in case we need reinforcements. Go with honor for your tribe and family, and leave your war pipe and nail clippings with me. If you don't return, we wish to have something to bury or burn."

Cloudstrike and one other nodded, leaving their war pipe and a small leather bag with their nail clippings inside. Sladestone would bury or burn the bag and pipe if Cloudstrike and the other goblin were to die in battle riding their warhawks. The risk for a goblin and the fear they would feel so high above the ground of Vineland gave all that knew of what they were to do a sense of gratitude and celebrity. They sowed despair in the sky and could die quickly, from a stray arrow to a buckle breaking on the warhawks' harness.

* * *

Austin wore his lightest gear, strapped down tight, a short sword, a tomahawk the Union Dogs preferred to wield, and two knives. They ran on the east side of the Razorshine River for about an hour and waded into the rushing water. Swimming relentlessly, they made their way to the edge, soaked and exhausted, gripping large shale stones to avoid getting washed away. Austin swallowed some water, tasting copper and a hint of sulfur, which reminded him of how he felt after a battle or tournament. The west side of the river was calm, and he could hear animals scurrying in the forest undergrowth; it was darker as the pine, maple, and ash trees were outnumbered by the oakthorn and the dangerous black willow trees. The black willow emitted a poisonous fog that drifted around their trunks. Large ferns covered much of the ground if not for the trees.

Elora led them down a deer path, looking for the Gothine be dammed lodge hours before sunrise. Pap had given Austin an order with a General Casting seal on it to be broken at first light.

They walked another trail for a while and found the edges of a village, but the inhabitants were gone. They circled a homestead recently abandoned. How many Austin could not tell? The coals of the fire were still warm, and food had been prepared and eaten. He drifted to the other side of the camp and met Parker Hillview and Elora.

"Killed a goblin and a dwarve coming back from taking a shit. They were joking with each other when I split their heads."

"What the fuck are dwarves and goblins doing taking a shit together?" Austin asked.

"What are they doing taking a shit in a latrine someone dug?" Elora coughed.

"I dragged the bodies back into the latrine pit. They were armed and painted up for battle, so they were unfriendly."

"This crossing is going to be worse than before," Elora shook her head. "Let's find this lodge and get back to my dad as soon as possible."

They moved quickly north of the village and followed a footpath, giving way to speed and less to quietness. After another hour, they broke into a meadow surrounded by pine and oakthorn trees. The field was overgrown, unprepared for the coming season; in the middle stood a scarecrow with two birds sitting on it.

"Those are fucking baby warhawks," Elora hissed.

"This must be the field the lodge used for grain and crops, circle right, stay out of sight of those fucking monsters, and we should see the lodge to the north of the field," Parker said, looking at the birds. The morning mists were starting to take shape, and the birds cackled at a personal joke between themselves, looking like giant mutant crows.

All three ran similarly, one hand free while the other carried a tomahawk for protection. At the next stop, Austin thought he could open the missive given to him by Pap. He hadn't heard anything south yet, so the crossing could have gone well. He breathed hard and deep as they stopped near the beginning of a path north of the trail, the field now behind them.

He felt something change as the two giant birds stop cackling. They left in enormous swooping circles and headed south toward Pap and the rest of the expeditionary force. Austin looked back, and Elora didn't say anything. She shook her head as if reading his mind.

Bits of dusty sunlight broke through the canopy as morning crept into the wilds. Austin found a bright spot on the side of the path and used his hands to tell Elora to wait. He cracked the seal, catching his breath, and squinted to read the scroll, not understanding. It mentioned a wooden case with treasure or gold would be found in the lodge cellar. They were looking for a family heirloom, a knife, or an ornate axe. He read the word *"paragon"* and closed the message.

Elora and Parker quickly read the order from General Casting, returned it to Austin, and pushed on.

An oakthorn tore at Austin's arm, cutting through his leathers, and he started to bleed but kept running north, following Parker and Elora. His legs tired, and shortly after, they stopped. It was another clearing, but this time, they found the remains of the lodge. It should have been a principal structure three floors high, with a basement and separate cellar. All that remained was the overgrown, burnt-up shell of Holy Imperium grandeur, the remains of what a noble could build eaten away by fire and nature. They walked the perimeter of the lodge ruins.

Quietly, they made their way inside the ruins, searching through the debris. The order told him to search the lower floors, now covered by ash and burnt timber. He was looking for a wooden case where this heirloom would have been placed. A large movement of birds could be heard behind them, and then the echoes of screams and metal grinding together.

Austin looked back at Elora and saw pain and worry in her eyes.

* * *

Pekka put his archers on the lower left half of the crossing under the cover of an ancient fallen tree and another group of archers above the path that led to the river ford to provide support. They quickly released two volleys into the air as the first force waded into the water, the arrows arching overhead into the undergrowth on the other side. No screams or hits were heard. The

Blue Templar drew up their war horses, made no attempt to stay quiet, and even blew a horn as they started crossing the river. No birds or animals were moving; the forest was silent except for the water moving downstream across slick moss-covered stones and sharp shale underneath. The shore on the other side held large rocks on the left and right of the crossing, leaving a flat shale stone opening covered in fine sand. This led to extensive open paths, each big enough for a wagon to use, leading into the Blightbriar Wilds and beyond into the mountains. The side the Holy Imperium held mainly was pine and maple trees, except for two black willow and oakthorn trees that created a canopy gate at the river opening. Another set of black willow and oakthorn trees twisted together, creating a gate-like opening on the other side of the river ford. The branches were twisted and gnarled, and the trees consistently put out a low green fog that made eyes water and caused a rash if anyone neared it. The horses pushed to the center of the path after the few Union Dog scouts crossed the river and quietly passed the large river stones and off the beach. Leslie and Keyla drifted softly into the ferns and undergrowth of the Blightbriar Wilds ahead of the foot soldiers and the rest of the force.

The foot soldiers crossed next, and Pap crossed after finding no resistance. He wore a fortune of plate and mail armor, helm down, and immaculate war sword in hand with two other Wildcat knights at his side. The brutish Blue Templar and monks followed. Pap made his way off the stone shore into the sand and onto the nearest path across the tree line gate above them. The forest canopy let misty light in the early morning, and Pap only heard his sour breathing inside his helm. He felt the first bolt hit the side of his arm and nearly lost his horse as his training kicked in. Pap gripped the saddle with his thighs and shifted his horse. His war horse kicked out, hitting a camouflaged goblin who sat in a long fern, killing it instantly.

As before, enemies lay above in tree limbs unseen before now. Pap raised his good arm, and the army shifted and moved to the lower trail closer, leaving Pap and two other knights on the main trail. Pap started hacking at the ferns, and the other knights did the same; Keyla and Leslie came running out of the forest's darkness toward Pap.

When Keyla and Leslie came close to Pap, the three knights had trampled a half dozen goblins and dwarves and one smaller orc with their horses. Pap's arm bled, the bolt from the crossbow stuck in his shoulder.

Keyla and Leslie were out of breath and had also seen battle. A portion of the force was now either in the water or the lower part of the river crossing, moving their way up the shore onto the other path.

"They're coming!" Leslie said. Pap nodded and waved his arm again, and Pekka, on the other side of the river, blindly let loose waves of arrows over the heads of the knights into the darkness of the forest. The archers had adjusted and moved directly onto the river's shore to gain further reach into the forest. The arrows fell before the Holy Imperium soldiers, and they heard grunts and groans as their enemy died. Pap had hoped to now flank their enemy moving toward the ford's lower part. He could see their bodies in the distant overgrowth, human goblins, dwarve, and the taller orcs outnumbering his force. The clash of arms was met as the shore gave way to the bank and the lower, wider path the rest of the Holy Imperium force took. The Blue Templar were slowed as several enemies high in the tree canopy peppered them with arrow shafts, hitting the horses, causing a break in the ranks, as the enemy now met sword to sword, spear to shield with the Holy Imperium force, some on the shore, some on the bank and a few struggling at the start of the path into the Blightbriar Wilds.

"Shit, we need to clear those trees. Leslie, Keyla. Can you find those fuckers!" Pap yelled.

They both took aim and hit two of the enemies in the trees. One was behind them, sitting in the gate tree branches. Pap looked back, lifted his helmet visor, and steered his horse back toward the river.

"Keyla, Leslie, you two hold this path; only retreat if outnumbered," Pap ordered. He looked back at the crossing when he saw a large bird swoop down and pick up a foot soldier crossing the middle of the river like an owl grabbing a field mouse. The soldier loped across the water one moment and gone the next as the large predator warhawk spread its wings to grab and leave with its prey.

"The enemy, there is more coming! We must fall back!" Leslie screamed.

"Good Maker's legs," Pap said aloud. "Warhawks, look to the skies! Warhawks." The soldier fell on top of two others at the front of the line, causing carnage and confusion. Another bird dropped two pots of burning pig grease on two Templar. Their screams were muffled inside their helms as they burned and shimmed, and the smell of the burning fat and the flesh inside was baking as they expired. Another force came above Pap, and he steered his horse to meet it. A large female orc warrior appeared, shoving a massive oakthorn spear into Pap's horse. He fell hard but saved his legs from breaking. The two other knights were pulled down from their horses after killing several goblins and one well-armed orc. Leslie and Keyla fell back, hoping to help Pap and get him away from the overwhelming force in front of them.

* * *

Knight Commander Sladestone saluted her sword toward Pap and held The Servants Guide, a tomahawk in her other gauntleted fist. She held her great sword, nearly six feet long, with ease in one hand. Next to Sladestone stood two lessor orcs, each a sword and war hammer in hand, well-made and well-used.

"Leave my home," she screamed at the invader. "Bleed for my trees and feed them!"

"For Vineland," Pap screamed as he faced Sladestone. Leslie and Keyla placed a shaft into each of Sladestone's guards and prepared to defend themselves as further soldiers of the Holy Imperium fell in behind them on the cusp of the shore and the Blightbriar Wilds. The roar of a ruin bear could be heard downstream as it ripped apart a Blue Templar soldiers' leg and horse beneath it.

Alysha - Desperate Choices

Silence only lasted for a moment as the dust spread, and the vacuum of the moment ended. The melee above continued. Screams of agony and booms from further stones hurled by catapults and trebuchets blasted the city walls of Grimwood above. The lands around the city were already under the control of the Holy Imperium and the harbor, and soon the city would fall. The soldiers above attacked the gates. They celebrated as arrows sped through the air, finding armor, shield, and flesh of the city's sparse defenders.

Stunned, Alysha looked at the stone, and Felix's remains under it. The urge to escape clutched at Alysha and Helena.

"He's gone," Alysha choked.

"We can't go forward; we must risk going back to the stairs on the eastern side and into the forest." Helena tried to shake off the fright for her and Alysha's safety.

Helena pulled Alysha up as she gasped in pain, her earlier injuries on fire. They ran through the moat, stones crashing down all over the place, bouncing off the walls above, missing their mark, and dropping into the moat. The randomness of death takes its toll throughout the city.

"I am sick of this place, sick of cities, sick of everything," Helena hissed.

A volley of arrows fell onto the bridge as they passed into the cover of black willow trees.

"Masks on until we get to the stairs. Stay on the path," Alysha ordered. Every step she took away from Felix's remains seemed to clear the fog from her mind, her focus returning. "Let's get the Hades out of this place," Helena said with determination.

Both were beginning to feel the aching dread of their situation deep in their bones. The effects of Felix's elixir were wearing off, leaving them groggy.

They dashed toward the stairs, their lungs burning from the effort. Grimwood townspeople clashed with Holy Imperium soldiers in the moat off to their left. A merchant and her guards attempted to escape with their lives. Bundles of goods, now useless, were left at the feet of a mausoleum opening. Black Willow Falls was swarming with activity; the base of the crumbling eastern bridge into the city was crowded with commoners and other soldiers battling Holy Imperium forces that had made their way from the harbor. Alysha saw a bearded man far off swinging a giant war mace, bashing a Grimwood archer in the chest with an underhanded swing as the archer defended a young boy, his efforts useless as his chest shattered. The bearded man in armor and a monk's cowl stepped on the child as if he were an egg and smiled with happy rage. The city of Grimwood burnt above; a tar-filled smoke spewed out of the eastern gate above them, drifting down into the moat and mingling with the poisonfire fog.

She knew the bearded man at once, Jared Blackheart, the menace of Wolf Hills. Adrenaline surged into Alysha, and she slowed. Helena continued quickly to the stairs at the broken bridge on the eastern bank of Black Willow Falls, unaware Alysha was not following. Alysha looked at Jared at a distance, stood taller, and took her mask off. He stopped his assault on a family as they braced against a tombstone. He pointed his mace and shouldered his shield higher, yelling at her, challenging her.

A voice deep inside her came through all the chaos.

Avenge my lands.

Alysha heard a muffled cry as a soldier struggled with Helena, ripping her mask off. The soldier was grabbing at her waist and had thrown her onto the ground as she punched and scratched at him, digging a knife into his arm.

Alysha breathed deeply and replied defiantly, "Not today, but soon." She rushed toward her friend, dropping the soldier to the ground with a flying knee to his chin. She smashed his face with the hilt of Stormkiss. Helena's knife went in and out of the soldier's armpit three times, and she breathed in a gory and glorious smile, spitting the man's nose out of her mouth.

"I'm getting you a better knife," Alysha said in a desperate breath.

"Maybe some better armor, too," Helena said as she stood.

"Up the stairs, let's go," Alysha pushed Helena on.

She felt drained yet thrilled to remain alive and tried to buy Helena time. Helena took two stairs at a time, using her hands to steady herself up the steep incline, but her pace slowed as the height increased, along with the danger of falling. Alysha turned and saw a Genteel Monk facing her.

The Genteel Monk didn't expect his prey to turn around with a vicious-looking axe in hand. He screamed, and Alysha kneeled, shoving her axe head into the monk's armored stomach. It penetrated the chainmail and leather behind it. She stuck the other end into the ground, and the monk's inertia finished the blow. She pushed him over, pulled out the axe, turned to the stairs, starting the long climb. Halfway up, Alysha gasped, sweating and cursing loudly. Arrows pinged off the steps below her, and she was numb to their danger. Soldiers at the bottom of the stairs slowly started pursuing them.

She rolled her eyes and followed Helena up the stairs. They climbed the winding stairs on hands and knees. A towns person above them lost their grip and tumbled down, rolling past them on the right, bloody and screaming. They hit two of the closest soldiers and knocked moreover. The stairs had no rail, just stone cut into the side of a cliff in a zig-zag pattern. Alysha's ears rang, and her breath and feet were the only noises she heard, except for curses below her, which were muffled by distance and occasional screams from Black Willow Falls below. Finally, she saw her friend's hand at the top, waiting to pull her up.

"Almost there," Helena gripped Alysha's arm and pulled her to safety.

"Others are coming," Alysha heaved over the side and fell, face blue, kissing the moss-covered ground. Helena heaved a heavy tombstone next to Alysha and pushed it down the stairs they climbed, smiling as it crushed their pursuers.

"Let's get into the woods. I hope any that follow choke on the poisonfire fog." Helena brushed her hands off on her trousers and hauled Alysha to her feet.

* * *

Alysha and Helena wandered through the Grimwood forest, passing oakthorn, ash, maple, and black willow tree groves, creating a canopy of darkness and fog. Some of the long grass near the black willow trees was sharp as a razor and cut through clothes like a knife, while other paths led to wildflowers and berries, offering no harm to the birds and foxes in the area.

They stopped and drank water from water skins, trying to move back in the original direction they ran before they made their way into Grimwood a few days ago.

"My guess is Holy Imperium soldiers patrol the outskirts of the forest and may even be inside it looking for people or soldiers using it for cover," Alysha said.

"No idea where we'll go or how to get out of here, but at least it's not the madness behind us."

"I saw Jared Blackheart back there," Alysha said.

"You think you could take him with that axe of yours?"

Helena looked at Alysha.

No voices spoke in her head, just a silent understanding.

Alysha shrugged. "I think we only have each other at this point. Get out of the Grimwood, head south if we can, and back to Wolf Hills to regroup. Worst case, we head south and west and hit the swamp. That place could hide us, hide a whole army, but it could swallow us up, too."

They went to the forest's edge and ate a strip of dried meat. They sat by an old oak tree surrounded by heavy brush, a light gray fog circling the area. Alysha felt safer as squirrels and birds nattered throughout the region; she knew they would not be about if the poisonfire fog lingered. She saw glimpses of sunlight drifting through cracks in the Grimwood canopy. The forest above and behind dulled the battle at the city's gates. The distant thunder of stone smashing and screams of terror echoed through the trees, darkened by the foliage. They walked for two more hours until they hit the forest's edge.

Crows and vultures argued in the sky above as they drifted on the currents of the fires now consuming the city, the smoke blocking the sun's warmth.

Tall grass, chest-high, sprouted at the forest's edge, obscuring sight lines.

"What are you doing?" Alysha asked.

"Climbing a tree to see what we have to deal with. Help me up," Helena barked.

Alysha offered Helena a foothold with her hands. "Besides, you've got too many bandaged-up wounds to slink about a tree like this."

Alysha agreed silently and pushed Helena up, supporting her legs and behind. She watched the grass momentarily as Helena scaled a huge ironwood maple tree. She listened but still heard animals and birds about as if nothing was happening, even as one of the largest cities on the Erie Sea burnt behind them.

Helena hopped down after gathering scraps and cuts on her hands and face.

"Off to our right is a group of four soldiers on the road. Looks like Holy Imperium scouts taking an early dinner. It's an open field from here to the road, mostly this tall grass with a few trees, then a road, another overgrown field, and further on, woods and what feels like familiar territory."

"What does the west look like."

"From what I saw, Southtown and Weston are controlled by the Holy Imperium, and from the smoke, I would think Grimwood is done for it."

"As soon as it's dark, we start through the grass, heading south and east back toward Wolf Hills, trying to stay away from the few trees in the area. Use them as guides, but keep your distance. The scouts will do the same, but press closer to the trees."

"You think they'll search the trees?"

"They don't know the area, so they will use them as guidelines searching for refugees or raiding parties if Grimwood has any fight left in them."

"If we meet the scouts?"

Alysha paused. "We fight and most likely die or split up and hope one of us escapes."

Helena frowned. "I'd rather die with you than become another slave."

Alysha looked at Helena, hoping it wouldn't come to that.

"A few more hours until we make our break. Let's move to a safe spot to run from and rest."

* * *

Brett mixed oats with bacon fat and threw in some chives he had found on his last patrol. Working as a scout for the Holy Imperium had its advantages, and fresh food was one of them. He scratched at his ratty beard and thought of his wife Matilda back home.

"Ruddy army gets to take Grimwood and all its spoils, and we get bloody refugee patrol," complained the youngest scout, Richard.

"It's better than leading a charge up a ladder to get your head caved in, I tell you what," said the oldest scout, Brett.

"That the last of the bacon?" Richard sniffed about the small fire Brett had made.

"Yeah, we eat and then ride for some time, rechecking the line, then break and take another ride near dark."

"Andy, you big lump, what's our refugee count, by the way?"

Andy was returning from taking a shit, wiping his ass with a well-used cloth.

"I reckon at least twenty moved to the outskirts of the mire prison camp. That is a nice bonus for the four of us."

"Right, it is. Better to make a few coins than getting killed trying to scale some Maker-forsaken wall, Richard."

"Jesse should be back soon with Ty; then we'll make another circle and hope we don't meet any regular Grimwood soldiers," said Ed, the fourth Holy Imperium scout.

"Oh, piss on that. I doubt any are left; the plague took most of them, or they ran off west before we laid siege. I bet toward the Republic of Wind, I say. This is a cakewalk, my friends. We could be in real trouble if we head west."

"You think the prince wants to take all the major city-states, Brett?"

"If they're all as easy pickings as this and don't bend the knee, I don't see why not. Wait until this plague weakens the city and lay siege when they are near death."

"Sure, as hell, I hope I don't get that blasted Smoldering Plague."

"Makes you squirt from your pooper and bleed from your eyes before you go," Richard said, laughing.

"Better off killing yourself," Ed nodded and looked away, thinking of a lost friend.

"Don't say that, Ed. Maker, Servant, and Child, don't say that," Richard said.

"Andy, you may be whip-smart with those numbers and memorize entire plays, but that doesn't mean we are immune to that sickness. I served up north during the Crimson Struggle and saw shit that would turn an orc into a coward, and none of it was as bad as watching my friends die of the Smoldering Plague," said Brett.

The bacon crackled in the pan with the oats, so Brett added watered wine to the mixture, creating a form of gruel.

"Grab your spoons and cups. Let's eat and go get us a few more scalps and captives. I ain't looking to serve another campaign to another city-state. I want to go home."

"If this is so easy, they may redraft us to serve another campaign," said Richard.

"Shit, I know, can't do much about compelled service, royal bastards, the whole lot," followed Brett.

"Finish up. We got a horse coming in from Southtown. Looks like one of ours. Could be the boss."

"Look alive all," Brett said, kicking dirt into the scant fire, upsetting he couldn't relax a bit longer.

* * *

Alysha could smell the scout's food, and her stomach cramped from a lack of real substance. They had little to survive on and hoped they could hunt for game once they got out of Grimwood. It was a genuine concern but not the most pressing now. First, they needed to escape. They had enough water and miserable rations for two days. She figured that would get her and Helena into better hunting grounds. She looked to the sky, unable to tell how late it was, but tightened her gear and threw down anything that would slow her, keeping only the meager rations and one waterskin.

"You ready to do this?"

Helena fixed the sword at her hip and checked her knife as well. They looked like a wreck, a mixture of bandages, torn clothes and mismatched leather straps, armor pieces, uncombed hair, and a fierce will to survive.

The women squeezed between two oakthorn trees, cutting up their clothes further, but withheld any curses coming to their dried lips. As they pushed past the natural tree-formed wall of Grimwood, they found it near twilight.

Alysha saw another grouping of trees and brush on the other side of the tall grass. It would take time to make it through, but she liked the odds. She figured scouts tended to ride near the oakthorn tree line of Grimwood, watching for any refugees attempting to escape through the natural openings of the forest. They tried not to leave too much of a mark from their forest exit and harm the grass but knew it would be unavoidable. They saw a portion of the grass worn down by horses and jumped past the path and back into the tall grass. She heard shouts at a distance to her right, and Helena tensed up and moved closer to Alysha, holding her breath.

"Looks like a family of four over here. Grab your ropes team," Holy Imperium scout Ed yelled.

"Don't move, don't move, we understand. Just trying to ensure you're safe," Andy said trying to calm the family. His smile hid the violence about to befall the family.

"PLEASE NO, we didn't do anything wrong!"

"Mercy, Mercy!"

There was laughter and, finally, a scream and a struggle.

"Keep moving," Alysha said, "while they're distracted." She was sweating and angry at herself and her weakness for not offering help.

They moved forward into the grass, away from the patrol, when Helena stopped and squatted, quietly pulling out her sword.

Alysha grasped Stormkiss and held her breath to listen.

Kill them and water my grass, something inside Alysha commanded. She felt confidence and strength run through her.

She heard a horse as Helena shifted and moved back further into the tall grass, trying to hide. The horse pushed through, barely feet away, and moved toward the commotion before them. They circled for multiple steps behind the horse and caught sight of a road.

"Saw grass moving over here, Brett."

"Hold up, wait. Think Ed and Andy found refugees. Sounds like they are having some fun."

The scout named Richard moved toward Alysha, his back facing them, as the other scout, Brett, pulled away on his horse.

The grass was thick and ran high as a saddled horse. Alysha didn't want to, but she gripped Helena by the shoulder, pulled her close, and whispered. "We'll see each other again soon, but we must split up. Head back to Wolf Hills, find the thorn burrow on the other side of the river, and hide there. I will distract them and meet you there. Cross the road and into the next field of grass."

Helena grabbed Alysha and held her by her shoulder for a moment. She pushed her away, and Alysha's eyes filled with fear of never seeing Helena again and anger at the soldiers for forcing this choice onto her. She felt the movement of a horse nearby and wanted to stay, wanted more than moments, angry smiles, and bitter laughter between pain and fright. Alysha pushed Helena away and called out.

"I'm here, you worthless pigs."

Alysha wiped her eyes and stood moving, thinking of what to do next. She needed to get them facing away from Helena so she could cross the road.

Two scouts moved toward Alysha as she held her axe. Brett held back, waiting to see what was happening four horse lengths away from Richard, who slowly approached Alysha.

"You there! Hold."

Alysha snapped back. "You hold. I lost the other three of my party and my horse. There's a crowd of refugees and soldiers from Grimwood on the edge of the forest over there." She pointed in the direction she and Helena came from. "They took Bob, my buddy, with a crossbow and knocked me from my horse. Hob said to run to the road for further support. Let's go before Hob's overwhelmed."

"Richard, I told you to," said Brett, making his way closer through the grass.

"No time for that, boys; follow my path on your horses. The grass is pushed down there. I'll run behind," Alysha said, standing before Richard.

"Where you from, soldier?" Richard asked, smiling down at Alysha.

"I'm a merc the Genteel Monks hired in from Counselor City."

"Ha, Monk's must be hurting if they are hiring mercs with the likes of you."

"I dunno, Richard, that axe looks dangerous enough," Brett said, but he didn't aim his spear at her.

"It is, it is. It took a few heads when we burnt some towns south of Counselor City. Let's go, my boy. Need some help so we can clean up this damn place."

She got close and could smell the bacon and wine they'd just eaten. Her stomach grumbled.

Richard offered his arm.

"Right up you go, if you're a merc, then you won't mind riding with me." She pulled at his arm, dragged Richard down into the grass, grabbed the saddle,, and hopped onto the horse. It kicked and fought against her and trampled its previous rider.

"The fucker, Maker's sweet breasts, Richard, what did you do," Brett said, peering over the grass looking for his friend and only finding Alysha on the scout's horse. "Stupid kid." The grass was so high it hid the mess she had made.

She squeezed her legs tight, gripped Stormkiss, steered the horse over Richard's trembling body again, and swung her axe. Blocking a swift spear blow as the blade passed, the wooden shaft got caught on the curve of her axe head. This knocked the wind out of her, and they grappled. Brett, the scout, had the height and weight advantage. She grabbed the spear shaft and twisted again and down, pulling at the soldier and the spear until she felt the weight shift. The scout didn't expect that, so he lost grip on his horse and fell with her. They stumbled and rolled into the tall grass, and she cut herself on Stormkiss, but so did the soldier. Brett's cut was deeper, and he moaned.

"Fuck I don't need this shit."

He tried to stand, but Helena came up from behind and pierced his back and chest with her sword.

He gagged and groaned before the warm blood spilled from his mouth and piss released from below.

"Can you stop hurting yourself, please," Helena said, looking at Alysha, who looked even worse than she did a few minutes ago.

"Just get the horses. They said there would be more coming shortly. And thank you for coming back."

They mounted up and moved across the road to another field. Behind them, two groups of riders carrying torches searched for their missing comrades and more refugees. The light faded by the coming night, and smoke from the city of Grimwood fell.

"Where, too? Back to Wolf Hills?"

"No, something tells me we must go to the Litchbury Mire."

A priestess can be found at the tower in the swamp.

"What for?"

"I'm betting we'll find some people that may hate the Holy Imperium as much as we do."

Austin - The Forest is Bleeding

Elora and Parker circled to the left of the lodge, and Austin circled right, poking his head into the skeleton of what remained of the hunting lodge. He saw broken glass and burnt timbers, but nothing else remained. Everything was taken by whoever destroyed it or by the flames. Austin jogged to the end of the house and stood, his hands on his side, taking a breath. His feet ached now, and he didn't relish the swim across the high and fast Razorshine River afterward. He saw a flash of light against the broken glass and scared himself, tripping over a burnt, broken timber and falling onto his back. He lay on a wooden floor, weakened by the fire. The floor groaned and gave way, and he dropped into a cellar.

Austin's back flared up in pain as dust and debris fell over him. He growled and looked around, rolling onto his hands and knees. He'd fallen into the ransacked wine cellar.

Elora tried to quietly yell down. "Austin, you, ok?"

"Yeah, I fell. I'm in the cellar. Give me a second."

He investigated the empty cellar and found the floor near the wall dug up. Stooping to examine the whole, he found a large rectangle box smashed open, its contents long gone. Austin thought of the missive and spun around, kicking in frustration, and worked to see if anything else remained. He failed, though. Whatever General Casting was looking for was long gone.

He moved to climb out of the cellar.

Parker lent a hand as Austin made his way up.

"Can you run?" Elora asked, looking desperate. "The crossing started."

"We don't know what happened here, but there is no heirloom, and everything else is gone. This place was looted before it was burnt. We need to get back to Pap now."

"Let's get the fuck out of wilds," Parker agreed.

"We push back towards the river, wade in, and take it downstream, crossing at a swim," Elora commanded. "Let's go!"

They ran carelessly, not concerned about any noise approaching the river. Elora caught another footpath as Austin and Parker followed. They picked up speed at first sight of the water. Elora saw a movement to her left and ducked. Austin instantly threw his tomahawk and pulled his sword at the dark shape. It could have been a child or a bear; he didn't care; he just needed to hit the river and cross. Anything on this side of the river was an enemy. The axe fell into a human dressed in leather and light furs, their face painted for war. The soldier sat on his knees, an axe embedded in the arm that carried a well-made steel mace. Austin followed, cutting the man's throat, pulled the axe out, and continued running. A moment later, he heard a grunt, and as his momentum kept him going, he jumped and turned to see Parker on his hands and knees, crawling towards Austin. He'd two large arrow shafts, one in the left leg straight through and another in his lower back.

"No," he said out of breath. More arrows followed, and Parker fell to the forest floor feathered with several more shafts. Austin sprinted towards the river at a zigzag, hoping to avoid the arrows that continued to fly at him and Elora. Elora splashed into the water and dove down; Austin followed quickly, losing sight of her as stones and arrows flew over his head, the crisp rushing water taking over his senses as he swam, the shock of the cold water half drowning him as the river carried him toward the sounds of battle.

* * *

Austin washed on shore on the Holy Imperium-held side of the river, gasping and sputtering, coughing up blood from a cracked rib. He moved his arm limply and moaned as an arrow shaft jutted from the top of his shoulder. He lay on his stomach and shifted the arrow. It pierced his leather jerkin but hit the metal rings that helped strap it down and went past the cloth and into his shoulder. His arm and fingers moved and worked, but painfully, the pressure of using his arm nearly caused him to faint, and suddenly he was moving, dragged off the rocky riverbank and into the canopy of the woods, a mess of ferns providing cover. He smelled pine and wet leaves as pain shimmed down his arm. Elora, her face severe but with a half-smile, had scrambled to get him under cover.

"Parker didn't make it. He took three arrows in the back and fell. I couldn't save him. I couldn't," said Austin in wet exhaustion and pain.

"Fuck!" Elora barks. "This whole mission is a mess. I hope Prince Damon gets his money's worth out of this shit; I've lost too many friends. We don't have the soldiers to fight what they have over there." She stopped complaining, forgetting where and what they were dealing with, and squatted, looking at the arrow lodged in Austin's shoulder.

"Hold still. I am going take this out," she sighed. "Going to miss Parker. A great scout and dutiful with horses." Elora looked to the other side of the forest for a moment. The bonding from trauma secured them to each other with every breath that remained inside. Elora sat Austin up, smiled back at him, smacked his face hard, and pulled the arrow out. Austin grunted but didn't scream, not knowing what was across the river and if they were tracked somehow as she staunched the wound.

They heard the battle down the river, the crying of horses and men.

"We need to get back to the Union Dogs and Pap," Elora breathed, steeling herself.

Austin counted to three and held his breath as he got up, black spots dotting the corners of his eyes.

Elora smacked his face again. "You feel that?"

"Yeah, quit fucking hitting me."

"You have battle fog from the run and the arrow; I'm making sure you're awake, in the now, and not dizzy and seeing fairies and shit. Okay?"

"Yeah," Austin nodded. "I won't be much in a fight, but my fingers move, and I can run, I think."

Elora took a leather strap and a wet cloth and strapped his arm down tight. "We'll get you mended up when we get back. Don't fall behind. We need to keep going. You can still swing the tomahawk but don't worry about using it unless you see me in trouble. We'll circle to the back and see what's happening. Let's go," she commanded.

Austin obeyed.

She was off, and Austin followed, his head dizzy but clearing. The pain and adrenaline pushed him on further. They made it to the front of the Oxfell Gate, where a makeshift triage was set up inside the compound walls. Soldiers lay on the ground as a surgeon and his apprentice evaluated and treated the wounded. Blood, moans, and death lay in heaps. Austin felt it was one-fourth of the force they came with on the ground. The moans and cries came from the few living. The dead hadn't been separated yet. He hoped Pap was okay.

Elora walked through the soldiers asking for her father but didn't see him. Austin wasn't sure if that was good or bad.

They walked towards where the reserves should have been but found the area empty. They soon neared the river ford.

The soldiers had crossed and died in twos and threes as before, but this time, a platoon of soldiers had made it across to establish control for a brief time, but the archers on this side of the river couldn't cover them. The shafts in a circle of bodies were like nothing Elora had seen before. It amazed her that so many arrows and bolts could be placed into a body. She saw her father across the river surrounded by Union Dogs, the Imperial Army, and Blue Templar soldiers, all dead.

Austin saw his body through a haze of mist. In the shadows, he heard the roar of a triumphant war cry, heard someone cry "loose" from the edge of the river, and saw a reign of arrows drop into the shadows. Pekka Deeran, who oversaw the archers, continued the command.

He looked on and saw bodies of knights smashed against rocks further downstream as if they had fallen from a distance. The bodies lay maimed, the armor sliced open, heads pummeled by large stones and rocks, legs severed at the knee, arms and hands a distance away from the rest of the corpses.

Austin thought of the two large warhawks he saw earlier and wondered if there were more of those beasts in the sky and looked up to the opening canopy of the tree line.

"Sir Pekka, what's the status," yelled Austin.

Deeran looked with a deep stare Austin hadn't seen before and shook his head. Austin turned back to Elora as she stood on the shore, her gaze fixed on her father, dead on the other side. Arrows whizzed by at a distance, hitting the shore. Austin tore his eyes away from Elora and saw squire Hopesinger near Pap, covered in slashes and arrows, her arm missing above her elbow, eyes open and lifeless.

They watched as an orc clad in mail and armor walked over to the circle of corpses and pushed the dead away from Pap. The orc looked to be a war chief or leader, as her presence stopped all action around her.

"What in the Maker? Archers," yelled Pekka.

"Wait," Elora said. Pekka paused, and they watched as the orc commander bowed towards where Pekka, Austin, and Elora held the river with the remaining dwindling number of their forces. The orc, over six human feet tall, was clad in armor that would match a belted knight. She took out a tomahawk and knelt by the corpse of Pap. She opened his chest and forced her hand down, ripping Pap's heart out of the cavity. Elora choked audibly, tears falling as wrath and grief rose inside her. The orc took a bite from the heart and pounded her chest as she held her tomahawk aloft and roared in triumph. She put the heart back into Pap and stood and bowed again. Rain started to fall, and the orc howled to the sky.

Elora, uncaring about herself, moved toward the river slowly, the rain drenching her. She ignored any cover or the enemy force visible on the other side. A mixture of goblins, elves, orcs, and dwarves watched on. The water rushed around her knees, splashing away dirt and blood.

The enemy started to slowly chant "Wrathfall, Wrathfall, Wrathfall."

The storm from above washed away the blood from the orc's hands and face as she chewed, swallowed, and walked back into the forest's shadows. The chanting ended, and the rest followed.

Austin jumped toward Elora, splashing into the water, "Take cover, Elora, now!" He grabbed her with one hand as she stood in the open, uncovered in her anguish. He couldn't carry her; his arm was too weak, but he hoped his voice and concern would help carry the message. She looked on into the rain, watching as the orc that had eaten her father's heart was met by a goblin, and they disappeared into the darkness of the Blightbriar Wilds. She turned back as archers traded shafts across the river, a boundary between the two forces separating Elora's grief and revenge.

The Holy Imperium task force didn't have the soldiers to cross again to retrieve the dead. The remaining force pulled back, taking what they could. Austin saw Newt Crashbury as she walked back. "You see a foot soldier named Jaden?" Austin asked hopefully.

"They fell with Pap during the crossing and didn't make it to the shore; one of the warhawks grabbed him and gutted him. Left parts of the body spread across the river. They were all over the sky, spooking the horses, causing the knights to fall into the river." She spoke. "Monsters are real sir, the monsters we were told about when we were younger, they're real." She mentioned this coldly as if it happened every day. "Got to get back and grab more arrows to keep those fucking creatures at bay. Sir Pekka is in charge, and Brother Walder is injured. Brother Walder led the retreat after Pap and the others were killed. He saved many lives."

"I don't know what to say," Austin paused and looked back at the river from the cover of the forest. *What the fuck were they doing here?* His mind shifted from grief to disbelief, trying to understand why they were here in the first place. The rain came down straight and loud, making the water rise like the sky and river were merging. "I expect our enemies to counterattack. Let's get back to camp and prepare."

Austin looked at Elora but didn't say anything. She turned back to the river, spat, and watched the soldier retreat. Austin didn't like to say retreat, but they were returning to the cover of their fortified camp to dig in and hope their enemy didn't come with enough strength to wash over their palisade walls.

"Let's get whatever messages Pekka has and get out of here."

"We can't just leave him out there." Elora choked. "They'll eat him. We need to get his body back."

"I don't see how that's possible, at least right now. I think what we saw was a sign of honor, Elora. I think that orc eating the heart was supposed to be respectful."

Elora looked at Austin with anger and grief. "Why the fuck did we even get sent here?"

"General Casting and Prince Damon sent me and this task force to secure the hunting lodge and look for something. To look for something that was already gone." Austin said defensively, yet his heart wasn't in it.

"Prince Damon sent us on a fool's quest to find a Paragon of the Maker, the tomahawk that fucking orc has in her belt," she said.

"I think so, yes."

"Foolish children's stories got a lot of good people killed. This is all a joke. Now, what do we do?" Elora looked tired.

"We tell Prince Damon and General Casting they need an army to get it back. That they need an army to protect the cities from the Wrathfall."

The river rose. Elora saw now it was going to wash a lot of the bodies down and away, never to be found.

"We'll leave early tomorrow morning," Elora said. "We'll clean up your arm and go."

The remaining soldiers fell back to their war camp and lit torches. Sir Pekka Deeran was now in command, while Brother Walder either recovered or died from his wounds. Austin visited the man, who had one of his monks sitting by him in prayer. The surgeon had amputated the bottom of his left foot. He was delusional, in and out of sleep.

Austin held his hand for a moment, trying to be positive. The camp was in a sorry state. Deeran would need help.

"I could use you, Austin, you know that. You can help me organize and keep this place clean," Pekka said as he stood in Pap's tent, his tent now.

"I can't do much for a short bit," Austin lied. His arm was tolerable, and he could fight if necessary and ride, but it would be weeks before he would be useful. "I think it's important I report directly to the capital; those are my orders, which would be best for you and the soldiers here. You need replacements."

"I sent your squire Newt to the nearest keep on the Kings and Queens roads, requesting any militia or soldiers available to meet me back at Hawkhallow

Village. We'll dig in deep there and fortify the Hades out of that position. Lots of open ground around it. We'll see the fuckers coming and fill them with shafts before they hit the walls. Going to build a few siege engines, too, and just start tossing stones into the other side of the river. Do you disagree? You may speak freely, Austin,"

Austin turned around momentarily and looked at the tent and Pap's effects. He would grab a few personal items to take back as Jasper may want to remember Pap. He also didn't want someone taking up Wildcat symbols and tainting the Prince's Royal Guard.

"No, it wouldn't be smart to remain so close. I don't want to give up this camp, and we may have to retake it, but I don't think we can hold it with the current state of the force."

"I think what we face across that river is bigger than imagined," Pekka said. "We could defend ourselves better in an open field of battle."

"At least you'd see the warhawks before they attacked."

Pekka Deeran put his hands behind his back and stretched.

"Goblins, elves, orcs, dwarves working together. They had humans among them. I've been to cities not segregated out west; Grimwood was open to elven tradesmen, and the Republic of Wind had open borders as the name suggests, but nothing like this." He stopped and stepped towards Austin. "We saw the warhawks. They're real. This is not some storybook. If they have warhawks, who knows what else the wilds hide. We'll hold the village. Get us support."

Austin nodded, and they shook hands.

"When do you leave?"

"Break of light tomorrow; Elora is coming with."

"I suspected. And what of the rest of the Union Dogs?"

"They remain under your command until their contract is up. If they wish to negotiate, you have General Casting's backing. Elora is giving orders to their new leader now. I thought she would be back by now, though."

Pekka laughed a little. "I don't like her, but she's a competent commander. They're well-trained killers. I misjudged her, but not by much. I bet she went to go grab her father's body."

Austin glanced at Pekka, but that thought had never occurred to him. He didn't wait to be dismissed and charged out of the tent and toward the front, stopping at the last outpost.

Two soldiers stood on watch, each with a horn in hand.

"You go out there, you die. I ain't going to stop you, but if you don't come back, your family isn't getting your back pay," said the guard on the left. He wore a tight brown and red beard.

Austin wasn't wearing any of his Wildcat uniform. They thought of him as just a scout.

"Did someone slip through this way, another scout?"

"She didn't even let us stop her. She just asked for the safe word to return."

"How long ago?"

"Maybe one, two hours."

"Shit," he said and looked at the two soldiers. "Password?"

"Lightning."

"And the challenge?"

"Maiden of Storms."

"Be careful, once of the Templar hear about this, they'll string you up for heresy," Austin said. He put his hand to his tomahawk and jogged into the night. This was stupid, but deep down, he knew Elora would do the same.

* * *

He kept low and was aware of the pain in his arm. It moved in the sling as he shifted in and out of the brush and trees. He stayed off the main trail where the sentries guarded as if the enemy would use the main trail to attack. He shook his head reminding himself. The rain from earlier had passed and the moon shined in brief glimpses through the forest canopy. Owls hooted, and he heard squirrels or mice darting for their lives, easing his anxiety. Austin continued moving towards the river, wondering if the warhawks could see at night or if something more dangerous haunted the forest when the sun dipped below the horizon.

Austin crept to the left flank where the archers had initially set up and provided cover during the attack, figuring it would be the best view to see where Pap fell. On the other side, all the bodies were gone, dragged away. It looked as if the area had recently seen a flood. The only signs of battle lay on the Holy Imperium side of the river.

Goblins could see well in the dark and were quiet predators. It was why the war camp had lit torches around the base, to blind any that may attempt to crawl in and cause chaos or slit throats.

He watched and waited, looking between two trees, and imagined goblins circling the area. The enemy had guards just as the Holy Imperium did.

Shortly after, something shifted to his right, and he adjusted the weight he squatted at, preparing to defend himself. A stone landed deep to his left at a distance in the darkness. His focus shifted, and he saw movement in the forest undergrowth, shadows moving in the night, pushing, and slithering towards the noise and away from Austin's direction.

A hand crept up to his mouth, and a knife jabbed at his back.

"You're improving, but I can still smell your musk."

Elora let go of his mouth and sheathed her knife.

"No bodies left, let's get back and rest up; Pap's gone." Though she tried to hide it, saying those words pained her.

They moved back to the base camp, carrying only sorrow. They rested briefly before leaving for Hudson City hoping for answers and to gain more soldiers to battle what they had come to call the enemy, the Wrathfall.

The Gloomspire Gate - The Choice of Freedom

The stones were solid and untouched by civilized hands. Forged in the depths below Vineland and through the push of time, the winds of autumn, the cold breath of winter, the spring storms, and rays of heat from the Profane gods shaped the two cliffs on each side of the knight commander. She felt the power of the original four races: the elves, the goblins, the orcs, and the dwarves. Her hand gripped into a fist as she thought about the last race that came to the shores of the Erie Sea long ago like a disease, humanity.

Nirinath Sladestone could smell their fires across the river now. If she tried, she could hear their absurdity and loudness as they disturbed the forest across the river. They came now like King Christopher before. They came to conquer, farm, breed, and consume all that was beautiful and pure.

The Gloomspire now held families, and they were building culture and a new life among themselves. The orcs and goblins among the people known as the Wrathfall were writing and printing their histories. They thrived and grew by befriending the lost elven tribes, the clanless dwarves, and even human outcasts and former slaves.

The Holy Imperium had come to take all of this. They came seeking answers with swords, spears, and shields. If it wasn't the Holy Imperium, it was Great Brightland before them, or the Legion of Carigreed, or the Nation of Stouya.

The hunting lodge was initially left alone. They'd allowed the so-called royal humans to hunt until they took too much until the royal greed and lust spilled blood and broke innocence. When the hunt burnt a home of a mixed family. Knight Commander Sladestone took it upon herself to lead the blood revenge. She unleashed the warhawks first to sow fear and then came with blade, arrow, and fire, leaving none alive. For those who fought well, she was treated with respect, and she did so to the wounded, and this battle was no different. She remembered the slick blood and taste of the commanding knight's spirit across her lips.

"Bring the scouts. They will have a choice to join us in our freedom or continue their ignorant service to their prince who wears a tin crown," said Commander Sladestone. She could feel the fallen spirits seeping back into the earth after the battle.

A dwarve, two orcs, and a strong human guard brought three soldiers to Commander Sladestone. They were bound at the feet, legs, and hands. All three were wounded, but they would survive if treated properly and quickly.

Commander Sladestone stood above the first.

"You have survived a battle against my army. We are the Wrathfall. We seek to make our holy lands safe for our families, friends, and loved ones. This Prince Damon and his Holy Imperium seek domain over us, wish to make slaves of our children, rape, murder, and burn our crops and villages. You can join us in this fight, live free among the Wrathfall, start a new life, or stay at Prince Damon's royal side as his puppet and servant. What say you?"

Kenneth Coinfell, looked up into Sladestone's green eyes. Blood was splattered across his face; the two crossbow bolts were taken out of his shoulder, and he bled from wounds on both legs. He would survive if Falstaer Vicorm allowed it.

Kenneth was a mere boy, old enough to fight but not old enough to be a man. He shook his head. "I don't understand," he spat. "You ate his heart; you ripped out Sir Meldguard's heart."

"You are a young one. You don't know our ways; the Wrathfall is a united group; the word you use is culture. We are dwarves, elves, even goblins, and the great orcs of the east and west, and if you wish, yes, you, my child, maybe one of us." Commander Sladestone placed her large hand on Kenneth's face, smashing his lips together, "Even a weak human is welcome here. Now choose, I have work to do."

She released the boy's head, and even though she could easily crush it, she waited.

The Rain Miser Falstaer Vicorm sighed. "He will deny us; nearly all of the humans do so."

"I'm dead, anyway. Never would I join you, savages." He was defiant yet weak, and his body sagged as Commander Sladestone slid her tomahawk, the Servant's Guide, across Kenneth's neck without emotion.

Commander Sladestone moved on, wiping her axe head clean. The other two scouts looked on, soaked in fear and agony.

"This goes the same for both of you. I saw you fight; my soldiers feel you are worthy of redemption."

"How could you, how could you eat Pap's heart! You fucking pig," Leslie screamed and cried.

Keyla Dirkbuckle was delirious from pain and fever as the ropes strained against her skin and muscles. The wounds in her back warmed with the last pumps of adrenaline, defiant even in the end.

"We of the Wrathfall are not beyond who we are and where we came from. If I find a warrior suitable, as an equal, as a great enemy, I will honor them to my gods. I sacrifice and take their strength and give them a rightful seat at my table upon my death as an equal by tasting of the heart. It is the essence of all they signify and have been. This is an honor. Unlike the ears, noses, and fingers your kind sells back in the cities as gifts and trinkets."

Leslie Greathane looked at Keyla, blood dripping from her eyes. She had fallen early in the battle and was swept down by the river to be found by goblins. She hadn't known about what occurred to Pap until Kenneth mentioned it. She thought through her fevered pain she'd be eaten alive, but they made a stretcher and carried her up onto stone stairs and towards the sky; she felt as if heaven were near in one way or another.

"You can save us, heal us if we join you?"

Sladestone looked at her. "This is the Rain Miser; if it is possible, he will heal you; when you join the Wrathfall, you will be saved."

"Choose now before your lives slip from your hands or mine," Falstaer said bluntly.

The orc and goblin looked down on them.

Keyla and Leslie looked up at this powerfully built orc and the goblin mage beside her. They were righteous in their fear and grasping to survive.

"Heal us, and we will join the Wrathfall."

Keyla slumped and passed out. Leslie took her friend's weight, and she felt her bounds cut. She gave no resistance.

A dwarve and goblin grabbed her by her armpits and placed her on a cool stone table. They had dragged four of them up stone-carved stairs. One of the prisoners died and was thrown off the side. Now she lay with Keyla, exhausted. She shook and felt blood leaving. Leslie heard the voice of a goblin, Vicorm, singing. She reached her hand out for Keyla and moved her head as if drunk. They had stripped off her clothes, and yet she could do nothing as her body was too tired and heavy.

"What are you doing? What are you doing to her?"

"Relax, my child. We're cleaning you with water and making sure you heal properly. I work with the knowledge of elves and goblins at my hands."

"Are you going to sacrifice us?"

The goblin giggled.

"No, we laid you down to cut your armor and clothes off. You will bathe in the purest waters you have ever touched, and I will do my best to bind your wounds and sing you to your health. You are too hurt to walk."

The goblin wore a large bird beak over his nose and mouth, sometimes muffling his voice. "Leaftoss, bring the stretcher and shower them in the waterfall there. Quickly, they are losing too much blood."

Leslie was naked as blood seeped from her wounds. The water touched her, and she shivered and screamed as she was submerged. She jolted and struggled, and then she was pulled from the waters, wrapped up in a soft cloth, and placed back on the stone table, now cleaned of her blood. The weird goblin wrapped her wounds and sang. The goblin's movements were daft and sure, and the song sounded mournful and sweet. The tune reminded her of a ballad about a young girl's broken heart. The pain in her wounds remained but lessened. She rolled her head over and saw Keyla jerking in the water as an elve and goblin pulled her from the water.

"Sometimes, when people join, they feel uncomfortable; I'm sorry for your friend Kenneth. He would have made a decent citizen of the Wrathfall," said Falstaer Vicorm. The goblin's nails stitched up a sword wound on her arm as it sang. She looked up at the goblin.

"Will she live?"

"You will. I have yet to know if your friend will make it, but I will do what I can, what I must. Your lives are as important as my children's lives now that you are the Wrathfall. Now close your eyes and rest."

Leslie's eyes flicked, and she watched as the goblin walked over to Keyla, singing to her wounds with a song in his heart. Her eyes flicked and closed, and she fell into the soft cadence of the Blightbriar Wilds and Castle Gloomspire behind her, lost in the mists.

Doc - Constitutional Convention

"We're going to be late, Doc!"

"Damn it, don't you think I know that! We've one more stop and then off to the courthouse." Doc smelled of bourbon and stress.

"They moved the secret meeting to a courthouse. How is this even a secret anymore?"

"The Holy Imperium will know everything soon enough, but we'll call it a preliminary meeting of the House of Lords if the matter comes up," mumbled Doc as he gripped his pipe in his teeth. "This isn't official, just an airing of grievances among friends. You may even call them allies."

"Just because we're in Affectus doesn't mean the Holy Imperium isn't in control here, Doc," said Maynard.

Doc stopped and looked at him, "The Society of Shadows runs deep here, deeper than any other city except the Crescent City, which is now the weakest I've ever seen since General Hammer Clinton took it over. The only ones not bought and paid here are the Order of the Blue Rose, and those, from my understanding, are extorted and look the other way," Doc finished and took a nip from his hip flask.

They walked quickly through the streets of Affectus, their boots knocking on the brick-lined streets of a side road, and approached an official-looking building where two city guards stood at the door.

"Doc, this looks like a constable's office. What exactly do you need here?" asked Maynard. "If you're supposed to talk in the next hour, you must prepare notes." His feet were tired, and he considered asking Doc for a sip of his flask, which consisted of a mix of bourbon, cold tea, and reefer leaves.

"Just because you're no longer my apprentice doesn't mean you get to tell me what to do, you bastard," Doc said. He stopped abruptly and patted his patchwork military jacket down, putting on spectacles that changed colors and aided his vision. "You should get a pair of these, Maynard."

Maynard sighed. He had already been told this a half dozen times. Doc put on the spectacles juggled his staff in the crook of his arm, took out a flask, and sipped. Usually, he would put it away, but circumstances had changed between them since Runt's death, so he passed him the flask, and Maynard took it. Doc watched Maynard grasp the flask and noticed his lack of fingernails.

"I should ask Maynard," Doc stopped. "Truthfully, this is what we do. It leads to nothing good. We curse ourselves to achieve feats nobody else can and do it to protect our friends, family, and, sometimes, something higher than that. Did you lose your fingernails to retrieve the staff, or was it the cost of your work with Runt?"

Maynard took a sip from the flask and coughed but didn't directly answer. "Doc, I chose this life. I was nothing without you. You gave me schooling, purpose, and a will to live. I won't squander it, and I won't give up what I have," he whispered. "I love having the power."

"I understand that, dammit, it's just that sometimes the price for it…"

Maynard looked at his hands and noticed that they lacked fingernails. The skin was not calloused, just a hard scab.

"Be careful, Maynard. You may not be my apprentice anymore, but that doesn't mean I don't-"

"Holy Maker's tits, I think you may say something nice to me."

"What I— fuck you, you worm," Doc snarled, rolling his eyes.

Maynard put his hand on Doc's shoulder, something he had never done before. "I don't claim to understand you, Doc. You're a shitty teacher and a worse friend, and you disappear when situations get bad, but sometimes you aren't a total asshole."

"Here, put these on for a second," Doc said. He handed Maynard his rounded, multi-colored spectacles. Maynard placed them on his face, and his eyes adjusted. He looked around the alley at the two guards and Doc.

"I would do anything for Vineland. Anything to create a place where my daughter or others like her could grow up in safety. She's gone, but I still dream of a day when Vineland is better. The Holy Imperium and Prince Damon are not the right ways to do it. I didn't want Runt to die. If anything, it should have been his brother who died."

"Stop, Doc," he ripped off the glasses. "Why did I see the color green on your face when you were talking."

"Simple Maynard, the glasses change color when people speak. Sure, they block the sun out, but they change color. Red is when someone lies. Other shades have other meanings." Doc took another pull from the flask, batted away an imaginary fly, and mumbled lightly to the voices nobody else heard.

"What does green mean, Doc?"

Doc grabbed his staff and walked toward the door, mumbling some more. Maynard could have sworn he heard the word sincerity.

"Nothing, nothing. Come on, we need one more to form our trinity," demanded Doc.

* * *

"Who're these two scoundrels?" said a thin female orc chained to a bench inside a constable's office.

"Watch your mouth, toad, or you'll get slapped around again. That crazy-looking man and his multi-patched jacket and the weird-looking kid wearing spectacles? That's Doc Young, battlemage from the Crimson Struggle. Killed loads of people up north during The Battle of the Reaping," said the jailer sitting at his desk with his feet up. "Ain't that right, you piece of horse dung?"

The orc chained to the bench sat up straighter.

"Fred, good to see you again."

"Doc, look at you. Look like a stacked pile of shit. I'm glad to see you sober and not chained to the wall like this one. What can I do you for?" said Fred, who was not sober and who looked like a fat piece of shit.

"Actually, I'm here for her." Doc pointed at the detained orc.

Fred, the jailer, sat up and straightened his jacket, which did not fit his rolls.

"Is that so? Rook here is scheduled to be deported back down south near Magnoliafield. Slave catchers brought her in, saying she left a plantation months ago."

"My name isn't Rook, you swine. It's Charlotte Rainspire and." The orc took a breath, shaking her shackles slightly. "And I work for *The Plain Herald* in Grimwood."

"She's an escaped slave. What do you want from her." Fred said, ignoring Rainspire.

"Fred, we've had wretched times together. You beat me over the head with a club and let me sleep in your fine dungeons for two days a few years back," Doc smirked at the memory, "but I need Miss Rainspire here for an assignment. She's telling the truth."

Doc looked at Rainspire. She had long, chin-length dark hair, which held a slight curl and was thinner than most orcs he'd seen. She wore horns still, but only two, and they were short, not the larger ones he'd seen on warriors on battlefields. No, he was sure she was telling the truth. Her face was green, and Fred's was a deep red when he spoke.

"I think maybe you're short on your bribes for the week to the Society of Shadows, so you found this one drunk in a wine cellar and are going to ship her down the road to pay off a debt," said Doc. Maynard shifted next to Doc and stood in a more defensible position. Doc smiled at that. "You know the leader of the society is due in for the big not-so-secret meeting today, right?"

Fred stood up abruptly. "Get out, or I'll-"

Doc's eyes started to glow for a moment.

"Sit the fuck down, or you'll burn when you piss for the rest of your short, miserable life, you shit stain!" Doc pointed to Gaston's Beard, and a spark jumped from the tip, dancing slowly to the ground. Rainspire shifted in her seat at the bench, straining against the chain. The spark started slowly jumping on the floor in fits, hopping towards Fred.

"Or you can take this token of our friendship." Doc threw a short bag of coins on the constable's desk.

Fred grabbed the money. "Okay, put it out, man! Maker, please put the spark out!" He pleaded, moving against the wall.

"Key, please?"

Doc snapped his fingers, the spark went out, and Fred threw the keys at Maynard.

"Hi, I'm Maynard, and this is Doc," said Maynard as he unlocked Rainspire's manacles. She wore painter overalls and a loose sailor's shirt underneath.

"Thank you, Maynard." She nodded to Doc, walked over to a cabinet, grabbed her tools, walked over to Fred, and spat at him. The gob of spit and phlegm arched and landed on his face. She stepped out into the sunlight and freedom.

They walked to the edge of the alley as it touched the busy main street. A farmer couldn't fit a cart through the alley without it getting stuck between the two buildings. Charlotte was busy putting her quills, knives, pencils, and other implements into the multiple pockets of her overalls. Maynard noticed she had also attached a belt, which held an assortment of pockets and a pocket knife.

"Alright, I'm grateful for that, but what do you want from me?"

"You're a reporter and artist for *The Plain Herald*, correct?" asked Doc. We're scheduled for a meeting shortly and think we might have a story." Doc handed her a flask. "It's whiskey."

She took it, tipped it towards Doc, winked at Maynard, and downed it. "I'm lucky to have gotten out with my horns still attached. You bought my freedom and want me to draft a story. Sorry, pal, I have other priorities, like getting the Hades out of here. Fred might fear you, but that bootlicker will come after me when you two are gone."

"Fred's a fucking shit stain and knows better to trifle with me. What I'm trying to say is, do you know how to take care of a tree?" Doc asked.

"You give it freedom and water it with blood," Charlotte replied, looking from Doc to Maynard.

"You work for *The Plain Herald*, a respectful rag, better than the *Post Examiner* up in Hudson City; that's trash."

"I worked for the *Post Examiner* a few summers back; the editor was pretty abusive and didn't pay enough," said Charlotte. "Made me work the slums section, making my folk look bad."

"And now you work for Grimwood's *Plain Herald*?" said Doc.

"You know that Grimwood is under siege or fallen by now, right?" questioned Maynard. "Prince Damon's moving against any city-state that doesn't swear full alliance to his crown."

"What?" Charlotte shook her head. "What are you talking about? I send missives there all the time."

"When was the last time you heard back? Or got paid, for that matter?" Doc asked.

Charlotte scratched at her face and shook her head, thinking.

"I haven't heard shit from the head office in a while, just the local paper here where I send my stories out," said Charlotte. "What makes you say that, Doc."

"We have on good authority that three of the four gates of Grimwood fell to siege not too long ago. The city was wrecked with sickness beforehand. By now, it's well under the control of the Holy Imperium."

"What about the Gray Vultures? I had friends in the city guards as well," said Charlotte.

"Most are dead from the Smoldering Plague," Maynard looked at Doc for a moment and patted his pocket. Charlotte saw he lacked fingernails. "Doc had received letters before we left Olde Ridgewatch noting as much, and I confirmed it through messenger bird before we got into the city. I had friends at the university there. My professor said she had moved the entire Grimwood Library onto Pinelight Island. The entire university had evacuated. Doc used to teach there."

Maynard pulled out a thin piece of paper and rolled a cigarette.

"You smoke," said Doc as purple smoke seeped from his pipe. "Nasty habit."

"Calms my nerves for this meeting, that's all." They talked as if Charlotte didn't exist. She began tapping her foot, taking in what they had told her. Maynard's hands trembled as he lit his cigarette, notching a copper filter. He rolled another and gave one to Charlotte, whose hands were unsteady as she processed the news before her.

"You mean it's gone? Grimwood, the paper, the university, all of it?"

"Books were saved, some of the faculty and the students. If the Smoldering Plague doesn't take them, General Flint's First Army will have finished the rest of the city." Doc paused. "Flint's vanguard in a siege would be the Genteel Monks, whose fanaticism will bring blade and fire."

"Fuck the prince," said Charlotte.

Doc and Maynard smiled.

"Look, I'm sorry for the shit news and all, but as we're going to this meeting that nobody knows about, yet everyone seems to know about, would you join and write a few stories, taking notes for posterity's sake?"

"I don't write for free, Doc. Every journalist knows that."

"I know Olivia Franklin at the *Hudson City Journal*. She'll take you on as a roaming reporter."

"That paper's gone," said Charlotte. "Prince Damon outlawed it this past winter."

"It went underground, and she needs the help," said Doc. Maynard stood back, taking in the news as much as Charlotte was. Since Runt's death, Doc had let his thoughts and plans spill out. Maynard was disgusted and amazed.

"How much does it pay?"

"More than what you are making now, Miss Rainspire," said Doc, and he smiled again like a cat full of a day's fresh catch at a pier.

"Cut your hand of your own free will, my friends." Doc sliced his hand gently.

"Really," said Charlotte. "A blood pact? That's childish."

"Trust Doc," said Maynard.

"Trees need to grow, Charlotte Rainspire," finished Doc.

Maynard cut his hand and handed Charlotte the blade. They all shook, and Charlotte was weaker yet happier afterward.

"Come on. Before we make our way to the courthouse, let's drink to cool ourselves off," said Doc. "This heat doesn't agree with my stomach." He coughed, stumbling away as if already drunk.

They walked into McGrave's Ale House. The building was full of people milling about and chirping with purpose and gusto. One of the oldest buildings in the city, the inside was filled with catacombs of dens and hallways connecting the large front-facing beer hall, a perfect place to meet in a large group or perform a back room deal in the shadow of candlelight. The two upper floors were used to sleep off a drunk or sleep with an old friend, and the basement held several cellars and passages out of the building and into the sewers.

Doc moved up to the bar, the scent of sawdust and piss filling his lungs. An old goblin sat in the corner eating crackers and sausage, five empty pints before him. He giggled to himself at seeing Doc, staying out of the light as he prepped his mind and body for work later in the evening.

"Three darks and three lights, please, my lady."

"Pay up first, Doc, or you'll get horse piss," the bartender shot back.

"What? Yes, of course," Doc said, slightly incensed. He paid and handed the drinks around.

"Comrades, to new beginnings and past sins." Doc raised his tankard.

"Huzzah," they all said, smiling, except Charlotte.

"Doc, you know I'll write what I see and not some propaganda, right," she said uneasily.

"You write what you see at this meeting; it's a grouping of fair-minded people like the House of Lords before Prince Damon disbanded it. Afterwards, you travel with Maynard and me. You'll see the horrors and tragedy the Holy Imperium wrecks upon this land, and you'll write about that, too. Write for what pays, my friend. Write for what pays. Now let's go, it's past lunch, and they started an hour ago without us. I heard the Gray General may even show up, and he's got a new friend now."

Charlotte finished her beer feeling light-headed and weak.

Before Maynard could blink, Doc finished his, but he was always like that. His thirst was insatiable and necessary. They constantly whispered and screamed at him if he sobered. The price he pays for power.

* * *

"Sinners, bastards, and criminals, the lot of you!" Doc yelled as he opened the Affectus Courthouse doors.

"Maker's tits, seriously Doc? You're going to get us killed," Maynard whispered loudly and then said, "Sorry, sorry we're late," as he bumped and shoved his way through the crowd.

A richly dressed older man held sway over a packed audience. He gestured with a closed fist, using his thumb as a pointing finger, and leaned into the audience's attention while others stood gossiping and watching as a tall, regal woman waited for her turn to retort in the middle of the courtroom. The windows of the courthouse were ajar, and heat radiated inside the building. Rum punch was handed around, along with clear and dark liquor bottles.

"We aren't sorry; Hades never apologize," Doc said; he breathed out a purplish smoke from his pipe which followed him like ink spilling on a scroll of paper and cut through the crowd pushing to the center of the courtroom. Maynard and Charlotte split off from Doc to observe the meeting.

"I haven't seen this many important people since I was at Prince Damon's court," whispered Charlotte, "as an undercover servant." She was leaning against a banister inside the center of the court, splashing ink on the floor and sketching as quickly as possible, leaning to her left and right to get a look at the speakers.

"Remind me who each person is, Maynard. I need names."

"Doc, you know, of course. The other two speakers are Brice Hitchson from Wheathold in the Rosewood Dominion. He's one of the wealthiest men in Vineland and owns plantations worked by serfs and slaves alike. There are rumors about him that echo throughout Vineland."

"I already don't like him. Who's the other one, the formal-looking elve? She's not from the Blightbriar. I don't recognize the beading in her hair."

"If my notes serve me correctly, that is Lady Braya Summerbrake from beyond the Stagger Wall, an emissary," Maynard said, thinking he should have brought something to drink with him. The heat rose along with the whispering and gossiping during the debates.

"Holy Maker," said Charlotte.

"Holy Maker indeed. She stands for the Hazefire Confederacy and may represent the Dawnworth and Honeybreak city-states," said Maynard. "That area is in constant turmoil and has been fought over more than the

Gloomspire. So regal or not, her say in that area would be up for debate by different voices."

"Nobody wants to hear from a coward more worried about his personal fortune than the community they live in," Doc said, interrupting Brice Hitchson as he walked to the center of the courthouse and accepted the debate between the two speakers. "There are nobles and merchants worth more than empires and countries, and you bitch about your tea as if that ran the world." The crowd inside gasped as they saw a mad bald man wearing shaded glasses and a patchwork military coat call one of the wealthiest men in Vineland a coward.

"Here, here, everyone quiet down and show each other respect," said the booming voice of Mercy Pitcher, who stood for the Union of Dockers from Lackmore. She pounded a gavel at a podium next to a large tub of rum punch. Her voice was stern, and she commanded obedience. "The floor presents Hunter Young, an emissary of Grimwood University."

"I should challenge you to a duel for calling me a coward. You jumped up, hedge witch!" Brice growled, smiled, and turned around, his arms out. "But I am a man of peace, and this city has an open policy of allowing all to be free of violence, so let me counter and say, Doc, the tea trade is suffering; the Holy Imperium tax is undercutting us."

"Well, it's not a tax then. They're undercutting your stolen tea. Raise the price of your tea, you idiots, or go legit. Do I have to do everything here," Doc growled.

"Doc, I didn't think you'd make it; I heard you were busy off playing chaperon with a group of misfits, a man with few friends, few brains, and no lands. Why are you even here?" retorted Brice, and members of the courtroom laughed at Doc. "If this were a real House of Lords, you wouldn't have a vote!"

"I say, I say, you barely represent the University of Grimwood, more or less the entire city," said a man squirrely in complexion but dressed sharply even for the hot temperatures radiating throughout the summer heat.

"That is Richard Ratwolf, Dean of Staghollow University. He's next to Dean Slither from Mount Nittany University and a student, Hattie, who I know," said Maynard, and he nodded toward them. They exchanged a moment, smiling. "Richard is most likely representing the interests of the entire Silver Ivy League and keeping an eye on matters for the capital. I would be worried about what information he sends back to Hudson City."

"I've had a hunch that the Silver Ivy League holds as much power as the East Thamesbridge Company," Charlotte whispered to Maynard, who had lost his attention as he looked back at Hattie. Charlotte rolled her eyes, somewhat annoyed and a little jealous.

Doc smirked at Brice Hitchson, turned, and formally bowed to the other speaker, Richard Ratwolf, who now stood next to Lady Bray Summerbrake.

"Lady Braya Summerbrake, please forgive my interruption. I'm blessed to be in your presence, and your every breath is a gift to myself and the rest of this group as we gather to discuss the future."

She nodded with poise. She was slightly taller than Brice and Doc, and her long black hair was braided in flowers, beads, and silver.

"Well met, Sir Young, well met. Your power and your," she paused and looked him in the eyes, "madness travels in stories even across the Stagger Wall. I am fortunate to meet you again." She stopped as she saw his staff and turned away.

The crowd attending the gathering sat if they could, but others stood against walls and each other. People in the back hissed and jeered, getting drunk on the punch. They fanned themselves with pamphlets. Maynard noted the pamphlets were called *Ordinary Wit*.

Brice looked around, smirked, and then turned, but Lady Braya Summerbrake interrupted.

"Behave better, Doc, or you will be removed. Everyone here is a guest in this city, and it is known for its love and not its rudeness. We have representatives from all over Vineland from as far away as the Republic of the Wind and further." Brice and Doc nodded to Lady Braya. Ratwolf retook his seat.

"Doc, we were just discussing taxes and the like. Will you let us continue?" asked Brice, changing his tone.

"No," Doc said, pulling out his pipe and removing his glasses. "Enough bitching. Threads are tangled already, and they threaten to spin out of control, dammit. I bring news of Olde Ridgewatch and beyond."

"Sir Young, we all have brought news. Did you read today's papers?" questioned Sybil Pierce-Veil from the crowd. "Your presence here alone is enough to get any of us killed; you are branded a traitor to the Crown Prince, terrorist leader, and delinquent of many debts. If you were to step into Cinderpool, you would be arrested and thrown into a pit with haste."

"She represents the City-State of Cinderpool," whispered Maynard.

"How do you know all these people? You're just some kid from Grimwood," Charlotte Rainspire mumbled as she wrote furiously.

"Doc and I traveled from Olde Ridgewatch after the Ridgewatch Massacre, and we gathered the news as we went. I also have a way with birds now; a friend taught me," he said with a short smile.

"I bring news of the slave revolts and the burning of villages, the Blightbriar Wilds, and the fall of Grimwood," said Doc. "A rebellion has started, Sybil; at this point, we need to find what each of our hearts stands for. Do we continue the same old ways of kneeling to a royal family whose riches come from the backs of our hard work, or do we stand up for liberty and a voice for us all."

"You speak of treason, and the rest is hearsay," Ambrose Slitbear yelled in the crowd. He and his wife, Prudence, dwarves from Colehampton, stamped their hammers down hard on the ground.

Doc patted his bald head. The heat inside the courtroom was unmanageable. Someone gave him a cold pewter cup of rum punch. A large cast iron cauldron stood off to one side, where everyone was dipping their cups. Doc took a sip.

"No, it's not hearsay. The City-State of Grimwood has fallen. Captured and destroyed by the Holy Imperium First Army. General Robert Flint stands on the city's stones and ashes and now looks west. Olde Ridgewatch is now in revolt; the townspeople and members of the Bastards of Liberty have taken Bawstone Keep, and the Holy Imperium has left the city to deal with the slave revolts in Lackmore," counseled Doc. He reached into his pocket, sniffed a mixture of tobacco and wizard salt, and sneezed. Maynard put his hand on his head, knowing Doc's frequent drug use to stabilize himself made his debating skills weak in front of his peers.

"He's saying all the right words, but he's not winning any friends," Maynard whispered to Charlotte closely; he pulled out a woman's fan and started to use it. Charlotte smiled at his lack of care for his own masculinity. Most of the men used *Ordinary Wit* to fan themselves. Charlotte was taking notes and sometimes manically making sketches with a quill and ink, splashing it around on papers and handing them to Maynard, who would fan the pages and put them in a leather folder.

"That is very plain to see," she said.

Members of the audience visibly gasped at the mention of the Bastards of Liberty, a rebellious offshoot of the Society of Shadows, and the confirmed news of Grimwood and Olde Ridgewatch.

A tall, muscular woman standing announced, "I am Mercy Pitcher from Lackmore. My docks are safe, along with the ships in port, but what Doc says of the revolts, there was many a house that treated their servants poorly, and so they were burnt down, and those that treated their slaves and servants well, their homes were left, but the slaves and servants ran. Lackmore is a strong city, and we live and die by the Atlantis Ocean, the hardworking folk thrive yet the nobles have felt the sting of their hubris." She seemed neither upset nor encouraged about the revolt. Her independence teetered on the day.

Brice Hitchson of the Rosewood Dominion scratched at his face, and Braya Summerbrake stepped back and bowed.

"I leave the floor to Sir Doc Young," Braya said, stepping away as two elven guards guided her to her seat and stood by her. They wore scaled armor and carried sabers with elegant guards. Doc knew their elegance was only a veneer for how dangerous they were, yet he feared Braya Summerbrake even more so. Those beyond the Grave Reach River had power and might the likes of which Vineland had not seen in hundreds of years.

"What do you mean revolt," yelled Brice. "What about General Ashburn, the army Sir Leadwall leads, not to mention the Bitterleak mercenaries? This little riot by these so-called Bastards of Liberty will be crushed. We continue to talk like this, and we'll all be hanged."

Ambrose Slitbear knocked his hammer on the floor again. "Remain peaceful, all of you." His wife put her hand on his shoulder and whispered into his ear.

Mercy Pitcher nodded thanks. "If folks like Dick Holmes and Lesia Surmount hold Bawstone Keep, they won't. They could last in there for years, you know that," noted Mercy Pitcher.

"The Holy Imperium moves against the city-states not under their control after the Crimson Struggle. It's plain to see Grimwood never knelt to Prince Damon. They held Olde Ridgewatch until recently under martial law; they will soon announce an alliance with Steelsburg as the Clearstone family will fall from power there. They hold the main roads from Grimwood to Hudson City now, and many of the corresponding holds, including all of the keeps in the Sword Belt except for the Gloomspire. Their southern army has encircled the Crescent City."

"Those places are far away. They don't encroach on the Rosewood Dominion," said Brice. "What of the Waterhurst, Magnoliafield, and Cinderpool city-states? What of the great city-state of Colehampton," Brice said, asking for help. His voice, although pleading, held a refined elegance to it when he spoke, and his eyes demanded an audience. He was a refined rapier, while Doc was a blunt hammer dipped in booze.

"Waterhurst struggles with pirates and taxes like other port cities," said Ezebell Milessent, the daughter of a pirate and smuggler. "The Holy Imperium has been nonchalant in stopping any such crimes in our city-state yet takes our taxes just the same."

"They don't want to sow the fields of the Rosewood Dominion with blood, no, but you're rich, so they'll suck the Wheathold dry with taxes, leaving the Rosewood Dominion a husk," finished Doc. "We have representatives from all those city-states today, including the far-off Republic of the Wind, Honeybreak, Colehampton, Crescent City. Other territories have sent observers and emissaries to voice their concerns and act, if necessary, to address these concerns."

Sir Martha Lowdale, Knight of the Wind, nodded in agreement with Doc. She stood tall in full armor, holding her two-handed greatsword across her arms, taking up much of the area around her, the blade sharp and dangerous as she was. The knight had not spoken in any manner, just observing the entire gathering. On occasion, she looked near the podium where Lord Washcreek stood near Mercy Pitcher, who stood for Lackmore. Maynard and Charlotte noted that sides and alliances were gathering during this meeting.

"You'll notice that nobody is here speaking directly from Steelsburg or the Crescent City as they remain in firmly the Holy Imperium hands," mentioned Maynard.

Charlotte nodded, "You think we may hear from them later tonight?"

Maynard shifted closer to her. "Yes, I think the real politics will occur tonight over strong drink and dark smoke, where sleazy handshakes and blood pacts reside." The debating continued as guests arrived and left.

"This is preposterous. Prince Damon is our sovereign and can do as he pleases under the grace of the Maker and all she holds dear," interrupted Brice. He threw his cup down on the ground, and it rattled, bringing the attention back to his sharp-featured face.

"Not everyone worships as you do, Brice," Prudence Slitbear said. "Your slaves don't worship the Maker. Don't the elves, us dwarves, and even our forsaken enemies, the goblins and orcs, worship as they will? Even the Nation of Stouya and the Legion of Carigreed worship a medley of gods. The Holy Imperium and its alliance with the old empire Great Brightland is a noose on our necks. If we wait, they will push us off the ledge," she stated hotly, speaking for Colehampton. Her husband was now outside smoking a pipe next to his hammer.

"The people are with us. Even as the Holy Imperium burn our books and pamphlets in the streets, the commoners whisper our thanks for educating them," chimed in Olivia Franklin, who stood for Hudson City. "They yearn for liberty." Her voice was sweet and sharp.

"Who authored this new book causing an uproar, saying such stories about Prince Damon, and who prints the pamphlets saying we have a right to speech, a right to worship as we wish, and a right to protest against our prince and lords? This is heresy," said Hendrey Coalfell, a dwarve from Magnoliafield.

Olivia Franklin stared at Hendrey Coalfell, who did not glance back at her. He smirked, knowing he had pissed off one of the more powerful mages in Vineland.

"I agree with Coalfell; we are business partners, and he feels the sting of this unrest and taxes. None of which is good for business," said Brice.

A tall man walked up carrying a spear whose name on the battlefield was the Holy Truth. He was powerfully built and wore his long hair, mostly streaked with gray and white, tied back. Behind him stood two well-armed guards, one an elve quiet and coiled, ready to strike like a snake, and another a short man with the look of a well-seasoned mercenary.

Every mage, witch, and user of magic felt the fear rise on the back of their necks seeing the short, well-seasoned mercenary, even if they didn't know him by name, as he dulled their powers. He reeked of danger, and his last name was unknown except to Doc, Olivia Franklin, and General Washcreek, and that name was a danger to himself, the last of a bloodline thought long dead. The back door opened, and a hedge witch watching the show in the courtroom slipped out quickly and quietly, fearing for herself. Her two goblin companions, both seen working in the taverns of the city, left with her. Ravens in the rafters cackled as she went.

"Every person in their home has the right to worship, read what they wish, and ask those in charge for better terms. It's why we're here. It doesn't matter who wrote the damn books," said General Washcreek, challenging Brice Hitchson. They were both from the Rosewood Dominion, comrades, and business partners but also, at times, bitter enemies.

"If they slander you, call you a pig fucker. Is that ok?" Brice said, turning on him. He carried no weapon and wore no armor; he represented power through money, conversation, and powerful contracts; he had some representation in the East Thamesbridge Company when it suited him, but the past year, he had reaped scorn on the company and its attempts to buy out his lands and holdings, and he was a known poet and gambler.

"I'm not a pig fucker, and I don't live the life of a man who has such stated of them, Brice," and Washcreek looked at him with contempt. Doc smirked as his body swayed. Maynard grasped at his seat, hoping Doc wouldn't fall over, but the man teetered and stood back up.

"What do you all suggest?" asked Richard Ratwolf, the largest landholder in the Hudson territory outside of Hudson City, who held the position of Dean at Staghollow University. "I'm besieged by the looming thought of the

Gloomspire as my land lies in its shadows. The prince taxes me, and my people aren't slaves but toil the ground, nonetheless. I can't face another war and fight more battles. I'm barely breaking even."

The doors opened, and Maynard gave a slight smile when he saw the person walking through. Abigail Holmes of the Empty Gauntlet walked through the door. She wore her cooking apron and carried a large meat tenderizer—this one a sturdy elven make.

"That's not a meat tenderizer; that's a mace," Charlotte laughed. "What in the Hades is happening."

"The bastards have taken Bawstone Keep and control Olde Ridgewatch. We have liberty and freedom from nobles and royals alike. I'm here to ask for aid and assistance so that we can live our lives as free folk the way the gods intended," she yelled. "We will write our demands to Prince Damon for equal rights and liberty that all shall enjoy, and if he declines, we'll take them ourselves."

Doc smiled, and the crowd of people inside the courtroom erupted in arguments and cheers.

"I yield to Abigail Holmes, owner of the Empty Gauntlet, who represents Olde Ridgewatch," said Doc, shuffling away to get more punch. *Now it really begins,* he whispered to the voices he defied inside his head.

* * *

Doc's hand shook as he put his pipe up to his mouth. He was visibly sweating. For years, Maynard watched him, his mentor and father figure, breaking down before him. Doc's truth-telling glasses had been adjusting for over three hours as merchants, nobles, and ordinary folk debated on how to collaborate with Prince Damon, rebel against Prince Damon, or find common ground with his Noble house in Hudson City and his gripe on key city-states of Vineland. Doc failed to light his pipe several times.

"Maker's tits, I can't even see straight with the lies, the half-truths, the fucking voices screaming inside my head Maynard. Half of them are even right, for Child's Sake!" Doc murmured.

319

"Who, the bunch of sparrows and hawks cackling inside or the owls out here who actually know what's happening," Maynard asked.

He walked closer, stopped the wind, lit Doc's pipe, and lit his pipe. Doc inhaled, and the voices of all the dead he killed subsided so he could focus. Maynard noticed Doc's muscles relaxed, jaw unclenched, and shoulders dropped measurably.

"This day has been too much," he said quietly, nodding to Maynard. "Night Keeper's sweet weed, thank you."

"Careful, Doc, smoke enough of that, and even here in Affectus, you could end up dangling from a pole while your legs danced in the air," warned a voice behind him.

Doc looked at Lord Washcreek. His two guards, one of whom Doc knew Samuel Hawthorn, stood off at a distance. Maynard acknowledged General Washcreek and walked away from the guards to where Hattie and Charlotte stood in a deep conversation. They smiled as he greeted them, and Doc and Lord Washcreek stood closer to speak. Olivia Franklin opened the courthouse's back door, known as the Judges Exit, and saw Lord Washcreek and Doc standing. Lord Washcreek lit a cigar and puffed, blowing white smoke into the air as it mingled with Doc's purple pipe smoke. It danced in the calm atmosphere, lingering for moments and disappearing into the sky. The afternoon sun dripped with heat as the group stood under the shade of a large thousand-year oak tree.

Olivia Franklin walked over and interrupted Doc and Lord Washcreek. She snagged Doc's pipe and took a hit while she fiddled inside her jacket for a cigarette.

Braya Summerbrake appeared through the courthouse door. Doc could hear two or three people debating inside the courthouse. Those with seats were considered lucky; others stood against walls. Braya saw the circle forming and made her way to them. The backdoor closed behind her.

"There will be a vote if you can believe it. We're going to write up a note, a bill asking for a series of rights for," Braya walked in as Olivia spoke. "A series of rights for everyone, human, dwarve, elve, and if you can believe it, even goblin and orc kind."

"It's what they're arguing about now, not that it will be sent to Prince Damon, but who will get these rights, these freedoms."

Doc raised his eyebrows over his glasses. Maynard looked at a distance and noticed the glass's colors had stayed the same. He was among friends, equals even. Olivia puffed on her cigarette, the copper filter hanging on her lip. Braya looked at Olivia, took it from her mouth as if they knew each other, inhaled the cigarette, and chuckled. Lord Washcreek looked for a moment and politely turned away from them. Braya snicked as she pushed smoke away from her mouth.

"This is an interesting day," said Doc.

"It is," nodded Lord Washcreek. "Who's going to write this bill to the prince?"

"I am. They know my pen is mighty," said Olivia.

Doc laughed, knowing her quill was one of Vineland's most potent artifacts, a Paragon of the Maker.

"What's so amusing, Doc?" asked Braya.

"You know as much as I do." And he paused and looked at her and looked away towards Lord Washcreek and Olivia. "When will you write this thing? I have an acquaintance taking notes; I can get them after this, and we can use them for guidance for these requests. No, no," Doc said, mumbling to himself. He wiped the sweat off his forehead. "Requests isn't the right word, demands. When we write up our demands to Prince Damon."

"I'll write it tonight. We'll vote and break up this madness tomorrow. Everyone will go home, and we'll meet again here at the courthouse after Prince Damon's party when he's presented our petition," sighed Olivia with determination.

"What of those not speaking up or represented today," said Lord Washcreek.

"We shall hear from them tonight at the McGrave's Ale House; not everyone wants to be seen in the daylight, Lord Washcreek. The cover of darkness brings allies and fools alike."

Lord Washcreek nodded, "As long as we vote and agree, we move forward."

"And you thought I was mad, Lord Washcreek," Doc looked away and puffed on his pipe.

"Doc, this is one of the most important undertakings we've attempted since the beginning. If you come, I need you to behave," Olivia reminded Doc.

"I'm curious. How old are you two?" asked Lord Washcreek. He changed the subject as if he'd needed more time to consider this bill of demands. "I've known you both almost all my life."

"I am interested as well. I've heard of you two for longer than most humans have lived," said Braya.

"If we are to be united in liberty and do this proper, we shall be more forward about who we are, said Olivia. She looked at Doc and smiled like a cat that had just eaten a bird or squirrel. And maybe he had before he'd gotten to the courthouse.

"We are the first of what you call mages. We are disciples of Gaston," said Olivia.

Doc removed his glasses and coughed, "We were his first pupils."

Braya and Lord Washcreek stopped breathing for a moment.

"Even my people know of Gaston," and Braya bowed. "We now have more to discuss over drinks, my loves." She looked at Olivia and Doc. "I will meet you tonight at McGrave's Ale House," Braya said, subtly bowing to the two mages. Lord Washcreek turned lower out of respect, keeping his eyes on her with a slight sense of awe and lust. He looked back once, though, with a slight edge of fear in his eyes.

"I have a matter to attend but may stop by to see the final product before the vote," said Lord Washcreek. He followed Braya back inside the courthouse.

Doc smiled again as he felt the attraction between Braya and the general.

"Well, there we have it. The sparrows and eagles are inside, and tonight, we'll have an alliance of owls," Olivia said.

Doc snorted and took a swig from an uncapped bottle. "Better than a conspiracy of crows. Here, Olivia, you're going to need some more medicine. We have another hour or two of arguing over whether elves, goblins, and orcs have the same rights as dwarves and humans." Doc said as Olivia took a sip and turned to him.

"It doesn't matter what they argue. What I write will be undeniable."

Sorella - Two Birds and a Knife

"First civilians I've seen since the front," Austin said. His eyes were bloodshot as if he'd been riding nonstop. "What brings you Oxfell County?"

Elora moved her horse into a defensive position. She already had her sword out as if expecting trouble from the three civilians. She looked on intently. "You'll find nothing but trouble that way. The Oxfell Gate is closed, and savages across the river are attacking homesteads and villages. Prince Damon has sent a force to stop them, but it's been hard going."

"We don't recommend continuing; what takes you in this direction? You're not traders that I can see," Austin continued.

"No, we aren't. I'm delivering these slaves here to my sister. She has a homestead with two other families up the roads near the river. They needed an extra hand, and I found them for cheap," Grey Jim stated flatly, gesturing at Taug.

Taug snickered but hid her laugh behind a yawn.

Austin looked at the three of them. Sorella looked back up, taking in the situation.

"Looks like both of you have seen action. Our dignified Prince Damon even protects those on the outreach of the Holy Imperium," Grey Jim said.

"Enough to hold the pass but not enough to protect villages from raids. You're safer turning back," said Elora.

"The natives are restless on the other side of the river, and we expect raids, so I don't think it's safe for your sister if she's still there," said Austin. He was ready to move on. This conversation was going nowhere.

"We must check, at least. I haven't seen or heard from her in some time. I worry," said Grey Jim.

"Maker's Will be with you. If she's gone, make your way out of Oxfell County and back to Hudson City," said Austin. He moved his horse toward the road, nodding his head.

Elora sheathed her sword. "Stay away from the army at the front with the slaves. They are battling the enemy daily, a group called Wrathfall. They won't want to see an orc or an elve. Chained up or not, they'll kill your slaves, take your horses, and force you into soldiering. She rode away behind Austin.

"Thank you and Maker's speed. There is an inn down the road. They should have more news and food," said Grey Jim.

Sorella, Taug, and Gray Jim watched the group move on.

"That could have gone worse," said Taug. "They looked as if they'd been in a battle for days. War worn and in need of anything but more of a fight. We could have killed them, taken their horses."

"Not with an army in front of us," said Sorella. "Besides, they didn't have to tell us any of that information, seemed decent folk."

"We have an entrenched army ahead of us that is not friendly to orcs or elves, and they're blocking the only way across the river for weeks. Now what?" Gray Jim asked.

"I can't connect to my two birds; I sent scouting the area for us. This concerns me. We go off the road here, head towards the river, and cross at a shallow spot," Sorella considered. "Or we cross through the trees above."

"Maybe you elve, but neither Gray Jim nor I can jump on branches like a squirrel in heat."

"I cross and wait for you both to float downstream. I'll carry Gray Jim's long sword and anything else back and forth. If either of you fall in, I hope you both appear down-aways."

When the two riders were out of sight, they moved off the road, heading south to avoid hitting any foraging parties or scouts from the army at the front. They met the river late in the afternoon; its rushing waters were deep and powerful.

"This river is not manageable to swim," Gray Jim noted.

"No, it keeps the Blightbriar Forest at bay and stops the ignorant from getting in. You'll drown your horse and yourself if you fall in. Only the strongest orcs can swim across the river."

"And you, Taug?" asked Gray Jim.

"I'm a lover and a mage, Gray one, not a great soldier like you and Sorella." She smiled at him. "I can't swim that either."

Sorella chuckled.

"We have no rope. The only ford is guarded by the Holy Imperium; the next ford is not within our reach unless we make our way to the Erie Sea, and we don't have the coin to hire a boat," said Sorella.

"I know a spot," the orc chimed in. "Let us ride south for a day, away from the Holy Imperium, and let me think. We'll have a nice dinner. I saw wild mushrooms, and I'll catch a rabbit to make a fine stew."

Taug cooked her stew that night after gathering wild weeds, roots, and mushrooms near the river. She took her time, singing to herself. The melody calmed both Gray Jim and Sorella. Taug handed a bowl to each of them, and they dug into the meal as they watched the fire. Usually, Sorella was more on guard, which she found odd, as they were near a group of people that would either curse her and hang her or force her into their army, but she couldn't help but laugh as the fire sparked and hissed. She thought of Duncan and glanced up at Gray Jim and Taug. She'd noticed a hint of chemistry between them. Jealousy welled up as the thought of Duncan echoed deeply. She took out the note he'd left her.

Taug looked at her from across the fire, the last to indulge in the stew just starting to eat after cleaning up from cooking, still humming to herself. "Now is not the time, my queen. Wait until we cross before you read news from the past; the future comes from the sky," Taug sang louder now.

Sorella looked at the sky and the stars. It was a cloudless night. Her head swayed, and she felt a tiredness weigh upon her.

"Taug, did you poison us? I thought I smelled an odd mushroom flavor. I can't keep awake," Sorella fell over.

Gray Jim stood unsteadily.

"What have you done to us, you witch?" Gray Jim said in a drunken anger.

Taug laughed. "The wine dulls the mushroom effects some, my Gray Jim,"

"Your Gray Jim?" he asked with a smile and stumbled.

Taug stood and started undressing. Gray Jim's head spun, or was it the world? He couldn't say or even think straight.

"What is, why are you?" Gray Jim could barely put a thought into words about the mushrooms. Taug walked towards him and grabbed him firmly, naked. Gray Jim pushed toward Taug.

"You'll be with me, and then you will sleep, as you are mine now. Welcome to the Wrathfall," Taug said, bringing her lips to his. Gray Jim barely stood, and then he was on the ground with Taug moaning and biting him, and he gave into the bliss of another.

Sorella's eyes flicked open, revealing trees flying below her and the river passing as claws ripped into leather. Fear and fury stung from the betrayal of her traveling partner, Taug. She recognized the mushrooms too late before passing out. This woman she had trusted had misled her and Grey Jim. She turned her head slowly to see the large feathers of a warhawk grasping her, one of the largest birds she had ever seen. A bird thought long extinct after the creation of the Stagger Wall along the Grave Reach River. The warhawks were long thought wiped out along with dragons, their natural enemies. She closed her eyes and considered what her next actions would be upon landing and what the existence of such an animal meant.

* * *

Sorella awoke and immediately shifted into a squatting position, taking in her surroundings. She grabbed at a blade hidden in her boot and guarded herself, ready to cut and kill, and realized she was on a cliff near its edge. A stone arch stood in front of her, and an altar was nearby, fresh with blood dripping on it. Her feet shifted, and pain surged into her arms and legs as they bled from where warhawk claws shredded through her light armor and her leather trousers. The bird had flown away down past the cliff beyond her sight. Bird, she considered, more like a monster.

Taug stood behind her, staff in hand.

"Relax, my queen, you are safe," Taug said.

Grey Jim lay on the ground, crumbled, and cut up in the same manner as Sorella.

Sorella shifted and lunged, disarming Taug and shoving her boot knife into Taug's throat, breaking the skin. She had twisted Taug's arm behind her and pushed her to the edge. They saw a deep black night that only the Blightbriar forest could bring.

"Struggle, and I cut and push. Now speak plainly, no songs, no lies." Sorella didn't blink.

"Your breath smells of anger and truth. Move the blade, and I will speak," Taug said. "My Queen."

Sorella breathed and moved the blade back slightly.

"I drugged you so we could cross. I sang to the warhawks and my brother, the keeper of the birds, a goblin. The soup took away the pain of their claws and the fear most had of the flight. We are now away from the confines of the Holy Imperium. See, your two birds waited for you."

Sorella's two birds, her companions since given to her by Hunter Young years ago, perched on a stone arch.

Sorella let up the blade. Taug wiped the blood and licked it, as she had done earlier after they were tortured.

"Your two familiars, my Queen, trust me; now I ask again, trust me," Taug pleaded.

Gray Jim shifted on the ground behind Taug.

"I had the most fucked up dream last night," he mumbled.

Sorella released Taug's arm. "I must go to him and calm him. He will not like what I have done," Taug said quietly.

"Go to him and then more questions," commanded Sorella.

Taug returned to Gray Jim, "I'm sorry, my love," she said. Sorella couldn't hear what else was said. She looked out and down into the opening of the Blightbriar Forest past the Razorshine River and took it in, the front line for the war of Vineland below her feet.

Alysha - Separation Anxiety

Alysha kept her horse near the edge of the dense forest overgrowth as they moved southwest, keeping the battle of Grimwood to the north and east of her and Helena. The noise from the city-state of Grimwood disturbed the horses. They were skittish as crashes and screams echoed throughout the sky. Alysha pulled up, and Helena stopped behind her as she took in the view before them. In an open plain, a large palisade wall and several man-made wooden towers protected the corners of a newly erected camp in the middle of a road. It had appeared as they moved south on the horizon. She saw a group of six horses at a distance riding behind them towards the walled camp.

"Every move we make feels wrong."

"I hear you. Worst case scenario, split up and make for Wolf Hills. It may be your best bet."

"Alysha, you don't have to protect me. You know I'd rather be with you, die together, or live together."

I had maidens that guarded and protected me. A voice said in the back of Alysha's mind.

"Look, I have unfinished business yet." She felt the hilt of Stormkiss. "Blackheart."

"Yeah, well, that's a death sentence. He's always going to be surrounded by soldiers. Besides, if given the chance, I'd kill him, too, but that doesn't mean we have to be stupid. It will take more than two of us to get to him, Alysha. We'll need an army," Helena snickered.

"Look, I'm just saying if given a choice, you would save me, right?"

"Of course."

"Well, same here. I'd die happy knowing you were safe."

Two large birds above cackled a warning, and Alysha looked back.

"Those riders are coming towards us," Helena said with a start.

"Into the woods, follow me, keep your head down," Alysha said as if she were not herself.

Alysha rode her horse close to the saddle and could hear Helena behind her, their pursuers closing. At least six of them, perhaps more. They took a well-worn deer path deeper into the woods, riding as fast as their horses allowed them, staying silent and trying to make it harder for pursuit. They rode hard for an hour and slowed up to listen to see if they lost the rider behind them. The path they took led out of the woods and back into tall grass, the camp they initially saw now well behind them.

"We take the edge of the woods until we see another deer pass and head back into the woods. I'll follow. Go."

Helena leaned into Alysha, grabbed her hand, squeezed, and moved forward. Alysha followed, realizing she'd lost track of time as rain clouds gathered above them. She recognized a mixture of tall cattails and cord grass as she trotted the horses down the edge of the woods for another thirty minutes and then slowed. They let their horses rest momentarily, feeling like they had lost their pursuers. Helena took a sip of wine from a wineskin and passed it back to Alysha, who silently drank and felt relief. She saw a break in the tall grass and noticed the same break into the woods on the other side before them.

"This break will let us push into the Litchbury Mire, or we can head east and back into where it all began," said Alysha, unsure of herself and who she wanted to be.

"To Wolf Hills," said Helena with hesitation.

"Right."

They come now, something inside, Alysha said.

Alysha felt it before she heard it, and an arrow whistled before sinking into the haunch of her horse. The mare kicked up and grunted. "Push forward, go!"

The arrow came from her right, but they could only move forward, and with her horse lame, Alysha knew she would slow Helena.

Alysha saw two Holy Imperium soldiers, lightly armored, pushing through the brush of tall grass. One notched another arrow. She moved forward, leaning down onto her horse.

"Archers Helena!" Alysha yelled. "Get to the woods; I'll follow after I lose these two!" As Alysha forced her horse forward, Helena looked back as her horse ran toward the woods, and her face clipped a branch from a maple tree. Alysha saw an arrow fly by, barely missing Helena.

Alysha turned her lame horse to the right, splitting off from Helena, who went in the other direction, and Alysha decided to attack. She turned and grasped Stormkiss, maneuvering the reigns to her left hand, and pressed forward toward three soldiers. Alysha was outnumbered, but the speed of her movement and presence within their line unsettled the soldiers. She leaned down and slashed at the first soldier's horse before he could meet her. The hit was clean, and the horse faltered as its thigh lay open to Stormkiss. She adjusted further, spun in her saddle, and twisted back to defend herself from a wild slash on her left, steering the horse with her muscular thighs. She was through their line, and they scattered in the cattails. She felt her stitches nearly broken again, and her wounds were freshly bleeding. For some reason, she gained strength from it as some of her blood dropped to the ground. The horse she'd hit with her axe screamed and kicked its rider below it and behind her now as she pushed into the Litchbury Mire, hoping the other two would follow her and let Helena escape. She steered her horse further into the grass to dodge puddles and mud, but the arrow in her horse's thigh slowed it, and she quickly lost hope of surviving more than the next hour. She patted the horse, saying thank you. Alysha looked back, grabbed what she could from the saddle, slung a pack over her shoulder, slipped off the horse near a thicket in the grass, and pushed the horse off so it would leave.

"Hope this works," she whispered to nobody but herself. She squatted in the thicket covered by a bush and brambles.

"You see her?" A soldier's voice called.

"I saw movement ahead."

There was a shuffling of bodies and horses near Alysha as she held her breath.

"The other one, where did that one go?"

"Gone down a rabbit trail, no hope of finding them in those woods; let's hunt our pray here."

"Better find this one; she's armed; at least it will help explain losing a horse and Sam breaking his neck when he fell."

"Rogue soldier got lucky."

"Right, that is what we'll tell Shortstride."

Alysha breathed as quietly as she could, bugs and leaves surrounding her inside the leafy bush. They were close, and she felt they could hear her breathing, the pounding of her heart, and the blood dripping down her arm and leg.

They pushed their horses on.

"They're over there, I saw something!" They disappeared off to her left and south into the fog from the swamp.

More noise was behind her, and she pushed plunged into the Litchbury Mire. Bugs hummed and spun around the air above the tall grass over her head. She tried to separate the grass slowly and quietly so as not to splash the stagnant, dark puddles below. She found a dry path with moss and stones used by animals. To her left and right were large puddles and taller grass. If she veered off, the noise of moving in the water would give her away. She figured if she could find a small bed used by a deer, she would wait until dark, push back into the woods, and search for Helena. She thrust forward, away from the noise to her right, deeper into the swamp.

After several minutes, there was a break in the marsh grass, where she saw an opening and a dilapidated house with boards and stones leading to the porch surrounded by murky water. Trees with no branches stood like long dead spears from another time, surrounding the house. On top of them sat nests for birds of prey that circled the sky near Grimwood, ready for a feast not seen in years. The old trees were thick, and the nests looked larger than any nest she had ever seen. She remembered her mother Maria saying goblins rode the bigger birds into battle. She remembered laughing at this as a child but looking at the size of the nests. The memory didn't seem so funny. She saw a long tower in the distance if she squinted enough and wondered about it. She shifted into the grass to study the house and heard noises behind her.

"I found footprints, Colten. It's her. I know it," said a voice behind her.

"You don't have to announce it, you fool. She did have a nasty axe with her," said another voice. Colten heard a man garble his mouth before he spat something out.

The door of the house opened, and a hand beckoned her. Alysha looked on, confused, and searched for a way around the house but found the water unassailable. The hand beckoned her through to come inside. She noticed two of the largest birds she'd ever witnessed perched on the house's second-story porch, and with a swallow of any common sense, she parted the grass and rushed to the two-story cottage. The roof was a mixture of woven cord grass and wooden panels, and the rest of the house was a mixture of weathered Litchbury Mire wood and a dryer layer of dark silt hardened by the sun. Architecturally, she was unsure how the structure stood or even held a second floor. The door opened a crack but let daylight into the musty, moist atmosphere. As she entered, the two birds the size of dogs of war laughed chillingly as if they knew the worst was yet to come.

The older woman who beckoned her wore a long, elegant, yet well-worn dark robe. "You reek of pain and potential," the woman spoke hoarsely as if she had a sore throat.

"I need help, my lady. Can you hide me, offer me safety?"

"I can and shall, but payment will be needed later."

"Soldiers come for me," Alysha said, not thinking.

"They know not to come here, lass. They know better. Why do you think my pets that fly are so big. They eat what's good for them, but go now, go into the basement, pick a nice bottle of wine out, and follow. I will walk out and feed the birds."

The woman turned and surprised Alysha with her beauty. The woman wore a veil, but Alysha glimpsed enough to know the woman had young, regal features, surprising her and causing concern. The soldiers would do the same thing they had planned for her, yet she obeyed and went into the basement.

The woman pointed down into a hole with well-worn stone-cut steps.

Alysha thought three attendants fall, and three attendants rise, but her thoughts were not hers.

"No candles. They scare the slugs and bugs. Go pick a bottle and follow. I will be with you soon."

Alysha was unsure, but exhaustion and dizziness clouded her senses and thoughts as she followed the woman's instructions. She walked down the stairs and into the cellar. As the woman stepped outside.

"What do you I call you, my lady?" Alysha called back up the stairs at the last moment.

"Lady Blacklace Wightland. You know of me, I am sure. Now go!"

The door closed behind her, leaving Alysha in the darkness.

* * *

Lady Blacklace pulled her hood down, showing her dark hair flickered with silver streaks. She was no longer in her youth, but age also did not settle on her bones. She wore a dress of mixed lace and spun cotton from the southern city-states of Vineland, and her cloak was fine wool from Great Brightland. She wore rings of value and carried a clay pitcher.

"My my, what handsome soldiers we have. How can I help the likes of you?" she purred.

Both soldiers carried arming swords. They were thirsty for water and other vices, as soldiers tend to be during times of war.

"You there, witch, why aren't you with the rest of the villagers?"

"The answer to your question is simple: your leader, Shortstride, is known to me and left orders for all of you to leave this home untouched, along with myself. Do you not recall these orders?"

The soldiers hesitated. They wore leather-stitched riding armor and carried arrows and bows on their backs. The senior of the two wore his receding hair shaved down tight. He was missing an ear, but he made up for it by having a smashed nose from an earlier battle.

"Fuck Shortstride, we're looking for two pretty things on horseback or

333

foot, and they're armed. Do you know where they are? Might make it easier on you if you do." The broken-nosed soldier pointed his sword as he stalked closer.

"Lucas, the captain said to leave this area and the woman in the two-story house alone. Said it best for us and her if we don't disturb."

"You should listen to your friend Lucas. Yes, I have seen her. Please have a drink, and I will round up her horse. It took an arrow in the flank. I believe it's stuck in the muck near my house." She put down the clay pitcher.

"Come. Beer for the both of you. I am glad to help the Holy Imperium. I am sure the horse may have some documents or something that may help you with your search." She stepped away from where she stood and started walking toward a trail in swamp grass near them as if looking for something.

"See, now that wasn't so hard now, was it," smiled Colten, the other soldier.

Lucas scratched at his chin. "So, tell me, hag, why does Shortstride allow you to live undisturbed?"

She walked out of the grass with the lame horse. The two giant birds on her house cackled in delight. They moved back and forth and peaked on her roof.

"Servant's grace, those are some big birds," Colten said.

"They're warhawks used by goblins to ride into battle. These two are my pets."

Lucas drank the beer, which splashed against his lips and down his throat. The other soldier, Colten, took the clay pitcher and swallowed deeply.

"That is good. Thank you, ma'am."

"Don't worry about the bird's comrades. They'll not harm you now. They're scavengers and only eat the dead. Please take the horse. The birds would have warned me if someone came this way as they warned me you two approached."

"Was that the odd noises we heard on our way down the trail?"

"Sounded like whispers and laughter."

"Why yes, it was. You're both perceptive." She pushed her veil up and smiled, showing a painfully white tooth. "I do hope you had enough to drink."

"Why do you say that?" Lucas took the reins of Alysha's horse. He wiped his beard clean from the broth of the beer.

"Simply because the poison will be much more painful if you don't get enough. It should kill you about now."

"What did you do?" Lucas stopped speaking, his knees trembling, and he collapsed, trembling momentarily.

"There you are."

"Lucas, what no, what did you do to hmm," but Colten couldn't finish his words and choked and tore at his throat as his eyes bulged. He fell to the ground, convulsing and shaking.

"Oh, my lovely, you didn't get enough." The woman walked over and ran her finger across his neck, spilling blood onto the ground. Their horses kicked, and she looked at the gear on the horse and smiled. She took her time taking money, weapons, and anything useful off the bodies, leaving them naked near the briny shores of the swamp. She looked up at the birds and signaled, and they swooped down, laughing at their dinner. She took the horse's gear, pushed it out past the trail in the opposite direction of her home, and walked inside, looking at the tower in the distance and the poisonfire fog around its base.

Alysha fumbled around in the cellar; its absence of light consumed her vision. She found a shelf to the right of the stone-cut stairs with several bottles of wine and ran her hands down it to guide her around the room. She thought of Helena and wasn't sure if she had saved or betrayed her but hoped for her safety. "Judith, protect her as I continue in the darkness," she whispered and felt her eyes adjust, and realized that jars inside the cellar had bugs inside, glowing softly, allowing her to see the outline of the basement. She hoped Lady Blacklace could aid her and what the price would be to do so.

Alysha pulled on a bottle that came from the shelf with a click. The frame moved slightly as if to tip, and Alysha grasped at it, realizing it functioned as a door. She returned the bottle, grabbed another and a jar of luminous bugs, and opened the door. She entered and pulled it shut, walking into a carved-out cavern.

Outside the house's opening, a pair of eyes looked on as the birds finished

Hudson City - Challenge for Leadership

Hands shifted over the back of a woman's neck and slid down as it arched, and she moaned in pleasure and pain as those same hands dug into her skin, with enough pressure to push against Jasper further. Their hips slid together back and forth. He moaned, adjusted, and pulled another to his side, kissing him as the woman rode on top of Jasper, grinding and pulling away, lost in each other's haze of groans and bodies. Jasper breathed in deeply, trying to hold back looking at the woman on top of him and then deeply into the man's eyes as he bit down on his lip.

The Fools Flush brothel was in what most called the East Village and was shadowed by Hudson City proper, only a slight distance away. At the high sun, the city's towers would shade the village, and in some mornings, Elverstone Citadel at the edge of the peninsula would cast its justice and shadows as well. The area was where the commoners lived and where the servants gathered after long days of work.

Jasper Pinehard, leader of the Wildcats, spent his free time in the village areas where he found drugs, lust, and his most peaceful moments in situations like this, finding a moment of tranquility in a world where everything could get him killed.

The door slammed open.

"For Hade's sake, what in the fuck!"

"Master Jacob, I am so sorry; I couldn't stop this reprobate. He said he must speak to you and rushed ahead of me once I confirmed there was a Jacob Hardbone here tonight."

The woman shifted and pulled away from Jasper but stayed near the other younger man in bed.

"Austin, how did you return so quickly, and why do you look as if..." Jasper paused, not covering himself. "What happened to you, man?"

"Jacob Hardbone, I remembered the alias you used in brothels; I needed to see you before reporting. We took the tunnels through the Wolvenshire forests where the dwarves stock the city. I met our old friend Bradley Railhead. Paid him a brick of reefer, and he led us back under the Farover River and through the woods, as it were."

"Shut it, Austin, not here, not now." Jasper pushed his hair back. "Melisa and Bobby, you may leave. I will pay you in full plus a tip if this is never mentioned. Mother Echoes, did anyone else see these rogues?"

"So," Mother Echoes sighed. "You know this man and his brute of a partner?"

"Unfortunately, I do," Jasper sighed. "Do what you can to ensure everyone who may have seen these two is happy.

"I will, he came in through the back way with another. She awaits downstairs, full of piss and venom that one," said the brothel owner Mother Echoes.

A hand pushed Mother Echoes away from the door.

"So, this is the man who leads the Wildcats in all his spender," Elora said.

Jasper stood and saluted with a slight hiccup, his body taut. Austin and Elora gazed for a moment.

"Well, I see why you must pay for it. Get dressed, man-child. We've lost friends and lovers to deliver our news, and if we don't act quickly, we'll lose more,"

"Right, right, it must be bad if you interrupted my play time, Austin, and brought a woman of poor taste and bad eyesight," Jasper finished.

Austin watched as Mother Echoes brought Jasper a pewter cup of witch pepper. After having had too many goblets of wine the night before, the drink was an excellent pick-up, and they both could use a cup. They left after Jasper dressed and downed the drink, which tasted of bubbly vodka, sugar, and spices. After a few intersections, they found the back entrance of a closed tea shop and knocked three times. A slide opened inside the door. Austin shook his head, and Elora looked at Jasper.

Austin whispered to her, "Yes, he knows everyone and can get in anywhere." Elora rolled her eyes.

"Long Live the Prince," a voice said behind the door.

"The prince drools like a drunk goblin," Jasper repeated.

The door opened slightly, and Jasper pushed inside, guiding Austin and Elora. They sat down, Austin and Elora across from Jasper.

"Speakeasy, my friends; this place keeps secrets like a dragon keeps gold," Jasper said as they slid into a well-used booth at the back of a wine bar. "Tea shop during the day, wine bar and opium den at night, gracious people here, better wine, and best drugs." He lit a pipe and passed it, exhaling. Austin picked it up, capped it with his finger, put the coal out, and looked at Jasper.

"I need you clear-headed for this, Jasper," Austin said, his eyes tired.

"Fine, fine, who's the wench," Jasper said, ignoring Austin's remark with a smirk.

Elora hit Jasper's shin with her boot under the table, causing him to flinch; his head dipped closer. She grabbed his hair, slammed his face into the table, and sneered at him through clenched teeth. "My name is Elora Meldguard. Meldguard, have you ever heard that name before? My old man was sent off to some forsaken river to fight monsters and orcs while you drank fine wine and fucked whores."

Austin grabbed Elora's hand and released it from Jasper's head, pinned to the table. Austin grasped the side of his face, sitting up, and rubbed it. "My face, ahhh. And my shin, you kicked my shin. Okay, so that's true, but when the Prince of Vineland orders you to do something, you do it." Jasper whined, looking hurt and pained in pride and body.

"Jasper, did you get any of my letters? Did General Casting or Prince Damon get any of my letters?" asked Austin.

"What, no, we got reports but no letters," breathed out Jasper.

"What did the reports say?"

"That Pap and your squad had everything in hand. Austin, you should have written to me; I was worried, my friend; you look like Hades and have made a nasty little friend," Jasper said. "Austin, what the Hades is going on here?" he asked.

Hades, Jasper's face hurt. He was so confused. One minute, he was having a lavish threesome with his two favorite prostitutes, and the next, he was in a whole other threesome, getting his face shoved into a table and questioned like he was under torture.

"Jasper, this is Elora. She was the leader of the Union Dogs, a mercenary group hired to assist our expeditionary force in the Blightbriar Wilds; she's Pap's daughter," he stopped. "Was Pap's daughter. Jasper, Pap's dead,"

Jasper's eyebrow went up, and his face lost all color. He looked away momentarily and breathed deeply as he took in the news. He stood and bowed. "Your father was better than me. I never deserved my position."

"Yet you took it anyway," Elora spat back.

"Only after he said I should take it," insisted Jasper, looking hurt. "When your best friend is prince of all of Vineland and asked you to be the leader of his personal guard even when you've never led anything but an orgy, you don't fucking say no, thank you. You do as you are told and surround yourself with the best people. That's what I did," Jasper said in a yelling whisper. "He was the best I could surround myself with." He looked away, not showing the hurt that welled in his chest. He looked back at her.

They stared at each other. She nodded. Jasper turned and walked to the bar. He spoke to the bartender, who gave him a bottle and three cups.

"They get the bottles from beyond the Stagger Wall," said Jasper. "Please, red wine for memories, to be among friends in grief," and he handed a cup to each of them. "Stand, both of you."

They were escorted into a private den. A curtain separated each area as smoke, music, and laughter crept through in muffled tones. The place was rife with smoke from an assortment of pipes. The curtain was closed behind them. Jasper waited for a moment and held Elora and Austin back from sitting.

"Elora, kneel now." Jasper stood up tall and in command of the moment. Austin had seen him like this while guarding Prince Damon in public. He was all business.

"Kneel Elora Meldguard," he drew his sword. Elora looked at Jasper, then at Austin, who nodded, and she bent to one knee and looked down on the ground.

Jasper placed a blade on her shoulder, *"Knowledge, obedience, and duty to Vineland. I bleed for you, and you will bleed for me, and we will bleed for the land."* Jasper placed the sword against her other shoulder, cut his thumb, grasped her hand, and cut her thumb. "I bleed for you, and you will bleed for me, and we bleed for the land we walk. Rise, Sir Elora Meldguard, you are now a member of the Wildcats."

Elora stood slightly stunned.

"Your father was the best of us. I was lucky to be in his shadow."

That sat, Elora was unsure of what to feel. Austin continued.

"It wasn't a bunch of bandits; we believe an army is situated in the Gloomspire near the hunting lodge. We lost half of the soldiers we brought and were reinforced by further Templar, monks, and local conscripts. Pekka Deeran retreated from the Razorshine River to Hawkhallow Village. They will push the Oxfell gate when they can, but the crossing between the two gates isn't held. Jasper, we're at war."

"What are you talking about? With whom?" Jasper tried to grasp at all that had occurred.

"This isn't combat in a field lined up with horses and calvary Jasper. The enemy is goblin orc, dwarve, elvish, and human," Elora said.

"And Sir Pekka Deeran is in charge?"

"He's doing his best, but the Templar don't follow orders, and the Union Dogs took the brunt of the casualties."

Jasper grasped at the table, thinking.

"We saw graffiti at the lodge we investigated. It was hard to trace what it meant. *Wrathfall* written in a blue paint."

"Are you joking, the Wrathfall?"

Elora and Austin looked at Jasper, not smiling.

Jasper put up his hands.

"Okay, okay, I can see," he stopped. "You both have seen some shit."

"They strike at night mostly and from undercover in the day; if we kill one, they pull the body back. They use archery to good effect, blades, bows, traps, and more," said Austin.

"If someone is caught outside a fortified outpost, the only thing that is found is a bloodstain on the ground," Elora finished.

Austin opened a pouch and pulled out what Jasper thought was a broken shield.

Jasper picked it up, "This is a beak, a giant fucking beak from a,"

"Warhawk."

"I found it on the other side of the Razorshine River. The birds snatched up a soldier in full plate and dropped him from the sky onto rocks. Other men were shredded into meat and bone and dropped into the river."

"Our archers couldn't reach them; they can strike anytime," said Elora.

"This force, the Wrathfall, are they a threat to the farms in the domain of Hudson City in Oxfell County?"

"Jasper, they are a threat to the capital."

* * *

After talking, Austin, Elora, and Jasper made their way to the Wildcats' barracks. Austin went to his room, and Elora was assigned to Pap's room near Austin. "Elora, welcome to the Wildcats. Your father would be proud," Jasper said. Rest. I need to report this to General Casting. I'll return soon."

She nodded with no smile.

Austin and Elora slept the rest of the night and into the morning and were awakened by Jasper, who had a servant bring morning Thamesbridge tea before he entered Elora's room. Austin followed Jasper.

"When we're out of uniform, you will speak to me as you will; when in uniform, you will do as I command, and if not me, all those above me, including Prince Damon himself."

"As you command," Elora said. "Permission to speak, Sir Jasper."

"Granted."

"Why me? Why not another noble's son? Why not someone else?" she asked.

"Austin has you in his confidence, and that says enough. Besides, I'm creating a special unit to investigate corruption and treason within the Holy

Imperium. The three of us have permission from Prince Damon and General Casting to investigate anything that could disrupt the masquerade. That means unruly slaves, the Bastards of Liberty, or imperial messages that have gone missing," Jasper said with his eyebrows raised.

They entered the Wildcats' common room, which remained empty. Everyone was on duty or resting in their rooms.

"We should be preparing the city for a siege, not throwing a party," Austin said.

"We're outmatched politically and by force now that we're spread so thin across the city. I can only afford you two to investigate this matter and report your findings to me. Your letters never got to me, General Casting, or Prince Damon, so your first part of the investigation is to find out what happened to them." said Jasper. "I'm making a mess of the Wildcats. Your father, Pap, was much better at organizing the Wildcats. I feel we've been outmaneuvered." He stopped and cautiously looked around, making sure they were truly alone. He whispered, "The Order of the Blue Rose are either undermining Prince Damon or have him under their thumb."

Clearing his throat, Jasper continued, "Austin vouched for you, Elora, and your dad was one of a kind. What I say is only for us." He drew closer. "I don't even know him anymore. Prince Damon was my best friend, but he's moved on. He's out of my grasp. We were-" he stopped. "I'm just a guard to him now. I'm no longer in his confidence and scared for him and Vineland." He said, louder now. *"Knowledge, obedience, and duty to Vineland. I bleed for you, and you will bleed for me, and we will bleed for the land."*

Austin waited; he'd never seen Jasper, at least sober, like this.

"I'm still his," but Jasper didn't finish his sentence. He only moved on, slightly pained. "We must protect Vineland to defend the ground Prince Damon walks on until our blood is coated in it."

"And of the Gloomspire, the Union Dogs, and my father's sacrifice for Vineland?" Elora asked.

"That's just it. This issue is at those crossings of the Razorshine River by the lodge, Casting believes you. Detrimentally, he's sending nearly all the Wildcats available to the front. We spoke while you slept. It leaves us with a skeleton crew. Prince Damon has already hired the Blue Templar to supplement our guard duties and a mercenary group that will arrive shortly to provide further protection during The Triumphant Masquerade. I now have six Wildcats guarding Prince Damon; we used to have twelve. There are the city and tower guards, but Casting stripped half of them to send to the front; we're stretched thin, and the Order of the Blue Rose grows. I also have news: someone who will join the Wildcats until he forms his honor guard for Prince Damon's wife-to-be."

"Prince Damon is getting," Elora guffawed. "Married?"

"We do not gossip, and we do not speak of the court's affairs, Elora. You will take to the grave what you witness," said Jasper, overburdened and unsure of himself.

Austin smiled. He enjoyed watching Elora discover a new purpose as a Wildcat and the confidence it gave her.

"This is all ridiculous," she said.

"This is necessary. Joseph Blackheart, the Brokenhearted one, will join the Wildcats as he prepares and creates an honor guard for our soon-to-be queen."

"Wait, what?" Austin said.

Jasper looked at them.

"Prince Damon will become King of the Holy Imperium on the same day of his wedding to whatever fortunate woman he chooses, and she will become queen. That day will solidify the Holy Imperium." Jasper was stern in his command, and Austin saw his eyes tremble.

They stood stunned but nodded. Prince Damon was taking a step with or without the mad king of Great Brightland's blessing.

"When should we expect him?" Austin said. "He's supposedly the best sword in the Holy Imperium, a hero of the Crimson Struggle, and helped win our side at the Battle of the Reaping."

Jasper bristled, "Best sword, sure, sure." He paused and ran his thumb over the handle of his sword. "He'll be making his way here now; he's our second in command of the Wildcats if I were to fall. He's got much to learn about the position."

"Hope his head gets through the door," Elora said.

Jasper snickered. "For now, all he knows is that you are on an assignment of the highest order, and he gives you free leave to continue your assignment. You only report to me or General Casting." He paused and whispered. "Myself or Casting."

They stood in the barracks of the Wildcats, notably empty.

"We'll find you new squires, considering we left or lost two already. Tidy your shit up; the hero of the Battle of the Reaping will be here soon." Jasper walked away as the anger in his voice faded with him.

"The Brokenhearted one will be a Wildcat," Elora said. "You ever met him?" she asked, unloading her pack on a cot in her tiny bed chamber.

"Yes, we've crossed swords sparring several times,"

"Is he as skilled as the songs say?" she asked, trying to sound casual. "Better than my dad, better than Jasper?"

"With a sparring sword, he's fair. We break even, but they say when he uses Twilight, he's unstoppable."

"A magic sword? I don't believe it," Elora said.

"You should; when I bleed a soldier with Twilight, the sword sings to me in a soft moan as if it just finished someone off in bed," said a voice at the door. It was cocky, reminding Austin how Jasper sounded when they first met.

"You two look like the Servant's tired feet. Where have you been?"

"The Blightbriar Wilds, fighting orcs, warhawks, and goblins," said Austin, staring at Joseph Blackheart with his long cold dead eyes.

"You joking? You must be." Joseph Blackheart stood and looked at both now-seasoned warriors. "You're clean at least, but the looks in your eyes, you've seen something. And all I've done is feast and bitch and moan about fighting some tournament," Joseph complained. "Tell me what you know; tell me everything; I must be reassigned to the Blightbriar front."

"Sir Blackheart, from the sound of it, you may never leave this city again."

"You heard the same then; Prince Damon has forced me to guard some sloppy princess he wishes to bed."

Austin and Elora felt uncomfortable as Joseph Blackheart complained about being a knight and guard to the future Queen of Vineland.

"I'm Sir Austin. This is Sir Elora. We're both Wildcats, but we have an assignment from General Casting," said Austin.

"I heard as I came up the stairs, and Sir Jasper filled me in."

"Sir Elora, you weren't sworn in with the rest of us; why is that?" Joseph asked.

"We're recovering from the front, and Sir Jasper granted me the status upon news we provided him; I saw no need for pomp and circumstance."

"And neither of you see a need to wear our Wildcat uniform?"

Joseph stood in full uniform, crisp and shiny; everything was in place except for his sword, which was not the traditional blade worn by the Wildcats. He carried the dark blade, Twilight, its ink-black handle juxtaposed against the white sheath.

"We are wearing light mail and leathers of common mercenaries but carry the rite of Prince Damon; our investigation will lead us to places Wildcats can't go," said Austin, realizing he'd already said too much.

"Interesting, you-" Joseph stopped and shifted his head. "You smell that?"

Austin and Elora looked around.

"Fire. I smell fire," Austin said.

"Out the window, what is burning in the villages?" Elora said.

Joseph moved closer as they all looked out of the tower, and at a distance, they saw smoke and flame.

"Blue Templar, I see their flag there; someone is on horse circling the large burn pile," Joseph pointed.

"What are they burning?"

Joseph laughed. "They burn heretics and books before the celebration as requested by Prince Damon himself. The Path of the Blessed is bright with the fires of the sinners," said Joseph Blackheart, almost in a daze.

"It reminds me of the stories of the Purge before the Crimson Struggle," said Elora.

"Nothing I ever wanted to live in or take part in," said Austin.

"You're a Wildcat now, like me; we aren't just living in it; we are known participants in the history of this land now; we'll witness history and never be able to speak of it," Joseph said. "Have you ever read any of the books *The*

Lonely Nights of the Milkmaid, The Early Mornings of the Lonely Milkmaid, or the new one, *The Milkmaid at Twilight?*"

Austin shifted his weight; his locker held all three, along with the outlawed *Ordinary Wit* pamphlet.

"When I was younger, sure, I had my way with *Lonely Nights of the Milkmaid.* Who didn't?" Austin said. It wasn't a lie, and it wasn't the whole truth. They could hear screams of agony and triumph from below in the streets.

"I hate the smell of burnt flesh," Joseph complained. "It reminds me of the Crimson Struggle and that last battle up north. As many as I killed, as many as I could, we were outmatched. We didn't realize they would strike as one against us," Jasper looked down, lost in thoughts about a past battle. "The winds and fires," he whispered, "you can never get the smell of burning out of your nose." He stopped talking momentarily and put his hand on the hilt of the Masterstroke, which calmed him, and he collected his emotions. "Still, nothing makes me happier than blood on my blade. You know what they sing in the taverns of me," he stopped and sang aloud. "Happiness is a bloody blade, swipe swipe," he cut through the air with his blade, its darkness clipping the air. "Happiness is a bloody blade, thrust thrust."

Elora looked at Austin sideways as they watched Joseph in this awkward moment, and he sheathed the storied weapon.

"Everyone hates the smell of burnt flesh, Sir Joseph; think of the ones burning. My first time in the capital, and this is what it's like. Not sure what's worse, the Wilds or what you all call civilization," Elora said.

"I hope that's all of them, the heretics, and those books. That filth." Jasper changed direction.

"You think the written word could do so much harm that you would ban them, burn them. You think people are so weak they can't judge what is right and wrong, truth and fiction," Elora countered.

Joseph stepped back and shifted his weight, guiding his hand to the handle of his blade.

"Oh look, Austin, a woman has said something that contradicts the Brokenhearted one's thoughts, and he grasps for his manhood because uncomfortable thoughts disagree with his own," Elora said.

"We burn these books and heretics to protect the innocent, the children. The pure," said Joseph. "I wouldn't think the prince would let a heretic into the Wildcats."

Elora and Austin adjusted their weights, shifting into a defensive posture.

"Joseph, we both come from old and noble families. Who are you to tell me what I can and can't read? Do you not feel my judgment is as good as yours?" Austin said, trying to argue yet keep the situation from escalating.

"You ever burn anyone, Joseph? Did you do the actual burning of villages, the raping, the tying of knots, and the setting of the fire when on campaign, or did you just order it to be done and wash your hands clean?" Elora said, eager to push the matter.

"We draw blades in here, and I'm the only one who leaves," said Joseph. You are nearing the point of no turning back."

"You're the one getting defensive, Joseph. We're having a debate, and you immediately took steps to escalate a simple conversation into a bloody showdown. Men are eager to draw their weapons when confronted by an opposing viewpoint that makes as much or more sense than theirs."

"What in the Maker's tits is going on here? I step away for just a few squirts with a servant and return to near anarchy; we are not fucking orcs here; take your hands off your swords; we have work to do. Joseph, take a squad and try to keep peace in the villages; the Order of the Blue Rose is making a mess down there; try to stop them from killing more people. Elora and Austin, you have work to do. Later tonight, all three of you will explain why you were about to kill each other when we should be trying to keep this place together!" Yelled Jasper.

"Sir Jasper, there are no squads, just a dozen Wildcats sworn in with me. The rest are on duty."

"Shit, grab Sheriff Hearthelm and his goons, and tell them they are to keep the peace, not help with the book burning. That is a direct order from the Wildcats, who are above the Order of the Blue Rose in this city. This entire process is going to cause a riot," Jasper commanded. "No fucking swords. Use staves and axe handles, for Maker's sake." Jasper scratched his mane of hair. "Austin and Elora, you also have work to do, so get out of my sight. Now, off with you!"

Joseph left first, and Elora and Austin gathered a light cloak shortly after and left.

"I hate being in charge; I wish Pap were here," Jasper said, looking as the sky around the tower darkened from burnt books and flesh.

Ben - Skillets and Schemes

Wild deer and squirrels moved in the distance, and flowers and green shrubs sprouted everywhere on the sides of the streets and paths the group traveled to Hudson City. Angus had sent a letter to Duncan indicating that Cordial and himself were escorting Ben and Stu to the capital on official business for the Holy Imperium at the first tavern they found outside of Olde Ridgewatch. Angus tried to hint it was less of an official business trip and potentially something else entirely. The tavern had messenger birds, and Angus had paid a high price to deliver the message to the Windmill Pub as they headed south.

They had been on the road for days and neared the city-state limits of Lackmore. Angus caught up to the three as they stood on the side of the road in reverent silence, looking at over twenty separate crucifixions in a tilled field. Families hung on stakes shoved in the ground, their feet tied to the posts a few inches from the dirt. Birds of prey picked at some emaciated bodies, their chests stretched and sunken in. The youngest looked to be five summers old.

"What the fuck is this?" Angus asked. "You humans and your horrible ways of killing people. Letting the birds pick at your dead. Fucking vultures."

"The birds or the humans?" asked Ben.

"They broke the law, Angus. They got what they deserved. Look at them; some looked elven, or likely they practiced magic," said Stu, even as he gagged at the smell of the dead.

Cordial looked at Angus and said coldly, "At least we don't strap prisoners to stones and roll them down hills."

"Well, there is that," Angus shrugged. "You're right, you handsome bastard. Better them than us. Why would two entire families be crucified?"

Ben looked on. "I think they were harboring a hedge mage or were found with some illegal pamphlets."

Stu pointed, "Yeah, one was burnt at the stake, most likely a witch. Any magic practitioners must be brought to the Holy Church and have an anchor ring placed on them or be subject to the harsh laws of the Blue Templar. The Holy Church must purify those who defy the law and nature itself."

Ben stopped looking at the dead sinners, feeling guilty for having conflicting feelings upon seeing the corpses.

"They broke the law. They deserved what they got," repeated Stu, trying to justify the horrors before them.

Ben said quietly, "Is this how we're to govern the people? Is this what the Holy Imperium, the Maker, wanted?"

"The pamphlet and books nailed to the posts above the dead are now considered illegal," Cordial said, shaking his head from left to right. "You no longer have to be born with old magic or be an elve, goblin, or orc to be indiscriminately killed; they'll get you for reading, too."

"One looked to be called *Ordinary Wit*; the other was *The Milkmaid at Twilight*," Angus leaned close to an older-looking corpse.

Behind the corpses, the homestead smoldered on the ground. The posts, some in the form of two angled crossed sticks, others poles shoved into the ground, had marks from animals as they reached up and feasted on the feet of the victims.

Ben continued to look up at the dead, his mouth open, his mind spinning, and said aloud to everyone, "Anyone really think crucifying a child is the right way to teach people laws and rules?"

Ben now looked at Stu.

"What?" He spluttered. "No, but they should know not to harbor witches and mages; those people can destroy entire cities if left to themselves?"

"Stu, who do you think delivers babies or heals soldiers on a battlefield?" Cordial snapped. "Mages and witches. Magic has existed since humans first stepped foot on Vineland, and the only people abusing it now are humans in control of it." He said disgustingly, "Let's get moving; they're bringing in the flies and mosquitoes; we got a long walk ahead of us to Hudson City."

* * *

The fire crackled and spat, teasing the four companions as they sat around it with its red and orange glowing flames and warmth. They had seen two more groups of crucified townspeople over the past few days. The summer season had hit Wolvenshire, the forested area outside of Hudson City, and the great canopy of the Wolvenshire woods brought relief from the heat after traveling south for six days. They were getting closer to Hudson City. The roads had been easy for them after they had stolen four horses from a gang of highwaymen while they slept.

"Angus, you are a breath of fresh air on the road. I know we've been together for a bit, but now that we aren't being hunted like a bear, the food has been some of the best I've had while traveling."

Angus burped and took a swig from his canteen. "As long as someone washes the dishes, that's fine by me. But I will wash my pan; it's saved my life more than once or twice. So, tell me, Ben, we've been on the road for a bit; what's the plan here? What are we trying to accomplish?"

"I dunno, I thought maybe that the son of General Benedict Ashburn, wishing to speak to him, would get me an audience with General Casting."

"You nobles always thinking your name means enough to open doors and get what you want," Cordial said. "Get me within twenty feet of anyone, and I will put a bolt in their throat." Cordial pointed a nasty, looking one-handed crossbow at Stu. "Doesn't matter if their name starts with a royal or noble title. Everyone casts a shadow, and the society makes sure nobody forgets that."

"That's illegal, you know," Stu said weakly, scratching his newly grown beard. "Don't point that thing at me, Cordial. Makes me nervous."

Cordial moved the crossbow away. He also carried Stitch's double stilettos in memory of this fallen friend.

"Cordial, you know the city. What's the best course of action? I don't think killing anyone is necessary, but if I could just talk to General Casting, let him know what is happening all over Vineland, what Angus saw, what's happening in Olde Ridgewatch, and the crucifixions on the road down here. I think he'd do something about it; General Casting and my dad are old friends; he would have to listen," he looked into the fire.

Angus stirred the fire and the debate. "You really think he'd listen to a bastard of a soldier who left his post and traveled with a known felon, a drunken exiled dwarve, and your best friend. You could be taken in as deserters. Plus, you took part in the capture of a Holy Imperium fortress by rebels. You have blood on your hands, both of you. You really think he'll make you knights? Ben, I'm here because I failed your brother, and your dad and General Casting might be old friends, but this is an impossible undertaking. I'll do my best to help, but this may not go how you wish."

"We're not deserters. We're messengers," Stu stood up. "Ben has orders from a general of the Holy Imperium to deliver messages to General Casting or Prince Damon and, and-" Stu faltered. "This all sounds ridiculous; why am I wasting my time here." He looked away.

Ben stood and turned to his friend.

Angus and Cordial looked at the young men, their ages and wisdom showing on their faces. Ben scratched at his face, hand on his knife blade.

"We can make a difference. Let's seek an audience with General Casting or at least one of his assistants. I know my way around a court; we should be able to talk to someone to get the messages delivered." Stu said, turning his back on Ben, Angus, and Stitch. It felt as if he was trying to talk his way into justifying everything he'd done.

"Words will only carry you so far, Stu. If they don't listen, we'll force them to listen or make a spectacle out of them," Cordial said. Ben looked at Cordial, the fire reflecting in his eyes.

Cordial smiled, and Angus turned away.

"You've come so far. The Holy Imperium did wrong to Ben's family, but if you cut an eye out for ever wrong, the world would be blind," Angus said. He tossed Ben his bottle of whiskey. "That's why we drink, numb the pain of regret, and a life turned sour. Now pass it around to Stu when you've had a nip."

Stu looked at Ben.

"Would you really kill a general, your father's friend from when they were younger to, to what end to punish Prince Damon? To punish the Holy Imperium?" he asked, looking at Ben and then at Cordial.

Retribution, Ben thought. *Blood for the earth so that the trees grow strong.*

"My family. Runt, Mom, Alysha, they didn't do anything. They lived in the wilderness, away from court politics and games. And they suffered for it. I didn't think politics and the court would be so involved in the military, but I saw it daily; you saw it, too," Ben pleaded with Stu quietly. The fire snapped, and the darkness of the night loomed behind them all. Ben played with the handle of his knife with his thumb. He sipped the bottle and offered it up to Stu, who took it, drawing closer for a moment. "The people at court think they're above us and step on folks' necks every chance they get; maybe they need to taste some blood in their wine and a little fear."

Stu looked away, "You're talking about my dad and mom, too, you know." He handed the bottle back to Angus. "Fuck this; tomorrow I head home, I won't say shit about you three, but I am done, done with this shit."

Cordial said. "Stu, relax, pal. We aren't going to kill anyone; I mean, we feel like we should, but it's not going to happen; it would be impossible to do it. Our emotions and grief take over sometimes. I want Ben to talk to someone important, potentially one of the most powerful people in Vineland; if you, Angus, and I can help, we will. Ben's father is a general leading thousands of soldiers; there would be no reason the son of that general would not get an audience with General Casting, even if it was just for a moment. No need to leave my friend."

"No, this is ridiculous; I shouldn't have left Sir Donald's lance and followed the three of you," Stud said, standing away from the fire, wanting to distance himself from them and their treacherous talk.

"Go wash the dishes in the creek there; I will join you in a few; gotta wash the skillet," said Angus. He stood and drank off the rest of the bottle and smiled. "Oh, that's good. I'll be down to wash my hatchet and knife shortly. It'll keep the wolves away if there are two of us."

353

Stu grabbed a torch, the cups, and Angus giant skillet and walked away carrying it like an axe on his shoulder.

Cordial stood up, "I'll help wash up, Angus," and he put his hand on one of the stilettos.

Kill Stu, Ben thought. He brushed his fingers against his knife handle.

Ben looked at Angus and Cordial.

"I want to talk to them, to one of the councilors controlling the Holy Imperium. General Casting would be best. They *must* know what's happening. I'll help Stu; you two relax by the fire," and he pushed past them and walked into the darkness where Stu had left.

* * *

The water trickled by the stones, dead fall tree limbs, and last autumn leaves that lay decomposing in the damp night air. Stu scrubbed at a pot with a piece of lye soap and then splashed water into it.

"You need help with Angus's skillet, fucking thing is heavy," said Ben from behind Stu lightly so he wouldn't scare him in the darkness.

"He said he uses it to cook and split heads. I can see why," Stu said. "Cut my thumb on a pour spout."

"You really leaving because you think we're deserters?" Ben asked.

"Ben, I don't want to, but what you and Cordial are talking about, this Society of Shadows he's in? It's too much." He paused, put the pan down, and washed a large spoon.

"Seriously, an organization found in every city that regulates criminals and runs contracts, and some hedge mage runs it. Do you really believe that?" Ben said. "I doubt it exists. They're just spinning stories. My dad hired them because two on the road isn't as safe as four on the road.

Stu sighed. "What do you really hope to accomplish in Hudson City? You've never been there; getting close to someone important will be impossible. The city has more people than the entire Commonwealth of Erieland.

Ben stood quietly, envisioning the crucified people on the road. The injustice of the act lingered in him, feeding something inside him, a wraith, a vengeful spirit. He shook his head, not understanding what was happening inside him. *A true knight doesn't do such atrocities*, he considered.

You killed before; do it again, another voice said back in response.

Ben touched the hilt of Dawn's Breath.

"Would it help if I showed you the papers my dad wrote, giving us leave to journey to Hudson City and request an audience with General Casting?"

Ben gripped the knife and patted his jacket's side pocket, which contained several messages directed to General Casting.

"I don't even know anymore, Ben," Stu stood and looked on. "What we did back at Bawstone Keep, people saw us."

Ben pulled out two sealed letters showing his father's seal and another one opened, supplying safe conduct to the capital as messengers for the Holy Imperium Army and directing them to General Casting.

"I am to deliver the letters and will speak to him directly about the crucifixions, the Olde Ridgewatch massacre, and riot, my brother and family, all of it. We'll get in, and we'll talk to General Casting."

Stu read the open letter under the torchlight. Two were still sealed with the Ashburn family seal.

"And if he doesn't listen?"

"I'll kill him," Ben whispered so Stu couldn't hear, touching the handle of his knife. The water of the stream trickled by.

Stu turned to read the rest of the letter written by General Benedict Ashburn.

"What if General Casting just posts us wherever he wants instead of making us knights? He's pushing us out of his army, Ben. Your father, he's getting rid of you. You have no idea what the other letters say, do you?"

Ben looked confused.

If he leaves, he will betray you; he knows too much, kill him.

"I am to deliver the letters, and General Casting will then give us leave to join Prince Damon's Court or place us in another position. My father wasn't clear on what we were to do after," Ben now said, confused, his head foggy, thoughts unsure.

"Whatever." Stu shook his head, jaw set. "You deliver these messages, I'm done; I'm going home. I can't stand the army anymore; you, Cordial, Angus. This is fucking ridiculous. Fuck it, I leave tomorrow. Do this shit by yourself. We were supposed to be knights, Ben. Belted knights! Now we're running messages for your father. He didn't even give us a proper guard! It's you and me, two failed archers and two hired goons who knew your dead brother."

Ben turned as grief and loss seeped into his heart.

"I'm sorry. I'm sorry. I shouldn't have brought it up. I know-" Stu stopped. "I know me killing him haunts you."

"Wait." Ben froze. "You? You killed Runt?"

"I saw you drop your crossbow; it fell, and the bolt slammed into the slave next to your brother. A snowball hit me in the face, and I pulled the trigger; it hit a boy, who I now know was your brother. I killed him. It could have been you, but I think I did it."

"All this time, and you didn't tell me you fucking killed my brother." Ben whirled on Stu, venom dripping from his words. Tears streaked his eyes, and rage filled his ears, making them ring. Stu looked at his friend.

Yes.

"How was I supposed to tell you? You were going crazy and have been drunk or high most of the time. And then the thing at the Bawstone Keep," Stu was yelling now, too.

"I grieved over murdering Runt for days! I still do. How could you!" Tears streaked his face in anger and despair, his hands shut tight and then opening, his breathing labored between sobs.

Stu came closer, "I'm sorry, I never." He came over to hug Ben, his friend, his comrade, the only person he'd confided in, and Ben grasped him, shoving Dawn's Breath deep into Stu's chest. Ben's eyes flicked white, and he left himself for a moment as the cold, hard truth of death dripped down Stu's chest.

"Liars and traitors to Vineland and my family. You all must die," Ben whispered into his friend's ear, but Stu no longer listened. "May Jupitor's summer sun never shine on your family again."

Doc - Alliance of Owls

"We hold that our voice to speak, to write, and to worship shall not be infringed by the maker, heir or other as to..." A knock at the door interrupted Olivia as her quill shook up and down, the ink bottle near it full of darkness deeper than an abyss. She looked at her scroll pinned to the table by four daggers and breathed deeply, protecting herself and the scroll on which she wove intricate spells.

"How do you water a tree?" asked Olivia.

"You give it freedom and your blood," replied a muffled voice.

"Enter," she said, and the spell locking the door was released. "Lord Washcreek, apologies if I don't stand. I'm in the middle of something important."

"It's fine." The gruff general shook his head as he entered the room. "I'm here to observe Olivia Franklin at work," he smiled. She felt him coiled in his chest but somewhat at ease as well.

"Doc went to get refreshments, including something for you and Braya," said Olivia. Braya had followed General Washcreek in. They smelled of sex, and Olivia could feel the attraction between the two. She could also tell there was a whiff of lust towards her and noted Washcreek's appetite.

"How did you know we would be here now?" he questioned.

Olivia stopped moving her quill and sat back from her table. The room was off from the main bar at the McGrave's Ale House. The window was blocked off with a black sheet. She sat at the remaining table with stools for three people and a leather couch off to the side. Bookshelves held up the walls, and an old map of Vineland pre-Crimson Struggle adorned another wall.

"What Doc and I do, we've done for years, Lord Washcreek. My specialty is knowing, writing, and governing ideas. Doc's is fire and other specialties thanks to what he learned at the end of the Crimson Struggle."

"Right, I forget such notions even after Doc saved my skin twenty-thirty years back." Washcreek closed his fist tightly.

Even now, Lord Washcreek carries his spear, the Holy Truth. It never left his hands, just as her quill was always near her, and Doc's staff never left his. She smiled, glad to know they held three Paragons of the Maker and went back to writing, her quill weaving and spinning words of revolution and liberty.

Lord Washcreek changed the spear's shaft depending on where he was attending. He used a longer pole for battle; as he was in the city, he carried a shorter version. Tonight, the blade shaft was the size of a short sword. The spear point was safely tucked under a wooden cover, so it looked like an uncomfortable walking stick, but Olivia knew what lay under it.

* * *

Doc nudged his way to the busy bar. He was calm tonight, only buzzed enough to keep the voices at bay. No wizard salt, and definitely no warlock coal or Gothine tears. Yee gads that would be a touch too much. He'd smoked enough reefer in the back alley with a bum. He'd met the hedge witch who left the courtroom early in the proceedings and downed a glass of bourbon after walking back inside to keep the edge off. Doc had been attempting to behave so as not to upset his betters. He knew his strengths and weaknesses and didn't want to shake the foundations of a better Vineland, a better tomorrow. He looked around the bar and saw familiar faces.

Mercy Pitcher from Lackmore sat in a corner eating a meat pie and drinking wine with Ezebell Milessent from Waterhurst. Over her shoulder and whispering to them was Brice Hitchson from the Rosewood Dominion, who sat next to a scout named Crux. The scout, Doc knew who worked under General Hammer Clinton, based in Crescent City. He looked up from talking and nodded towards Doc, who sniffed slightly and tipped his pewter mug at him.

"You there, bartender," he demanded. The goblin drinking earlier in the day now wore an apron and looked back at Doc. He was the size of a dwarve but skinnier with sharper features, and his goblin skin was off-grey and delicate.

"Interesting way to position yourself, Truestaer; how's your brother in the Wilds fairing?" Doc asked. He handed the goblin a small bag. "My compliments, I gathered a few mushrooms and a packet of reefer on my way to the city." The goblin nodded and gave a smirk. "Hits like a horse kick. I indulged with your local bum out back in the alley."

"Careful with her. She works for the shadows," Truestaer said.

Doc smirked, "Soon, we all will," he mumbled, biting on his pipe.

"Things progress in the Blightbriar Wilds, and they await word from here. It looks like your gathered friends are not pleased to include us," the bartender named Truestaer poured cups of ale and wine and placed them on a round lid for Doc to carry. Next to it, he placed cheese and cured sausage. Music played in the corner, a jolly tune for a sad, windy night by mandolin and cheap piano. The duo was originally from Grimwood, having moved out years ago. Doc had met the duo called The Off Keyes on the road and mentioned Affectus as an excellent place for them to resettle. Some windows were open, and the music drifted outside, but the gossip and secrets stayed indoors.

Candles lined the tables, and owl lamps lit the sides of the walls. Laughter and arguments challenged each other across tables, and wine and ale soaked the knotted and uneven floor. The crowd was lively, and the conversations were deep or shallow, depending on the group. Gossip and debate drifted around the smoke of cigars, pipes, and cigarettes. A few games of cards were thrown around tables, and games of dice challenged fate and the wits of a few true degenerates.

"Ambrose and Brice will follow, if not lead us eventually. They must publicly show their hatred to keep their business clean. Besides, as much as Brice seems to be against elves, dwarves, and the like," Doc leaned in closer as he paid for the drinks. "You should see his lover and their children. He'll protect them and himself, and the two align with what we hope to accomplish."

"As you say, Doc," said Truestaer. "From what I saw today, this will be messy." The goblin poured more ale for those around Doc as he smoked tobacco out of his pipe. Doc looked in the bar mirror, and it shimmered for a second. A tall man stepped out of the shadows to his right. Doc chuckled, knowing how much it would take for a mage to travel through a mirror from one place to another. Only one or maybe two people knew of the talent, and Doc only knew one who could do it. Johnathan Huber, a pupil of the mage Gaston, had made an appearance at the bar; he co-led the Society of Shadows in Affectus and other cities and was the last of his family name. He wore a similar patch quilt military coat that Doc wore, but his hair remained, and he covered his head with a tricorne hat. Nobody had noticed his entrance behind the bar except for Doc and Truestaer. He nodded, twisted his mustache, and walked toward Brice Hitchson.

"Shit, the boss is here," mumbled Truestaer to himself. Doc looked at him.

"How much for some goblin panic, my old friend? You got anything fresh from the wilds?"

Truestaer shouted so others could hear. "I don't serve that swill here, you ingrate! Now take your drinks and let me work."

"What! Fine!" Doc shouted, and smoke poured from his pipe. He looked at his friend Truestaer and then at the mirror behind him near the shelves where the bar stored bottles of liquor and barrels of ale and whispered. "Later tonight, meet Franklin and me for a drink after the others leave," someone nudged Doc. He gripped his staff and carried the drinks, mumbling and yelling at those in his way.

"Make way, make way, these drinks cost more than your life, you rats and vipers!" A red velvet smoke trailed from Doc's pipe, which he grasped in his teeth. Anyone annoyed by him soon forgot he had passed and continued their conversations.

* * *

"Come in."

The door opened.

"Well, here we are now. Even the esteemed Braya has showed up in a hidden room of a seedy tavern tucked away in a city of vice and sin," said Doc. "I am surrounded by owls and crows alike pecking away at the underbelly of Vineland." Doc bowed like a server, balancing a tray full of drinks in hand and a staff in the crook of his arm.

"Champagne for the ladies, whiskey for me, and a whiskey punch for Lord Washcreek. The tavern is full and brimming with gossip and stories. I've sent my newly acquired writer and Maynard to haunt the town tonight and pick up what facts they can find. When we finish there will be much work to do. I saw a flash in a mirror behind the bar when speaking to an old friend who represents interests in the mountains, and the man who represents Affectus has arrived. Johnathan Huber has entered, representing the city and the Society of Shadows."

Lord Washcreek bowed. "I'm blessed to be in such company." Washcreek nodded to Doc and Olivia. "Doc, thank you for the refreshment. You still remember what I enjoy. These friends of yours are not tof folk I typically deal with. Criminals and mages and such."

Olivia sipped the champagne and returned to writing as if in a trance. Her hand moved at a fantastic speed.

"Says the man who owns slaves and traffics in their sales, says the man who commits to killing every orc he passes, says the man who hangs goblins from trees and cuts off their genitals." Doc laughed. "I've known you since your youth cutting down cherry trees with a magical spear. Do not think your sins cut as deep as his; Huber is more forward about it. Everyone casts shadows during the day, and at night, everything is darker. If we're to build something better, we should include the rogues and vagabonds to ensure they can improve themselves and their families."

"Johnathan Huber is the last of his family and wants nothing but revenge," countered General Washcreek. "I was in the basement of this place looking at the wine cellar, and this den of vice was cooking up wizard salt and drying reefer in a room right next door. And I can hear the prostitutes in their work inside the rooms above the bar."

Olivia snicked, and Doc raised his eyebrows. "You don't know what happened to me, do you, Lord Washcreek? I want revenge as much as Huber does. He will be in after you and Braya leave. It will take different perspectives to build this new country, to build over the ruins of the Holy Imperium."

Lord Washcreek gripped the Holy Truth tightly and tried to stare down Doc, who brushed off the menace like a father ignoring a toddler.

"Sausage and cheese as well, you sly little fox. Thank you," said Braya, taking a bite and changing the subject. The two men broke up their posturing.

"You may both enjoy what I've gathered, and I've ordered another plate as Olivia will need some sustenance after her work," Doc said, looking at how thin she was now growing, the magic taking so much of her away.

Braya nodded. She wore no regal clothes and kept her hood on. A dark, expensive set of trousers and lightly woven elvish armor could barely be seen under a nicely fitted commoner shirt.

"And Samuel Hawthorn is in another tavern. I know his presence can complicate things," said General Washcreek.

Doc nodded while taking a hit from his pipe. "I appreciate his presence when I don't need to do anything. It calms what's inside my head but leaves me utterly defenseless." Doc alluded that Samuel Hawthorn was one of the last living relatives in all of Vineland related to King Christopher Goldthorn. Samuel Hawthorn's family, in some distant relation to those impressive families, managed to escape the slaughter and years of warring. He was now under General Washcreek's mentorship as one of two guards always near him.

Braya nodded, walked behind Olivia while she worked, and gently rubbed her hand down her back.

"This bill is astounding, but will it pass a vote?" asked Braya.

"This is more than King Christopher and Erica the Red proposed," said General Washcreek.

Braya sneered. "I hope to piss on their graves one day; you people hold them in such high regard."

General Washcreek nodded, "I have only the histories given to me, written by our scholars. I'd love to hear the first people's interpretation of the history of Vineland. Would you allow me to read them?"

Braya nodded. "Maybe someday, General, if you release your slaves working your tobacco and cotton fields." Washcreek scratched at his face and looked Braya in the eye, not shying from the truth.

"I am not beyond change, Mistress Braya; it's what makes a competent commander."

"If you sign this document, you'll have to do so," Doc said. "Free your slaves; this document gives everyone the same rights."

"Nobody will sign it," said Braya. "I came to observe your peers, but too much money and hatred is bred into their veins. The first peoples will never be free without a fight."

"I agree, nobody will," advised General Washcreek. "People are too stuck in their ways, stuck in their hatred learned from their parents, learned from their religion and those damn pamphlets Prince Damon puts out. Besides, it would shake the economy of the Holy Imperium to the ground."

Doc laughed and took a sip of whiskey to stop himself. "More free peoples mean more taxes on those peoples. Those taxes build schools, roads, houses built of stones, and hospitals. Think of the good this could do. We'll make them vote to raise their taxes, and they will love us for it."

"If you can unite them, eastern Vineland, this united city-state may finally catch up to the first peoples out west. Eventually, you may even threaten us," said Braya.

"The heathens are no threat to the Holy Imperium," said General Washcreek in a prided tone.

Braya laughed. "That is not what you were saying to me earlier on your knees, my general," She looked at Olivia, who turned away. "You prayed to your god so loudly." She smiled. "You may call me a heathen in bed, but do so in anger, and I will castrate you."

Doc snickered and passed his glass of whiskey and a piece of cheese to Olivia as she started to write forcefully again.

General Washcreek composed himself and returned to the document Olivia worked on, his ears burning red. "You're proposing a legal working here to protect the civilian population by a regulated standing army, the ability to carry weapons but also regulate them, even commoners."

Olivia stopped her pen. "Yes, like the dwarves, like the elves, like the goblins, and orcs, they all allow anyone to carry a weapon, but we'll be civilized, there will be training, there will be laws so that it's not madness in the streets, at universities, and churches. The words well-regulated here are for the militia and the common people- if everyone owns a sword or crossbow, it would be mayhem without."

Washcreek took a step back. "The crossbow is the most dangerous weapon I've seen on the battlefield next to a compound bow and you two mages. It's too easy to use and impersonal, but limiting swords and axes, all of this, I don't know how it will be regulated."

"Prince Damon and his Council of Crows limit commoners from carrying swords and crossbows already; this puts it down on paper," Doc said.

"The Clearstone family, as they fought for Steelsburg and retreated to the Gloomspire, approved crossbows to be used by all, General Washcreek; it's how we will win the coming war. We need the Clearstone family on our side; they are exiled now and no longer allowed in Steelsburg above or below, and we will help take it back. Lines are drawn; I'm just putting them down on paper," said Franklin. She was visibly wasting away. Doc handed her more food.

"From what I saw earlier, most folks don't want a war," said Washcreek.

"We've been at war with Prince Damon and those like him since before his birth," said Braya. "With Great Brightland, the Legion of Carigreed, and the Nation of Stouya. They have sent my kind into slavery and committed atrocities against my cousins, goblins, and orcs for years. Until we fought back, until warhawks carried their children away, until we burned them from the skies above and built a wall to show them, we would take no more. You must fight for your freedom and continue to do so with every breath you take." Braya crossed her arms.

"The Holy Imperium doesn't want war? It's already here. It started when General Benedict Ashburn's soldiers slaughtered us in the streets of Olde Ridgewatch. The people of Olde Ridgewatch took Bawstone Keep and can hold it. They need our support." Doc put his hands down on the table; looking at the bill, Olivia stared back with a frown.

"Doc, your glasses are gone," said Olivia quietly. "You trust everyone here?"

Doc didn't hear or did not care.

"What we do and say is treason to Prince Damon and his Council of Crows," General Washcreek hesitantly said. "There will be so much blood."

"It's how you make liberty trees grow, general," said Doc. Olivia nodded. Braya shifted her weight towards the door, not acknowledging the comment. "There will be no kings in the united city-states of Vineland, just us."

"I know Prince Damon must fall and what must be done. It's difficult knowing and seeing it come about. I've only served and never conspired," said General Washcreek.

"What we are doing now could change much. All of Vineland," said Braya. "Let's hope it's for all its peoples and not a privileged few." She looked at Washcreek. "Free your slaves and be a man, not a hungry boy on his knees serving a bastard prince."

Olivia was scribbling faster, her eyes white, her hand a blur, the paper, the quill spewing a yellow stout smoke. It was quiet for minutes as they looked on. She stopped and put the quill down, her eyes returning to normal.

"When we finish, we sign with blood. We sign with all of ourselves because if we don't, we fail. We must be willing to give up everything to bring a better tomorrow to those who come after us," said Olivia, whose eyes were white and bleeding.

Braya, General Washcreek, and Doc looked at her and said nothing until Doc said, "If you are committed, then so am I."

"What happens next?" asked Olivia, dazed. She was herself again. She wiped her face clean. "The future, the next steps are foggy," she said. She started eating what was left on the plate weakly. Her darker hair now held strands of gray and white. Doc had noted she'd aged years yet retained the beauty she always carried. It was always hard watching a peer use the arts.

Doc took his pipe out. "We bribe. Twist arms, break heads, and make deals to get this passed. And then you're going to get this bill copied, and we are going to tie them to bricks and throw 'em through fucking windows until the royals realize the revolution started, and it's too late to stop it."

Washcreek said. "I dislike the politics. It's worse than war."

"Politics and war are the same coin. Only with politics, sometimes there's less blood," said Doc. "On our trip here, Maynard and I saw peasants who had lost what little they had. When they lose control, they will lash out at those in power. Take away the brothels, tax the beer and wine, and make the tea harder to get; a plague or a bad harvest will cause bricks through windows, riots in the streets, and mobs marching. This document will push them toward Hudson City and away from the merchants and landowners of Vineland."

Olivia stood up. "If the peasants are starving and the prince announces what he's having for dinner, the nobles will taste the fires of fear and pain."

Braya and Washcreek looked at the mages.

"Your Prince Damon will lash out; this document will not bring peace. It is a warhawk painted white like a dove," said Braya.

"If I sign this document, I best start getting soldiers together to defend the Rosewood Dominion from Prince Damon's wrath."

Olivia looked at General Washcreek. "General Washcreek, you best get an army ready to defend all of Vineland, not just your own home."

Hudson City - Burnt Hopes

"We've been to all the rookeries connected to all the bridges?" Elora said.

The royal rookeries rested at the top of the great bridges of Hudson City and were the main contact points for incoming and outgoing mail via carrier bird. They were also the stopping posts for any correspondence or messages from royal messengers. The public and government officials used the birds and the bridges for information, gathering gossip and general knowledge of the area.

"We've confirmed every rookery has a monk sorting through the mail. My gut says they all report to the Order of the Blue Rose," he stopped himself as they walked and checked the knife at his belt, thinking. Elora and Austin walked on a busy street in the West Village and saw a soldier in chainmail, leathers, and a cloak and livery of the Blue Templar.

"Not a full-on Templar yet, but they're recruiting," said Elora. The press of people on the busy street forced them to stand close to each other near the building as they waited for the soldier to pass. Her breath smelled of wine and mint leaves, and her body was taut with stress; Austin ached to reach his arms out and pull her closer, but he guarded those thoughts and concentrated on finding out who had intercepted his personal correspondence.

"We have no evidence, but all my senses, all my thoughts, point toward the Order of the Blue Rose, stopping my messages from getting into the hands of General Casting."

"What are we going to do to prove it?" asked Elora as they stepped out of the alley and away from each other. They slowly followed the soldier who had passed, trailing him at a distance. Not on purpose, but something felt off. "We're not at war with them, but it's a power struggle. I don't want to get involved, but we're slowly spinning into a conspiracy here without proof."

"I think I need to go to confession…" Austin sighed.

They were still close to each other in the crush of the crowd, but Elora stopped after Austin said this.

"You do that into the Holy Church?"

Austin nodded. "My beliefs won't change even if the Path of the Blessed is blemished with sinners."

"You know I'm not welcome in places like that. I can stay outside while you confess your sins," Elora said. "They call people like me heretic and profane because I worship the first people's gods."

Austin looked at her, and there was resentment in her eyes. Elora had been thrown into the chaos of one of the largest cities in Vineland, and her discomfort was evident, not only at coming up short on evidence of Austin's missing messages but also at the fact that he was heading to a place that would burn her at the stake for her religious beliefs.

"You taught me a lot in the wilds. Now, it's time to learn how to deal with court politics and the unnatural laws of the capital. Let's get the horses and make our way back towards the street of towers," he said. "Confession clears my head, and I can gather more information from a source."

* * *

"State your business." said a Copperhead guard as Angus, Cordial, and Benjamin walked toward the gates of Warhawk Kiss Bridge. The foot traffic moved off to the side of the bridge, the central section allowing carriages and wagons to come and go from the city. The traffic was constant during the day, and during holidays, the bridge remained open at night as thousands moved in and out of the town. Angus took a sip from a brown bottle and wiped his mouth, already a little drunk.

"We hear the city guard is recruiting; these boys and I have done some," Angus burped loudly into the bridge guard's chest, "similar work."

"You don't look like much, you three, turn around. We don't need any more mercs in Hudson City. Unless you have a sponsor, no entry allowed."

The guard, adorned in shoulder armor and a leather cuirass with his copper half helmet and Hudson City livery, frowned at the three. Angus stepped back, out of sorts, his head spinning.

Ben was about to speak up when Cordial stepped in front of them.

"I am Valentine Cordial Wightland, the son of Viscount Wightland," Cordial said with a change of stance and a slight poshness. He palmed the guard three coins and shook the guard's hand harshly, his voice like warm butter on bread. The guard looked down and saw the tattoo of the Society of Shadows on the crease of the inside of Cordial's elbow, as well as a black feather with blood on the end. "If you don't know the Viscount Wightland himself, I'm sure you know of Brother Hewitt or Sister Temperance. They're personal guards to Bishop Devon of the Maker's Holy Church here in Hudson City." Cordial laughed, looking at Ben and Angus and then back at the guard. "Now, you're holding up the line; move yourself so we can continue. These two will join the city guard or my father's ranks."

Cordial placed his hand on the guard's shoulder and bumped him, smoothly lifting his purse and walking past the guard, knowing nothing would happen. Angus took a swig of the bottle and handed it, empty, to the guard. Ben followed with a quick skip in his boots. The guard said nothing and was too tired to stop the three of them. He just yelled, "Next," as another group moved to his gate to pay their toll to get into the city.

"I knew you had noble blood, but your father's a viscount. Do we call you lord now," Angus teased.

"No," Cordial said flatly. "My father and I had a falling out when I was younger. The family is very devoted to the Holy Church to get into the graces of their peers after my grandmother disgraced our name."

"Younger? You're less than twenty-two summers old, boy," said Angus. "Try living past one hundred years like a real dwarve. This city smells like burnt sausages and human grease. Reminds me a bit of home deep underground." Angus smiled slightly.

"Not much older than me," said Ben. "My father used to spin tales of the

Wightland sisters, Lady Grapeseed, Lady Rowan, and Lady Blacklace."

"Grandma Grapeseed is something special, I will tell you that," Cordial said. "Great cook and full of wit and wonder. She taught me the skill I used to lift that guard's purse and alchemy."

Ben could smell fresh bore skewers and fish and turned toward the smells. He saw a fishmonger stall next to a general store, next to an herb shop, and the people and places continued on. He'd been in large cities and castles, but nothing compared to the capital of Vineland.

"Keep walking, turn to the right at the second intersection, and watch your pockets. This is where thieves and shills love to work," Cordial said. "I'm no lord and no longer welcome at House Wightland by my father or brother. They took other directions in life, so we're stuck with lesser accommodations. I doubt my sister would recognize me either."

Ben looked up and around as tower shadows blocked out certain portions of the sky. He wondered how they heated such massive buildings during the dark winter nights when the god Stribog angrily dropped snow and wind from the sky, and his wolves patrolled the Wolvenshire forest.

"The wonders of the dwarves never cease," said Angus as he admired the poured stone towers sunk deep into the cobblestoned streets. "They just take your breath away."

"I've never seen the towers inside the city. My father was exiled before I could get here. I only saw them at a distance," said Ben.

"Stop looking up. Ben or my friends in the shadows will mark you as a rube and rob you, leaving you nothing but a fig leaf to cover your asshole and pecker," said Cordial, walking quickly. "Keep up and follow me."

The streets were a fine cobbled stone, and they looked as if the cobbling allowed drainage into the gutter.

"This is a well-built area," remarked Angus.

"It is, but other portions as we get away from the river are a little more to our liking, and we aren't even near where we want to be yet. May take a day or two to figure out how to get into the Nightingale Theater."

"The celebration's in three days," said Ben, unsure of himself. The city's size and mass of people had humbled his earlier thoughts on reaching a Holy

Imperium inner council member. He thumbed Dawn's Breath, and a thought drifted into his mind, *have faith in the shadows, my knight.*

They stopped at the corner of an intersection and moved off to the side, letting foot traffic and carts pass. Some of the inner sections had Copperhead Guards directing traffic; it was so busy.

"You think we can make it all the way to General Casting and speak to him through all these thousands of people? Stu may have been right," Ben said. "This is hopeless." He pushed his fingers through his hair.

"I don't think we'll even make it out of here alive," Angus finished.

"Probably not, but we'll try. The shadows are known to be resourceful. If we pull this off, you may be allowed to join. So, let's enjoy ourselves these last few days and at the party, come what may," said Cordial. "Revenge is bittersweet, and the life before the end is the sweetest."

They made their way to a wine cellar and a dirty table.

Angus had been quieter ever since Stu's death outside of the forest. Ben and Cordial discussed their plans to reach Hudson City and get into Prince Damon's Triumphant Masquerade party. He now chewed on a wad of tobacco and spat at the floor, turning to Ben as Cordial was away grabbing drinks.

"Duncan told me to stop you two from getting into what you're planning. Fine fuckin' good that did, considering that Stu is dead," Angus paused and looked at Ben with bloodshot eyes, darkened and slightly wet. "I would have done the same thing to Stu if he'd done what he did. Little bastard. Just do your best. What you've been through, you deserve a voice, even if it's yelled into the darkness."

Ben looked away, feeling guilty. *Or yelled from the darkness.*

Cordial placed three pewter cups on the table, waking Ben from somber thoughts.

"My friends, we're in the greatest city this side of the Atlantis Ocean. Now we need to secure some masks that will be used by the staff at the party. From there, if the opportunity presents itself, Ben can slip the messages to a member of the prince's council," Cordial said with a smile that did not meet his eyes. His bright teeth showed as he eyed a server. Ben drank his port wine down quicker than Angus, raising his hand for another as he fingered the blade at his side.

"I want to at least try to get the messages to General Casting," said Ben, thinking of his father. Cordial looked at Angus and Ben and nodded, knowing they could be dead in three days, and the only thing that mattered was the last taste of friendship, love, and drink that lay ahead of them.

"We get inside the party and seek an audience or at least a word with General Casting or someone close to him. We'll never get close to Prince Damon. Ben can deliver his messages and try to clarify what happened in Olde Ridgewatch and what he found out about his homestead. Angus and I will ensure that we have a way to escape if something happens."

"This is asking a lot out of you two," said Ben.

"Your father hired us to guide you to the city and get you to General Casting, Ben. Angus is not only part of this but a member of your family. Let's try to do it right here. It's up to you what happens once you get close enough to General Casting," said Cordial.

Ben shifted in his chair and turned to the dwarve. "Angus, what are your thoughts."

"I'd like to see you become the best of us, Ben. That's what I want, and that's what you want."

A thought lingered in Ben's mind, *join the shadows, become your own knight.*

* * *

Austin prayed again on his knees, asking for forgiveness for the joy he felt in taking a life, for the cursing of the Maker, for the times he spent with Elora and her two partners while under the stress of battle, for the drunkenness and drug use, and for not feeling the love Austin knew he should feel and for what he was about to do.

He looked up from his prayer and saw her. A Nun of the Holy Church. His confession was short and came at the end of the day when he knew she'd be finished with her sacraments. He'd done this before, praying and waiting to see her float by. She was an angel he could not hold or long for, yet he did. Austin lusted for her like no other, and she was unattainable. Her eyes were pools of grayness, but they shifted and changed when he spoke to her through the veiled window. His every thought for her, his every moment in her presence, felt like a sin to the Maker herself, yet he steadied, asking deep inside if this was what courtly love felt like. His thoughts teetered between a woman he'd never be with and one that challenged him and his every thought and action.

Today, Austin needed something from her. She came as if summoned and knelt within whispering distance as he performed his penance.

"They listen when you confess; it's best to never give too much," she whispered.

"I came to confess." He waited a moment. "I've come for you. I come to see your eyes and to hear your breath."

He felt her smile, felt the warmth of it even if he couldn't see it.

"You honor me with your," she hesitated. "Devotion."

Austin gambled. "We lost many Maker-fearing soldiers in the Blightbriar Wilds, and I fear for the city and those inside. My messages to my superiors never made it into their hands. Does the Order of the Blue Rose control the royal messengers and the tower's rookeries?" he asked.

They knelt in the middle of the chapel under the Holy Church, separated by their choices and the Maker. She knelt before him one pew in front, off to the side, and he prayed behind her.

"Yes, the church and its power grow, for the blessing of the Maker is upon us, and Hudson City and its most holy Prince Damon, but those in power fear," she waited. "They fear those they cannot control, the wicked, and the unholy."

"Does the Order of the Blue Rose conspire against the Wildcats and Prince Damon?" asked Austin.

"Not against Prince Damon; they unite behind Prince Damon, for he is bathed in the Maker's holy light. The Wildcats, the city guards; they are to be replaced," she finished, made the sign of the blessing, and stood.

"I've said enough. Soon, the Holy Imperium will purify all of the wicked and the vile. Now be safe among those who speak the truth."

She stood, and somehow, Austin didn't understand and needed more.

She looked at him briefly and walked away, lost in prayer, losing herself to worship as Austin's thoughts veered towards the scheme of what Prince Damon planned.

"What is your name," he pleaded quietly, still on his knees. She had started walking away.

The nun stopped and walked back to Austin, a knight of the Wildcats, and she removed her veil and pulled her habit off. "I am Jocelyn, Jocelyn of the Blue Templar. Order 1776 will replace the Wildcats the city guard, and do much more. Join us or perish in the light and fires of the blessed. Shed your cloak and join us as we punish the sinners and slats infesting the Holy Imperium. We are first among the Maker; all others shall bow to us in the Maker's light."

Austin's mouth opened, but he said nothing. He bowed his head, lost in thought and confusion, averting his eyes. The nun stood for a moment longer and looked at the knight, judging him.

"Choose the Path of the Blessed or the shadows," she turned and walked away. "The time of chivalry died when Prince Damon marked this land the Holy Imperium."

Austin felt a cleaner understanding and frustration at his situation, chained to his oath. He looked back down, ashamed. Jocelyn walked away, her steps loud and echoing in the hollow church. Austin now understood that she had been a member of the Order of the Blue Rose the entire time and that they may be at odds with each other.

Austin walked out of the Holy Church as Jupitor's rays from the sun shined down on him, casting shadows on others. The days had grown along with the shadows, and he feared for Vineland.

Elora met Austin a block away, eating an apple. She offered him a bite, and he took it, the juices tasting sour yet sweet, almost pure.

"What'jah find?"

"My contact, her name, I just learned." Austin looked away from Elora, who stood with her hands on her hips. He looked off to her right into a darkened alley. "I learned her name, Jocelyn. I thought she was a nun; she's been a Templar the entire time. I've been confessing to her since I first joined the

Wildcats. She said, as much as we've surmised, The Templar has a written order, order 1776, which will remove the city guards and Wildcats and replace them with the Blue Templar. The Holy Imperium is to become a pure religious state." He kicked the ground. "We're bound to protect Prince Damon. We're bound to protect the state, the royal bloodline."

"You bound me to this even though I'm—" she paused and forced Austin to look her in the eyes, grabbing his face. He looked Elora in the eyes and saw hope. "This is madness, all of this," Elora was frustrated as much as Austin was. Why did my father even join the Wildcats?"

"Pap was close to General Casting's father, who died on the Plains of Ursula. Umar and Jezebel Everfall, before they fought our mage, Sir Hunter Young, slashed the front lines of the Holy Imperium, killing my father and General Casting's father faster than an angel's first breath. That's what Pap said. Pap lay over their bodies as the winds whipped against the earth around him, slashing through his plate armor, mail, and into his back; Pap protected their wrecked bodies as the three mages tossed lightning and fire like gods on the battlefield."

Elora looked at Austin. "He never told me."

"Nor I. It's written down in the *A History of the Wildcats*, in our barracks. I'll show you when we return to the tower. Let's head to the Groanwitch neighborhood."

"When I took the oath," he said and then whispered. "I swore my allegiance, my life, to Vineland.

Knowledge, obedience, and duty to Vineland. I bleed for you, and you will bleed for me, and we will bleed for the land.

She nodded. "I did, too."

* * *

"Where're we headed now?" Ben asked Cordial, who was now the de facto leader of their trio.

"We're heading to an old friend who owns a bookshop. The owner's daughter works in the kitchens of Nightingale Theater, where Prince Damon's party is being held. All the dignitaries in town will be there, this town will be alive with parties and dances to celebrate Prince Damon. There's a rumor he will choose his wife and announce it soon."

Cordial stopped again in the street.

"Short lesson about Hudson City. All of this from Trinity Cloudreach to the peninsula's tip is Hudson City. It consists of boroughs, neighborhoods, and strongholds. The Hudson city-state expands well past the peninsula, but we're in the heart of the Holy Imperium for our efforts." He walked over to a stall selling hand-rolled cigarettes, bought a box containing twenty for a half-penny, and lit one off a taper from the stall keeper. "I love and hate this place; it destroys the best and only keeps the strongest, but you can find anything you want here." Cordial blew smoke out of his nose and offered one to Ben. Angus took another and lit it.

"Mom always said this shit would kill you, but it doesn't really matter now," Ben said.

Ben grabbed the cigarette, lit it, and coughed, feeling light-headed and fuzzy.

"First time?" Cordial asked.

Coughing, Ben croaked a "Yeah," as he put his hands on his knees.

"Ok, then quickly, the tip of Hudson City proper is the Elverstone Citadel, protecting the city from pirates and navy attacks," Cordial pointed quickly in a direction as if this were nothing new to him. "That, along Fortress Green Hill opposite Elverstone Citadel, controls the mouth of the Farover River. Raven's Keep Island sits in the middle of the river as another protection. Hudson City's Elverstone Citadel is the largest and busiest of those fortresses." He yawned and continued, "Between Elverstone Citadel and the giant Trinity Cloudreach, you have other towers built and connected by bridges and walkways. Royals and nobles don't have to touch Vineland ground for days if they don't want to."

Cordial held his cigarette between two fingers, spat off a piece of tobacco to the side, and took a hit from it.

"We came out of the Warhawk Kiss Bridge into the Butcher and Blade district. As you saw, merchants, fishmongers, and the like gather there. There are two main villages named the West Village and East Village, and below them, before you get into government buildings and towers of the city, you get an odd intersection of a gang-controlled portion of the city. That is where we head to see my friend. He owns a bookshop in the Groanwitch neighborhood."

"It's a world unto its own," said Ben.

Angus put his hand on his shoulder. "Don't fall in love with the city, lad. Cities don't love you back, just like a bottle doesn't."

Ben laughed, "Angus, that never stopped you from drinking."

Angus shook his head and snickered. Ben took in the city, felt a shiver of fear, and despised himself. If he could do it, get close enough with the blade. Ben thumbed it now. Would he, could he stab Prince Damon or General Casting, or would he ask to join the Wildcats or join the city guard and become a Copperhead? He thumbed Dawn's Breath and kept his thoughts to himself. Why was he even considering such a thin? *Why not?*

"I take it this Groanwitch neighborhood is known for witches, then?"

"They burnt and hanged scores before the Thornbriar War, from what my grandma Grapeseed said. Now, the Society of Shadows protects the neighborhood the best they can," said Cordial. "The shadows of the noble's towers sometimes feel like they suck the life out of those below them. Darker places keep torches and owl lamps lit all day. The Ruby District is where all the plays and shows are performed, and even the nobles come down from their towers to enjoy them. Which is the neighborhood where The Triumphant Masquerade will take place. The actors, poets, and workers live in the surrounding neighborhoods and walk into the area to work. Slave quarters are housed below ground, at the factory where they work, or on the thirteenth floor of a tower. If the tower is tall enough." He knocked his copper cigarette filter on a wooden post.

"If you're walking a neighborhood with owl lamps, you're safe; if you don't see a single owl lamp and you're dressed nicely, you put your life in your own hands. The Ruby District has owl lamps, Hades Kitchen does not, Groanwitch has a few, the West and East Village have two each, and the Butcher and Blade neighborhood has one. Flip a coin if you feel safe in any of those."

"Penny for the poor." A rough-looking man walked up to Cordial.

Cordial immediately pulled out a large knife. "Fuck off, you alley rat; come any closer, and I gut you so bad your mother will think shadows got to you."

The man, who looked hobbled and near starved, ran off quicker than his initial walking gape let on.

"The fucking gangs and street toughs here will give it to you if you give them an inch," Cordial said, putting his knife away. "Don't let anyone even close to you that looks like trouble."

Holy Imperium affairs breathed and sighed in Hudson City. Outside its stark towers, the life of the city pulsed and pushed about with messages, merchants hustling and hawking their wares, and rogues and puppeteers walked the streets together, leeching money from all in their own ways. Barons bought street food as they stepped out of carriages, restaurants, and inns, capitalizing on the sheer number of people bustling through the alleys and streets. The city smoked, drank, and snorted drugs and never slept, as during the night hours, servants, slaves, and hired hands delivered packages, food, and merchandise while others picked up trash and burnt garbage in a never-ending drudgery of organized mania.

Cordial finished another cigarette as they walked four blocks in the Groanwitch burrow and finally into a bookshop. He flicked the last bit into the street and pocketed the copper filter he used to hold the paper and tobacco.

The door rang a bell as they entered. Ben smelled the musty scent of knowledge, parchment, leather, and well-oiled wood. He saw two dim owl lamps hanging from the ceiling, lighting shelves stacked with papers and books. An older man sat in the middle of a half bar sipping tea and reading *The Milkmaid at Twilight*.

"Paid my dues to the Copperheads already, boys; now go off with you."

"I ain't a Copperhead here to speak to you and Gertrude about Velma; I have business done only in the shadows."

The older man scratched at his face, looked up from his book, and cleaned his nose, wiping his hand on his trousers. He snuffed the candle near him and rechecked it to ensure it was entirely out. A small fire at a bookstore could lead to the end of business and the loss of a fortune of knowledge.

"Cordial, I haven't seen you in ages. Look how you've grown."

Angus shifted his weight as he stood behind Cordial. Ben studied a series of books on a shelf and suddenly thought of Runt and how he would have loved to see this place. He ran his fingers down the spines of the book. His sister Alysha would have enjoyed it, too. Those two were always lovers of the written word. Now Runt was dead by his friend's bloody hands, and Alysha was gone to the winds of tragedy.

The man stood from his seat and closed his book. He was a taller, older man, crooked like a river, but still had an opposing frame and look.

"Gertrude, an old friend is here asking about Velma," he sneered and looked directly at Cordial.

"You know she got rid of the baby, you piece of shit," Hershel said.

"I know she did, Hershel, I know," said Cordial. "We had discussed this previously, and you said never come into this neighborhood again. So, ask yourself why I would do so unless something more important than my word was at stake."

"Let's see what my old battle axe has to say about this," Hershel said.

"What, who's here? Why you noble of a whore!"

Through a door on another side of the room, an older woman jumped onto Cordial and began scratching and tearing at him. He defended himself moderately, and Hershel, the older man, just cackled behind the counter, yelling "Getim, Getim" through a few missing teeth.

Ben and Angus grabbed the older woman gently.

"Ma'am, Ma'am, we mean no harm and only come asking for help," Ben said sincerely.

The older woman, Gertrude, hissed and swung at Cordial, who was taking stock of himself on the floor. Ben wrapped his arms around the older woman's frame as she hollered and screamed in Cordial's direction until she finally moaned and stopped.

"Let me go, let me go, young man," she gasped, hair in her face. "I'm done now. I'm done."

So, Ben let go of the woman gently.

Herschel walked out from where he stood, hearing something besides the fight that had broken inside his bookshop. He walked right over to Cordial and his wife, who made herself presentable and caught her breath, and he acted as if they didn't exist, moving past them to the door.

"Quiet, the lot of you." He peered out the greasy window of the shop, cleaning a section to see better.

It was near evening now and hard to see, but Hershel saw a group of monks and city guards walking in the street, heading toward the shop.

"Gertrude, grab the money and your best books and get behind the bookshelf. Take these lads with you; we may hate Cordial, but he'll know what to do."

"What? What is it, my sweet? This boy owes it to take care of any trouble we have. It's the least he could do for what happened to Velma."

"These three don't have the strength to stop the Order of the Blue Rose. Maybe it's nothing, but I want you to be safe," Hershel said, his mouth trembling.

"Cordial, if you had any love for Velma and us, you would do your best to protect Gertrude and Velma. Now, all of you get to the back!" Hershel said this with anger and concern in his voice. It was a command, and they obeyed, feeling the sincerity and strength in his words.

Ben could see the torches outside the shop through the greasy window.

Gertrude moved to the back, grabbing a box of money and three books from the shelves. She pointed out books to Cordial, Ben, and Angus as they shuffled into the back of the shop to a large bookshelf, their hands stacked with books.

She pushed against a brick, and Ben heard a click.

"Trick wall, there is more behind it," said Angus. "I love a secret room."

"Cordial, help me. I'm too old to shift it anymore," Gertrude said, an enemy now an ally. Cordial moved to her side quickly and pushed. The shelf was on a wheel and moved shakily. "Everyone down into the cellar, now," Gertrude ordered. "Velma will be home tomorrow morning. She has a room above the Noble Lamp Inn; you'll be safe there. "She smiled.

They all walked into the cellar, where they found a short printing press in the center of a dusty floor surrounded by stacks of more books and lines hanging newly printed pamphlets. It smelled of ink, parchment, and spilled wine.

Gertrude pointed at another set of stairs, "Tell Velma we love her. The deed to the Three Strands Bookshop is with the money in the box there. No matter what happens, she must stay safe and send our love. I must attend to my husband upstairs and speak to these Templar myself." She returned up the stairs and closed the secret compartment behind Cordial, Angus, and Ben. Ben stood there holding a stack of books and papers and looked at Angus, who also carried several books.

"She went back," Ben said.

"This printing press, there's a reason they're being raided," said Angus. There was a sudden scream upstairs and shuffling of feet. The sound of books and shelves collapsing followed. Ben gripped his knife, and Angus and Cordial looked at the hidden entrance to the shop. "You have a story to tell us later, Cordial, about what you have done to this family and what you owe them."

"That is years of love." Cordial ran his fingers through his hair. "I owe them plenty and want their legacy to live on." Guilt and understanding shone through him as he climbed the stairs, latched the shelf, and locked it. "Come what may, love is eternal, like a song or the wind," he said into the darkness behind the shelf. He took a moment lost in his thoughts or a prayer in the darkness.

Ben noticed one of the leaflets hanging was the pamphlet *Ordinary Wit*, deemed illegal by Prince Damon in a recent decree. Hershel and Gertrude, two older commoners running a bookstore, were traitors to the crown, printing propaganda against Prince Damon and the Holy Imperium. He smiled and thumbed his knife. They were in the right spot, and the danger was getting closer with every breath he took.

"Take the money, grab those mail satchels, and those books there. We can't take the printing press, but grab the stack of pamphlets in case the Templar find the cellar," Cordial whispered as he started ripping down every illegal pamphlet he could find. "We'll head to the Noble Lamp Inn."

"Can't we fight them? Can't we do something?" Ben said in confusion and anger. They heard shouts and struggles as bookshelves were knocked over and loud crashes.

"Lad, we are going to do something; we are going to make sure their daughter is okay, give her the news we have, and think more on it later. We can't fight Templar dressed in full plate and chain mail," whispered Angus as they went out the cellar stairs to a back alley.

Cordial looked at Ben. "If a book is so dangerous to the Holy Imperium, then they are too weak to govern us, and we must be free of their yoke."

"You sound like one of those Bastards of Liberty the *Post Enquirer* writes about." Angus showed Cordial a bent front page of the newspaper. He skimmed it quickly.

"It's about the massacre in Olde Ridgewatch, so yeah, I guess I'm one of them now, and-" he stopped as they rounded the corner of an alley and checked to see if they were safe to get away and looked at Ben. "So are you two."

They moved through alleys on the other side of the building. Ben looked as they crossed between two buildings and saw a crowd had gathered carrying torches, and he heard screaming and yelling as they piled books into the center of the street. The townspeople were out now and joining the spectacle. A pile of books and pamphlets, and three well armored Templar leading the way along with a dozen monks carrying whips. They didn't see Gertrude or Hershel. One of the Templar dragged a piece of wood and placed it in the center of the books as more threw wood and books around it.

"My brother is with them, helping to build the book pyre," said Cordial in disgust.

"I hate mobs," Ben mumbled to himself. Angus put his arm on his shoulder, and Ben looked down at him.

"Well, lad, after what you've been through, I can see why. Let's see this lass and tell her what's happened."

* * *

Austin and Elora walked under the long shadow of Trinity Cloudreach Spire into the Groanwitch neighborhood and smelled smoke from the area's plaza, surrounded by shops. A large arch built to commemorate a victory stood at the park's center. They were discussing what they knew of Austin's messages and the failed communications between the front line near the Razorshine River and Hudson City and came to the crest of a slight hill as townsfolk gathered, attempting to look further down the cobbled street. Austin went towards the gathering, pushed back by an exhausted Copperhead. Elora veered off from the group to get a better angle and view what everyone was trying to see.

She found an unobstructed view and looked down on a crossroad blocked by a pile of pamphlets and scrolls from offices and shops. A platoon of monks and six Templar had marched in the heat, baring torch swords. The Holy Imperium needed only a flimsy excuse to purify commoners as heretics and unfaithful, all at Prince Damon's orders. She looked on as a member of the Order of the Blue Rose pushed an older couple towards a stack of books and two stakes.

"They wear their robes with pride and righteousness, yet they have no dignity in their actions," she said aloud. A young boy stood beside her and spat in agreement on the street.

"You there! What's happening?" demanded Austin, accustomed to getting answers. The crowd looked down the hill, separated by the distance and Copperheads.

"Piss off, yokel, or I dent your head," said the guard. He carried a large wooden stave with a steel knob at the tip. Other Copperheads used spears to keep the crowd from moving down the hill to where a mob of Templar secured an old couple, booksellers by the looks of it, onto a pole in the middle of the pile of books. The man's head was clearly split open, the woman's face beaten in, and she continued to squirm and scream at the crowd in defiance.

"I'm a Wildcat for Prince Damon, off duty. I demand to know what is happening."

"Are you now? Well, I suck a witch's tit at night, mind you, so piss off," the guard said and pushed the crowd back. Another guard grabbed his cudgel and swung into the crowd; Austin pulled a dagger from his belt, slid it quickly toward the guard, and bared the Wildcat emblem under his vest.

"All right, all right, the rest of you bugger off." The overworked guard yelled. "We got nobility here. Back up, back up." And he spat at the crowd.

Down below, Brother Hewitt opened a flask and doused the books with what Austin knew to be holy oil. This flammable oil wasn't sacred, as elves and dwarves cooked with it. Elora pushed her way toward Austin.

"That's Brother Hewitt and Sister Temperance," Austin said. "Guards for Bishop Devon."

"The leader of the High Church? Why would he have his two personal guards lead a book burning?"

"They've done his dirty work before. Jasper and I saw them break up a party we attended. They busted heads and made a mess of a fine time. They're rigid in their beliefs."

"Bootlickers," Elora said.

Sister Temperance prayed at the other end of the pile, and dozens of followers knelt before her.

"That's Father Losh Miller. He's led mass when Bishop Devon fell ill," said Austin.

"These books are full of sins, perverse with smut and heresy against Prince Damon, against the Maker herself. We do this to protect our families and children from Gothine," the monk preached to the crowd, some on their knees around the pile of books and the couple tied to the post in the middle. Others stood as part of the group of Templar and monks carrying torches as if at a holiday mass. "Repent, my brothers and sisters, from your ways. Bring us your books, your pamphlets riddled with vile elvish words, those books that undermine the Holy Imperium government, those romance novels that question your morals. We burn those that call for liberty from the greatness that is Prince Damon!"

Elora and Austin watched uneasily.

"We can't do anything to stop this, can we," Elora said quietly.

"Not directly, no, we cannot, but we can make slight changes. We can make a difference." And he paused. "Maybe," he said even quieter.

The guard looked at Austin and Elora.

"You two don't look like noble Wildcats that guard our loving and caring Prince Damon. Where's the rest of you? At least the Blue Templar does something about these menaces that talk about our prince and speak evil of the Holy Church." The guard spat on the ground. "The Wildcats, a bunch of wild peacocks, is what you are, all shiny in your cloaks and armor, walking around and not doing anything but taking up air."

Austin and Elora walked away. He'd previously been to the Three Strands Bookshop and sparked a conversation with the older woman. There wasn't anything wrong with the owner or the store. It was a wonder before. Now its door lay open, the shop's contents torn and destroyed.

Father Losh Miller and other church followers in the crowd raised their hands as Brother Hewitt Wightland took a sacred torch, presented it to the books in a godly salute to the Maker, and threw it into the pile. Sister Temperance Wightland prayed at a distance with townspeople hand in hand, many of which carried long, slender torches. The flame from Brother Hewitt touched the first few books and spread toward the couple. The oil caught, and flames simmered higher. Austin and Elora watched as it traveled slowly. Flame and smoke mingled and sizzled as the couple's heads shifted back and forth. Eventually, flames overcame them, and they stopped moving.

It was grotesque what stood for the rule of law in Hudson City, what Prince Damon ordered, and the Order of the Blue Rose had executed. He looked down, knowing that if the Wildcats were not in the Blightbriar Wilds, he could have been burning books and executing villagers at Prince Damon's command. Ordered to kill people Jasper and himself had drunk with and made love to.

Austin looked at the crowd, the followers of the Holy Church, and what occurred did not feel sacred and true. It wasn't just monks and Templar causing the chaos. He noticed younger men and business folk throwing books on the fire.

Some of the townspeople shook their heads, and a few gasped at the sight, not caught up in the fanaticism of the moment. Elora looked at the pile of books and noticed something odd just off to the side. She watched a dwarve and two men carrying messenger satchels leave the alley near the ruined bookshop. She squinted and saw books peeking out of the one man's satchel.

She grabbed at Austin as he looked at the odd group while the crowd basked in the biblioclasm. The dapper-looking man put up the hood of his cloak and led the other two away from the crowd, lost in the light of the putrid flames of the Maker.

Austin put his hand on Elora's leather-armored shoulder. "Affairs are getting complicated now. It's hard to see right from wrong. We'll let them go. Bet they're connected to the shop and not our stolen messages. We know who the enemy is at this point. It's just a matter of proving it."

"The Union Dogs have acted savagely before, but somehow everyone agrees, everyone allows this, and nobody fights back. When people cower in fear and let it happen-" Elora said.

"It makes it worse," Austin finished.

As they walk back to their barracks a page caught on the wind flipped, flew in the air, and landed in front of them. Elora picked it up, read it, smiled, and handed it to Austin.

"The lands burn with plague, riots, and rebellion, and Prince Damon sits on his throne saying his royal blood is purer than our mothers and fathers before us. Rise Up, resist, and take back our lands! Join the Cause."

Austin folded the partially burnt sheet in two, folded it again, and stuffed it into his pocket, gripping his short sword pommel. They looked back as flames burned more books, and smoke dark pitch drifted into the night, words searing and forgotten forever.

Alysha - Swamp Burial

And suddenly, Alysha's eyes opened.

"What happened?" Alysha said, rubbing the back of her head as she lay on the ground, a cloudy light above her peering down from an opening, and darkness crept around the edges of her eyes. A voice echoed in the cavern where she lay.

"Helena?" Alysha echoed to herself.

"No, no, come, come, deary, you have much to explain," said the older woman who had helped her earlier. Her hand pointed to the side of the cavern, and footfalls and handholds appeared against the wall. She climbed hesitantly, even as her lungs greedily sucked in the stagnant air from above, and her eyes adjusted to a grayer steadier light as she climbed.

"Did you carry me? What happened?" Alysha felt like she might throw up, and the dizziness did not lessen.

"Let us get out of the tunnel, my deary. You hit your head on a trellis that keeps the tunnel from caving in. This place isn't safe for the likes of us. Large rats and spiders that goblins ride call this place home. They like to tear the flesh off the young first. Come, come, let us go up," said Lady Blacklace, who licked her lips, which Alysha did not see.

Alysha climbed into a room surrounded by walls and a set of stairs to the corner. The one window above her head was barred up, and the surrounding stone was cold and unforgiving. She felt the loneliness and anguish of the place when she placed her hand on the smooth stone surface of the wall and realized how thick the wall felt.

"Where am I? Is this a prison?"

"Of a sort, welcome to the Litchbury Tower. I am the only inhabitant, Lady Blacklace Wightland, exiled and imprisoned in a cursed tower in the middle of the forsaken Litchbury Mire." The woman bowed slightly. "Those soldiers will bother you no more. I believe you have news for me. I do love news. Come, come, we have hundreds of stairs to walk before we are comfortable."

They walked up winding stairs to the point of height beyond the tallest tree Alysha had ever climbed. She stopped twice, dizzy from the growing heights. Alysha noticed the tower held multiple floors, housing unused fireplaces, rooms for sleeping, prison bars, and an open door that looked like it led to a mixture of an apothecary and torture chamber. The tower could accommodate hundreds of people. It looked as if it was part of an unfinished keep or castle.

They remained silent for a while as they spun up slowly on the well-worn stairs.

"You stink of Rowan and her faith in gods."

"I'm blessed by Judith and the spring seasons. I'm Alysha Wolfthorn."

The older woman frowned and shivered.

"It seems you are. You bring a storm's kiss with you, I see. A whole army has followed you and ruined the grand city-state of Grimwood," and the woman smirked and then pointed her lips.

"My lady, you have me at an advantage. I can offer as much information as possible if I can rest and heal. I hope to see my friend Helena as soon as I can. I also have money on me, but not much."

"Money is useless to me. I can't leave this swamp."

They stood at the precipice of a door after finishing their climb to the top of the tower. "Well, let's have some tea and speak of my sister and what has become of Grimwood, and then we can talk of payment."

Alysha felt Stormkiss's handle against her worn-down hands and flexed her fingers as it lay strapped against her back. She thought of the stories of the lady of the Litchbury Mire and those giant birds of prey she had seen earlier.

"You carry a Paragon of the Maker."

"If you believe in that rubbish."

Lady Blacklace smiled.

"My, you have spirit. It's been so long since someone with spirit has been here," the crone chuckled mirthlessly. "Please sit. I will make tea."

Alysha's thoughts were not her own. Her head ached, her mind stuttered, and she entered the room cautiously.

Lady Blacklace allowed Alysha to walk into the tower room, where she found a minor fireplace used for cooking built against the side of the wall. She sat on a well-worn, cushioned chair, placing Stormkiss on her lap. Alysha watched as the woman, who looked in her forties, moved around to make tea. She moved to a box and tossed a dark loaf of bread at Alysha.

"It's a day old, sorry, it's not so fresh. So, tell me, how is Rowan? She was living in a backwoods hole called Wolf Hills," said Lady Blacklace, almost as if she knew the answer to the question before asking.

"It was Wolf Hills, my home." Alysha waited for a moment. "The town was burnt, and she's gone."

Lady Blacklace poured the tea from her large cast iron kettle. The kettle's iron was black and rusty, with white ware at the pouring mouth from years of use of Litchbury water.

"Our town was attacked, and the survivors were enslaved. We were all forced to march towards the Erie Sea, and she escaped, and that's when I saw her shot by an arrow as lightning struck on top of a hill."

"Go on, dear, go on."

"Several months later, after winter," Alysha looked away at the window. "I was attacked on that same hill by Holy Imperium soldiers."

Lady Blacklace spat on the ground in disgust. "Prince Damon and his Holy Imperium and his shit of a father, all of Great Brightland. They can go to Hades," said she, full of venom and vileness.

"I fell near the same area by a religious sight, and again the lightning came. I awoke inside the hill, in a goblin hole, where Rowan, who had lived by me since I was born, was tending to my wounds. I don't know how; I saw the arrow strike true and the lightning fall. She could not have been alive, and yet she was. When I finally came too and stood, she mumbled a prayer and faded into nothingness."

Lady Blacklace didn't say anything; she just stared at Alysha. She sipped her tea and, placing it down, smoothed out the sleeves of her dress, which looked like a well-worn and faded black lace wedding dress. Her face held no emotion, and she said, "That is a fascinating story. Here you are."

Alysha was still determining what she should say or do.

"So Grimwood fell?"

Alysha shifted her feet slightly as she sat and sipped her tea. It tasted warm and pleasant. "Yes. My friend and I tried to warn those in charge, but the city was in chaos from the Smoldering Plague," said Alysha.

Lady Blacklace smiled at this. "They watched in silence as I sat up here innocent of my crimes, and then they started to shit blood and bleed from their eyes," she said quietly. "From the smoke and fog coming from the north, yes. You don't see the dead from here, but the winds carry its cries and pain. You don't hear the clash of steel and grunt of flesh tearing but feel the wrath of fires burning and taste the ash and despair in the rain as it falls. Grimwood, the city is no more, yet the cemeteries gain fame and new clients, while the old forest stands ever present and watchful of the city's new rulers."

Alysha finished her tea, feeling better and almost safer now.

"Let me see your wounds, dear. I'll bind you tighter. I know a thing or two of potions and healing."

The tea warmed Alysha's chest as Lady Blacklace tended to her. Her anxiety calmed, and she felt sleepy.

"Why are you here all alone, Lady Blacklace?"

"Because I cursed Prince Damon at court, sweetie, as you heard me before. I cursed him, I cursed the foul mage Hunter Young, and all of Great Brightland cursed them and swore vengeance on all of them. And so, they knocked me out, chained me up, and sent me to this forsaken place. My family is of royal blood, even if it is a very distant touch of it, a sliver, so they could not kill me, but they could disappear me, and so they did. I am not the first woman silenced by a set of walls, and I will not be the last."

Alysha's eyes grew heavy. "That would not warrant such a punishment?"

"Would it not," Lady Blacklace looked at Alysha with pity. "There was also something else, the last bit, the yelling and screaming, which was just the last bit. Something else had left a stain on me that lingered on that Council of Crows that rule the land. It was a trifle thing, I attempted to kill Prince Damon before the war ended, but they could never prove it."

"Wait, you attempted regicide?"

"You act as if you are offended. You killed my sister, and I didn't react this way. Know your place, commoner."

"I was not at court, but my father is Benedict Ashburn. I am no commoner; I am of fine blood, same as you."

Before Alysha blinked, Lady Blacklace put a long, thin blade to Alysha's neck.

"You lie, little pig; you said your house name was Wolfthorn. You killed my sister, and you're the daughter of a general of the Holy Imperium. Tell me one reason I shouldn't kill you."

Alysha shifted her weight and tensed her hands.

"I can feel the adjustment, cow. Move or shift again and you'll have a new hole to breathe from. Speak plainly and quickly."

"Just because I was surprised doesn't mean I'm not upset you failed." Alysha smiled. "I want Prince Damon dead, too, but I need to get to General Flint and Jared Blackheart first."

Lady Blacklace eased up on her blade and slipped it back into her sleeve.

She stood, laughed, and bowed.

"Well then, Miss Wolfthorn, it is. I believe we shall help each other. Now let's get you fixed up."

Alysha relaxed.

"Lady Blacklace, I didn't ask for this, for your sister's death, for the fall of Grimwood, none of this."

"Did you ask for revenge? Deep down in your thoughts and prayers, while you were a slave, a servant, while your mother died, through your tears, did you beg for revenge? Don't answer. You already know there is a toll for all requests like this. The bell of Hades tolls for us all. I am afraid my sister was part of the toll, and the city of Grimwood was too."

Alysha's shoulders dropped, and sadness settled in next to exhaustion. Both of their teacups were empty. All that remained were the dregs.

Alysha rose quickly. "I need to go, and I need to get to Helena."

Lady Blacklace stood taller and thinner next to Alysha, whose arms bulged, yet she felt meek and humbled next to this thin, birdlike woman. She looked at the cup and spun it slightly, looking at the dregs.

"Your friend made it into the woods. She's safe, but you are no good to her in the swamp. Too many soldiers and too much madness of war nearby. You will stay and rest, and we will take steps to suppress the Holy Imperium until help arrives."

Lady Blacklace walked to the window, her black lace dress and long cloak with bulging black feathered scales hung on her frame. Alysha realized she carried a thin rapier as well. She called through the window, and Alysha saw the sun blocked out twice. Lady Blacklace pointed in one direction and then another and called the birds again. She waited, and they replied with birdlike screams.

Alysha's vision blurred, and her tongue felt dry.

"What did you do to me?" she fell forward, and Lady Blacklace turned around and smiled.

"Silly cow, silly cow, there is more to this than just you now."

Alysha was half awake as her body dragged against the floor and up another set of stairs. She sagged and struggled against Lady Blacklace as she was placed on a table. There were bindings and chains, she heard as her wrists and ankles were bound.

"What are you doing? I thought you were going to help me."

"You are a strong cow. If you didn't have woman parts, I'd say you were a bull. That poison I gave you should have knocked you out for days, yet only a few minutes and you remained semi-awake. Intriguing Alysha. You are truly touched, but no matter."

Alysha's head rolled, and her vision cleared. She lay in another room at the top of the tower. The windows were open, with no glass or protection from the elements. She rolled her head and found herself on a stone table bound by chain and leather, still clothed but unable to move. She waited and constricted, hoping to pull whatever strength she had left inside her to slip from her bindings.

"What are you doing to me?" she demanded, playing for time.

"I cannot leave the Litchbury Mire. Once I was exiled here, Minister Shannon bound me with magic older than any I've ever worked with. She is more powerful than she lets on. But *you* can leave, Miss Alysha Ashburn, so I will leave as you."

"You'll what?" asked Alysha, shifting her neck to look at Lady Blacklace.

"It's a delicate thing. I've done it with giant war birds and have done enough research to know if it's possible to do it from human to human. The elves mastered jumping into animals long ago, but now the powerful ones are beyond the Stagger Wall, and there is so little left as Prince Damon and the nobles enslave the elves when they have so much power within them." Lady Blacklace paused and walked around, sliding her willow-like hand up and down Alysha's body. She barely touched her, yet she showed how powerless Alysha really was.

"You can't be serious; this isn't possible; you rant and ramble like, like-" said Alysha.

"Like a witch?" And she cackled with glee. "My sister gave her life for you, brought you back from the dead, gave you powers you can't even comprehend, and you think skin jumping, you think it's not possible?" Lady Blacklace laughed. "If you are blessed by a goddess, I will jump into your body, and you will slide into mine. If it doesn't work as I intended, we will remain in your body, and I will force your will to bend to mine. It's complex, but we have time now. I must brew herbs and wait for the moon to rise tonight."

She walked over and forced more strong tea into Alysha's mouth, this time cold and bitter. Alysha shook her head and gagged, but the witch held her head firmly and forced it down, watching as Alysha choked and snot bubbles popped from her nose. Alysha's restraints shook, and her body convulsed against itself.

"So strong, so strong. I can't wait to see what you are capable of. What I can do with that axe and these muscles."

Alysha's eyes fluttered, and she tilted her head to watch Lady Blacklace as she walked towards the window. "Now, how long must I wait until the sun sets and the moon rises?" She tilted her head to the window.

Alysha's eyes dimmed a faint white and faded, and she tried to reach for her axe Stormkiss that lay far away, willing it, forcing it, begging it to move.

"Not much longer. The sun sets even now, Alysha."

Alysha's attention was drawn back to Lady Blacklace who now mainly spoke to herself by the large window.

"This war will unmake many a life, and-" The witch's voice cut off. Lady Blacklace stumbled, falling closer to the window.

Alysha's eyes widened. A knife handle stuck out of the old witch's back; her hands gripped the window, and her left knee bent. The blade sunk deep but not enough to kill. Alysha had no clue who had thrown the blade and what would come next. She tilted her head barely as Lady Blacklace turned, holding a thin blade in her hand. Alysha knew the instrument was sharper than a razor.

There was movement near the table where Alysha lay, and someone charged, holding an old spear. Rushing past her, the spear was jammed into the witch's stomach. There was no war scream, just the smack of the tip of the spear into Lady Blacklace's stomach.

"Ugh!" Boots and slippers scraped against the floor. Alysha recognized Helena as she and Blacklace pushed against the spear. Helena bent her knee and pushed the shaft toward Blacklace's chest, driving her back into a wall. The knife blade dug deeper as Lady Blacklace hit the wall. Ichorous blood spewed from the witch's mouth, and the edge of the knife protruded from the front of her chest. Helena relented momentarily, but Blacklace still stood, unable to speak. She touched the blade and smiled maliciously, blood coating her teeth. She hissed and lunged at Helena, pulling herself through the spear shaft.

Alysha's eyes widened. *This woman should be dead already.* She grasped at the chains that held her to the table, trying to escape and help her friend. Helena held onto the spear with all her strength. Lady Blacklace swung her thin blade but missed Helena, unable to make up the distance between the two. Helena continued to push against the shaft as Blacklace hissed through the blood seeping out of her mouth, but they were no longer against the wall. The old woman coughed shortly, losing her breath, and Helena took advantage and pushed harder, dipping her hips and bending her knees for leverage. Blacklace took a step back, lost her balance, and Helena forced the spear shaft up and forward. Lady Blacklace tumbled out the window and met the swamp hundreds of feet below. The grass and dark murk of the swamp groggily started to take her body into its waiting arms as Helena looked down.

"Gothine's shit, where did you come from?" Alysha spluttered. Helena rushed over and started to take the restraints off Alysha.

"Me? I followed you after the guards chased you into the swamp. What kind of madness did you get up to?"

"Get me out of this, would you?" Alysha put her head down and shook it from side to side. "Helena, my head's a bit foggy, but I think those children's stories about the witch of the Litchbury Mire might have been true."

"You don't say! I stumbled over a pile of bones in that tunnel I walked through; they were not adult bones either. Let's get the Hades out of this place. I heard what she wanted to do; I was waiting on the stairs, trying to pick the right time. I grabbed this spear in the tunnel on the way in."

Alysha sat up on the stone table.

"Is she dead?"

"If the knife in her chest didn't kill her, the fall from one of the highest towers I've ever seen most likely did. Swamp ground is soft, but I don't think she'll be an issue any longer."

"Let's hope not."

Alysha stood on wobbly legs like a newborn colt. Helena grasped her shoulder, and Alysha half-smiled and held onto her friend. It felt safe to be close to her, and she breathed deeply.

"Thank you for coming back."

Helena looked at Alysha, then around the room and back at her.

"You did it for me when I didn't expect it; favors returned."

It took time to walk down the worn stairs of the tower, and they looked out of some of the smaller arrow slits the tower provided to get the lay of the land.

"The only way out is through the tunnel below," said Alysha, feeling more like herself. "I'd rather not sleep here tonight. I get the feeling if we sleep here, we may never be able to leave."

"Agreed, there is something wrong with this place. It's no refuge."

"Out through the tunnel and to Wolf Hills if we are lucky."

"Let's just get out of this tower first. That witch knocked me out and dragged me through the tunnels, so I have no idea which way to go."

"Alysha, I don't want to get lost in the tunnels; dwarves have good eyes down there, but so do goblins, orcs, and spiders."

"Right, let's head back to Wolf Hills. Revenge or not, we need rest and to rethink all of this."

They each made sure they had flint to start a fire and carried two torches, one lit and one as a backup, and started down the tunnel. They quickly became lost, however, as the neared an intersection. All the possible paths looked the same.

"I don't remember seeing this before. Do you remember which way?"

"Not behind us, for sure. We just came that way; this is madness."

"The darkness in this place, I don't know how the dwarves can do it."

"I remember Angus from the tavern would tell us about the huge cities in Steelsburg below ground when he had one too many hard ciders with Mom," Alysha said, trying to lighten the mood as the darkness crept near them.

"Still can't imagine it. All the world above pressing down on us all the time. You were the only reason I came this way. I felt like you came this way, I didn't know."

Alysha gripped Helena's hand. "I appreciate it. We can't keep each other safe through all this, but we can try."

"You know, I don't think we'll ever be safe with these Holy Imperium assholes around," Helena said.

"The best we can do is kill as many as we can before they kill us," Alysha finished.

She smiled in the darkness, gripping Helena's hand tighter as they chose one of three paths, hoping it was the right choice, and moved forward into the darkness together.

Hudson City- Subterranean Kitchen Shrooms

T he Nightingale Theater stood in the shadows of Trinity Cloudreach Spire in the neighborhood known as the Ruby District. After the ground was mined for gems and minerals, it was filled back in, and cheap buildings were placed on top. The buildings couldn't hold the same heights as the towers but were close enough that the nobles invested in them, creating a series of museums and other lively entertainment. Down the main road was known as Hades Kitchen, where troubadours, playwrights, actors, and poets from the Ruby District lived in slums, cheap hotels, and shanties for the season. Hades Kitchen lay near Groanwitch Village and bridged the West and East Villages along the peninsula. Thousands of people moved and lived on the peninsula on the edge of Vineland, creating art, living life, and making news and fashion that other cities, territories, and city-states copied and envied.

On the day of The Triumphant Masquerade, the kitchen below the Nightingale Theater was packed with staff working non-stop preparing for the night's events, except for the two main event coordinators, who habitually enjoyed each other's company during mid-day tea. The party would not start until dark, and guests would arrive by carriage. Chef Oloff Burnstew and steward Vladimir Richpike left the kitchen under the theater for a short break when Angus walked into the kitchen and was at once met by another cook in charge.

She looked down at him and smiled. "Another cook, I see. Good. We need help over there by that stove. I will be with you shortly. Get to work on those potatoes," said the older lady. So, Angus started peeling potatoes after putting his large cast iron skillet down, a sack filled with spices, and an assortment of mushrooms and peppers.

"Sorry I'm late, but there are parties and celebrations at every park in the city, and the roads are blocked with folk drinkin' and celebratin'. The commoners love a public holiday. I was assigned to work appetizers; I specialize in fried foods."

"You'll work where I tell you to work, dwarve. I am Chef Grapeseed; you may call me Chef."

The woman gave Angus a hat to keep his hair from the food. "Thank you for braiding your beard and mustache; you're a professional, I see you brought your own pan and seasonings. Excellent. I'll get you started after the potatoes are peeled," Chef Grapeseed said with a stern smile.

There was a crash behind the woman, and a trifling steam fire broke out. "Maker's tits!" She yelled and left Angus to his job. Angus looked around and planned his next moves. Another cook stood near him, prepping for the coming celebration. The dwarve smiled, took a sip from a hip flask, and offered it up. The cook took it, drank and handed it back. All kitchens working under high pressure were the same. Angus knew he would be fine and could complete his surprise to help Cordial and Benjamin in their mission to get closer to a member of the Council of Crows and escape if need be. He had no delusions that something would happen and a diversion would be needed. He never liked royalty and nobility anyway. He briefly considered his mother, took a sip, and started peeling potatoes.

Time passed, and guests arrived. Angus worked the kitchen directly below the stage, where the masquerade guests drank, danced, and gossiped at the start of the night's events. After sorting the potatoes, he worked the grease station next to the line cook. His station was a large cast iron pot with bubbling grease and lard of pig, rat, and horse fat used to fry potatoes and other viddles for guests. His co-worker was the tall older woman with faded white and gray in her tight bun. She cooked a large batch of clams and mushrooms. He smiled sheepishly; the woman was an expert, and working near someone who knew their job felt good. Angus fried potato sticks in a vat of lard and did batches of mushrooms he'd brought in for the occasion. They would not kill anyone, but the hallucinogenic effects would give the party goers a memorable night as they tasted colors and saw ghosts. He recommended that the servers entice the guards with his food on their breaks and hoped this would help Cordial, Ben, and himself escape the theater if things got fouled up. Before he started in the kitchen, he'd also placed rags soaked in a flammable liquid throughout the basement floor below the theater in case a fire was needed to mask their escape. He drank a large mug of witch pepper as he cooked. The woman working the sauce station said "Behind" and scooted by Angus, reaching into the bag next to his, where she pulled out a few mushrooms. She stopped and looked at him.

"Chef, would you like a sip," he said and whispered, "It's witch pepper." She smiled and took a long drink from the cup. They were two equals in a busy kitchen. Other workers moved around the large kitchen; it was loud, and everyone was a moving part of a bigger team, keeping the nobles happy and enjoying themselves upstairs. Knives cut pieces of beef, pots stirred, and cheeses were cut up and taken upstairs. The smell of garlic, rosemary, and other exotic spices drifted.

"Chef Oloff Burnstew and steward Vladimir Richpike are tasting the final dishes as they go out the main door. The appetizers go out the side doors and are given to the nobles and merchants of local stature. Please ensure your work goes out the side doors. I don't want Burnstew or Richpike to taste any of your specialties," she said and returned to work.

She knows about the fairy mushrooms, he thought. Their eyes met; they looked familiar, like Cordials, but more tired.

Chef Grapeseed looked back at the two bags on the floor next to the giant pot where Angus had dropped a load of fried potato sticks. The fat bubbled, servers entered and exited, going up spiral staircases to the main floor. One bag held the fairy mushrooms he'd grabbed the night they buried Stu's body. The mushrooms induced feelings of euphoria, heightened a person's sexual appetite, and made people feel the music, taste color, and touch a place deeper inside themselves. The dwarves considered them sacred, but he was beyond those traditions. He wanted to fuck with the people in charge and knew before one could enjoy the mushroom, the body would reject it, forcing the person that ate it to throw up uncontrollably after gestating for about an hour.

He looked at the other bag of mushrooms and saw several different types of potatoes and mushrooms mixed, including, he could have sworn, a few reaper mushrooms. The woman smiled.

"You are going to make some of these guests have a challenging time tonight, Mr. Dwarve," her voice was noble and educated. She grabbed a petite fairy mushroom from his bag. She split one in quarters and ate it. Then, she gave another tiny piece to Angus.

"You know your proteins. I like an educated cook. Enjoy this for a few more minutes. Finish whatever you are doing and leave this place before they blame you for what I am about to serve these noble guests," she said quietly.

Angus looked back at her saute pan, which was as big as his personal pan and weapon. It held several pieces of what he thought he saw in the bag: rot mushrooms, whose effects were like those of the Smoldering Plague. This woman, this noble woman, was poisoning the guests above.

"Yes, my lady," he whispered, pulling out another batch as she tossed a few cut-up pieces of rot mushrooms. What was he to do? They would blame the cooks, and she had said he should leave soon. Would they blame her? Was she going, and why should he care?

They finished more batches of deep-fried stuffed mushrooms, sauteed onions, garlic stuffed in breaded cheese, and a medley of fried potatoes and mushrooms for the guests, and then they washed their hands together.

"What is your name, Mr. Dwarve? It has been a pleasure working next to a professional such as yourself."

They were off in a room that led to a hallway below the theater; the kitchen was a short walk away. Actors and entertainers used the rooms to prepare before their performances. Angus could hear a series of grunts and slapping as someone enjoyed themselves in a room beside them. She had removed her cook's jacket and was wearing a modest blouse and tighter dress as if she were going to the party.

Below the theater where Angus now stood were the dressing rooms for the performers, a kitchen, and a series of tunnels that allowed the theater to receive supplies from other areas of the city, all used by dwarves. Where guests sat, the ceiling depicted the night sky and twinkled with cleverly made dwarve lamps to look like stars at night. The ceiling above the dance floor and stage held catwalks hidden by a thin plaster mold ceiling where one could walk, and dwarven smokeless lights adjusted and used to provide pristine views of the party below. The guests laughed and mingled with each other, waiting for the night's events to start.

"Angus, my lady," he said, strapping his knife and hatchet to his side. He held his washed cast iron skillet in front of him.

"I am Lady Grapeseed Wightland. Please ensure my Cordial leaves this place alive, Mr. Angus; it is unsafe for him or yourself now." She tossed the cook's jacket into the trash and produced a mask.

"How did you know?"

She gave Angus a dog mask the servers wore.

"I am a disgraced lady and a mother. I knew when you entered the city. I run my Queendoms from the shadows of the capital, and my fingers reach further beyond the capital. The other, the Ashburn boy, is going his own way and may either serve the Imperium or fight against it; either way, he will bring it to ruin along with his sister. Join me now upstairs and take Cordial away as the nobles attending tonight will know the wrath of the Society of Shadows.

* * *

Austin and Elora wore Wildcat armor and adorned their festive Wildcat masks as they walked with Prince Damon into the hall and onto the stage, making their way for Prince Damon's entrance. No dancing was to occur until the curtain lifted. Prince Damon entered and started the official event of the night. The crowd on the other end was loud and enjoyed songs and entertainers.

The stage where the dancing was to occur and where Prince Damon now stood was used for theater productions and plays. Two separate bands were set up in the sunken section, where an orchestra typically played. The grand piano was above the orchestra section and to the right of the stage, not covered by the curtain. There were two small walkways to the left and right of the sunken orchestra section, with stairs leading up.

Everyone behind the curtain was already wearing masks. Prince Damon, wearing the same mask as the other wildcats, laughed and stood unsure of himself with an ornamental sword at his hip, blade ever slightly pulled away from the sheath as he spoke to Jasper and Joseph, who were closest to him. Austin was curious if the prince was nervous. In the past, he'd seen the prince push the sword in and out of the scabbard before a meeting with the Council of Crows. The prince was fidgety and constantly needed the attention of those around him, like a hungry lion cub. Behind Prince Damon walked General Casting, dressed in a fine suit and a raven mask, along with his own guard and footman. Victor Parish wore a tightly fitted mask of a crow but stayed in the shadows, only appearing to provide General Casting and Prince Damon drinks and whisper news. The tables off the side of the main stage held an assortment of appetizers and glasses of champagne and were lit by candelabras. Behind Prince Damon came Bishop Devon, Brother Hewitt, and Sister Temperance, all wearing plain white faceless masks with eyes cut out. The lack of imagination was evident as they were the plainest guests in the hall. The bishop had made some effort with a red hood holding gold and silver sequins around the edges.

The Templar each carried a spiked mace and torch in the shape of a sword, which they could light by grinding the shaft of the mace across the tip of the torch. The animosity between the Wildcats and Templar was apparent. After the scuffle at the book burning, there had been fights between off-duty Wildcats and roaming bands of Blue Templar, leading to both groups getting thrown into stockades and paying fines. The city guards could do nothing between the two groups as they were appointed by Prince Damon and above city laws and regulations. Austin shifted, searching the corners, now seeing a third-armed group of guards dressed in large bull masks and heavy plate armor. If he could get to Jasper and speak to him alone, Austin would have to confirm if they were allies or potential enemies of the Wildcats and Prince Damon. He guessed they could be guards of foreign dignitaries as they wore no insignia of the Holy Church, but such matters would be reported to the Wildcats so that security would be unified.

His promised meeting with General Casting and Jasper would be later tonight, and he just needed to get through this party without political drama or infighting.

They waited behind the theater curtain as Prince Damon was to enter through the curtain first, followed by his Wildcat guards, General Casting, and Bishop Devon. The rest were to take a side door to join the crowd. The music played in the orchestra was an ancient song sped up to give energy to the crowd waiting for the entrance. Austin and Elora were to be his two closest guards tonight, along with Jasper and Joseph. The four soldiers nearly looked the same, except Prince Damon wore an ornamental sword, and Joseph wore his blade, Twilight. It was the idea to always have at least two guards on Prince Damon's person or nearby, but nobody would know who the actual prince was because they all looked the same. Prince Damon hoped to learn more about his suitors without them knowing it was him. All four guards were asked to speak to Prince Damon's potential suitors and report after the party. Austin was determined to remain by Prince Damon's side as long as possible. Jasper and Joseph were given overnight duty after the party. He wasn't sure if either would be sober. After Austin met with General Casting, he would stand guard at Prince Damon's door to cover for whatever illicit choices Jasper made tonight. His duty was to protect Prince Damon, and his duty was to protect Vineland.

"Thank you, everyone, for coming tonight," a voice said in front of the curtain. A slight pop like a glass breaking was heard, and Austin stared at the curtain as the audience gasped. Light showed from the edges of the curtain for a moment.

Magic

The voice was Aleister Saltdrift, who, at the last minute, assisted with the event's entertainment and displays. Jasper heard the man was a battle mage from Great Brightland, but Austin felt the man was a charlatan. Prince Damon had fallen for him and wished to keep the man close to his side like a new pet.

Here we go.

The music stopped as someone in front of the curtain requested silence.

"There are now fifteen major city-states of Vineland, and all have pledged allegiance and fidelity to Prince Damon and his Holy Imperium."

Austin thought, *several pledged fidelity to those who walked Vineland*, technically. He'd read the treaties and messages from the city-states that had not bent the knee. Prince Damon altered what he'd seen and took it as allegiance to him and his government.

"Tonight, Prince Damon of House Farover, Royal Leader of the Holy Imperium, and victor at the Battle of the Reaping, champion of the Crimson Struggle, presents to you all The Triumphant Masquerade!"

Austin frowned under his mask as he heard history rewritten for entertainment and ego and then tensed up as his work was about to begin. He shifted his weight, looked at Elora, his partner, and breathed out audibly. Austin raised his eyebrow with a smile and wanted to reach out to her, to give her assurance, to give himself confidence, but steadied himself. What was happening to him? He was a knight of the Wildcats, a protector of Prince Damon. No, no, that is not what his oath said.

Knowledge, obedience, and duty to Vineland. I bleed for you, and you will bleed for me, and we will bleed for the land.

In a quick moment, his mind shifted as the curtain rose. He must speak to General Casting and Jasper tonight. He glanced at Elora again. She wore the uniform and sword and carried one tomahawk opposite her short sword. The sheath looked like the other Wildcat's weapons but remained shorter, and the blade itself was what she used in the Blightbriar Wilds. Only the handle had been cleaned up. So much for everyone looking the same tonight. Jasper had approved of the weapon and her short sword, which the Wildcats used, as her fighting style was not as direct as that of other guards. Austin realized that he and Jasper were the only two that completely matched wearing Wildcat masks. The other three, including Prince Damon, had weapons that could tell themselves apart. He sighed, unsure if it really mattered.

Prince Damon shook his hands loose, and the audience in the theater stood fans out, drinking, applauding, and hollering, lost in a cult of giddy, mindless ignorance and grandeur. It was a gilded event filled with the city's best and brightest. In the back and around the edges, servants and guards stood. Outside the event, the commoners drank, danced, and partied, all content for the moment.

"Huzzah!" the crowd in the back yelled.

The curtain rose, and a solo light from the back of the room showed onto Prince Damon dressed in his Wildcat mask. Prince Damon stepped forward, and the curtain quickly closed behind him, blocking the four guards.

"All hail Prince Damon!" said Aleister Saltdrift. He bowed towards the prince, and the crowd echoed back.

"Hades, open the curtains back up, you fool!" Jasper yelled at the dwarve managing the curtain, who was wearing a dog mask. His braided beard swung as he finished closing the curtain. He stood to the side as the rest of the party barged past him to get into the middle portion of the theater.

"Forget it, out the side door, out the side door," giggled Joseph. Austin thought his voice sounded off, but then again, so did Jasper. It had to be him, though he'd never give Twilight to someone else. It was a family heirloom, a powerful tool, and, some believed, even the first sword ever made.

Elora grabbed Austin, and they split left. Jasper and Joseph broke right, and the curtain remained closed. The production crew was sure to lose their jobs and potentially their hands for their mistake. Jasper would see to it.

Austin and Elora rushed through the side door into the crush of the overcrowded party, where the guests mingled with each other again. The orchestra music playing loudly.

Elora pushed a noble person in a mule mask out of the way who stood looking at the designs of the arches that held up the theater. She urged to pull her weapons out but saw no cause to do so. The goal was to remain as close to the prince as possible so that he would remain anonymous while moving about the guests, but it didn't make sense to her, and this entire process was becoming a burred mess. She wasn't even sure who the threat would be and searched for Prince Damon or Austin. She bumped into a dwarve wearing a dog mask. She swore it was the same one who closed the curtain.

"Excuse me, would you like a mushroom?" he offered her. She blinked, looked at the near-empty serving plate, picked it up without thinking, and then put it back down. "Maybe later, on duty." Then she looked up, saw a man wearing a Wildcat mask, and rushed toward him.

Elora felt unease pass by as servers served guests glasses of champagne and ale and plates of appetizers that smelled lovely. Her stomach grumbled in hunger. She breathed in deeply and challenged herself to focus on keeping Prince Damon and the rest of the Council of Crows safe.

Hudson City - Welcome to the Masquerade

D ragons slithered through the dance floor in a hall of dwarven owl lamps and mirrors. The colors sparked and twisted, dancing between the light flashes from the lamps and reflecting off the candelabras on tables and chandeliers above. Smoke filtered throughout the room from candles, cigars, and long-stemmed rolled cigarettes. Wolves prowled the edges and wandered through a forest of delicacies, hunting for their prey. Large bulls the size of orcs stood at attention in full plate armor around the corners of doorways and walls while sprites and squirrels mingled with eagles and one ugly cat by a mountain of champagne glasses. Prince Damon's grand Triumphant Masquerade had begun.

Duncan's beard held sweat and stress as he walked around the hall of Prince Damon's celebration of the Holy Imperium. Earlier, he'd thumped a duke in the back of the head at a posh tavern while he took a piss, knocked the poor sod right over the head with a brick. The duke was dressed like a giant tortoise. Duncan didn't know if he killed him or not but took his costume, mask, and invitation either way. Luck was on his side, and the man had a beard like his. Duncan had taken the man's shell, put its cloth cover over his shield, and wore it on his back, a straight sword held inside it. A palace guard searched him as he came through the Nightingale Theater when he offered his invitation, completely ignoring his costume. A Copperhead hired to watch the door after a long day of guarding crowds during a parade earlier yawned. *Three cheers for the overworked and underpaid*, Duncan thought. A grand tournament was to be held in a day, and the Copperheads had their hands full, keeping groups of knights from killing each other in the wine stalls and brothels throughout the city. Now, Duncan needed to find his friends and get them the Hades out of this place. He knew deep in his ageless bones that something terrible would happen. The guard's nonchalance about letting him inside was a blessing and an anxiety; it looked as if anyone could quickly get into this party and were doing so.

The Triumphant Masquerade was unlike any event he'd attended before. The entire neighborhood around the Nightingale Theater was alive and fed off the gathering of nobles and royals inside. As a squire, he would attend his knight during formal feasts that included dancing, gossiping, and the occasional drama, but all of it was civilized and according to etiquette. Tonight, the elite were forced to be low-brow and join in an odd mash-up of sophisticated dancing with touches from the lower classes. Prince Damon tried to show that he was one of the people and encouraged nobles to gather around him in his notoriety. Bitterleak Burgers were available, and jugs of beer were passed around along with fine wines from Dawnworth. The dancing was not formal; there were bows and requests, but there were no dance cards, and the dancing did not save room for the Maker between each other as guest's hips touched each other for longer than a moment. The older nobles gasped and shook their heads, yet most guests enjoyed the scene, and there was much laughter. Everyone wore masks including those of a mythical warhawk, simple boar's head, or deer, and he thought he saw a creepy cat and rabbit walking around. The cat had the same walking style as Cordial. The guests frolicked and mingled carefree of sinning in the light of the Maker, laughing and grunting like animals as the champagne, beer, and witch pepper were in everyone's hands. Duncan walked around the floor, looking for the ugly cat he saw and wondering if it was Cordial. He passed a plate filled with lines of wizard salt, and he smelled a mixture of smoked Gothine tears and reefer in the distance near an open door.

"There are so many people here. This is an impossible task," he said to himself as a tray of mushrooms passed near him, hands grasping for a piece here and there. Several costumes were intricate, while other guests stuck to formal attire, with just an animal mask on. Still, he saw shabby get-ups, not associating with the royals and nobles, ragged jackets, and poorly made masks standing at the food tables as they sucked down pork and beef pieces with delight. There were two bands and a separate piano in the hall. One band prepped and readied themselves for a song while the other played. After passing the entrance, he stood near the top of the open theater doors. Below him, people sat and watched a mass of nobles and royals dance on the theater stage. There were two queues to make it up to the stage, and other areas between the seats were broken out into informal dance groups.

A server wearing the mask of a dog walked by, offering an appetizer plate. This was not the first time he'd seen an identical dog mask. Duncan waved them off and looked around further. Animated gossip floated around groups of party goers spoke of book burnings, the Olde Ridgewatch Massacre, and echoes of rebellion. The stories traveled through the smoke-filled air, drifting to the fake night sky above. His eyes stung as he realized all servers and staff wore the same masks. Duncan noticed large guards dressed in bull masks and plate armor arranged at the side of the walls in the theater. They were as big as him, if not larger, almost inhuman. Duncan shook his head; Prince Damon was too righteous, too racist to employ a group of orcs as guards. A man, well-muscled and wearing a wildcat mask, walked by. Only one or two drank, yet all wore swords and light armor.

He'd traced Benjamin, Cordial, and Angus to an inn called the Noble Lamp after finding an old lover of Cordial's named Velma drunk with her three other friends. Velma had lost her parents, Hershel and Gertrude. They were dependable folk, from what Duncan could remember. He'd known Hershel, having served at his side in battle before Hershel met Gertrude. Velma had easily said that Cordial and his two friends had taken shifts at the Nightingale Theater tonight to serve wine and appetizers to the nobles dressed as dogs and given her a purse of coins to spend in grief for her dead parents.

* * *

"You look for General Casting Ben, and I'll make sure we have an open way to our escape route," Cordial said at the top of the stairs, servers going in and out of the doors. They spoke together quickly.

Ben looked at Cordial. "If General Casting allows me into court or knights me, I won't need an escape route."

"True, but he may also attempt to have you arrested as a traitor," Cordial said but looked away.

"This was a terrible idea," Ben said. "General Casting will never speak to me. I'll never be a knight."

Cordial was about to walk off but turned around and got closer to Ben so he could see him through his mask holes. "Then you stab him, and I'll slit his throat, and we'll show these royal crows who's in charge of Vineland."

"We'd never get out alive," said Ben, breathing into his mask, fighting back tears. The fear of what he was attempting to do nearly caused him to cry.

"Angus has us covered. Just find General Casting or Prince Damon, or look for the leader of the Wildcats. They'll find us someone to talk to. Once you have him, find me, and we'll figure it out," said Cordial, and he left, handing stuffed mushrooms to guests who took them with glee.

Ben breathed into his dog mask and passed a guard dressed in full plate armor wearing a full bull mask. He raised his eyebrows and served the rich and powerful bacon-wrapped dates given to him by one of the kitchen staff downstairs. Sweat dripped down his back, and he only felt at ease when his hand brushed the handle of Dawn's Breath under his coat. The other side of his jacket held two sealed messages for General Casting. One asked General Casting to serve justice to those that burnt the Ashburn's homestead and surrounding town, and the other requested permission to have Benjamin Ashburn join the Wildcats with his father's, and last commanding knight Sir Donald Williamson's, recommendation. The catch was that someone at court considered his brother a wanted criminal before his death and he did not know who. There was a risk in everything he was trying to do. The thought of the massacre lingered, and the events he'd taken part in at Bawstone Keep played through his head.

Earlier, Cordial and Ben had smoked a cigarette laced with reefer before sneaking into the server's quarters to get closer to the royals and nobles at the party. The basement area where Angus cooked held a series of rooms and an open dining hall for the staff containing three main exits, each guarded by Copperheads. There was also another door used for throwing garbage and bringing in food and equipment, which is how Cordial and Ben snuck in, as Angus was already inside and left the door open. They quickly slipped upstairs, grabbing a tray from the kitchen. Angus had warned them not to eat anything. Once they were upstairs, the cigarette and its contents wore off quickly. Ben was walking around a massive group of guests and had no clue which one he was looking for. He saw a woman wearing jewelry worth more than his entire town of Wolf Hills. There was a table with a fountain of champagne that guests could dip their cups into.

"Who pays for all of this," he said to himself, and a voice echoed in the back of his thoughts. *The poor, the common folk, everyone under the boot of the royals and nobles. Only you can do something about it.* He shivered and continued to walk through the crowd. He was fighting more than second thoughts.

He'd heard royal suitors from across the Atlantis Ocean were in attendance. Ben circled them as much as possible. A husky man in a ferret mask nodded to a woman in a bright red dress wearing a bunny mask.

"Prince Damon will dance with each prospective woman and announce his choice to marry at the end of the night here," said the ferret. "You best find him and see if you can get a dance; you never know." Ben offered the two a look at his plate, but they did not even see him. He left as the woman, in a shrill voice, said, "It's all a gamble, and we won't even know what he's wearing until the end."

A game of dances and deceptions had begun. *Find him and seek what is right.*

He thumbed the knife under his jacket gently, and it calmed him. He felt weirdly alive, knowing he could be dead before the night ended. Or a knight.

A shadow knight.

Ben walked the center aisle between the seats and saw couples talking and kissing with masks on in full public view. Sections of the seats were blocked off from three sides, and groups sat in their little sections, blocked off from the rest of the party goers. The boxes above were loud and full of party revelers, drunk and high. Champagne glasses broke, and the music played off

411

the walls. The masks freed everyone from their inhibitions.

The curtain for the main stage remained closed as a willow-like man walked on stage, and the crowd hushed. Ben stood near the servant's door, about to enter, as the man began to speak.

"Tonight, Prince Damon of House Farover, Royal Leader of the Holy Imperium, and victor at the Battle of the Reaping, champion of the Crimson Struggle, presents to you all The Triumphant Masquerade!"

Ben waited and watched the announcement, noting what Prince Damon wore. Then, he walked downstairs to grab another tray, considering his next step. As he did, he passed a group of people coming through the hallway and out of the door he had just entered. Several were dressed similarly to Prince Damon, with the same outfit and wildcat mask.

* * *

Victor and Victoria stood at the party's edge drinking rich red wine, dressed in acceptable evening attire, including feathered capes and sharp crow masks.

"We'll be dining on anything particular tonight, my love," she said to Victor.

"If all goes well, I'll have a special treat for you. One of our friends has provided us with a young, suckled sow. Vladimir Richpike found the sow, and I bent Chef Burnstew's arm to prepare it for us tonight. It should be ready soon."

"Even after all these years, you amaze me. So, who will Prince Damon choose tonight, Victor?"

"If we played it right, he'd choose Charity Mapleton and secure a better treaty with Carigreed. I would also be happy with Grizel Vickers, but that is a weaker choice, as Great Brightland has started another minor skirmish with the Nation of Stouya across the Atlantic Ocean."

"Oh, this drink is delectable. What year is it?" Victoria asked.

"It's young but full of body and energy, isn't it?" Victor Parish said with a sharp smile. It's a taste of what tonight will bring."

"You know there are others he may choose. Kara Giannini is making the rounds tonight, and Laura Speers is also here. Her assets are marvelous. Even

I could not look away. You know Prince Damon loves an entertainer."

"I met her when I spoke to Mae Bergen. We were talking about her poem *Spiderweb of Litchbury Mire*," he said, looking at Victoria.

Her face reddened with anger. "Don't you ever mention that to me again, you prick. We destroyed those three witches, and that bitch Mae goes and authors an epic poem about them making them famous; I will rip out her fucking heart and eat it!"

Guests walked by, looked at the Parish couple, and shook their heads. Victor tipped his glass of wine at them with his predator-like eyes and placed a pale hand on Victoria's shoulder. "Please, my love, my job involves gathering information and controlling situations for Sir General Casting. You know I must have uncomfortable conversations with our enemies and those who follow them. Besides, Lothar Waterguard defends her and knows of us."

Victoria looked at her lover, Victor. "He knows?"

"Yes, my goddess, but he will not act if I don't betray him."

"Betray him of what? That he's sodomizing a queen's daughter? This wine has soured. I am moving on to something sweeter," Victoria left her partner's side, following a hired dancer as they moved towards the stage. Victor smiled slightly, took a drink from his glass, and wiped the red from his lips.

* * *

Duncan looked for Angus, but the few dwarves he followed were members of the Blitzsteel family, including Ella Blitzsteel. A fear rippled through him. Even if they had never met, she had witnessed his near execution, and his miracle of survival set off a civil war with the Blitzsteel family on the winning side. He quickly made his way away from her and her entourage, knowing Angus would also keep away from them.

"Fuck, I need to get out of here." He shifted the shield on his back. He looked around and figured he would stick out with his size but realized the guards were even larger than he was, and formidable knights of renown were in attendance, including some he'd met in battle, like Joseph Blackheart. Duncan's mind always prepared for an inevitable clash of will and might.

Maker, I'd love another go at him.

A foreigner bumped into him on purpose from behind and mumbled something about "mutts" in a broken common tongue.

Duncan nodded down, did not look at the man, and said, "I beg your pardon." He waited for a reply, not wanting to cause a scene. This man was clearly looking for a fight, still wearing a light armor kit, unlike the rest of the guests dressed in formal attire.

The noble stood tall as Duncan, sniffed through his giant red horse mask, and situated himself. A hand touched his shoulders, and he relaxed.

"Come, my Red Hare, come. We are to enjoy tonight. I wish to dance," said the woman. Lothar Waterguard walked away but looked back at Duncan, a glare of respect in his eyes. Mae Bergen moved on, Lothar Waterguard followed, and anyone in their way parted to make room.

Duncan relaxed his stance as he bowed to the two foreign nobles and took a deep breath.

"Big fucking giant horse of a man," he said quietly to himself. A woman in a sleek dress giggled next to Duncan. They stood shoulder to shoulder but did not make eye contact.

"Lothar Waterguard is known as war itself in the lands where he is from, the Four Queendoms. They say he embodies one of the four that ends all life on Midgard," said the woman wearing a crow mask, her skin pale and white.

"I'd hate to meet the other three: pestilence, famine, and death," Duncan said, forgetting his place and the event he attended. His beard stuck out from the sides of his mask, and his hair was tied back and covered in dark grease.

"Maybe you already have tonight, my love," Victoria said without looking at Duncan. She walked towards the stage where the two foreigners had cleared a path with poise and confidence. Duncan's eyes followed the familiar gate of the woman in the black crow mask and feathered cloak.

He shook his head, *no impossible*, and moved slightly in another direction.

This whole endeavor was useless, but if he could find Prince Damon and stay near him, Duncan could stop whatever Cordial, Benjamin, and Angus had thought up. He moved toward a kitchen entrance door and watched servers come and go, hoping to see one of the three as they walked through the doors. Those working moved quickly, and the kitchen area's loudness would burst through as the door opened, the noise hitting the waves of music and boisterous chatter from those attending the party. He grabbed a drink from one of the servers passing by and took it down quickly, cooling him off. As he cleared his eyes around his mask, he scanned the edge of the dance floor and, again, saw the woman in the feathered cape and crow mask. It caught his breath and made his heart skip for a moment. She looked the part, but he needed to see her face. It was impossible. He knew she was dead and buried. Could that have been Victoria Silvercrow? He started to walk towards the dance floor and away from his mission, lost in deep-buried memories and sadness.

* * *

Austin and Elora shifted around the crowd as Prince Damon, other nobles, and royals danced and laughed onstage. They made no question that they were working as guards while Joseph and Jasper took turns dancing with different women who thought each was the prince. Austin himself had a round with Laura Speers and Kara Giannini and followed who he thought was Prince Damon outside on a balcony.

Jasper turned and smiled, smelling of champagne and smoking a reefer cigarette with a short copper filter. Austin knew at once it was Jasper and not Prince Damon. Prince Damon preferred wizard salt and could not stand reefer.

"Shit, I thought you were the prince," said Austin.

"Alas, I am not."

"We're supposed to be on guard tonight," Austin said as Jasper stepped outside on a balcony near a hallway. Austin closed the two doors behind them. On another balcony nearby, two lovers necked and moaned on a hard marble stoop. Jasper watched, smoking; Austin tried to ignore the lewd display.

Jasper smiled behind his mask.

"It's over. The Wildcats are no longer," Jasper finished his glass. "We can still meet with General Casting later tonight, but Prince Damon informed me the rest of the Wildcats are marching to Olde Ridgewatch in two days to take back the city. I have no idea how; we don't have the soldiers."

"What of us? What of the prince's protection?"

"The four of us are to find him a princess, and you and Elora will join her royal guard."

"We get to play pimp and babysitter, this is outrageous!" Austin could barely hold back his anger. The couple looked up from their frolicking, straightened their masks, and left.

"Don't stop on my account, I was really getting into it over here!" Jasper yelled, but their door closed. He turned to Austin. "This is what you signed up for, Sir Austin."

"There's more, isn't there," Austin said flatly.

"We'll discuss it tonight with General Casting." He flicked his reefer bud on the ground and stepped on it. "There's hope, but it's slim. Come, let's dance and guard Prince Damon. We're surrounded by the best in the city, and there's food and wine for all." Jasper's smile warmed Austin's heart and the stress he felt as the sands shifted under him.

Jasper opened the door, stopped, and touched Austin's shoulders like a lover and friend. "You're a respectful knight, Austin. Better than me, even." He breathed in. "The changing of the guard and adjustment, it's not easy, but we'll survive. Tell me, do you know how to care for a tree?"

"I know to answer that question correctly is treason." Austin's eyes watered.

"Is it now? Such an avid reader, but can you dance the macabre of light and shadow?"

Austin was left outside, and Jasper moved through the crowd toward his prince. Austin followed, now even more confused, back into the heat of the theater. He watched as who he thought was Sir Joseph, carrying his beautiful sword Twilight, stood next to Sir Jasper while everyone danced. Austin relaxed a little, knowing momentarily that Prince Damon was safe on the floor and that his comrades were doing their job.

The prince took another dance with Charity Mapleton of Carigreed. They bowed, and Charity, a tall woman with blond hair, squeezed Prince Damon's hand, hoping to make a connection before the next song sparked up, and they moved, gliding around the floor. The music was slow but building, and Prince Damon shifted partners mid-dance, took Princess Grizel Vickers's hand, and spun and switched partners again. This time, he held Candice Saltdrift from Great Brightland. He placed his arm around her waist and turned ever so slightly to stay closer to her. Prince Damon looked on as he saw Joseph, with his sword, and Jasper talking right outside the dance floor, sipping champagne, and he lost his composure.

* * *

Sir Joseph stumbled and grasped Candice's hand again, feeling helpless without his sword at this side as he danced. He played Prince Damon's part tonight, dancing with princesses and actors while Prince Damon dressed as another Wildcat, drank, and laughed with his best friend Jasper Pinehard of the Wildcats.

This was his life now, a guard to one of these women. Prince Damon had allowed him this as a curiosity, and he knew it as a ploy for safety. Only Prince Damon and himself knew they had switched masks and swords. He wore the same wildcat headpiece as the other guards except for the baby crown on top of the headpiece. Prince Damon laughed again, placing his hand on Joseph Blackheart's sword. It was the first time in years that Joseph had not had his sword near his hand, and he felt weaker and less sure of himself.

The music hit its peak, and he spun Candice Saltdrift around, taking in her fragrance as her hair drifted in the air; if he could choose any of these women, it would be her. She radiated all he loved in this world. Candice was dressed as a dove with a white and blue feathered mask. As the music broke for a moment, another woman slid in, and Candice drifted off to another partner. He took this new woman dressed in dark crow feathers and grasped her arm, spinning her into him. Victoria Parish looked past the wildcat mask at Sir Joseph Blackheart.

"You are not Prince Damon. Where is," she whispered in anger.

"How dare you? I'm Prince Damon," he said but did not finish. She grasped

417

him closer, crushing his pelvis into hers, and he shifted uncomfortably as they slid across the floor. She asserted her dominance and led, turning her hand over his.

"There are those that will die tonight, and no side is safe," Victoria said. "Choose us, and you will live."

"I would die for Prince Damon," he said. "And his soon-to-be queen Candice."

"Would you now? Because he would not die for you." The dance ended, and the guests bowed; those in the audience watching clapped while others continued to eat and drink. The guests fanned themselves off, and the music began again, this time the lights dimming through the works of the lavish owl lamps; the crowd started moving again, twisting and turning on the floor.

* * *

Duncan watched in the shadow of a column as a man with a wildcat mask danced with the woman in the feathered cape and black crow mask. He became lost in a memory of his lover, Victoria Silvercrow, who had died along with his stepbrother Victor years back from the Smoldering Plague, and now Duncan was seeing a ghost. Even now, the complications of family and his birth, the bastard of rape from the notorious Bearfric the Righteous Hand and his mother. Later, his mother fell for a man, Haerton Parish, and their relationship brought him something he'd never had before, a brother. They were two brothers born from violence in one family. Later, the Smoldering Plague took all he knew from the world. He buried his family and his love with the help of his closest friend, Sorella, Victoria's sister, who was half elvish. Duncan was forced to live half in one world and half in another, and rarely at home in either, just as she was.

Duncan stepped back away from the crowd, his head spinning, and something sharp stabbed him in the side near his turtle shell. His body twisted, and a strong arm grabbed his shoulder.

"Next to me is a soldier in heavy plate that will cut you down like the big cow you are. Now follow me like we are talking about old times." They started walking. "Now, brother, tell me what the fuck you are doing in Hudson City."

* * *

Cordial and Ben were serving drinks around the edge of the dance floor when drums from the symphony below started playing loudly, booming across the theater and causing conversations to ebb.

Cordial passed by Ben. "Have you seen Casting?" Ben asked.

"He's wearing a raven mask, and his servant is wearing a crow one," Cordial said. "Here, drink." He passed Ben a short pewter cup.

Ben slammed it back and wiped the side of his mouth.

"Witch Pepper should clear up your head and help the nerves."

He felt a rush of adrenaline. Ben's heart felt like it might beat out of his chest as he tasted the sour cherry and vanilla-flavored bubbly liquid. Cordial was knocked into Ben by another group of guests, who were oblivious to the staff taking a short break, and Ben nearly fell. Cordial grabbed his back. "That hit you quickly, my friend. Are you ok?"

"Yeah, I-" he looked at Cordial's eyes. "It's been a long night," Ben said.

"His servant walked into a room on the other side of the stage. If you follow him, you'll find General Casting, I think. The servant is dressed in formal attire and a feathered crow's mask. Casting has on more formal attire only slightly more conspicuous." Cordial fixed his jacket. "You're a principled man, Ben; you'll make a fine knight; leave the shadows to people like me."

Ben looked at Cordial oddly, feeling lighter, like a weight had left his shoulders.

"Okay, let's meet at the bottom of the left-hand kitchen doors in one hour," said Cordial as he walked away from Ben.

Cordial shifted Dawn's Breath on the inside of his coat, having swapped knives with Ben when he accidentally knocked into him. The lift, complicated for most, had been done hundreds of times by Cordial. He touched the handle of that beautiful knife and smiled widely.

You will sever the spine of the Holy Imperium tonight, and the sun of Jupitor will shine on its bones.

* * *

Ben crossed the edge of the dance floor towards the room as he saw a tall man with a crow mask and a prominent man dressed like a turtle enters a side room. He patted his jacket for the two letters and knife, steeling his nerves.

* * *

Cordial slipped into the shadows as he neared a group of nobles and royals. He went to the latrine to drop off his serving plate and wipe his sweaty hands down, trying to figure out how to get closer to the prince, who he knew wore a wildcat mask. He dipped his hands in a wash bowl, wiped them clean on his pants, adjusted his mask, and walked back out.

The only wrong choice is no choice at all.

When he returned to the party, the dance floor cleared, and a man wearing a wildcat mask stood in the spotlight. Cordial moved down the hall to where there was a crush of guests, including two men with wildcat masks standing off to the side.

* * *

The night had drifted into the morning; it was time for the unmasking, after which there would be one final announcement at the closing ceremony. Ben watched the scene on the stage with his back to a door that would not open. There was a conversation going on, but it was difficult to hear. He watched the stage at a distance, and his vision was guided to another as someone pointed toward the ceiling.

* * *

Austin watched as a man dressed in a wildcat mask stood in the spotlight, surrounded by hundreds of guests. The party goers were hemmed in by wide rectangular tables and lesser circular ones holding grand desserts and candles, giving the finish to the party a faint glow as the owl lamps were dimmed for the presentation. The theater was packed, the seats full, the aisles filled, with more people standing in the wings laughing, gossiping, and fanning themselves. Many were no longer of the noble class as the party was as big outside as inside. All windows were open, and most doors as well. Austin saw Elora shifting back and forth outside the spotlight as the prince spoke, looking for any danger. He smiled and nodded at her, and she nodded back. Austin continued to watch the crowd, not Prince Damon. He glanced up out of luck and saw a significant net holding thousands of flower petals above all of them; *Maker* Austin thought *if those fell, it would cause a fire.*

The man speaking onstage dropped his arms, and the nets opened. Austin looked at the man on stage again as the crowd moved toward him, thinking it was Prince Damon. But the voice was wrong, and so was the man's height and build. The petals—thousands of them—slowly drifted down, spinning and twisting toward the crowd.

"We've been guarding Jacob Blackheart the entire time," Austin said in astonishment.

Prince Damon was wearing Jacob's sword, Twilight. The crowd below yelled in excitement as the flower petals drifted down. Guests took off their masks and cheered and danced as the music started back up.

A man cheered and gagged and threw up right onto Austin's leg, a brown and green affair smelling of sour apricots and wine.

"Get a hold of yourself, man," Austin said. "Elora, find Prince Damon," but she did not hear anything as the crowd's noise grew louder in jubilation at the big reveal. Austin saw Elora pushing through the crowd toward Austin.

Dwarven-made owl lamps hung on the theater's walls, but all the tables held long candelabras. The guests looked up as they took off their masks and laughed as they found out who they were drinking or dancing with throughout the night.

* * *

Cordial kept his mask on and looked on, not knowing what was happening, standing next to two men dressed as wildcats nearby. He slid into the shadows like they were his friends, his form blending and shifting in the darkness. He grasped the handle of Dawn's Breath.

Make history. Let them know the old gods still hold power.

One of the men dressed in a wildcat mask lifted his arm to drink, watching the petals above, and Cordial slid his knife out. There was a scream from the other end of the theater on the balcony as someone lost control of themselves and hurled their undigested food over the side onto the crowd below. He shifted his weight and brought the blade up quickly and smoothly, pushing it into the armpit of the first, forcing it deep and up, and then pulling out. The man he stabbed, his feet gave, and he fell into the other. The crowd was thick, with guests nearly elbow to elbow, as the flower petals floated and the band played on.

* * *

Jasper laughed and breathed as the flower petals floated in the air. He pointed and glanced at Prince Damon, his best friend.

"Brilliantly done, my prince, brilliant," Jasper said.

He took a drink with a smile. Maker, they had come so far, from running fields when they were young to running through the excellent brothels a few years ago, to their tumble together before the party just a few hours ago; his prince said it would be their last and meant it. Now Prince Damon was moments away from announcing his engagement and wedding, where he would crown himself King of Vineland. Jasper swallowed, and pain streaked up into his shoulder and chest, and he gagged. His feet gave, and he stumbled.

"What are you doing? Are you drunk? This is my moment!" Prince Damon complained as Jasper, the oaf, fell into him like the alcoholic idiot he was. Prince Damon could never understand why he kept company with such a low brow fop, and then pain seared through his side, and he put his hand down and found blood.

"Guards," he tried to say, but only a whisper came out, and he fell. Jasper was on top of him, his legs shaking. "Guards."

Nobody came.

* * *

The flower petals slowly fell, the party goers screamed joyfully, and the revelers removed their masks. Hugs were given, laughter exploded in corners and at tables, kisses of passion and a few angry slaps occurred as hundreds of revelers engaged in unmasking. High Judge Sternball took off his mask next to a beautiful woman and threw up, blood seeping from his eyes. The woman screamed.

Another guest started to shake and spew the food they were eating. And more continued to throw up and defecate into their pants and dresses. Streams of shit hit the floor under the lush gowns of the nobles, and somewhere in an open door, an older woman laughed as her revenge spread across the party. A tablecloth caught fire as the flower peddles met a candle.

The smell caught on as quick as the fire, the panic of the petals catching fire at the theater twisted in the air like half of the guests holding their stomachs in agony as they slipped and fell in their own vomit and urine. Their friends discharged the insides of their guts onto the floor through their mouths and behinds. The theater seating was sloped, and the guests struggled to leave their seats and move up or down towards the exits; they fell and clogged up walkways as the fire caught quickly, slipping and sliding in the vomit, urine, and liquid shit of their peers. The band had continued at the start, thinking the event was part of the extravaganza, but stopped as Laura Speers screamed, blood seeping from her eyes, and fell into the orchestra pit from the stage.

"Open the exits!" Austin yelled to the large guards in full armor. He hoped they'd obey his demands. Elora elbowed and pushed her way toward Austin.

"We need to find Jasper and Prince Damon. Joseph Blackheart has been wearing Prince Damon's sword and mask all night. The prince is with Jasper."

"We need to find General Casting; I have not seen him all night," Elora demanded.

"Shit, that looks like the Smoldering Plague," Austin said.

The next step in the show was for Prince Damon to return with his soon-to-be queen and present themselves as a couple for the first time, but that would not happen. They were to meet in the back with General Casting, Bishop Devon, and the four Wildcat guards. Austin moved to the left side of the stage. A table tipped over on the other side, glass shattered all over the dance floor, and people slipped. Austin and Elora saw Brother Hewitt stumble while Murrow Edward vomited; the smell started to drift through the crowd, mixed in with smoke as tapestries hung on the walls caught fire, and the close hands of dread grasped onto everyone. A man had taken his mask off and started coughing up blood, spitting on himself and other people.

"Fire!" an owl screeched, and he took off his mask to reveal he was a wealthy merchant from Groanwitch whom Austin had met in a brothel. Another person murmured, "Plague, plague, this man has the Smoldering Plague." In an instant, the entire party shifted from a grand masquerade ball to a tragedy of unknown proportions.

* * *

"How are you alive? I buried you myself." Duncan said.

"You buried me and Victoria. You are correct," Victor said. "You two don't let anyone else in this room unless it's Victoria Parish."

The two brutes in bear masks and silver and black armor nodded. "As you wish, my lord."

Victor smiled; all pretenses were lost now.

"You've come at an exciting night, brother," he said, looking up at his half-brother Duncan, who was as tall as the two orc guards. "The Holy Imperium has embraced my siblings of the north. As of tonight, all of Hudson City is guarded by House Moosewell, who lead the Burnside Alliance at the tip of the Erie Sea and Atlantis Ocean under the veil of Prince Damon's new king guard, the Bullfurs. House Moosewell has civilized and united in the north."

Duncan fell back into a small office. Victor took off his raven mask.

"Victoria is alive?" Duncan asked.

"My wife, my lover, lives as do I."

"Your wife, impossible. Not even the greatest mage has escaped the

Smoldering Plague. How?"

"You know we're different; you're a half-dwarve, and I am half-orc, the violence of our births made us special. How often does that happen."

"That doesn't explain Victoria," Duncan said. He removed his shield from his back and shifted into a defensive position.

"Relax, brother. We are reunited; you come on an astonishing night." There were screams and crashes outside the door. "You have found your brother and your first love alive and well; it's time to celebrate."

"I came to save someone from making a mistake. I fear I failed again," Duncan said.

"Always wishing to play the hero for someone else and failing. When will you start playing the part of who you are, brother?"

Screams could be heard outside. Victor was tense and in control of the room where he and Duncan stood, but the crash of a table, the pounding of feet, and the smell of smoke made the tension rise between them. The confusion simmered into rage directed at Victor Parish.

"Come what may. Whatever we had is gone. I can stop this, Victor. Move away."

Victor drew a short rapier from its sheath; it looked like a toothpick. Duncan shouldered his shield and gripped a well-balanced short sword meant for slashing and stabbing.

"Always protecting with a shield and sword; you never learn that to win, you stick to the shadows and let time do its damage." Victor stepped into the shadows, disappearing, and silence fell.

"Whatever you are, whatever you were is gone and buried; you shouldn't exist; my brother is dead."

Duncan wasn't sure what was left or what was happening, but he knew that Victoria had died with child, and Victor as well to the Smoldering Plague. Their eyes bled, and no breath came from them as the soil fell on their bodies years ago.

"You and Sorella buried us, and I had to crawl out of the fucking ground, and little would I know the woman you loved and abandoned was sitting at the foot of her tombstone waiting for me." He spoke now behind Duncan.

"How?"

The door opened, and the shadows shifted.

"It's simple: when you carry the life of another, they take from you, but they also give as well; Victoria made a choice to survive just as I did, and we're going to force Vineland to destroy itself for having to make this choice."

"You savage necromancer," Duncan yelled as Victor emerged from the shadow. His blade pointed at Duncan.

The door behind Duncan opened, and he heard a voice long thought dead and spoke.

"Necromancy is a bleak word. We prefer vampire."

Alysha - Starkness of Violence

"You hear that?" asked Helena.

The shadows scratched and hissed, sending echoes through the cavern as Alysha and Helena quickened their pace. Alysha strained her ears, hearing underground creatures following them in the tunnels under the Litchbury Mire.

Helena whispered, "Something follows us."

"I thought it was rats and spiders, but it sounds bigger," Alysha breathed.

The tunnels were hollowed out stone and clay trussed up by old timbers that had tar placed on them to slow their rot. The work of dwarves and goblins who found a home in places where the sun of Jupitor never reached. They continued, moving quicker with the one torch between them. The air grew denser, and Alysha could feel the walls becoming more of a stone consistency than the original clay walls they felt as they left the Litchbury Mire tower.

Helena started running at a light pace and Alysha followed, both doing their best to not trip on a loose stone in the darkness. Behind them crawled the unknown and the fear rushing from it.

"We're heading north toward the Erie Sea," said Alysha, sure of her remark. "I'm not sure what's following us, but it will die or stay back once I start swinging Stormkiss," she said to reassure Helena even as they ran forward.

"You named your axe?" asked Helena as they turned toward the noise.

"Give me the torch," said Alysha. "Yes, I named my axe, and sometimes I talk to it," she said with an odd smile. She lit the spare torch and handed it back to Helena. Alysha tossed the old torch on the ground, still lit behind them, and took a defensive stance, holding Stormkiss with both hands. She stood at a side angle, with her left shoulder facing the torch on the ground, ready to swing.

The chattering sound came quicker, and Alysha's eyes widened as a spider larger than a dog came into view of the torch on the ground; astride the spider road, a slender grayish goblin was blinded by the torchlight.

"Hiss!" The goblin screamed, and the spider spat a gob of liquid, falling short of Alysha and causing the ground to bubble. She sidestepped and sliced a leg off the spider. It backed away and spat again, the acid hitting the flat of Stormkiss, and Alysha swung now in a short arc at the spider's legs, pushing her anger and frustration through her arms and into the blade. The goblin tried to jab at Alysha blindly with a wicked spear, but the spider fell after the axe split two legs at a high joint on the thing's body. It screamed in spider agony, and Helena ran as the spider and goblin tumbled over each other. She smashed the torch into the spider, catching its leg hairs a flame as it wailed in agony and crushed its rider, dying in flames.

"Run, Helena! There's more," Alysha screamed as the dying spider's body lit up the cavern behind them, showing six more spiders with goblin riders rushing toward them. They ran from the putrid, burning lump of flesh in the only direction they could.

"How many more?" Helena asked, moving away from the foul-smelling animal.

"More than we can manage," said Alysha.

They ran, the sound of hissing, and dozens of feet followed. On occasion, a spear would hit the ground at a distance in the dark as they continued to push further from the spiders. The cave path slowly made its way up and away from the inky darkness of the Litchbury Mire.

"There, light. It must be morning," huffed Alysha.

"I'm almost done. My feet and legs, they don't want to go anymore." said Helena. She was sweating and speaking only between breaths, but they continued to move as quickly as they could.

Alysha was winded, the adrenaline now gone, "Let's keep going, most cave goblins and spiders get blinded by light, whether it's the sun or a bright torch."

Alysha grabbed Helena's hand, and they pushed forward into the early morning light, holding onto each other as the sun's rays seeped into the sea cave. The echo of the spider's legs and goblin's hissing faded behind them, and their anxieties slowly subsided.

They broke from the tunnel into a partially lit cave, the sea giving off a greenish tint from the stones below the waves.

"There, the path leads off," said Alysha. "Let's put some more distance between us and this cave, I don't want to be crept up on by spiders when night falls."

Helena leaned against the cliff wall, arching her back and taking in the rays of the sun breaking from a cloudy sky and Jupitor's blessing arched into the cave opening.

The sound of the spiders disappeared, replaced by the light waves of the Erie Sea. They walked towards the opening, leaving the darkness of the swamp cave behind them.

"What is this place?" Helena asked, running her hands against the wall that led toward the Erie Sea.

Alysha left herself as she had done before.

"It's an altar to my gods. The Holy Church calls them the Profane; we call them the old ones. This is an ancient place, and it's why the ones that followed us stopped. The only blood that should be bled here is to be given and not taken."

Helena looked at the altar carved and aged by time and the Erie Sea deep into the cave wall just outside the entrance. Four etched statues, worn over time, still connected to the wall. She knew that the woman before her was her friend and something else entirely.

Alysha walked closer to the altar, and Helena followed.

There was ivy guiding its way up and down the walls, with flowers that gave off a slight glow as the light trickled in.

"The one closest to the Erie Sea is Jupitor; the Holy Church wrongly calls him a sun god. He's known as the brother of light, of summer, herds, farmers, famine, and thirst; he blesses the warm season," said Alysha. Below the sun and behind the man stood a bull and sheep. He carried a sheep crook, a spear, and a knife at his belt.

"The Holy Church says all sorts of things and looks the other way. Their Path of the Blessed says everything is a sin," Helena frowned. "I'd hate to even consider what they thought of me this past year."

Alysha put her hand on Helena's shoulder. "Doing what we can to survive is not a sin." Helena looked back and smiled.

Next to Jupitor stood a statue, shrouded in shadow, the deity partially hidden by a large, gnarled tree. Jupitor had stood solid and bare-chested, with a sun carved out of the cave wall and lines pointing down his face, youthful and powerful. Yet the this deity was cast behind a tree, with bare branches, a dagger and tomahawk lay at its feet, along with food and fallen leaves. Two birds stood in the empty tree branches, one mouth open, one closed.

"As Jupitor is the mid-day sun, Sif, Wraith of Twilight is the shadow of autumn, the lover of the harvest, feasts, slaughter, bringer of war."

"Are you giving me a history lesson?" Helena questioned forgetting herself, looking at Alysha's back. Alysha was touching the face of Sif, she looked back and Alysha's eyes dripped with black tears. She turned back to the altar.

"Her face is beautiful and inviting, and the other half is hidden in shadow, the destruction of war, both necessary and horrific," Alysha said. Her voice, not her own.

My Sister Sif is coming soon.

Helena wanted to ask, wanted to interrupt Alysha, and reached out to do so, but before she could touch Alysha's shoulder, her friend turned her head. The pupils of her eyes were gone, and black tears of blood surrounded the bottoms of the downcast white eyes.

"It is not history; it is before, it is now, it is what will be."

And Alysha moved to the next carving.

This carving stood hunched over and looked much older than Jupitor. He looked like a hardened man, worn but unbroken. He wore a fur cloak with a shield and sword strapped to his back, and bears and wolves stood beside him.

"Stribog is the bastard of the silent night, winter cold, and father of wine, snow, and sickness. He takes his toll without asking, awake or asleep. When he comes knocking, there is no stopping him, only hoping he comes with wine and ale, not plague and snow," Alysha said.

Helena was frozen, unsure what to do. Alysha did not look back this time. She grasped Helena's hand, and her hand jerked as if a bee had stung her. A shiver went up Helena's arm and into her heart.

"Steady yourself. You are the dark clouds, and I need to create the storms that come," said Alysha. Helena felt the shiver roll through her; her lips parted, but she did not speak. She wept, but tears did not fall; she felt weak yet stood bound and stronger now.

"This is Judith, Maiden of Storms, servant to earth and animals, the early morning after a long night bringing growth and lust, giver of vengeance and forgiveness."

Helena saw a young woman with a deer and a fox. She wore no clothes but stood bare and surrounded by clouds. She carried a bow and a quiver of arrows and a bowl filled with water. An axe lay between the two animals at the statue's feet .

Nobody lives forever; live for yourself, live for those that you love, and live to nourish the lands that give their all.

Helena looked on and placed her hand on Alysha, where Stormkiss was strapped to her back. She touched the shiny black rippled steel, and Alysha smiled like a cat purring.

"And those are the four deities, the old ones," said Alysha, shifting away from the altar. She was breathing again, and her eyes looked normal.

Helena was pale and frowning.

"You disappeared there," Helena said. "Someone else was speaking."

Alysha smiled, "There is one other deity, but even in this old place, they are not spoken about or worshiped. The followers of the Maker call him Gothine, the fallen servant. To us, Gothine is the beginning and the end, the caretaker and creator; there is no need to worship Gothine. To others, they call them the trickster, liar, slave, and devil. Gothine cannot be worshiped because one does not comprehend the beginning and the end without falling into the abyss." Alysha lifted her head slightly, lost in her thoughts. "If Gothine were to come, the world of Midgard would fall into oblivion." Alysha shook her head as if to clear her mind and touched her eyes with her hands; moving away from the altar, she kicked a broken statue of a figure wrapped in a cloak. Helena looked down and assumed it may have been Gothine, as there was an empty place for the statue to stand above the others.

"Do you hear me?" Helena asked with concern.

"I do, Helena. I wasn't myself there, but something came over me," Alysha said and shook her head, pressing her hand to her forehead and pushing some of her hair back.

"There is no stopping what's inside of me; there is no fighting it; it's like defying a storm, like riding a wild horse. All I can do is just hold on," Alysha looked at Helena, their hands still touched; the buzzing of bees inside of Helena had gone, and all that remained was the cool touch of Alysha, like a spring rain coming on at a distance. "Stay with me. It's all I have," Alysha said with a weak smile. Helena looked at Alysha and nodded back.

* * *

They followed the trail out and up to the shore. The water became more transparent as they walked out. They climbed for an hour; the threat of the spiders lessening with every step. They crested the top of the cliff, leaving the cavern and the rocky stone steps below. The shore of the Erie Sea lay before them. Alysha looked back in the distance and saw the smoke from the destruction of Grimwood on the horizon. She shook her head, aggravation rising as she felt like she failed to save the city and its people.

The shore was rocky until the water break, with a minor patch of sand before the water touched the land. Alysha saw multicolored stones: deep red, dark blue, and orange. Even after all the turmoil, she took in the beauty of Vineland with every breath. Beyond the rocky shore were sloping hills of sea grass that held paths used by locals and wildlife. They continued walking the shore and rested at midday. They ate, taking in their provisions. No fire, just the sound of the waves splashing and pulling away from the shore. Every time the waves hit; Alysha felt stronger, more alive.

"I'd come back here under better circumstances," Helena said. She wiped her face clean of sweat, and Alysha came over and brushed a hair out of her eye.

"How? Would you bring a knight, or a merchant's son on a sunny Erie Sea picnic?"

"Alysha, I'm done with all that. Never really liked them anyway, but it was better than digging ditches." Helena looked away. "I could use some other company if I came back here, a bottle of wine, maybe some bread, and cheese."

Alysha breathed in and handed Helena a hard biscuit they'd found in the tower on their way out and a piece of unknown meat, could have pickled frogs for all she knew.

"I'd come back with you Helena. I would, but there's something inside of me." She looked up at the sky for a moment, not feeling like herself. "A lot of people need to die before I can relax," Alysha said seriously, not looking at Helena, her voice not her own. Then it changed back, and she changed the subject. "Here. It's not wine, but it's clean water and it tastes like the seasons changing." Alysha passed the water skin to Helena, and she took a sip. It tasted like spring melting into the summer, and she closed her eyes and moaned quietly to herself, thinking of better times.

Helena caught herself and broke the tension. "Ahh, Litchbury Mire's finest water filled with mosquito tears and snake piss."

Alysha looked at Helena and laughed. "I'd love to come back here, Helena. Maybe the Erie Sea would wash away all the blood and grief from this last year. We could watch a storm come in. I love a hard rain."

"Me too," said Helena.

They smiled at that. Alysha walked over to the sea and washed her hands clean, fingers numbing from the chilly water.

"See what I grabbed from that old witch's desk?" Helena thumbed through two books with sheets of notes bound together. "My Ma taught me a thing or two of herbs. These books have recipes in them for making salves and potions." Helena stopped. "And poisons," she added curtly.

"I'm sure we'll need some of that here if we get time to make some," Alysha said.

"I also grabbed this short vest, which holds six or seven colored vials with liquid inside. I think this green one is for killing ants, and this red one makes fire or smoke."

"Hob and Bob taught me to blacksmith and to use the tools and weapons I made. No idea about alchemy Helena, sorry no help there. Just don't try any of those on yourself. Can't lose you, you're the only friend I have," Alysha said to Helena. She looked around, trying to understand where they had come out of the cave.

"I think we're west of Grimwood, Helena. We ain't making it back to Wolf Hills unless we backtrack, and those spiders and goblins aren't something I want to deal with. I don't know how far the Republic of Wind's borders are, but it might be safer if we make our way there."

"Ahh, I heard soldiers back at Counselor City say they hoped to take Grimwood, potentially The Republic of Wind next."

"I don't know much about them other than they have two capital cities and rotate where their court is depending on the season or threat, either from the Grave Reach River or the Erie Sea."

Helena shook her head, "The only thing we ever learned about that was through songs during the winter when Stribog's strong hands gripped the valley. My parents use to sing to us during the coldest nights to keep us from losing all hope. They mentioned the Goshawk Knights of the Wind and the Gray Vultures riding to storm pirate caves and fighting off elvish raids."

"Hades were those stories wrong. Where was the vaunted Gray Vultures to defend Grimwood?" Alysha shook her head. "They never talk of the famine, and disease and raping in those songs do they, just the grand gestures and heroic deeds." She stood, wiping her hands on her pants.

Helena closed her book filled with poison recipes, but Alysha stopped her. "Read for a moment. I am going to see where this path leads. I'll be right back."

Alysha carried Stormkiss with her and walked for about fifteen minutes, finding a footpath that led east to west; after traveling south further across the path, she got the feeling there would be a main road, further down, blocked by light bushes and trees.

She walked back quietly and found Helena asleep like a fawn curled up in soft sea grass, and she had nearly stepped on her.

"You look so sweet, but dream time is over. We can take a footpath west and hope to find a fishing village or shack to get news or trade."

Helena yawned, and Alysha smiled and turned away.

"A few more hours; it's so quiet with the waves."

"I know, but it's best to get moving."

Alysha offered her arm, and Helena pulled herself up. They stood close for a moment, their hair whipping around each other in the wind. Alysha pulled away first, fearing what would happen if she remained that close to Helena. She swallowed that fear down and they moved down the path and west.

* * *

They walked the path quietly for over half the day with only the sound of the waves and the occasional deer or sea fox crossing their path. Helena carried a half spear and the Wolfe family sword at her hip. She tried her luck but didn't come close to killing anything.

She was picking up her spear from her last failed attempt.

"You're getting better," said Alysha, who laughed lightly.

"Shut it, just shut it," said Helena, and they walked on, kicking sand and stone on the hardened path.

"The animals are fleeing west like us. I bet there will be refugees heading that way on the road as well. That could be good or bad; we could get news, but-" Alysha said.

"Refugees are easy pickings for Holy Imperium scouts and bandits," Helena finished.

They walked on, but the road became rocky and split in two directions. Two large birds hung above them in the sky, circling.

"I bet that path leads to another cave like the one we came out of. We take the other one and head inland," said Helena. Alysha nodded, and they moved inward toward the road.

They walked further and found the path, as Alysha suspected, leading to a main worn road. It was the width of two, sometimes three carts, well-worn but taken care of. It was crushed stone and sand from the sea, with trenches to help drain water during storms.

Alysha looked left and right and saw and heard nothing. As far as they could see, nobody was traveling on it.

Helena put her arms up in an *I don't know* motion, so they started moving west on the road. To the left of them, as they walked, were mist-bound trees and bushes and the high swamp grass of the marsh behind them; to the right were the sloping hills and dunes, sometimes broken up by stone formations or patches of vegetation.

"What do we do if we see someone?" Helena asked.

Alysha considered for a moment and answered. "If we see soldiers, you mean. I don't think anyone is looking for us, at least anymore. We carry weapons openly and pledge no affiliation to the Holy Imperium or Grimwood. Let them know we're looking to join a caravan heading to the Republic of Wind as guards," she said, but she was unsure of herself. She was unsure of many things now. She was afraid if she saw Holy Imperium soldiers, she'd end up losing herself and killing them or die trying.

"Okay, maybe we'll get lucky and find a caravan to walk with into the next large town," said Helena.

They walked quietly on the road for hours, lost in their thoughts. It was as if each was surveying what they had been through. Two different journeys in life broke them apart, changed them, and brought them back together in the face of the horrors of war, the powerlessness of slavery, and the starkness of violence. They were a part of these moments in their history, a greater lore and story they could not imagine.

"Never been this far west. Have you, Alysha?"

"No, but I feel I have. I know we're on the edge of the Litchbury Mire, which means the lands beyond are mostly the domain of the Republic of Wind. Hob and Bob told me one night about how Grimwood fought the Republic of Wind over farming and grazing lands for cattle and horses long ago. Eventually, they made peace except for one city that refused to acknowledge either the republic or Grimwood."

"What happened to this city."

Alysha stopped and looked at Helena.

"They combined their armies and burnt the entire city to the ground. Pulled the stones from the walls and made fences to divide the lands between the two grand powers of the Republic of the Wind and Grimwood."

"Maker's sweet tits," said Helena frowning.

"I doubt the Maker had anything to do with it, Helena. I wouldn't give that deity any power by cursing or praying."

"You don't believe in the Maker, Alysha?"

"We weren't raised that way, and you know that, besides, she doesn't seem to be a fair steward for Vineland. Look at its bloody history."

Helena was unsure how to maneuver the conversation, and she'd not really mentioned the moment in the cave where Alysha wasn't herself. There wasn't a fear there, more of a feeling of inspiration.

"I guess I should know that. I remember your mother taking Runt, you, and Ben into the woods when we were younger before Ben left to become a soldier. I followed your mom as she took you to a hill with an altar. I watched from below; I couldn't follow further without being seen. I thought at first you were having a picnic, but when you walked down, you were all quiet in contemplation, lost in prayer."

Alysha laughed a little. "It's funny that you have a memory that I barely can hold onto in my mind. All I remember of that hill now, that altar, is Rowan, our old neighbor struck by lightning, and after that-" Alysha paused, the memories not worth remembering.

"After what?" Helena kicked a stone down the road, still moving west.

Alysha took a deep breath. "I returned there with Hob and Bob to get firewood. We were harassed by Holy Imperium soldiers. Ryan was there from Wolf Hills but was changed; he was no longer the blacksmith's apprentice we grew up with. The Holy Imperium soldiers killed Hob and Bob and were going to hurt me. More than hurt me." Her voice stuttered for a moment. She cleared her throat. "So, I showed the Holy Imperium soldiers I could use Stormkiss. Ryan died shoving a sword into my chest." Her finger traced the scar below her neck. "The metal was found from a fallen star, darker than a standard sword's steel, but it shimmers."

"That is some work," said Helena, running her hand over Stormkiss as they walked on a worn road. She let her hand glide onto Alysha's hand for a moment, smiling at each other. They heard the noise of horses before they saw them.

"What do you think we should do?"

"Keep walking; two of us are not a threat to those on horses, and if we run, they could run us down." Alysha squinted. "Looks like four total. They're coming at a slow pace, so there is no hurry. If they pick up speed coming towards us, it could be trouble. Loosen your knife and sword. If need be, stab hard and true with that spear first."

The two groups moved closer to each other, the distance shrinking slowly.

"If there's trouble, try for the horses first. Get them off their horses, and we may survive.

"Looks like two with spears and one without; the third is a prisoner," said Helena.

"Holy Imperium scouts, is the prisoner a Gray Vulture or someone from the Republic?"

"Hard to tell," said Helena.

They moved closer, and Alysha waved at them as they moved to the side of the road near the tall grass of a farmer's field, trying her best to seem friendly, yet deep inside her, a voice echoed to kill them.

"Hail heroes of the Imperium. Is there an inn or town nearby? We need rest and news," Alysha said with a smile, masking the burning anger inside.

"What are you two wenches doing on the road?" asked the lead soldier with a sheathed cavalry sword.

"We lost our horses to that infernal swamp, heading north looking for work. Now we need a warm fire and hot food at a tavern," said Helena.

"Work, you say," said a red-bearded soldier in the back. He shifted in his saddle as if to let the unspoken act of moving his crotch say enough. "I have something on which you can work."

"There are two more coming along here. Make way. We must get our gift to Brother Jared Blackheart," said the leader.

They follow the Maker and deserve darkness, a voice whispered inside Alysha.

Alysha looked at the captive. He was a young man with a cloth tied around his mouth, hands tied to his saddle, beaten, and worn. He was wearing the colors of the Republic of the Wind: navy blue, white, and orange. The soldiers remained relaxed, not even pointing their spears at Alysha or Helena.

"If you hadn't lost your horses, we'd hire you two on as soldiers for the front line if you could carry yourselves well, and if not for back in the tents to earn your keep."

The three Holy Imperium soldiers laughed. Alysha frowned, gripping her axe tighter. She looked up through her unwashed hair and at the prisoner, blood spilling out of his broken nose and tears in his eyes.

Hagen will guard you just as Helena does.

She said nothing as she punched the top of the axe's head into the horse's stomach. The horse screamed wildly and kicked up, releasing the axe head. The soldier on top with the red beard fell over, and the horse followed, crushing the man.

"Fucking Hades," Helena said as she took her knife, wrapped her hand around the boot of the scout next to her, and cut into the back of the knee, slicing it through leather and into the meat and bone. Her hand was wet with blood; she quickly pulled the knife down four knuckles deep from knee to ankle and stepped away. The pain was immediate for the soldier and then numbing as the blood sprayed from the wound. He reached down and fell headfirst.

"Ahh, ahh, wench stabbed me!" the soldier screamed, gripping his leg, shaking.

Alysha ran over to the man, now on his back, as his horse bucked and stumbled, falling into the grass. He raised an arm as she brought Stormkiss crashing down into his chest and neck. She pulled it out quickly and saw the remaining soldier tied up with Helena, her spear broken with one piece lodged into the man's upper thigh. They pulled at each other as she grabbed the soldier's reins; Helena received two heavy blows from the soldier's fist. He wore riding gloves and not gauntlets, or she would have been knocked out immediately. She held on, giving Alysha time to run over and pull him from his horse. The man fell with a slump, grunting and heaving.

439

"Kill me if you want, but there are more of us, you bitch."

Helena stabbed him with her sword awkwardly as Alysha brought the butt of her axe down on his face. The blood splashed onto their hands, shirts, and faces. They breathed in and stood.

"We're never going home, are we?" Helena asked, heaving in the air, adrenaline pumping through her temples.

"You asked me to always tell you the truth? I don't think so, no."

"Are we going to die?" Helena asked Alysha and herself.

Alysha looked down for a moment and up at the sky, turned, and smiled sadly as tears of blood dripped from her eyes. "If you die, nobody will be safe from Stormkiss, and I will pull lightning from Nirvana for you and burn everyone with my wrath."

They looked at each other and breathed, bloody, beaten, and determined to carry on.

"Shit, here come more," Helena turned west to look at what the horizon brought. "What do we do?"

"We kill them, or they kill us, Helena, that's it. It's that simple." Alysha walked over and stood next to her. "We rise like a storm."

Alysha's pupils were gone; only the whites of her eyes remained when she spoke to Helena. Alysha marched toward the two horses, bearing down on them. Their spears pointed directly at her. The two horses were frothing, charging full-on toward them, closing the ground quickly.

Alysha continued, meeting the two soldiers on horseback. She raised Stormkiss to her shoulder and started to run.

The sky darkened, thunder rattled, and lightning flashed momentarily.

The lead horse faltered and veered away as Alysha threw her axe horizontally. The axe, its star metal frame spinning, struck the animal entirely in the face, cutting through it and into the first rider, killing both instantly. They split and fell into the other horse, forcing the animal off to the side where the rider fell head over the horse onto the ground, stunning him as he broke his arm and collar bone. Alysha ran over to him as he struggled to breathe, pressing her knee to his throat and pushing on his chest, suffocating him. There was no scream, just a weak struggle as his lungs gave way to Alysha's strength.

"Tell your maker I'm coming for her," she growled. Her eyes were white, her teeth bared, and blood poured from her nose and eyes. "Tell your maker I will destroy all she has built and bring this land back to those who made it."

The soldier of only one year in service died gasping and spitting, his ears ringing in pain and prayer to a god that didn't listen.

Alysha stood and walked back in a daze, her fingers cramped; she cradled Stormkiss after cleaning off the muck of blood and gore from its blade.

Helena stood there in silence, unsure of what to do, in the presence of her friend and something else entirely.

"Are you safe, my love?" Alysha asked, her head tilted, her eyes white as if they were back lit by something holy and pure.

"We just killed five soldiers and survived," said Helena. "Bout as safe as we can get."

Alysha stood tall and firm, her arms toned, and her eyes pure white, pupils gone. Helena found grace and anger about her, and her movements were structured with confidence and power not seen before. Then Helena fell to her knees, either stumbling or out of homage to the figure before her. Alysha bent down, gripping Helena's chin with her bloody hand. The sky above dimmed, yet Alysha held a hallow of brilliance.

"There is no need to kneel," Alysha said.

Helena's hair hung in her face, and tears streamed down. She told herself she was not weak and equal to Alysha but knew the might and awe before her and could not fathom what her friend had become. She closed her eyes and willed herself to stand and examine her only friend's face. And Alysha was there. They stood and grasped each other. Helena saw Alysha's eyes, normal now, dark from the blood smeared around them, her smile streaked with even more blood. They pressed their foreheads together, and for a moment, they were one.

"If I lose you, I lose my last touch of all that is myself and what binds me here."

"I know, I know that now," whispered Helena.

And their lips met. Helena felt Alysha's strength, tasted the wind and rain, and felt her strong arms around her. The kiss ended before it began as the pull of Vineland's viciousness and misery gripped them with every breath they took.

I am awake now.

Alysha pulled away quickly. "I hear," she paused. "Horses are coming, a dozen or so from the west," she turned and indicated.

"Shit, the prisoner. We should get the horses and run for it," said Helena.

Helena went after the prisoner who had fallen off his horse and was struggling with his wrists to break free near a bush by the road. She cut the man loose from his bindings.

"It's okay, soldier, you're safe," she told the man. The man, a full-blooded elf, was in wretched shape, face battered and discolored. He smiled and opened one one eye, the other eye swollen shut. His ears had been clipped short. Helena cut his gag, and he breathed in deeply.

"Thank you. I thought I was done for," he pushed his sandy hair away from his beaten face.

"We need to run. They're more soldiers coming from the west," Helena pushed him along, seeing that he could walk. "You really look like shit; they take you for a spy?"

"A spy to the Holy Imperium, scout to my commander," he grimaced in pain. "A little of both when needed."

They ran back to Alysha, who had grabbed the remaining horses. They bucked against her in fear. She steadied them, whispering words in a long-dead language.

"They'll be on us before we get far. We should meet them on steady ground and kill as many as possible before they overwhelm us. You, Hagen, grab the bow and arrows. We may survive if you can even up the numbers a bit."

"How did you know my name?" the elf asked in confusion.

"Hagen, this is Alysha. I guess Alysha already knows your name," Helena said awkwardly. Alysha nodded and turned back to the west and at the sky for a moment, whispering to herself.

"Twelve well-armed soldiers are bearing down on us. I want to survive, so start acting like you want to survive, too," said Alysha, trying to keep the power inside her from taking over.

Before either could act, the scout Hagen looked at her with one eye, grabbed a horse's reins mounted gingerly, and bucked his horse, taking off toward the riders.

"He's eager to die. I like this one," said Alysha.

"You seem to pick the most interesting friends," said Helena.

Alysha and Helena mounted their horses as well. Alysha reached over and squeezed Helena's shoulder.

"Fight to live and love Helena. That's all we have right now."

They rode after Hagen and toward the coming soldiers. Alysha noticed Hagen had not drawn his bow. They galloped on and noticed the soldiers slowing as they moved closer. They added Hagen to their group and enveloped Alysha and Helena. Alysha sat with Stormkiss drawn. Helena held her horse's reins and gripped the knife at her belt, feeling safer than a sword on horseback.

"Wait, they're with me. They're riders of the wind, the Goshawk Knights," said Hagen to Alysha and Helena.

"Hagen, we thought you taken or dead," said the lead soldier.

"As you must, and I thank you, Captain Dedric. These two maidens saved me."

Alysha sat on a white horse with streaks of black across its hide—like clouds in the sky. Her eyes were smeared with blood, and her face held the remains of a horse and soldier. Helena sat next to her, looking worn, bloody, and headstrong.

"Ladies, this is my captain, Sir Dedric Valter," said Hagen.

"We aren't ladies, far from it," Helena said.

Captain Dedric looked around at the gore, the dead, and the two-armed women covered in blood and laughed slightly to himself.

"Look at these two maidens, killing Holy Imperium scouts like the Maker herself falling from the sky."

Alysha's eyes turned white, yet her new horse did not shy away from the goddess sitting astride. It stamped its feet in defiance of the soldiers before it.

"I'm the maiden here," said Helena, wiping the blood and gore from her hands and face. "Best get off your horses and kneel before the goddess before you." Helena moved her horse to the side, so she stood at an angle. Alysha sat tall in her saddle, bloodied and worn down from the trials of the last few days, yet the past continued to echo inside her. The defiance of a goddess seeped through her white eyes. The soldier's horses stepped back, nature knowing when to fear a change in the weather.

"And who is she supposed to be?" Captain Dedric asked.

"I am the storm," said Alysha. She wiped the curved blade of her axe and gripped Stormkiss defensively, feeling the breath of Judith deep inside her.

* * *

To be continued in Union of Steel
Book Three of The Conspiracy of Crows Trilogy

Dramatis Personae

The Conspiracy of Crows Trilogy
Five Known Races of Vineland - Humans, Elves, Dwarves, Orcs, and Goblins

The Holy Imperium
Prince Damon of House of Farover
The Council of Crows
Minister of the Treasury: Madam Diana Thompson
Minister of the Navy: Admiral Howl
Minister of the Army the Lords: Thomas Casting of the Longview family
Minister of Education: Victoria Parish, secretary to the Council of Crows
Minister of Laws: High Judge Sternball
Minister of Letters: Stephanie Shannon of House of Breechrun
Bishop Devon: Leader of the Hudson City Holy Church
Lord Protectors of the Holy Imperium
East: Thomas Casting
West: General Jacob Blackheart, Fourth Army
North: General Robert Flint, First Army
South: General Hammer Clinton, Third Army

Members of Court
Murrow Edward: editor of *The Post Enquirer* Newspaper
Jessie Stainfurd: wife of Murrow Edward
Victor Parish: footman and fixer for Thomas Casting
Sir Leadwall: second in command to General Hammer Clinton
Lord Rotherham: Owner of the Featherbottom Hunting Lodge
Vladimir Richpike: Steward of House Farover
Father Losh Miller: works with the Wightland siblings
Brother Hewitt Wightland: guard of Bishop Devon
Sister Temperance Wightland: guard of Bishop Devon

Hudson City
Oloff Burnstew: master chef
Sheriff Hearthelm: sheriff in Hudson City

Mother Echoes: Mistress of the Fools Flush Brothel
Conway & Winston: writers for *The Post Enquirer* Newspaper
Hershel & Gertrude Quilmark: owners of The Three Strands bookshop
Velma Quilmark: daughter to Hershel & Gertrude

Ladies of Wightland
Lady Grapeseed Wightland: a disgraced lady of Prince Damon's court
Lady Rowan Wightland: assumed deceased
Lady Blacklace Wightland: oldest of the Wightland sisters, exiled from court

The Wildcats
Jasper Pinehard: captain in the Wildcats, the prince's closest friend
Austin Casting: a guard in the Wildcats, cousin of Thomas Casting
Sir Michael Meldguard: "Pap" in command of expeditionary force
Emma Hopesinger: squire to Jasper Pinehard
Newt Crashbury: squire to Austin Casting
Joseph Blackheart: "The Brokenhearted One," youngest son of Jacob Blackheart
Brock Rustblade: former captain of the Copperheads.

Grimwood
Alysha Ashburn (Wolfthorn): middle child of the Ashburn family
Felix Wolfe: brother to Junior Wolfe, a student at the University of Grimwood
Grim Vultures: Military Order of Knights for the City-State of Grimwood
Dorta Benders: Professor of the University of Grimwood
Brett, Richard, Andy, Jesse, Ty, Ed: Holy Imperium Scouts
Bill, Kavin: Holy Imperium soldiers in the vanguard
Quinn, Michael: city soldiers of Grimwood

Counselor City
Helena Catseye: prostitute
Edwin Flatrock: town guard

Captain Steller: Captain of the Counselor City guards.
Robert Flint: Redcloak general of the Holy Imperium First Army
Ian Shortstride: scout, close friend of Robert Flint
Brandy: City Guard
Edgar: Holy Imperium Messenger

The Genteel Monks

Jared Blackheart: leader of the Genteel Monks
Bernard Caldwell: Jared Blackheart's lieutenant
Sister Softfellow: priestess/nun of the Genteel Monks
Professor Nester: accountant for the Genteel Monks
Claudette Leigh: scout

Hagarville Valley

Dean Slither: dean of Mount Nittany University
Hattie: student librarian

Olde Ridgewatch

Benedict Ashburn: Redcloak general of the Second Army
Alfie Von Dyke: squire to Benedict Ashburn
Fredrick Burrow: leader of the Black Eagles
Sir Donald Williamson: semiretired knight
Stewart "Stu" Slickback: archer in Sir Donald Williamson's lance
Benjamin Ashburn: son of Benedict Ashburn
Dick Holmes: manager of the Empty Gauntlet beer hall
Mitt: cousin to Dick Holmes, runs the Windmill Pub
Taug: orc slave

Hawk Hallow

Sir Pekka Deeran: captain of the Holy Imperium soldiers
Brother Lucious Walder: leader of the Blue Templar
Jaden: archer Holy Imperium

Union Dogs
Elora Meldguard: leader of the Union Dogs
Keyla Dirkbuckle: second in command
Leslie Greathane: scout
Kenneth Coinfell: scout
Parker Hillview: scout

The Wrathfall
Nirinath Sladestone: orc & knight commander
Falstaer Vicorm: goblin called The Rain Miser
Cloudstrike: goblin & leader of the warhawk riders
Leaftoss: healer

Bastards of Liberty
Wyatt Duncan: failed squire and half dwarve
Sorella Silvercrow: elve, a member of the Society of Shadows
Valentine "Cordial" Wightland: member of the Society of Shadows
Angus: dwarven mercenary cook
Hunter Young "Doc": the last battlemage of Vineland
Maynard: hedge mage
Gray Jim: mercenary executioner
Charlotte Rainspire: orc & journalist for *The Plain Herald & Hudson City Journal*

Steelsburg
Dufin: owner of the Cracked Brick Tavern
Betsy: wife of Dufin, runs the Cracked Brick Tavern

The Dwarves of Steelsburg
Cormac Clearstone: head of the Cormac family
Morrin Clearstone: daughter of Cormac Clearstone
Heddwyn Clearstone: son of Cormac Clearstone
Rodric Blitzsteel: head of the Blitzsteel family

Gruff Blitzsteel: son of the Blitzsteel family
Ella Blitzsteel: heir of the Blitzsteel family
Gwawl Blitzsteel: honor guard to Cormac Clearstone
Griff Grudden: city guard
Gruff Blitzsteel: city gatekeeper
Toplin Bitterspear: guard of Steelsburg's northern gates
Fredrick and Lawrence Bitterspear: felons

The Bent Plow Company
Gunther "Gunny" Wilmot: captain of the Bent Plow Company
Bo: Gunny's second in command
Hilda: daughter of Bo
Ralph: member of the Bent Plow Company

Other Players
King Geordie of House Troulbuss: Great Brightland
Queen Layla of House Troulbuss: Great Brightland
Lord Washcreek: known as the Gray General
Bradley Railhead: dwarve who provides supplies to Hudson City
Roland of Eaglespire: knight of Owl Pillar and Eaglespire Towers
Olivia Franklin: editor of *Hudson City Journal*, mage
Samuel Hawthorn: mercenary/witch hunter
Princess Charity Mapleton: Legion of Carigreed
Princess Grizel Vickers: The Nation Stouya
Princess Gabriela Clawford of Bitterleak: Greatmaw
Princess Candice Saltdrift: Great Brightland
Aleister Saltdrift: brother of Candice Saltdrift
Laura Speers: actress
Pearl Daniels: Laura Speers attendant
Kara Giannini: renowned ballet dancer
Mae Bergen: poet from Four Queendoms
Lothar Waterguard: knight & bodyguard to Mae Bergen
Professor Leifus: Professor at Coldpine University

Haerton Parish: father to Victor Parish

The Union of Steel
Republic of the Wind: Sir Martha Lowdale
Honeybreak: Lady Braya Summerbrake
Grimwood: Doc
Steelsburg: Morrin Clearstone
Colehampton: Ambrose & Prudence Slitbear
Cinderpool: Sybil Pierce-Veil
Crescent City: Crux Brewmail
Gloomspire: Truestaer Vicorm
Magnoliafield: Hendrey Coalfell
The Rosewood Dominion: Brice Hitchson & Lord Washcreek
Waterhurst: Ezebell Milessent
Hudson City: Richard Ratwolf
Affectus: Olivia Franklin & Johnathan Huber
Lackmore: Mercy Pitcher
Olde Ridgewatch: Abigail Holmes

Known Gifts of the Maker/ Paragons of Vineland
Spear: The Holy Truth
Staff: Gaston's Beard
Wand: Maker's Quill
Knife: Dawn's Breath
Shield: Midnight's Veil
Sword: Twilight
Bearded Maul: Stormkiss
Tomahawk: The Servant's Guide

The Silver Ivy League
Grimwood University
Crimson Yard University
Mount Nittany University

University of Coldpine
Nestbarrow Noble University
Imperial College of Splitpoint
University of Deerspring
Winworth University
Chaindale University
University of Spearfield
Staghollow University
Maplepoint University
University of Baywallow
Blindpost University
Marblestone Imperial College

Illicit Substances of Vineland

wizard salt
reefer
witch pepper
warlock coal
Gothine tears
briar stew
goblin panic

Acknowledgments

Thank you for taking the time out of your day to read my story. I'm grateful to so many people helping me get through this book. Ty Tracey, our conversations and texts continue to push my work and keep me from the abyss. Kavin from Space Mage Press, thank you for your guidance and for lifting my work to the next level. David Gardias, your artistic talent, and vision for my covers continue to mold my words into reality. To my fellow writers, reviewers, and the reading community I communicate with daily on social media, your reassurances and comments keep me sane and writing. To my wife, son, and daughter, thank you for reminding me of the importance of time away from my writing and continuing to anchor me in a sea of strife.

About the Author

Matthew Zorich is an Ohio based writer who constantly daydreams of work he's yet to put down on paper. He graduated from the University of Akron with a degree in journalism. Comics, novels, and periodicals lay all over his house while several cats, his two children, and his incredible wife put up with his book hoarding. Along with reading, he appreciates long walks with loud music and enjoys a fine bourbon while gaming with his friends.

You can connect with me on:
- https://www.raccooncountypress.com
- https://twitter.com/MatthewZorich
- https://www.facebook.com/MatthewZorichauthor
- https://www.instagram.com/matthew_zorich_author
- https://bsky.app/profile/matthewzorich.bsky.social

Also by Matthew Zorich

Bastards of Liberty, The Conspiracy of Crows Book One, is a third-person multi-POV grimdark fantasy novel set in Vineland, an alternative version of America where elves, knights, goblins, and mages wander cobblestone streets and lurk in the forests. The book features found family, deep world building, political intrigue, magic weapons, and historical touch points.

Bastards of Liberty book one of The Conspiracy of Crows Trilogy

As Prince Damon's Holy Imperium consolidates power, Vineland faces an unstable peace. Join Runt, Alysha, and Benjamin Ashburn as they venture through Vineland after tragic events forever alter their family and country.

Could one family's tragedy provoke a revolution?